NOBODY'S CHILDREN

A novella collection
written by
Kate Orman
Jonathan Blum &
Philip Purser-Hallard

Published by
Big Finish Productions Ltd
PO Box 1127
Maidenhead
SL6 3LW

www.bigfinish.com

Range Editor: Simon Guerrier
Project Editor: Ian Farrington
Managing Editor: Jason Haigh-Ellery

Bernice Summerfield was created by Paul Cornell
Draconians © the estate of Malcolm Hulke and used under licence

ISBN 978-1-84435-281-4

Cover art by Lee Sullivan © 2007
New Worlds design by Stuart Manning
Logo designed by Simon Holub

First published August 2007

All Mimsy Were the Borogoves © Kate Orman
The Loyal Left Hand © Jonathan Blum
Nursery Politics © Philip Purser-Hallard

Thanks to Bryan Burford, Finn Clark, Stuart Douglas,
Sharon Gosling, Joseph Lidster, Bea Purser-Hallard,
Eddie Robson, Steve Tribe and Nick Wallace

Printed and bound in Great Britain by Biddles Ltd
King's Lynn, Norfolk

To the next generation: Max, Lucas, Charlotte, Ella, Leo, Charis, Isaac and Rachel… And to Maurine Brannigan, for raising a ridiculous number of children of her own.

All Mimsy Were the Borogoves
Kate Orman

1

uman beings are obsessed with sex. I learned this defining fact about them long ago, early in my training, when we began to study their biology and cultures. Disguised as an ornamental plant, in the quarters shared by the two humans Summerfield and Jason, I was suddenly in a position to learn a great deal more.

Human fertility is not limited to part of the year; accordingly, neither is their interest in trying to make each other pregnant. Mating permeates every aspect of their culture: law, art, religion, warfare. They have developed endless variations of the act. They experience euphoria merely *thinking* about it.

My first reaction to learning this was typical of most Mim. Human beings seemed like animals, driven helplessly to rut. A cruel trick of evolution, to marinate intelligent brains in overwhelming hormones. My classmates and I pitied them, even as we laughed ourselves silly.

It wasn't actually my intention to observe them. In fact, in human law my presence was illegal, and in human culture would have been considered extremely offensive. To hide from any hotel staff that might enter, I'd taken the approximate form of an ornamental plant I found in the room (a Kapteynian madder-lily, according to its label). I hadn't expected Summerfield to return to her room with another human, let alone her mate.

3

So there I was, one of two identical flowerpots, sitting side by side on a small table right next to the bed, the traditional location for human mating, which is most usually performed lying down.

Mim don't do *anything* like this. I can't think of any analogy that might help you understand what I was about to see; was already seeing, in fact. The entire business can take tens of thousands of seconds. (And that's only the actual mating. Courtship can last *years*.) Compare the elaborate human social rituals of preparing and eating food. It's hard for us to understand how these complicated behaviours can benefit the species, but if you think of them as methods of social bonding, they make more sense. Human offspring are raised in small numbers by small numbers of adults; mating and eating together reinforce the bonds within those groups.

I suppose the closest thing we have is the sinking theatre. But let me tell you, that's not much like what I saw. For one thing, drama naturally diminishes towards the end of a story; but humans reverse this, with the most dramatic events occurring at the *end* of their tales. My personal theory is that this is directly derived from their experience of mating, mimicking the increase in effort, which culminates with the mysterious experience called The Orgasm.

Some of it you've probably seen for yourself: the kissing with the mouth, the caressing, the pressing together of the bodies. (Often this process will stop short of actual mating.) Summerfield damaged her partner's garment while removing it, which made her laugh, but seemed to excite both of them. They spoke to each other in soft growls; I seldom understood it, though Summerfield called her mate 'Jason'. They were intently focused on each other. In fact, at times I think I could've walked out of the room, flowerpot and all, without their noticing.

At length Summerfield's mate began to caress her sexual organ with his hand. Her response was dramatic and vocal. It was shortly after this that they connected their bodies together. There was a moment where neither of them moved; then their motion became highly coordinated. It was like a fight-dance in the sinking theatre.

Jason's movements abruptly changed into a series of jabs. Summerfield clenched her teeth and grunted through her nose, repeatedly, matching his rhythm with her own movements. Her mate said several taboo words; she had closed her eyes tightly, but he was staring at her intently.

They both stopped moving, catching their breath; then he lay down on top of her. They uttered a few exclamations, as of astonishment.

4

You see how difficult it is to convey the experience from the outside? I understood from my training and my reading that The Orgasm had been exchanged, and yet everything that happened took place deep inside their bodies, and more importantly, deep inside their minds.

It took them several minutes to recover fully, during which they mostly lay still, occasionally stroking each other's bodies.

'I'm squashed,' protested Summerfield. Her mate obligingly moved off her and lay to the side. 'So. Do we think I'm pregnant yet?'

'I dunno.' Jason propped himself up on his elbow to look at her. 'Stand on your head so the sperms go in.' She gave a small cry of amusement and hit him with a pillow.

Shortly afterwards, they left the bed and began replacing their garments. Jason consulted his timepiece. 'What was it we said we were getting?'

'Peter's towel,' said Summerfield. 'Look in the zoo bag.'

Jason rummaged in a bag decorated with colourful animals while Summerfield replaced her shoes. 'Got it.'

'Get a move on,' said Summerfield, indicating Jason's remaining garments.

'Do we have to go back right away?' he protested. He began to caress her again. 'I think my sperms need a bit longer to work their magic.'

'You and your sperms!'

Jason grabbed his garment and chased her out of the room, both of them giggling (that is, laughing like human children). When the door closed, the silence in the room was intense.

'Well,' I said out loud. 'That was interesting.'

'You're telling me,' said the madder-lily.

2

For a moment I'd thought the madder-lily was a fellow Mim, but she turned out to be a very embarrassed hotel guest. I returned to my own form, shrank down to the size of a human fist, and hid in the bathroom when the staff came to move her to the correct room.

When Summerfield returned, some hours later, I think she took me for a cleaning tool. She filled the tub with hot water, and sat down in it, removing her garments first. She let out a long sigh, which I couldn't interpret.

Perched on the side of the tub, I expanded slowly back to my normal size, whistling softly to get her attention. I didn't want to startle her any more than I had to, but I inadvertently knocked a bar of soap into the water.

She saw me and screamed at the top of her lungs.

'Don't be afraid,' I said helplessly. 'I'm not an assassin, I'm a diplomat!'

'Bloody crukking hell!' she yelled, splashing about in panic. I decided that the most effective thing to do would be to hold still and say nothing. 'Turning up in my bath is not very diplomatic!' she hissed. She was calming herself with admirable quickness.

A little late, I remembered the taboo on nudity in some human cultures. 'I'm not looking,' I said.

'Oh, thank you. That makes it all better.' She climbed out of the tub, pulled on an absorbent garment, and went into the main living area. I followed, growing a long, thin pair of legs to speed my progress.

She sat on the sofa; I climbed carefully onto a chair where she could see me. For a moment I imitated her posture, crossing my temporary legs, but this seemed to disconcert her, so I reabsorbed their shape instead.

'All right,' she said. 'You're a Mim, you're not an assassin or I'd be dead by now, but you're a trained mimic, so you must be a member of the diplomatic corps. So your story holds up. But you're here very unofficially. The usual channels don't include my bathtub.'

'There is no diplomatic corps any more,' I said. 'There's no Mim government.'

She sat forward a little, adopting a sympathetic tone. 'What happened on the Mimsphere...'

'Every living thing on the Mimsphere was destroyed.'

'... surely some of your leaders must have survived the catastrophe.'

Already Summerfield was questioning me. You can see she has a quick mind: be careful of it. I said carefully, 'I myself am not from the Mimsphere, but one of our colony worlds. Humans call it Proxima Longissima. The Mim name for it translates as "Holiday Home".'

Summerfield picked up a terminal from the table beside her, held it in one hand, and tapped in instructions with the other. 'Proxima Longissima... biosurvey ID blah blah, common name: Neither Here Nor There. Ha! ... 54 per cent ocean, oxygen atmosphere, no land life. Mim colony world annexed by the Draconians on... that's barely a month ago. Over eight million Mim evacuated before the invasion.'

'I can't give you exact numbers, but there are a number of Mim still trapped on PL. Including my children.'

'Your children?' said Summerfield, in a softer voice.

'All of them,' I said. 'I've come to beg your help in rescuing them.'

Summerfield was visiting the planet Phaaag Zenbrou for a holiday of her own, with her father and her son as well as her mate. (Was there some significance to their gender and number? I'm not sure.) I met these others inadvertently, disguised as a garment of animal fibre, as Summerfield took me to the hotel's business facility.

We passed by the elaborate series of fountains, the centrepiece of the hotel, where they were relaxing.

Summerfield's father was there – it was easy for me to tell them apart, as I've been trained to recognise small differences in shape, size, and pigmentation. He gestured and called, and she had no choice but to attend him. 'I like your new jumper,' he said.

'Thank you.'

Her sole child, Peter, was playing in one of the fountains with other children, mostly native infants. (You haven't seen a Zenbrouli? They have two thick legs, a baggy head, and numerous prehensile tentacles surrounding their mouths.) I had a sudden envious urge to disentangle myself from Summerfield's body and join them in the cool, splashing water.

Summerfield's father – my briefing named him as Isaac – was watching his grandson play, with obvious pleasure. 'Jason says you're hoping to give me another grandchild,' he said.

'I think a little brother or sister might be good for Peter,' said Summerfield.

'You're not worried there might be problems? When his sibling grows up and doesn't grow a coat of blue fur?'

Summerfield said, 'I love the fact that he's surrounded by alien kids at the Collection. He's picking up bits and pieces from a dozen languages and cultures – it's all going to seem so natural to him. But I worry occasionally that it might make it more difficult for him to relate to human beings when he grows up. A brother or sister who's human on both sides could make a difference.'

Isaac gave her a look expressing amusement. 'Wait until he's a teenager,' he said. 'When the hormones kick in, he's not going to be asking Zenbrouli or Kapteynians to step out with him. He'll discover the human race with a vengeance.'

'Or the Killoran race. Probably both!' Summerfield laughed, then stopped short. 'Grief! I'll be almost sixty. Peter – and his hypothetical sib – will think I'm an alien.'

'I suppose that's one advantage of our long separation,' said Isaac, feigning seriousness. 'I missed your difficult adolescent years.'

Summerfield responded onomatopoeically, imitating a sarcastic laugh, then an adolescent voice. 'Daaaad? Can I have the keys to the time machine tonight?'

Isaac was amused. 'Tip-toeing around time's back stairs like this is best left to the harmless or to the experts.'

She fingered my wool, then realised what she was doing and stopped. 'Yes, well, the less said about that, the better.'

'Indeed.'

Summerfield blew out a sigh. 'I dunno, Dad. I'm getting too old for

9

the whole adventuring lifestyle, I think.' She said this loudly, for my benefit. 'Even when I don't go looking for trouble, I'm always getting dragged into one damn thing or another. It's not good for the complexion.' Isaac said nothing. 'Can I really kiss hubby and the kids goodbye, go out and get shot at and blown up and taken over and so on, then just come home again to the slippers and martini?'

'It is a full-time job,' he admitted.

'It's like that cartoon where the sheepdog and the coyote are only enemies when they clock in for the day.'

'In a war, your colleagues become an ersatz family, even while you're protecting the one back home.'

She gave him a tender look, which he didn't see, as he wasn't looking at her. She said, 'That's exactly how I feel. As though I've been fighting a war, for as long as I can remember.'

Isaac steepled his fingers. 'Have you been fighting for your own children, or for other people's?'

Summerfield was so startled by this question that she opened her mouth, then closed it without speaking, then slumped down into the chair. 'I dunno. Maybe war's not the right metaphor. In a real war children suffer the most of all.'

'I had the advantage,' said Isaac, 'in *the* war, that I was fighting for my wife and my daughter.'

'Yes, you successfully integrated work and family there,' said Summerfield. 'I've got the opposite problem, I suppose. Or the same one? Whatever. I want to make my family and my work one and the same.'

Isaac raised an eyebrow. 'Who are you really talking to, Benny?' Summerfield startled, sitting bolt upright in the chair and staring at him. For a moment I thought she was going to give me away, but Isaac said, 'Are you trying to convince me, or to convince yourself?'

'I must have pretty terrific karma, to still be here, but surely one day I'm going to have used it all up. I want to see Peter's kids. And Keith's. Or Keithette's.'

Isaac gave a small smile. 'I'd like to see that too.'

She leaned towards him so that others wouldn't overhear, and hissed, 'What chance have they got, when *someone's* got a weapon that can switch off the life on a whole planet like switching off a light?'

Isaac didn't answer. He closed his eyes, as though the light was too bright for him. I had the sense there were old arguments that they were both remembering, but that neither one wanted to begin again.

'Can I take them to a yurt somewhere, in the wilderness, on some un-catalogued planet that no one else can find? Is there anywhere safe? Totally safe?'

'No,' said Isaac. 'Not for us.'

A long silence followed. Summerfield stood, and her father looked up at her. 'I have to make a phone call,' she said.

3

till wearing me, Summerfield went to one of the resort's interplanetary phone stations. It was a private room, with what I took to be comfortable furniture, set before a large flat screen.

'This could take a while,' she murmured. 'Do you want to change into something else? Only I feel a bit peculiar, wearing you like this.'

I pulled myself off her torso, which made her flinch, and took the form of a madder-lily once more: a harmless ornament on the phone room's table.

'I wish I could've introduced you to Dad,' she said. 'He's saved a lot of aliens. But there's not much he can do here and now.' I was curious, but she went on: 'Right. Human beings can have godparents, and Draconians have got an equivalent. Someone who'll foster your children if you die. With me so far?'

'I understand.'

'If you appoint me your children's godmother, then Kothar has to deal with me. Otherwise he'll use the excuse that Mim kids have got nothing to do with me and I've got no business interfering.'

'I appoint you my children's godmother,' I said at once.

Summerfield took a deep breath. 'Thank you,' she said. 'I'll do my best for them.'

She had the contact details for Kothar's private line, but nonetheless her call was intercepted by a minor Draconian official.

To an untrained Mim, of course, a human and a Draconian look identical. (Hence a terrible joke with the punchline 'But the Draconians were the green ones'. Heh. Excuse me.) Given the sheer variety of alien life you might be surprised that two species could share so many characteristics; you'd be forgiven for assuming they were related. In fact, most sentient species are descended from marine worms, so many basic traits are common throughout the galaxy: protective skin coverings, body parts adapted from locomotion to manipulation, bilateral symmetry, heads.

Briefly: Draconians have scales as well as fur, and you won't see that greenish pigmentation on a human being.

'My life at your command,' said the official boredly. 'The Ambassador cannot come to the phone. Regrets. May I make an appointment for you? Alternatively, may I take a message for you?'

Subtitles were popping up on the screen, translating the Draconian's speech into human language. Summerfield turned them off with a remote control. 'Hi, Jekhet. Tell his nibs it's me, will you? And that I hold his future career in the palm of my hand? Ta.'

The official gave her a wry look. 'Please wait.'

He vanished from the screen; it was replaced with video footage of Draconia's parks and zoos, with an unobtrusive musical score. A symbol in the corner indicated that we were not being observed.

We waited. Summerfield held her knees in her hands and moved her thumbs about, expressing impatience. 'I have a question for you,' she said.

'Yes?'

'Was that *I Am The Walrus* you were whistling in my bath?'

I was pleased that I'd done it well enough that she'd recognised it. 'Human culture was my major area of study, besides physical training,' I said.

'I am he as you are he... very appropriate for a Mim. Very Mimsy.'

'And that's Lewis Carroll,' I said, showing off. She was surprised. 'I took a course on the history of nonsense.'

'You did.'

'There are parallels in the sinking theatre... don't get me started, I'm known for being a bore on the subject.'

The screen pinged, and the official was back. 'The Ambassador respectfully requests details of your business.'

'Sorry, Jekhet. I could tell you, but then he'd have to kill you.'

'Please wait.' Muzak.

'It's hard talking to Kothar these days,' Summerfield told me. 'I can't know whether I'm talking to one of the butchers who razed the Mimsphere, or an innocent man falsely accused of an atrocity.'

'Whatever they claim, the Draconians were at war with us! Any other explanation is wishful thinking.'

'Anything's possible – hello, Kothar.'

'Professor Summerfield. My life at your command,' said the Draconian. 'You have information that may be to my advantage?'

'A little bird tells me you've got hold of my children.'

'Excuse me?'

'I want them back.'

He sighed theatrically. 'I know you'll explain these remarks.'

'I'm talking about Proxima Longissima.'

Kothar seemed amused. 'Then this represents a breakthrough in human-Mim relations.'

''Tis to laugh. They're my godchildren, Kothar. They were left behind in the evacuation, and now I'm claiming them.' She switched to the Draconian diplomatic language. 'It's my right and it's my responsibility.'

Already I had the sense of them as opponents in a strategic game, their words and their expressions recalling the players' efforts to steal the lead in the sinking theatre. Despite the seriousness of the subject matter, I think they were enjoying themselves a little.

'The Mim have announced a complete evacuation of Proksssima Longisssima.' He couldn't help hissing the alien words. 'Which your Earth embassy there ought to be able to confirm. They have transplanted thousands of their nurseries to their twin colony worlds near Teegarden's star. Are you really the godparent of Mim children?'

'I really am.'

'Then you should seek them there.'

Summerfield shook her head, indicating disagreement. 'I know for a fact that they're still on PL.' A thought struck her. 'Which means they're not alone – there have to be adult Mim there too, looking after them. Which means you *must* know about them, Kothar. You've got a resistance on your hands, haven't you?' She leaned forward. 'Why don't you let me take those kids off the planet for you? The adults would follow – you'd be killing two birds with one stone.'

Kothar feigned confusion. 'Would one of the birds be the little one who told you about the children?'

Summerfield was genuinely confused. 'What? Oh. Don't muck about, Kothar, I'm completely serious.'

'As am I. If the Mim had failed to remove their children, surely they wouldn't have announced that they had completed their evacuation. Unless perhaps they don't value their children as highly as you or I?'

'Nice try, Kothar. Keep in mind these are *my* kids. You know what mothers can be like when their children are in danger.'

'You are fierce enough at any time, Professor.'

'And don't you forget it. Those kids are the Mim's future. I don't need to remind you of their current circumstances.'

'Indeed,' said Kothar drily. 'If only I could be of assistance.'

She switched into Draconian again. 'You're formally denying, then, that my children are on Proxima Longissima?'

'Neither I nor the Empire have any knowledge of such children,' he responded formally.

Summerfield blew out a sigh. 'Lemme put you on hold, Ambassador.' Kothar's outraged expression was cut off by the soothing images of parks and zoos.

She checked the screen was locked, then said, 'He's dying to know who I've been talking to. Can I trade information with him?'

'You can offer the surrender of the insurgency on PL in exchange for the safe removal offworld of our children.'

She blinked. 'Can you guarantee that?'

'No,' I admitted. 'But there would be few Mim who would put the children at risk by refusing, especially now.'

'What about the Earth embassy? Can we get them to help?'

'They've got a tiny staff, and they're under pressure from the Draconians to get off the planet. President Fiona is also... not sympathetic to extra-terrestrial causes at the moment. I don't think they're in a position to do anything.'

Summerfield switched the screen back on. 'Kothar. How would you like to know what I know about PL?'

The Draconian said, 'I fear your information is faulty, Professor. While I was eagerly awaiting your return, I took the opportunity to check with our forces. Their planetary surveillance has found no trace at all of Mim anywhere on PL, on land or in the sea.'

'Surprise surprise.'

'As it happens, there's also a Lacaillian prospecting vessel passing through the system's Oort Cloud, with Imperial permission.'

Summerfield squinted. 'They've been selling footage to the news media, haven't they?'

'Indeed. Rather than risk a second front, we have allowed them to continue their project in return for information on the system's platinum group metals.'

'Let me guess,' said Summerfield. 'Their surveillance scans haven't spotted any Mim either.'

'Indeed. What's more, their records are neutral and public.'

'They *are* rather far away from the actual planet.'

'You will have seen their recordings yourself. Very detailed.'

'In fact, so detailed that you've asked them to withhold certain images, if I recall what the news media were saying only last night.'

Kothar sighed. 'What can I do to convince you?'

'Well,' said Summerfield, 'why don't you let me pop over there and take a look for myself?'

'Professor! It's a war zone!'

'A war zone? I didn't think you *were* at war. And, anyway, the Mim are all gone now.'

Smoothly, Kothar said, 'As I'm sure you're aware, there have been attacks by small Mim groups all over the Empire. No doubt you heard about the salted nuclear weapon smuggled onto our base at Ushumgallu.'

'Oh, yes,' said Summerfield quietly, carefully not looking at me. 'I was glad your security people got to it in time. There's been quite enough of that sort of thing.'

'Fortunately, it has been all quiet on PL since we assumed control – so far. But I could not guarantee your safety.' He looked her in the eyes. 'I respectfully urge you, Professor: stay clear.'

'I hear you,' she responded. There was a pause; then they both reached for their screens' off switches at the same moment.

Summerfield sighed. 'Owned,' she said. 'Yet again.'

I said quickly, 'I wish I could apologise for what happened at Ushumgallu. But I can't. The insurgency is broken into independent cells – even on PL, as I think you guessed. My group has no say in what another group does. We don't even know about it.'

Summerfield groomed the dark fur of her head. 'I understand. But if there's even a whiff of neutrons about you, you won't be getting my help.'

'I assure you, we have no such weapons. We're very resource-poor.'

She stared at me, as though trying to judge my veracity, but who can tell if a potted plant is a liar?

'I'm not sure what else I can do for you,' she said.

'Come with me to Proxima Longissima,' I said at once.

'You what?'

'I can get us there secretly. You could observe the trapped children for yourself – bring back images, and more importantly, your personal corroboration of the evidence.'

She twisted her mouth at me, thinking hard. 'Kothar was right about one thing. It is a war zone.'

'It is no place for the young of any species. You would be saving the lives of many children, children like Peter.'

'No,' snapped Summerfield, 'children not really anything like Peter at all.'

'I'm sorry,' I said at once. It had been a bad slip on my part. 'I shouldn't make the comparison.'

'This is what you expected to happen, isn't it? What you really needed – an outsider. An eyewitness.'

'I had very much hoped that words would be enough,' I said, honestly. 'But it's clear we must force the Draconians' hand.'

Summerfield was staring at nothing, thinking. At length she looked up at me. 'If your kids don't have a future, then ultimately, neither do mine. I'll come with you.'

I let the madder-lily's leaves and petals sag, expressing relief. 'Thank you.'

'Grief, I haven't even asked you what your name is.'

'Call me Lwpha,' I said.

Summerfield looked at me in astonishment, but said nothing.

4

Disguised as garbage, I fell towards home.

Summerfield crouched at the other end of the habitat, constantly shifting her position. The cylindrical space had not been designed for humans; she couldn't even stand up. I had anchored myself in a comfortable tub of wet sand, drinking Kool-Aid through a straw and watching her.

She had put herself as far away from me as possible. Humans are stressed by crowding; they will turn away from each other, ignore each other, to create an illusion of roominess. Similarly, staring is an aggressive signal: Summerfield glanced at me from time to time, but unless we were in conversation, she would not keep her gaze on me.

There may also have been an element of unconscious xenophobia. The average Mim, untrained in mimicking alien forms, will know what I mean: that subtle sense of wrongness about creatures from another biosphere.

I formed a speaking apparatus and said, 'Do I make you nervous?'

'No, of course not,' said Summerfield, with a polite smile.

I doubled my size suddenly and shouted, 'BOO!' The human attempted to propel herself away from me with a shriek, but of course the wall stopped her. She tumbled randomly in the zero gravity for a few seconds.

'Very funny, Lwpha!' she exclaimed (meaning the opposite).

It was the perfect moment to deliver my standard speech about Mim biology. I tuned my speaking apparatus and told her:

What interests me are the differences between us: that's what keeps the universe from becoming like the same meal eaten over and over. But in the interests of friendly relations, let me talk about our similarities.

Life means cells: self-maintaining bags of genetic material. Even the simplest cells soon realise that they can do better by cooperating than by going their own way. They swap genes, they form elaborate mats, they even live inside one another. Eventually, they hit on the idea of bodies.

Very simple bodies, to start with. A handful of different kinds of cells; nothing as elaborate as the countless tissues and numberless organs of the human body.

'They're not –' said Summerfield, touching her belly with her fingertips.

'As far as I'm concerned,' I said, 'they're countless and numberless. Where was I?'

... a handful of different kinds of cells, stuck together to form a simple structure. You'll find them on hundreds of planets. You recognise what I'm describing: the humble sponge.

Those sponges are the forebears of every other kind of multicellular life. Every worm, every crawler, every human and Draconian: there's a sponge in their ancestry if you trace their family tree back far enough. Once you've got a body, you just keep thinking of new things to do with it. Sex, for example. Legs. The collagen in human skin? Invented by Earth's sponges. The lipid-hunting cells in the Draconian immune system? Got their start in Draconia's sea-pillows.

On Earth and Draconia, sponges have survived for hundreds of millions of years, while other life forms have risen and fallen, come alive and gone extinct, over and over. Sponges have always just sat there, calmly filtering their supper out of the seawater. Something happened on the Mimsphere, perhaps half a billion years ago. We don't know what, but suddenly the native sponges were developing eyes, stingers, anything that would give them an advantage in the fight for food. Very soon they learned they could eat each other. And when that happened, one clever little sponge worked out how to make itself look like a rock instead of somebody else's lunch.

Inevitably, that meant an evolutionary arms race. Eventually it led to the conquest of the land by species who could carry the sea inside them, much the same way you carry it with you as your blood. And that led to us, the people that the human race call the 'Mim', after an ancient human word meaning 'coy'.

'Is that where the name "Mim" comes from?' she said. 'I thought it was short for "mimic".'
'Little-known fact,' I said.

Don't make the mistake of thinking we are merely arrogant sea-pillows or clever sponges. Our genetics makes yours look like graffiti and what you would call our nervous system makes yours look like tin cans and string.
And we're *trained*. We can change our colour, texture, shape, density, anything, in the blink of one of your eyes. Cut us in half, into a thousand pieces, and we simply stick ourselves back together again.
But when you get down to basics, we're not that different from you. We're made of cells, we have to eat and breathe, we can die.
And we love our children. Very much. So you see, in many ways we're all just the same.

While she was absorbing all of that, I formed a human-like arm. She watched intently as it lengthened and a hand sprouted from the tip. It was of a similar size to her own arm, and about as strong; our natural form is so massive that we can spread ourselves quite thinly without turning into helpless wisps.
I reached out of my tub of sand for another plastic bulb of Kool-Aid. 'What is that?' asked Summerfield, making conversation. 'Some sort of Mim nutritional supplement?'
'Kool-Aid,' I said.
'Oh.'
'I like to keep hydrated,' I explained, 'and the recycled water on space vessels tastes awful.' I was able to gesticulate in a human fashion with the temporary arm as I spoke. Summerfield watched this with what I began to realise was horrified fascination.
'Fair enough,' she said faintly. 'I don't know why I never thought of that myself.'
'I like the green one best,' I said.
'Right.' She hesitated, then said, 'You don't really make me nervous,

Lwpha. Although I admit the disembodied arm is rather macabre.' She hugged herself, floating cross-legged. 'It's just I'm hopeless at waiting.'

'I noticed that you brought a number of books.' I pointed towards her small satchel.

'I kept reading the same paragraph over and over,' she said. 'Too worried about being blasted out of space by the Draconians.'

It was a small but real possibility. We were travelling towards Proxima Longissima in a dead asteroid-mining ship, an old wreck whose decaying orbit would drop it into the ocean within a hundred kilometres of our goal. Our habitat was an empty chamber for manoeuvring fuel, into which I'd installed a small, portable life-support system and a couple of lights. We were invisible and our heat signature would be negligible.

What's more, the Draconians were still using PL's own air-and-space tracking systems, which we hadn't been able to destroy as we departed. They had secured those systems; our dead ship would have been tracked the moment it came within range. But I had also installed an identifier aboard which signalled that we were harmless space junk, no radioactives, nothing salvageable, certain to burn up and break up in the atmosphere. The tracking systems would automatically put the ship on low priority, after which it would be almost completely ignored.

A curious or paranoid Draconian could override that. They could tell the tracking systems to vaporise us before we reached the atmosphere, or hit us with a pulse once we were in the air to make sure the ship broke apart. If they felt like a bit of target practice, they could shoot us down themselves.

'We'd never even know it had happened,' I told her.

'Thanks, Lwpha, but that's not actually very comforting.'

Summerfield's anxiety was very probably the same as mine; worse, since she'd had little input into the plan, beyond insisting on bringing a chemical toilet. Until we actually splashed down on Proxima Longissima, we were both effectively helpless. There was nothing either of us could do but wait.

'I wish I could relieve your anxiety,' I said honestly.

She gave me a small smile. 'May I have some Kool-Aid?'

'Of course.' I politely put away the arm, and she pushed off and floated towards me. 'Have one of the red ones.'

The long minutes of arrival were the second-hardest part of the whole mission: a completely uncontrolled descent into the atmosphere, tumbling and jarring and blazing for thousands of seconds. Deep inside the junk ship, we were gripped by high-grade military crash webbing and saved from cooking by the armour plating on the inside of the tank, more than enough to cope with the white furnace of vaporising metal that surrounded us.

We could only risk deploying a parachute at the last possible moment. The chute's opening jarred us with painful violence inside the webbing. Later, Summerfield told me that the deceleration was so violent that she lost one of her teeth and had to have it medically replaced.

I had expected an even greater wallop when we hit the water, but it was surprisingly mild. We sank for tens of metres, slowing, then began to rise towards the surface. We both began to free ourselves of the crash webbing.

The moment we broke the surface, Summerfield kicked open the escape hatch. I had expected steam, but thanks to the armour, the outside of the ship was cool to the touch. She pulled herself up and out and dived straight into the ocean.

When I emerged, she was floating on her back, squinting up at the sky. For a startled moment I thought she was dead, but then she changed her orientation from horizontal to vertical and pushed her hair up out of her eyes.

'Hell, Lwpha,' she said. 'I thought we were going to cook.'

'Are you all right?'

'Yes.' She closed her eyes for a moment, just bobbing in the cool water. 'Oh, yes. How about you?'

I pushed our collapsible boat out of the hatch, then leapt out after it, plummeting with a splash into the ocean. I sent out a joyous series of chemical impulses into the water, then translated for her. 'Hooray! I'm back in the sea!'

Summerfield laughed. She swam over to me and we began assembling the inflatable speedboat.

Our splashdown had certainly been noticed: the automatic tracking systems would have alerted the Draconians, who would send out a patrol to investigate. We needed to get away from the junk ship, as quickly as we could. We were gambling that the Draconians would see it was just a bit of flotsam (a collection of bits, now, chunks of ship spread out over an area half a kilometre across) and let it continue sinking to the ocean floor. If they looked more closely, they might recognise our habitat's heat shielding for what it was, making our mission much more dangerous.

While I was checking the speedboat's engine, Summerfield tugged off her wet clothes, quickly dried herself, and pulled on her diving gear. I made sure to keep my attention on my work, although of course it wasn't anything I hadn't seen before. When I turned around she was covered by a simple dark blue garment, all one piece, with lightweight oxygen tanks attached behind at the shoulders and waist.

'What are those things?' I had to ask. I extended a long pseudopod to point at the flat triangular objects clipped to her belt.

'Flippers,' said Summerfield, eyeing the pseudopod. 'They go on my feet. To help me swim.'

The small boat lurched suddenly. I extended a pseudopod over the water, then retracted it quickly. 'A large xebec,' I explained. 'It may think we're a prey animal.'

'Yow.' Summerfield warily looked over the side, seeing dozens of the marine creatures swimming around the boat. Most were no bigger than her hands, but the one that had given us a curious push was longer than her entire body. 'Just how dangerous are these things?'

'Not at all,' I said, and then had to correct myself. 'That's not true. I'm used to proximity alarms and all the rest of it. There's nothing like that here now.' I looked out over the ocean. 'It's so strange to think of it as empty.'

'It's not empty,' said Summerfield pointedly.

'Empty of people. Empty of activity. No communications, no media, no wildlife patrol. Nothing works and nothing happens. You'd think I'd have got used to it, but I haven't. It gives me the creeps.'

'I suppose a war zone is a lot like wilderness,' said Summerfield. 'There aren't any rules any more. It's just you and the sharks.'

I think we can rule out xenophobia: when I took Draconian form, Summerfield was no more or less disturbed by me. Perhaps unconsciously, we took the same positions in the boat that we had in the junk ship. I sat in the stern, resting a newborn arm on the steering lever, while she took the small seat in the bow. The boat's speed lifted her above the water, so that I was looking up at her as we cut through the low waves.

She did seem even more careful than before to avoid my gaze, now that I had visible eyes. Once, when our eyes met unintentionally, she laughed. 'I sort of keep expecting to look back and you've disappeared,' she said. 'Turned into a fish, or a lifejacket or something.'

I smiled reassuringly, which I think startled her: a human

expression on a Draconian face. I said, 'Can I ask you a personal question?'

Summerfield stared at me, and for a moment I thought I'd misremembered the polite phrase, but I think she was just worried about what I was going to say. 'You can ask,' she said. It was a nervous joke.

'Do human beings consider mating a public or a private act?'

'Private!' she gasped.

'Mmm.'

'Oh, no, you don't! You can't ask a question like that, and not tell me why you want to know!'

'Your cultures seem to treat it as both,' I said. 'It's taboo to mate in public, but not to represent mating in public.'

She thought about that. 'Would a Mim say there was no difference between an act and its representation?'

I was intrigued. 'The representation is not a violation of privacy?'

'Not of the participants' privacy, I suppose, if they consented...' She gave me a piercing look. I prepared to panic. She said, 'You're very curious about our biology, but I know next to nothing about Mim biology.' I remained silent. 'I know you've kept yourselves to yourselves, and that's not stupid, and I respect that. But I'd better know something about your children if I'm going to help you rescue them.'

Still I hesitated. As an agent of the Mim state, it would technically be treason to give an alien information about our biology, even a close ally. I decided the safety of the borogove overruled all other considerations.

I began, 'We reproduce asexually, by creating internal buds, then releasing them into sea water. Those buds develop into free-swimming larvae, and those in turn develop into young about the size of your head, benthic and vagile, crawling around on the sea floor. They group together in a colony that human beings have dubbed a "borogove".

'The Mim you meet off-world all began their training in the borogove stage. We're taken to different environments, shown thousands of species. By the time we enter our adult phase, we can cope with everything from freezing cold to jungle heat, from being cut in half to being shot with a blaster.

'The youngest members of a borogove are barely sentient: no more so than one of your pets. Our intelligence builds slowly, in a long, steady curve, without the sudden spurts of development seen in your own infants. The trainees, I can honestly say, are the most intelligent of all.'

'Is that right?'

'I'm not boasting. We receive intensive education, which enhances the development of what you would call our nervous system. It's far easier for us to understand alien cultures, and we are generally more resourceful, more thoughtful, and more curious.' Which reminded me. 'You joked about time travel with your father,' I said.

'Did I? I don't remember,' she dissembled... and that was all I was able to get out of her on the subject.

To pass the time, I sang some of the songs I remembered from my training in human culture. Benny recognised *I'm Walking Backwards For Christmas*, which fell into the period of history she had studied, so I went on to the contemporary *I Am The Walrus*, illustrating some of the lyrics. Summerfield could not help but laugh as I let my ersatz knickers down.

'You must think we're sex mad,' she said. 'That it's all we ever think about.'

'For a sexually reproducing species, you're actually pretty average.'

'Oh, really.'

'I don't personally have an problem with it,' I explained, returning to my less comedic Draconian form. 'You can't help what evolution has made you.'

Benny sat back, leaning against the rim of the boat. 'You know, Lwpha, it's not as though the Mim have untied Mother Nature's apron strings.' I waited for her to explain. 'The two Darwinian drives that shape us – sex and death – they're really just one drive. To have children. From an evolutionary perspective, that's what counts, not how long we live. That's why Mr Spider can cheerfully let Ms Spider eat him after they mate. He's food for his children.' (I don't know what a 'spider' is, but the analogy is clear regardless.)

It was fascinating to get a human perspective on this, and you have to admit, she has a point. Perhaps humans have based their cultures around sex in the same way that we have based ours around the tending of the borogoves. Both of us driven by evolution. Her argument gave me an unusual sense, for a moment, that we were both children of the same mathematics: of the same universe.

'Is that what I'm doing, Benny?' I said. 'Letting myself be eaten, like Mr Spider?'

Her expression softened. (Not literally. I mean that she was expressing compassion.) 'If we were just evolution's puppets, Lwpha

– if all we cared about was our own genes – I wouldn't be here with you. Would I?'

She was right. In fact, perhaps she occupied a higher moral position than my own. I said nothing more.

I was enjoying the feel of the sunlight, the smell of the water. It was horrifying to imagine the Draconians using their weapon here, the one that had instantly killed everything on the Mimsphere. They insist they're not responsible. I doubt one sentient in the galaxy believes that.

'What about you, Lwpha?' said Summerfield, teasingly. 'Was it public or private when you released your gemmules?'

'I decline to answer.'

5

One reason I'd appealed to Summerfield was the fact that she was well known. Were we discovered, this could be something to bargain with. It would be much more difficult for the Draconians to 'disappear' a respected academic; indeed, a minor celebrity. People would notice, there would be protests. Her notoriety might even serve to shield me, to some extent.

She would not be Summerfield when we reached the floating platform, but rather Frymer, a human biologist who had been visiting Holiday Home when the Draconians had invaded, and had been timidly hiding ever since. There really was such a person: the insurgency had provided us with her identification, taken from her during the confusion of the evacuation.

Naturally, I've practised my Draconian form a great deal; I was able to slide into it in less than a second, impressing Summerfield. For a more elaborate mission I could have brought a real Draconian uniform, but in this case we judged that forming my surface to resemble clothing would be adequate.

'That really is something,' she complimented me. She reached for my 'sleeve'. 'May I...?'

'Of course.'

If my new voice startled her (I had changed my speaking organ to the gruff and twangy larynx of a Draconian) she was too interested in my false 'clothing' to react. She fingered my sleeve, even slid her hand between the cloth and my skin.

'You could actually take it off, if you had to, couldn't you?' she said. 'You could separate it from the rest of your body.'

'I could even abandon it. Although I prefer not to lose mass unless it's absolutely necessary.'

A thought struck her as she looked into my face. 'Lwpha – is that a copy of a particular Draconian?'

'No. An average of several individuals. Oh. You mean, have I killed someone and taken his place.' She looked a little guilty, as though she had accused me directly. 'I assure you, it was not necessary. In fact, it's far safer not to take the image of a specific person unless you are actively intending to impersonate them.'

Abruptly, Summerfield raised a hand to her face. 'Grief! It smells like a fish shop.' Inside my Draconian snout, I formed a working olfactory organ, and tested the air. It was full of the stink of burned or rotting marine life.

As our boat approached the platform, it began to hit small objects. The water was dotted with garbage – dead marine animals, empty food containers, slicks of machine lubricants, even Draconian bodily waste. I turned off my nose.

Draconians on the floating platform were signalling us with a flashing violet light to stand off. I slowed the boat until we were bobbing a few decametres away.

The platform was a simple, open construction, a square, twenty metres on each side, built from narrow, lightweight metal pipes. Above the water there were two storeys, with several small, enclosed spaces. It was all straight lines (but soft curves where two pipes came together), painted smooth and white: minimal, tidy, modest. Its purpose had been to gently investigate the ocean surrounding it, not to fill that ocean with the random filth of war.

The lieutenant now in charge of the place was very young, with only the beginnings of the beard permitted to his rank. 'Identify yourself,' he called.

'Trooper Kherue. My life at your command. With a human prisoner.'

The lieutenant's ADC scanned us for identifiers and explosives, then murmured a report to his commander. 'Come aboard,' called the youngster.

We floated over to the landing, an area knee-deep in water. Two troops splashed in, pulled Summerfield out of the speedboat before she could get out, and marched her over to the lieutenant. (I was glancing around, counting troops. There couldn't be more than a dozen Draconians on the platform, although others could be off on missions.)

The lieutenant gave me a sort of wry smile as I hastened after my captive: if she turned out to be important, it would mean promotion and prizes, so her captor would naturally stick to her like glue.

'Where'd you find her?'

'In a mangrove swamp near City Fourteen,' I said. 'She's a marine biologist – she was studying xebecs, apparently. High Command said she might be useful here.'

Summerfield piped up, 'Stop that!' We both ignored her, but she went on, 'It's not fair! Speak a language I can understand!'

The lieutenant asked me, 'There haven't been any queries from their embassy?'

'Not that I'm aware of, sir.'

The lieutenant glanced at his ADC. 'Get the kit.'

'At once, sir.'

It's simple to tell if someone is a disguised Mim. None of us can fool a DNA test: we don't even *have* DNA. Generally, just telling a Mim agent you're going to test them is enough. With their cover about to be blown, they will try to kill you, or escape, or simply do as much damage as possible.

The Draconians were moving hundreds of thousands of personnel onto Proxima Longissima. Our intelligence had observed them testing their troops as they debarked, but only very rarely in the field. They knew that some Mim were still on the planet, but they also knew that most of those were non-combatants, and a Mim civilian has no chance of mimicking an alien well enough to fool anyone. The best they could do would be to pretend to be a rock and blow themselves up when a Draconian sat on them.

In short, assuming they hadn't found our crash vessel's heat shield, there wasn't much chance that anyone at the platform would test my disguise. Especially since I was carrying a troop identifier that said I'd already been tested.

So, instead, they tested Summerfield. A Draconian in a military-scientist uniform emerged from one of the enclosed areas, carrying a miniature suitcase: a field medical kit. He tested Summerfield, taking a drop of blood from her finger and making her squawk with outrage: 'I demand to speak to the ambassador!' The troopers couldn't understand what she was saying, and the lieutenant didn't care, as long as that test came up negative.

Which it did, of course. 'Right,' said the man in charge. 'Lady-Captain-Savant Cheset, apparently we have here a marine biologist. See if you can find a use for her. You'll need to break out a translator if you want to make sense of her chirping.' I saw Summerfield's mouth twitch, but of course she said nothing.

I took hold of Summerfield's arm in a gesture of ownership. No one tried to prevent me from staying with her as she followed Cheset. My presence saved them assigning a guard to her.

Cheset herself was an unusual find; Draconian women are actively discouraged from pursuing intellectual careers. She led us down a clanking metal staircase to the underwater area of the platform, a low-ceilinged laboratory with a great glass window that looked out onto the water. Every few hundred seconds, there was a sizzling flash somewhere nearby in the water.

The Lady-Captain-Savant poked a clunky translator until it began producing something that sounded like a human language. 'Oh, give it here,' said Summerfield, and twiddled it until she was happy with it. Staying in character, she next turned to Cheset and proceeded to 'chew her ears' with a long speech about the rights of sentient beings generally and human beings in particular, including several demands to speak to the Draconian Emperor, the Earth Embassy, the Interworld Institute of Ichthyology (which I think she made up) and the media.

Cheset waited patiently through all this, then said, 'I've been stationed here without as much as an assistant, so I'm very grateful for your presence.' I think Summerfield was genuinely surprised; she stopped talking and stared at the savant. 'Technically, I outrank the lieutenant as well as your captor, so I'll be able to protect you.'

Summerfield gave an embarrassed cough. 'What exactly is it you're doing?'

'I'm attempting to study the biology of the Mim,' said Cheset. 'We think this pontoon was built close by a Mim nursery. It's unique on the planet. Presumably, the Mim were conducting some sort of research on their own children.'

There was a brilliant flash just outside the window: a large xebec had got too close to the platform, and the automatic defences had fired, charring it to the bone. Summerfield was blinking violently, her hands raised involuntarily to her eyes; I watched as the killed fish drifted upwards. Apparently the Draconians weren't taking any chances: anything large enough to be an adult Mim was being shot down before it could get too close. No wonder the place stank.

Cheset went on. 'The problem is that while the platform isn't mobile, the nurseries apparently are. Either some of the surviving adults have moved it, or it's migrated away for some reason.'

'Perhaps your defences frightened them,' said Summerfield.

I understood this was humorous understatement, but the Draconian only agreed. 'Better the smell of dead fish than the smell of dead Draconians.' Cheset glanced at me. 'Don't you find you get paranoid – every object becomes a Mim?'

'I know what you mean,' I said, also with humorous understatement.

Cheset knelt down, and opened a panel in the bench: a puff of cold air and a loud hum announced it was a laboratory refrigerator. She reached inside, brought out an opaque plastic tub, and hefted it up onto the bench, pushing the fridge shut with her knee. 'Here we are,' she said. 'This afternoon's effort, Savant Frymer, will be to discover the secrets of our little friend here.'

They both looked inside the container, and I looked too, unable to help myself. I suppose Cheset was too distracted by pride and curiosity to notice me.

It was a dead infant Mim. Summerfield carefully did not look at me. A series of expressions moved swiftly across her face.

Controlling herself powerfully, Summerfield asked the Draconian, 'Did you catch it and kill it?'

Cheset missed her tone, lifting the corpse from its container. 'We found it on the ocean floor. It must have been left behind when the nursery was moved.'

Summerfield glanced at me. I wanted some way to signal that Cheset was probably telling the truth. The dead infant had probably wandered from the edge of the borogove and failed to find its way back: it wasn't unusual. But leaving its body for the Draconians to find had been a clumsy mistake, one that could cost the Mim a great deal.

'I want your help in dissecting it,' said Cheset.

'Of course,' said Summerfield thinly.

Getting intelligence from Cheset was no difficulty: clearly, she had been starved for company. I was interested that the platform had been so poorly supplied with personnel. In fact, it emerged that Cheset had pushed for the Draconians to investigate the abandoned platform, then had been infuriated by High Command's lack of interest in her project.

'It's a symptom of madness!' she declared, as she cut paper-thin slices from the child's corpse. 'The Mims' biology is not just unique, it's uniquely dangerous. A chance to study them at this stage of development is invaluable!'

Summerfield held the little body beneath her palms. 'I suppose the High Command doesn't think of the Mim as a real threat any more – not after what happened to the Mimsphere.'

'They're fools. They should spend a few days here on PL if they don't think the Mim are still dangerous.' Cheset laid the slice she'd taken on the bed of some sort of microscope. 'Meanwhile I'm stuck here with the most primitive equipment you can imagine, trying to work out what makes the Mim tick.'

'What do you think makes them tick?'

Cheset didn't respond, eyes glued to the microscope. I knew what she'd be seeing: a mass of indistinguishable cells, with no hint at all of how they could change themselves, rearrange themselves in a flash.

Summerfield tried again. 'I gather the official position is that the Mim aren't even sentient. Just an incredible simulation.'

'Yes, well, that's –' The translator emitted a polite bleep. 'But how *can* they think? How is it possible, when every Mim's just a lump of primitive, undifferentiated tissue! It can't be a chemical signalling system. Yes, slime moulds do it, but they don't *think*. How can the Mim signal quickly enough, efficiently enough?'

'Why do you think the Mim were experimenting on their own children?'

Cheset looked up from the microscope with an impatient snort. 'One thing we do know about the Mim is that they don't value their children the way Draconians do. To some extent, they consider their offspring disposable. The children should have been their first priority – not their last.' Cheset seemed to remember who she was talking to. 'That would be true for your culture as well as mine, Savant Frymer.'

'The Mim probably say the same kind of things about Draconians.'

'It's scientific fact, not propaganda. Would you like to hear my favourite theory about the Mim?'

'Yes.'

'Have you heard of the Joyce-Gate hypothesis?'

'No.'

34

'They theorise that the Mim *are* in fact mindless slime moulds. That they're possessed by intelligences from another dimension. The Mim are mere –' the translator struggled '– sock puppets.'

Summerfield, who had seen stranger things in her time, did not comment.

Over the next several hours, there were many times when Summerfield and I could have exchanged glances, even a few words, unheard by the enemies around us. I had to accompany her at all times, even to the Draconians' improvised latrine facility, about which the less said the better. They didn't think to give her anything to eat until I requested a meal for her: she ended up picking the plants out of a couple of Draconian ration packs.

But we didn't look at each other, and we didn't say anything. I pushed her around by the elbow and pointed and we carefully avoided each others' eyes. We were taking our roles, our mission, too seriously to compromise them even for a moment.

So Summerfield said nothing about the shock of seeing that dead Mim child at the bottom of its cold plastic container. She must have wanted to say something consoling to me, to tell me she shared my sorrow, to say she had imagined what it would be like if Cheset had shaved curious slices from a chilled human infant.

In fact, I had been more angered at Cheset's casual suggestion that my people had been experimenting on the borogove. It was hardly the first monstrous accusation the Draconians had made against us. Most of them *after* the destruction of the Mimsphere, not before: what had happened to us was so terrible that it was unbearable to think we had not deserved it. We must have done something. We must be monsters.

For my part, I did nothing to reassure Summerfield. Of course it had been disgusting and distressing to discover the infant's corpse in the hands of our enemies, but it was only one child, and a barely developed one at that. Perhaps five weeks old, at the stage when it would have begun to detach itself from its hatching point and start moving about. It would have been about as intelligent as one of the animals humans enjoy cohabiting with.

For those hours we stayed close to together, in our roles as captive and captor, and communicated nothing.

Back in the laboratory, Summerfield inched the conversation around to the new location of the borogove. Cheset showed her some rough satellite maps of the surrounding ocean. 'We're certain the nursery wasn't evacuated from the planet,' she said, zooming in on the patchy image. 'There hasn't been time to move it that far. The dead child and a few other clues suggest it was moved roughly north-west – possibly to be hidden in this deeper area, here.' She tapped the screen with a claw.

'The satellites can't find it?' asked Summerfield.

'It must be camouflaged.' Cheset's choice of verb forms indicated sarcasm. She drummed her claws against the edge of the screen, thoughtfully. 'Surely the satellites have sufficient resolution,' she muttered. 'The Mim aren't just sentient, they're too clever for their own good.'

Summerfield said carefully, 'I heard that you weren't responsible for the destruction of the Mimsphere – that's what you're saying.'

'How would I know?' said Cheset sharply. 'I'm not sure there's any way *to* know. When it's in the Empire's interest, the politicians decide the facts.'

'I thought Draconian savants were the only ones permitted to publicly disagree with the Emperor.'

'It's one thing to speak, another to be heard,' said Cheset. 'The Empire's bureaucrats choose which savants will make reports, and when. They're also permitted to rewrite dissenting reports.'

'Are you saying they lie to the nobility?' Summerfield was honestly shocked.

'They don't have to lie. Change a word, add a word, and what was clear becomes doubtful, what was urgent becomes merely interesting.'

'Okay… I'm with you now,' said Summerfield ruefully. 'I've seen the same thing done by humans.'

Cheset said, 'I'd like to demonstrate the development of intelligence in Mim young. It might do something towards undermining the conventional wisdom.'

I said, 'They'll say you're on the Mim's side.'

Both of them looked at me in surprise. 'He has a point,' said Summerfield quickly. 'You'll be undermining imperial policy. If the Mim are just weeds, not people, the Draconians can do whatever you want to them.'

Cheset made a gesture of frustration and spat out a string of syllables. The translator spluttered and went quiet for a moment. The savant stared at it. Finally the machine offered: 'The speed of light is the same no matter whose arse I kiss.'

Summerfield gave me a quick look. We were both thinking the same thing: this Draconian might be an ally.

If the human was considering revealing our mission, I would have to stop her.

Cheset was saying, 'The more I learn, though, the more I think it will take a biochemist to do the job, not a zoologist.'

'You don't really believe the sock puppet theory, do you?'

I think Cheset realised she was being teased. 'It does explain the available facts,' she deadpanned.

'Listen,' said Summerfield. 'I think I –'

6

There was a moment, the thinnest slice of time, when I felt the shockwave hit my disguised body and break it apart like a wave knocking down a child's construction in wet sand. A high-speed hologram might have caught the agonising split second in which I stretched before I shattered: my face and shoulders smeared out into a great curved shape like a spoon, my legs shortening and lifting from the ground. I don't remember the shattering itself, of course. You never do.

7

The next thing I knew, I'd become a thin slick on the surface of salt water. It took hours to become myself again. Perhaps we're too used to the air; water actually carries signals better, but more slowly. The chemical messages my cells were sending out seemed to drift lazily through the water, instead of spiralling out at the speed of gunshots to find my missing pieces and draw them quickly together.

That long time was like going through childhood again. The way awareness and thought accumulate slowly, slowly, slowly, sliding together in imperceptible instalments. I was already a collection of chunks by the time I knew that anything had happened, that anything *was* happening.

I remember hazy dreams of flying through seawater, coolness and warmth, blue and white light. A deep memory of ancestral times? Or of the thoughts of a wriggling, oblivious larva?

Once I was awake again, of course, I could direct the process, accelerating the painful business of reassembly until I had back all the parts of me that I was going to. I had lost five per cent of my mass, probably more to dilution than whatever catastrophe had occurred. It was nothing. With my training, I can lose up to half of myself without serious damage.

Once I was able, I changed myself into a suitable aquatic form, copying a long-bodied creature from Ninmah 5 whose trailing fins form an elaborate disguise. Looking like a mass of floating seaweed, I began a search of my surroundings, trying to work out what had happened.

It didn't take long to understand: the platform had been blown to smithereens.

The stink before the attack was nothing compared to the stink afterwards. I formed a tentative olfactory organ, and realised at once that every animal for perhaps half a kilometre had been killed by the shockwaves.

I was floating in a sea of burst corpses.

Had Summerfield survived?

I moved between and below the floating wreckage for half an hour. Chunks of torn and melted plastic, and Draconian bodies, peppered the surface of the water. Denser objects had sunk to the shallow bottom: metal struts, gas tanks, the automatic blasters.

Anything the Draconians didn't clean up would be slowly integrated into the sessile life forms, like lost snorkels incorporated into a coral reef. On the sea floor, crawling animals were nibbling at detached limbs and climbing into sunken, opened corpses. I wondered if they'd be poisoned by the alien matter.

Proxima Longissima was stained, marked with alien stuff.

I was able to identify by taste even the most badly damaged bodies as Draconian, not human. I suppose Cheset was there, and the lieutenant with his wispy beard. I wondered if I'd bump into the dissected remains of the infant Mim, but I didn't.

Summerfield had not only lived through the attack, but she'd got away afterwards. In my dissolved state, I'd had no idea of the passage of time, so I was frustratingly unsure how long it had been since the explosion. I guessed it couldn't be more than a few hours, or there'd be Draconians all over the site.

It was time for me to get clear, before they arrived. I picked what must be roughly the right direction and began to swim.

I swam for hours. The world seemed different once the sun had been swallowed by the horizon and the empty sky began to be spattered with stars. Deep silence filled the waters, like a blanket hiding the day's murders. Before the Draconians came the sea had always been full of the echoes of chemical communication: drifting, leftover molecules from distant conversations. Now the water was clear and meaningless.

Mim have only colonised a few worlds. We are more selective than some other species; what's more, we take far more care to prepare a planet for colonists. It's because of the children, of course. They need specific conditions to thrive. Proxima Longissima, or Holiday Home, had a reputation as one of the best places to bring up kids. Not much industry, a very compatible biome (after a few tweaks). The Draconians claimed the presence of a school for Mim agents made the whole planet a legitimate military target. It was only a pretext, of course, but it still shames me.

Above me were the constellations of my childhood. I traced their outlines with delight, remembering all their names, the names of the brightest stars. I saw the smear of light that was the galaxy seen edge-on. I corrected my course a little, steering by the stars, and tasted the water again. I could sense just the faintest trace of Mim speech. My thoughts raced with excitement! I couldn't be far from the nursery now!

Kilometres behind me, there were yellow lights in the sky, moving over the ocean. The Draconians had come to claim their dead. While I had reclaimed my childhood, every cell freshly washed by the sea, sailing home!

With a shock, I saw that there was a light on the water ahead as well. I turned my fins and rushed towards it, dipping below the surface for speed. It was hard to judge the distance, but surely none of the wreckage could have drifted this far.

A small Draconian boat? One of their marker buoys? It must be floating above the main body of the borogove. Was it a threat to the nursery?

With a surge I realised what I was seeing. I sped towards the tiny red light. I had to get there before the Draconians spotted it.

I formed the most light-sensitive eyes I knew how to make, but without equipment, I had to get within metres before I was sure. 'Summerfield!' I called. 'Please respond! Tell me that's you!'

There was a wild splashing noise, as of a xebec disturbed in its peaceful dozing, and then a voice called back: 'Lwpha? Thank God!'

'Switch off your emergency light,' I said urgently. 'I can find you without it.'

'Right... right... done,' she said. Her voice had changed; she was dehydrated. I paddled slowly towards her, creating a light-organ, giving her enough pale illumination to see me.

'Grief,' said Summerfield. 'What are you supposed to be? You look like an enormous sea dragon.'

'I am an enormous sea dragon.'

'G'goo g'joob.'

In my new form, I was much taller than her. She reached up and patted the side of my jaw. 'It's good to see you, Lwpha, whatever you look like. I don't suppose you've got any of that Kool-Aid with you.'

'You seem uninjured.'

'Raw luck,' she admitted.

'Not entirely,' announced a voice, out of the darkness.

The chemical signals washed over me a moment later. 'It's another Mim,' I told Summerfield at once.

'We've been watching you for a long time,' said the voice. The Mim squirted a package of taste chemicals, containing his name, a little of his background, assuring me of his friendly intentions, with a hint of surprise at my association with an alien. 'Several xebecs have shown interest in you – all of them large enough to be dangerous. We frightened them off.'

Summerfield was treading water, tiredly. 'Then I'm grateful to you,' she called.

'We're dreadfully embarrassed,' said the insurgent. He was using a baritone human voice, probably copied from the media. 'We had no idea you were there. All the different cells of the insurgency operate independently.'

'Well, I suppose that's the disadvantage of having a disconnected cell structure,' said Summerfield. She looked at us expectantly, for some reason, then stopped.

'She needs sweet water,' I told him. *Urgently*, I signalled.

'Follow me,' said the insurgent.

There was a little group of the rebels hiding only a few kilometres away amongst a large reef. I carried the exhausted Summerfield on the broad back of my sea-dragon form. The others bobbed to the surface to meet us and to take a good look at their human visitor. The insurgent who'd met us disappeared briefly and returned with plastic bulbs of fresh water, which Summerfield gratefully consumed.

'How did you survive?' I asked her.

'I don't know,' she said honestly. 'I think you saved me. I think your body took the full brunt of the blast.' She pushed her wet hair out of her face. She could not tolerate the ocean environment for many days, even with her suit to protect her. 'If I lost consciousness, it was only for a split second. Like a film edit. There I was, tumbling underwater, looking at bubbles and fish and bits of the platform.

'As soon as I got my head out of the water, it was obvious what had happened. I confess, Lwpha, my first thought was that you'd done it – your real mission had been to smuggle a bomb onto that platform.'

'No,' I said.

'After treading water for about a minute I realised that didn't make sense. Why go to such huge lengths just to blow up a minor Draconian base? If the base was incredibly important, for some reason, then why not just drop the junk ship onto it? Either there'd been an accident, or it had to be other Mim. You and I had probably just got caught in the crossfire.'

I translated as one of the guerrillas explained: 'The Draconians aboard the floating platform didn't know that we can break ourselves apart. I disguised myself as a school of xebecs – individually small enough to be ignored by their automated defences – and attached about nine miniature explosives to the platform, under the surface.'

Summerfield said, 'I thought you were dead, Lwpha. I had no way of searching the wreckage properly. I wasn't even sure what I'd be looking for – whether I'd recognise you.'

The fact was, I'd been spread so thinly through the water that Summerfield had probably swum right through me. Possibly even ingested a few of my cells. I saw it would be wise to keep this information to myself.

'The only thing to do was to look for the Mim who'd knocked the platform out from under us. They might know where your children were, they might be able to help me survive. If I stayed in the wreckage, the Draconians would certainly find me, but I didn't fancy my chances of not catching the blame for the bomb.

'I started swimming in the direction of the nursery. Roughly. Very roughly. I don't think I really cared where I was heading, as long as it meant I got far enough away that I wasn't swimming through dead fish any more.

'After a few hours, I gave up swimming and just floated on my back. It was getting dark, I was parched, I didn't know where the hell I was. When the stars came out and I couldn't work out what any of them were... That *trapped* feeling...' She shook herself. 'I think I put the emergency light on more out of panic than anything. I didn't know who'd get to me first. I'm not sure I cared, as long as *someone* found me.'

'Some of the older children had been tracking her,' said the insurgent who had found us. 'Off their own bat. When we got their messages we scolded them, of course, and approached her ourselves.'

Summerfield said, 'You saved my life and I don't know your name.'

'But we endangered you in the first place! Call me Spong.'

'Spong?! You're taking the piss.' Benny turned to squint at me. 'You're all taking the piss, aren't you?'

I explained, 'She means your name is a joke.'

'Ooh!' said Spong. 'Tell us a human joke. Go on.'

Summerfield seemed embarrassed. 'Um... I... all the jokes I can think of are based on puns. Look, I seriously doubt you'd find any of the jokes I know funny.'

I said, 'We promise to laugh.'

She twisted her mouth at me; I had no idea what the expression meant. 'Okay. What should you do if a shark attacks you?'

'I don't know,' I chimed in, 'what should you do if a shark attacks you?'

'Punch it on the nose. If that doesn't work, hit it with your stump.'

She looked at us all expectantly. 'I get it,' I said, 'because the shark would retaliate by biting off your hand!'

'What's a shark?' said Spong.

Summerfield put her face in her palms. 'Tell you what,' she said. 'Why don't you tell me a Mim joke?'

Spong bobbed up and down with excitement. 'Right, well, there are two adolescent Mim sharing the same rock when a parasite crawls onto the rock between them. So the first Mim says, "Push the parasite off," so the second Mim tries to push the parasite off the rock, but ends up falling off the rock instead.'

'It's slapstick, I suppose,' said Summerfield, laughing politely.

'I'm not finished,' said Spong. 'So the second Mim climbs back up onto the rock. By now the parasite is gone. So the second Mim gets mad and tries to push the first Mim off the rock – but ends up falling off the rock instead!'

I broke up laughing – I hadn't heard that one.

'Was that the end?' said Summerfield.

'Yep,' said Spong, who was still laughing at his own joke. 'Didn't you get it? Do you want me to tell it again?'

'No,' I said, 'You'd only end up falling off the rock!'

The whole group fell about laughing for a few hundred seconds while Summerfield just watched us, puzzled. 'Right,' she said eventually. 'So much for the interspecies humour exchange.'

'Most human humour is about sex,' I commented.

Spong said, 'Tell us a joke about sex!'

'*No*,' said Summerfield, and that was the end of that.

8

ummerfield still had her camera and plenty of oxygen in her tanks. There was no avoiding the surprise any more. While Spong and his fellows arranged our escape from PL, I took her to see the kids.

We soared over the nursery, me in a torpedo-dolphin shape for quick and agile movement, she kicking with her feet extensions. The children were on the shallow sea floor, clearly visible. Summerfield moved downwards to take a closer look. Some of the older children reacted, producing pseudopods to try to touch her as she passed overhead.

It was exciting to think of a member of another species seeing something so familiar, so Mimmish if you will, for the first time. The borogove was a long, oval shape. The smallest, youngest infants were in the centre, either completely sessile or only beginning to move; the oldest were at the edges, in constant motion as they jockeyed for safer positions further from the edge, or actively explored the sea bottom surrounding the nursery. It was a great mass of new life, randomly edging across the sea floor a few decimetres each day. Normally, they would have rippled with colours; but they had been told to stay camouflaged against the seabed. When one of the younger ones changed to an inappropriate colour, its neighbours scolded it back into line.

Summerfield and I couldn't speak to each other and, with the goggles and oxygen mask on her face, it was impossible to read Summerfield's reactions. But after some minutes, she gestured that we should return to the surface, and I followed her into the air.

(You're probably wondering whether humans send out chemical signals. They do, but nothing you'd recognise the meaning of, certainly nothing like language. It's more like a soft background murmuring, or static.)

She pushed the goggles onto her forehead and took the breathing apparatus out of her mouth, looked hard at me, and said, 'Lwpha... we've been swimming for ten minutes, and we haven't finished travelling over the nursery.'

'Yes.'

'There are *thousands* of Mim children down there!' she spluttered.

'I'm afraid so. We evacuated hundreds of nurseries, but this one got left behind in its entirety.'

'Well... how many of them are yours?'

'All of them.'

'*All* of them?' She stared at me. 'Lwpha, how literally do you mean that? Are you actually genetically related to the lot of them?'

When I didn't answer, she slapped my flank, not in order to injure me but to express frustration. 'You can't keep this a secret from the galaxy any longer,' she told me. 'How can I represent your interests unless I have the whole picture?'

She was right, and there was no way to avoid it. 'You'll be the first alien who's ever been told.'

'I know,' she said gently. 'But there's no other way.'

I began my lecture.

'Each borogove contains thousands of our offspring; the largest may contain a quarter of a million. But on average, only a few hundred of those young will survive to adulthood. The rest are eaten by predators or by each other, or are killed by disease, genetic disorders, and so on.'

'Well,' she said tightly, 'you did say you were interested in the differences between us.' Summerfield kept her face composed, but I knew how she would react, how any human or Draconian would react.

'We know it horrifies you. However, listen. You don't hesitate to throw away your own gametes, millions of them at a time. A sizeable percentage of human embryos never come to term. For that matter, you make soldiers of your own young while they are still only in their

48

adolescent phase. Now, how is that different to my releasing my gemmules into the borogove to take their chances?'

Summerfield closed her eyes. 'It's going to be difficult to get this across to people. The Draconians will use it as another argument that you're monsters.'

'You've got to make them understand. First, that means you've got to understand. Once my offspring have become part of that borogove, I love the borogove. The whole colony with its thousand parts. I can no longer tell which of the individual young are mine; I care for every one of them, and so do all the other parents. Most of the others are here because they couldn't get the borogove off the planet, and they could no more leave it to the Draconians than you could have left Peter in the hands of the Fifth Axis.'

Her eyes snapped open at that. I went on without stopping. 'When a borogove is struck by disease, I suffer the way a human parent would suffer. If a borogove dies, I grieve no less than you would for any individual human child.'

'But that means hundreds – maybe thousands – of your siblings died. Maybe you're the only one that's left.'

'Oh, that's not likely. Given the average size of a gemmule release, there are probably twenty or thirty adult Mim who share my genome.'

'But still hundreds just like you – eaten by animals! Or starving to death because the other infants were quicker grabbing the food!'

'You must not picture them as human infants,' I said. 'You must remember they are themselves virtually animals.'

She waved her hands. 'I can't think of children that way! A baby can't do the cryptic crossword, but that doesn't make it worthless.'

'Summerfield,' I said, 'most of the ones that die, die very quickly, and could not have been saved. It's one of the reasons that asexual reproduction is superior to sexual reproduction.'

'Oh, is that so?'

'We can't carry hidden genetic disorders the way you can. We've only got one set of genes. Do you see?'

'But not all of them die that way. There's still the xebecs. Weeding out the weak.'

Spong appeared, attracted by our argument, I think. 'How can you explain about borogoves to an alien?' he said out loud. 'Isn't it all so different that they can't possibly understand?'

'I've got to understand,' said Summerfield. 'I've got to try to explain this to other human beings. If you love the borogove so much, Lwpha, how could they get left behind?'

'We're still arguing about how that happened,' I said.

Spong said, 'There was a first-rate emergency plan in place. Everything had been stepped up in readiness for the anticipated Draconian invasion.'

I added, 'We can't just pick the kids up and run. The borogove's got to be kept together, and it's got to be kept in seawater. But there were plenty of lifeboats assigned to the nurseries, plenty of ships ready to take them off-world.'

'And then –' Spong splashed the water all around himself.

'Panic,' I said. 'Not everywhere, not all at once. People losing their heads, so to speak, and abandoning their posts, even trained professionals.'

Summerfield said quietly, 'I've seen a lot of emergencies. People can just snap.'

Spong said, 'I was on a fast boat to a rocket when everyone aboard began to "freak out". People were fighting each other for no real reason. It was contagious. I jumped over the side. I heard that the boat crashed a few minutes later.' He added shyly, 'That's why I'm still here, in fact.'

'Was there any pattern to the outbursts?'

'There really isn't the data to say,' said Spong.

'I guess that's not surprising,'

I said, 'There have been a lot of conspiracy theories about it. Agents provocateur. Our own people stirring up riots.' It was an ugly thought; the Draconians couldn't infiltrate us personally... but in a population of millions, surely you could find a Mim who'd be convinced by bribes, threats, promises, trickery. There were eccentric political and religious groups who might have become scapegoats for that theory if they hadn't died with the Mimsphere.

Spong was telling the human, 'Some people claim that a chemical was released into the air or the water – something that triggered the release of alarm pheromones. The more people got a jolt of it, the more pheromones there'd be, until everyone was just jumping around in terror.'

'The smell of fear,' said Summerfield. She frowned, but didn't say anything more.

9

S ummerfield woke weeping. I looked down at her with concern.
'I was dreaming,' she said. She turned her body in the water so that she was upright, pointlessly wiping her face.

I had been towing her for hours. 'Were you able to rest properly?'

'I slept a bit,' she said tiredly. 'Do Mim dream?'

'The structure of our dreams is not the same as yours, but we do have an equivalent.'

Summerfield said nothing, only positioning herself more comfortably alongside my sea-dragon body. Spong came a little closer and said shyly, 'Can I ask what your dream was about?'

'A memory...' she began. 'Actually, it's a bit difficult to explain. I once met a creature that could distort time. It brought my son back from the future. Our son – Jason and me. He hadn't been born yet. Still hasn't.'

Spong thought this over at length. Finally he asked, 'What stage of development was the child at?'

'Just starting to talk,' said Summerfield. 'And running around. The age where they have an attention span of about three seconds.' She smiled. 'He was only with us for a short while.'

'Do you mean, a short while in the dream, or a short while in the original event?'

'Originally, I meant. The time distortion didn't last. Keith went back to his future.'

More thinking from Spong. *Caution*, I signalled him. *Crying is a spontaneous indication of sadness.*

Spong signalled his understanding, then said, 'When Keith went back to his future, was it as though he had died?'

Summerfield turned her head sharply to look at him. I released a spray of irritated signals and said 'Spong!' out loud for good measure.

'It's all right,' said the human, patting her gloved hand against my side. 'No, Spong, it wasn't. Jason and I were optimistic. I think later… But we're back together now. We're hoping to meet Keith again, one day.'

But Spong had got into a maudlin mood now. He swam closer to my hearing organs and (staying with spoken language out of good manners) asked, 'Where were you when you heard?'

I signalled the exact name of the city area, and translated loosely, 'Here on Holiday Home.'

'I was at work,' said Spong. 'Everyone just floated around in disbelief.'

There was an awkward pause, which prompted Summerfield to ask, 'What was your job, Spong? Before the occupation?'

'I'm a plumber.'

'Erm, did I hear you right? You're a plumber?'

'I still am,' said Spong proudly. 'I don't spend all my time spying on the Draconians. In fact with the occupation it's a more important job than ever.'

'Well, that's… actually, that's true. Good on you, Spong.'

'Just call me Mr Useful,' said Spong.

Summerfield put a tentative kiss on him, which he grasped was an affectionate gesture. 'All of this seems like something out of the sinking theatre to me,' he said wistfully. 'As a kiddy I used to change shape all the time, but these days it's only for special occasions, you know. I'm not one of those rude people who does it just to show off. I don't mean you, Lwpha, obviously. You lead such a glamorous life – out there amongst the stars, all those aliens! It all seemed so distant and unreal. Until the Draconians came. Now the outside universe is right in our pores, whether we like it or not.'

Spong's gabble cut off suddenly as we were both hit by a wash of signals. He did a happy little jump out of the water. 'What is it?' said Summerfield.

'A boat! They've managed to get us a speedboat – a collapsible Draconian skimmer, pinched from one of their supply dumps.'

She was looking out across the water, shielding her eyes from the glow of the tropical sun and the scatter of flashes on the water. 'I can't see anything.'

I said, 'They're about ten kilometres ahead of us. Hold on, Summerfield. We'll be there shortly.'

'You've really got to call me Benny,' she said. (I could never remember to do it.)

The insurgent cell had been hiding deep in the water, waiting for our arrival. They rushed to the surface as we approached (fast enough to kill a human or a Draconian as the pressure changed!), carrying the boat between them. Its aluminium surfaces flashed blindingly as it surfaced, forcing Summerfield to shut her eyes until we were almost upon it.

I hadn't seen how badly off she was until we got her into the boat. She tried to climb in, and lacked the strength, and I had to lift her in with a trio of pseudopods. She had already lost some of her body mass, probably more from dehydration than starvation.

The insurgents (six of them, no names) had brought some Draconian rations and some extra fresh water. Summerfield pushed the hood of her suit away from her head, and used some of the water to wash the salt from her face and hair. There were already small sores where her skin had been exposed too long.

'Thank you,' she said hoarsely. 'Tell them, thank you.'

I passed it on. They were already sinking rapidly, back to the anonymity of the depths. I'd never know who they were.

Spong examined the boat's motor. 'It's a simple engine. Mostly ceramics. Powered by ethanol. I can generate extra fuel myself if we need it.'

'That's clever, Private Sponge,' said Summerfield tiredly, 'how would you do that?'

I signalled Spong to keep his biochemical talents to himself, before she worked out exactly how he had been supplying her with drinking water. He shut up and started the alien engine on his second attempt. I let him know I was grateful he'd accompanied us.

'Rest now,' I told the human. 'Eat something.' I pushed the liberated ration packs over to her, and busied myself tying a cloth shade over the boat.

'I feel like luggage,' she murmured, fumbling with the catch on a ration box. 'You'd be safe if you followed the others – if you went into the depths – wouldn't you? But you've got to stay on the surface because of the air-breather. Because of me.'

'You're the whole point of the exercise,' I told her. 'You're our witness! Our proof!'

'The holograms,' she muttered, picking at a limp salad.

'Holograms can so readily be faked.'

'Witnesses can be bribed.'

I made a head, expressly to shake it at her. 'You're a neutral party, Summerfield. You're well known and you're respected. Without your evidence to back us up, we'll have little chance of saving the borogove.'

Summerfield swallowed a leaf, with difficulty. I pushed more drinking water to her. She took a long swallow and said, 'I suppose you could work out which ones, exactly.'

'Sorry, what?'

'Which of the kids in the borogove are yours? You could do a PNA test.'

It had never occurred to me before. 'I can't think of a reason to do it.'

She waved a leaf at me. 'Say you could only save a handful of children from the borogove. Would you prefer to save the ones that developed from your own gemmules?'

Spong called out, 'Are you two playing "Ethics"?'

'If you like,' I called back. 'I think that, in fact, I'd do the opposite. I'd save some of the children I know I'm not related to.'

'Why?'

'I can replace my own offspring, but not someone else's... Can I ask you a question, in return?'

'Shoot.'

'Is this related to the reason you wish to have a second child?'

Summerfield looked at me, long and hard, taking another large drink from the fresh water. 'What makes you say that?' she asked. 'Peter is genetically mine, after all.'

'It is a private matter,' I said. 'I shouldn't have asked the question. Please, let's act as though I didn't.'

Summerfield gave a sort of grunt to indicate her agreement, and went back to chewing at the salad.

Four hours later, we saw a Draconian battleship on our horizon.

Summerfield was dozing under the cloth shade. I signalled Spong: *Don't wake her.* If they put a missile into us, she'd be better off knowing nothing about it.

Spong killed the engine at once, so that we were drifting noiselessly, a tiny speck on the rolling waves. *Will they fire on a Draconian boat?*

Yes, if it doesn't respond correctly to their signals.

Spong asked reluctantly: *Should we abandon ship?*

I dithered. We could leave Summerfield alone in the boat and both dive well out of detection range.

You go, I told Spong. *I'd better stay with her in case they try to take her prisoner.*

Now it was his turn to dither. *I should stay. For the engine.*

Spong, I said, *let's not get any closer to extinction than we have to.*

He didn't send any further signals, but slipped over the side into the water. I dipped in a pseudopod and called after him, *Try not to lose track of us. If we do get through, we'll need you.*

He signalled in the affirmative. It took a long moment to reach me, as he was already sinking as fast as he could, getting a healthy buffer of water between himself and any explosions. *Good Mim,* I told him, not sure if the signal would ever reach him.

We still had a chance. We were a dot on the water, after all, effectively invisible to any Draconian who might be looking out over the ocean, difficult to separate from background noise on scanners. I extended a pseudopod to have a look at the cloth shade from above; as I'd suspected, it was camo, mirroring the water. We had a chance.

Summerfield dozed on through the heat of the afternoon as the battleship stayed on the horizon. They came no closer. After some hours, I realised that the shape was getting smaller; they were moving away from us, or we were drifting away from them.

It was nightfall when they were no longer visible, not even as a distant light. We'd done it. We'd held on, and they'd never even known we were here.

I sent out a loud series of 'safe' signals into the water; if Spong approached to take a look at us, he'd know we were in the clear. Draconian tech is a bit of a 'blind spot' for me. I wasn't sure I could even start the engine without his help.

10

We never even saw it coming. We never saw it at all.

In an instant the cloth shade was on fire and the boat was melting down the middle, sliced precisely in half.

Summerfield woke with an undignified yell as she fell through steam into the water. I fell backwards over the side, got tangled up in the shade's ties, and squeezed myself free, shooting out into the water like an eel.

'What the hell was that?' she screamed.

'Orbital laser!' I shouted, over the sizzling water and the burning cloth. 'Get away from the boat! Get away from it!'

She started swimming at once, as fast as she could without flippers, which wasn't fast enough. I submerged and came up under her, moving like lightning.

There was a blinding smell of ozone as a second invisible beam struck the remains of the boat. Steam burst out and covered everything. Summerfield would have been cooked if I hadn't got her away.

At least there was no explosion.

Spong was on fire.

I panicked. I reared up and stretched out and Summerfield tumbled off me into the water. She swam for the screaming shape floating ahead of us, somewhere in the heavy, stinking cloud.

She reached him before I did, and pushed him under the surface, first with her gloved hands and then with her entire weight: she literally climbed on top of him, despite the flames, forcing him under.

He went right on screaming under the water, releasing a continuous, deafening stream of distress chemicals, which mixed with the dreadful smell of burning Mim-flesh, something even Summerfield could smell. 'Is he all right?' she was shouting at me.

'Of course he's not all right!' I snapped back. Spong's panic was mixing with my own. His cries were beginning to die down, which was not a good sign. 'Fire's out. You can get off him.'

What was left of Spong bobbed back to the surface in a blackened lump. Summerfield exclaimed: Spong was still alive, still moving. I signalled him urgently to stop changing shape. *You've lost over half your body mass*, I had to tell him. *There's an awful lot of dead tissue fused to your body. Can you shed it?*

Spong convulsed. Some of the blackened flesh fell away, revealing living but scorched tissue underneath. He shrieked, a chemical rush of agony.

Don't, I said. *Best to leave it where it is.*

We had no first-aid kit, not even a simple analgesic. We had no way to signal for help, even from the Draconians. They might possibly send a vessel to grab prisoners for interrogation, but I doubted it: those beams had been meant to burn us or steam us. Like picking a tiny parasite off your exterior. Had the battleship spotted us and reported us? Or had an attentive satellite operator picked us up on a scan? We'd never know.

'Back in the sea,' said Summerfield. 'Again.'

It took Spong a couple of hours to die.

Summerfield was clearly horrified by his injuries. In some ways I think the horror may have actually been worse for her than for me; she couldn't really understand what she was seeing, nor any of the silent signals Spong was putting out. What she cradled in her arms until the sun went down, what she crooned to in a low voice, was a mass of unidentifiable cooked and raw alien flesh, endlessly shivering in pain.

A human suffering such trauma would have lost sensation in their body, and could not possibly have continued to function mentally. Although a great deal of his memory had been lost, Spong remained lucid until the last.

I asked him, *Do you want me to euthanise you?*

How?

He was right. I'd need tools. *Do you have a religion?*

Not really, he replied, and then said out loud, 'Perhaps now is the time to start. Summerfield – what are your beliefs about the afterlife?'

She looked at him in astonishment. 'Well, I… I don't –' She took a deep breath. 'One human belief system describes being alive as being a wave on the ocean. Uh, we rise up and return to the water.'

'Good,' said Spong. 'That's good. We don't end… we were water all along. What about you, Lwpha?'

'I joined the Enmity during my education,' I said.

'Well that's no help at all.'

Summerfield's expression said she wanted to know what the Enmity were. I groped for an explanation. 'The transcultural belief in an enemy god,' I said. 'Do you know it? A supernatural entity that promotes evil… like the Draconian spirit of chaos?'

'Knaubetj Three Horned Face? Lwpha, are you saying you're a Devil worshipper?'

I wasn't sure what she meant. 'There's only one creator: the evil spirit. The Enmity oppose it.'

'I admit,' said Spong, 'when that laser beam hit, I was thinking of the evil spirit. Silly, really.'

'Still,' I said, 'sometimes you can't help but wonder.'

'I don't think I believe in the Devil,' said Summerfield softly. She was stroking Spong's surface gently; he wasn't troubled by it. 'Just terrible weapons, and vulnerable people.'

'You were right,' said Spong. 'We do take the piss. We take human or Draconian names, which make us seem amusing, so that we seem less threatening.'

'That's not bad,' soothed Summerfield. 'In fact, that takes a pretty sophisticated understanding of our humour.'

'I didn't think of it myself. There was a list circulated. I like *your* name. It makes me think of seaweed in tropical sunlight. Waving softly.' And he was gone.

11

We let Spong's body go. Once the micro-organisms in the sea began their work, he really would return to the water, like a wave settling down. Summerfield watched the small, charred floating body for a long time, until she could no longer pick it out of the darkening waves.

'We're screwed,' she said aloud.

'Speak for yourself.'

'Lwpha, we're in the middle of nowhere. What do you –' She twigged that I was making a joke about our respective biology, and let out a long sigh.

The insurgency would have more sense than to come after us, under the eyes of the orbital lasers. The Draconians would not even be looking for us. I was sending out mayday signals, of course, but the evacuation had emptied the oceans of Mim and we were hundreds of kilometres from land.

'You're right,' I admitted. 'We are screwed.'

Summerfield floated a little distance away, and turned her back to me. It was a way to communicate anger; I thought she was probably also composing herself for death, perhaps pondering the stars. She unlooped the camera from her neck, the little plastic box that contained our precious evidence.

'If Mim or humans find our bodies,' I called, 'they might find the images of the borogove.'

'I have a better idea,' she said. The camera's flash startled me; she had taken a picture of herself.

I was next to her in a moment, pulling the camera out of her hands, but it was too late: she had already transmitted the image.

I examined the camera. Her transmission had been broadcast in clear; anyone within thousands of kilometres could receive and view the image.

'Oh, Lwpha. What's the point in secrecy any more?' she said.

'If the Draconians fish us out of the water –'

'– then we'll find ourselves another sympathetic savant,' she said.

I squirted water at her in frustration. She laughed, misunderstanding. I was tempted to swim away from her, taking the camera. It would be easy for me to hide from Draconian searchers. Of the two of us, I'd be a greater security risk under interrogation, although I'd also be more likely to die avoiding capture.

Oh, what was the point?

I bobbed next to her like an irritated buoy, and we said nothing.

Fifteen hours later, a ship appeared on one part of the horizon and a flyer appeared on the other, almost at the same instant. We watched, silently, as they passed back and forth across the water. For a long time they were beyond the range of our unaided vision; we couldn't see who the vessels belonged to. It hardly mattered. We had no way to signal them. '*Que sera sera*,' croaked Summerfield.

I had formed myself into a sort of floating couch for her; I could float without expending energy, and she could not. I turned back and forth, very slowly, so that she had an alternating view of the two vessels.

When they spotted us, it was very abrupt; the ship was suddenly racing at us, its shape swelling by the second. Only a moment later the flyer followed suit, dashing to our position.

The flying ship got there first. It had human markings on its hull. I half-expected one of those crude T-mats, but instead the vessel settled into the water barely ten metres from us.

The ship, a Draconian motor gunboat, reached us even as we were being hauled inside the flyer by a trio of human beings. Delirious with thirst and exhaustion, Summerfield wasn't making much sense. 'Put us back in the sea! They'll shoot you down!'

'They can't,' said one of the humans. 'We're a diplomatic vessel.'

Summerfield cringed from imaginary lasers, in the water and in the sky, as the flyer lifted softly and tilted, just enough to allow hectolitres of seawater to spill through the open door.

I began to realise that we had been saved not by a military vessel, nor some sort of rescue vessel, but a diplomatic car. It had not been meant for this sort of work. Nor had the people staffing it. As I learned, they were not soldiers or rescue workers, but general staff from the embassy, including two records-keepers and a cleaner. With current tensions, the embassy had only dared to spare one member of its security staff, and she was piloting the vehicle.

They had no medic, but were in contact with medical staff at the embassy during our entire flight there. The Draconian ship followed for most of the journey, harassing our pilot with constant demands, which she handled first with assertiveness, then with brief anger, and finally with humour; everyone aboard was laughing at her responses, a little hysterically, I think.

The flyer settled into the compound at the human embassy. The sound of the engines stopped, the door slid open once more, and we were suddenly surrounded by humans, applauding and cheering.

'We made it,' said Summerfield.

'Apparently you're not important enough to go to war over,' said the cleaner.

12

Summerfield returned from the medics' attentions looking well, if tired and sunburned. I had formed a body with two legs and a head, my usual form when amongst human beings. It is smooth, featureless, expressionless. And yet, she still knew, just by glancing at me, that something was wrong.

I told her what was wrong.

'Ishtar's pubic triangle,' she swore. I had to look up the reference.

The embassy staff had a darkened room put aside for the playing of media, with a giant screen that could be split into dozens of smaller screens so as to watch multiple channels at once. I took Benny there, and we drank Kool-Aid and watched the news.

The embassy had sent out our precious images at once, along with statements from the humans who had rescued us and a plea from the ambassador himself. They had soon been all over the news media, but not for the reason we had expected.

Kothar, voice of the Draconians, was on every channel. On many of them, he was commenting on *our* images. Even Benny's life-saving snapshot of herself, floating in the ocean.

Ours were not the only images. Kothar was displaying stills and footage of borogove after borogove. I could tell at a glance they weren't the one we'd visited, the one I love. Some were in the tropics, some were in colder waters, one was in a trench and two were almost littoral. All of them were on Holiday Home.

'In their haste to abandon Proxima Longissima,' Kothar was saying smoothly, 'the Mim also abandoned millions of their own children. Fortunately, Draconians value nothing more highly than children. We have been caring for these orphans ever since we assumed control of the planet.'

Summerfield looked at me.

'We never even suspected,' I said. 'We had no idea.'

'Someone must have known. Some of the Mim must have known their children were left behind.'

I nodded my approximation of a head. 'There will be frantic parents among the refugees. But we've got no government, no records. It could be weeks before we match adults to children. We can't even be sure how many borogoves the Draconians actually have.'

Summerfield instinctively reached out, but I had no hand or arm or even shoulder for her to touch. 'It was your children they wanted all along,' she said softly, horrified. 'When our pictures got out, they just switched smoothly to their back-up plan – as though they were going to tell the galaxy about the kids all along.'

I could read despair in her expression. 'It's better that we've forced them to this second choice,' I told her. 'Much better. With the borogoves hidden, the Draconians could have done anything they pleased with the children. Think of it, Summerfield: think of the experiments, the dissections.' I saw her swallow and nod. 'Now, the eyes of many worlds are watching them. That was always all we could hope to accomplish.'

She didn't answer me, but only sank down into the soft chair, and closed her eyes.

13

ad the Draconians thought to weigh Summerfield, we would never have escaped the planet. But then, why would they think of weighing her? Even a Mim wouldn't have thought of it. No Mim has ever done what we did. I don't think any Mim has even imagined it. And only a fully trained agent could have accomplished it.

The Draconians couldn't stop Summerfield leaving; and why would they want to? Her efforts had only confirmed their own PR. In fact, they *insisted* on providing her with a shuttle to take her to the Braxiatel Collection, to rejoin her own family.

They could do anything they liked to me, though, the moment I stretched a pseudopod outside the boundaries of the embassy. And so, after everything, the most dangerous part of our plan was still ahead of us.

We had practised and tested the idea several times before we left Phaaag Zenbrou, and we were confident, but there was no way to be sure it would work in the field.

Summerfield sat in the bathtub as I slowly disassembled myself, preparing. She stared as the water changed colour, soupy with my shed cells. 'Are you all right?' she kept asking me. After several hundred seconds had passed, I couldn't answer any more. We had joked that our trick would require total concentration. I had no cells left spare to form organs for hearing or speaking.

Once I had reduced myself to about three kilograms in mass, we were ready to proceed. In a gelatinous trickle, my cells began to merge with hers, passing softly through her skin. Slowly, cautiously, I broke my body into smaller and smaller pieces, until I was smeared through her bloodstream, individual cells floating in every part of her body. Had my cells been the size of human blood cells, it could never have worked; but they're far smaller.

I lost consciousness partway through the process, but once it had begun, it completed itself quite automatically, my cells drawing each other on with chemical signals. Stay together, said the alien compounds soaking through Summerfield's body, but don't stick together. Even a small accidental clumping could be fatal. In our tests, her immune system had simply ignored my cells; but there was no guarantee it wouldn't find some protein it disliked, especially now kilos of me were involved instead of small samples. If I triggered an immune response, her body would tear itself apart to kill me.

I would love to be able to tell you that I maintained some dim, magical awareness of my new environment. I was closer to Summerfield now, more intimate with her, than any human had ever been, even her mate, even her child. I rushed and paused, rushed and paused, through every one of those numberless organs. I wish I could tell you there was a mystical union of two children of different worlds, two life forms so similar and yet so totally different. I wish I could say I became one with the blood, the living seawater of the universe. But for me, it was only blackness and sleep. Had the worst happened, a deadly fever or an ugly blockage, I would never have known.

I can only imagine the hours of determination and dread she spent aboard the Draconian's shuttle. The longer we spent meshed together, the more likely that our fused bodies would begin to kill each other. The leftover bits of me? Benny just pulled the plug and let all those loose cells and clumps of spongy flesh swirl down into the sewers. We found out later that – just as we'd hoped – the Draconians wasted time and troops following my faint biosignals through the pipes. Even when they started to find clumps visible to the naked eye, they didn't guess right away, but kept searching until a savant put two and two together. On Earth, lizards drop their tails to distract a predator, and I'd done essentially the same.

I became aware again perhaps three-quarters of the way through the reverse process. Summerfield was in a warm bath, in her own bathroom back at the Braxiatel Collection, trying to read a book. Aware again, I drew my cells softly from her in a rush and floated helpless in the water.

She fed me with teaspoons of diluted soy sauce for an hour, until I had grown enough to form hearing and speaking organs. 'You are unharmed,' I squeaked.

'As far as I can tell,' she said softly.

'We'll do a full scan of your body,' I promised. 'But if any of my cells have been left behind, they will most likely simply die.'

Summerfield said, 'A lot has happened while you were out. The Draconians – they want to talk.'

Hope surged through me like a drink of clean water. 'Are they willing to return the borogoves?'

'I don't know yet. It's all come together in the last few hours. The Collection's going to host the negotiations. A Mim delegation is on their way here already.'

'The Collection is a Draconian protectorate,' I said, weakly trying to clamber out of the tub.

'Woah, woah! Stay put until you get your mass back!' I bobbed helplessly in the bath. 'The Collection has a long history of neutrality. We've hosted dozens of negotiations like this. We did it, Lwpha. We won. It'll be hard yakka, but we're going to work something out.'

'I have to be there.'

'You will be.'

Summerfield looked up as her mate entered the adjoining room. I went on absorbing amino acids, reflecting on the extraordinary experience we had just shared, and half-listening to their conversation. (I don't think they were mating, only comforting each other by close proximity.)

'I told Peter you were fine,' I heard Jason say. 'And he could see you as soon as you'd had a bath.'

'He's with Isaac?'

'Uh-huh. Learning to play chess, which has got him pretty distracted for a bit.'

Summerfield let out a heavy sigh. 'I think if there was going to be a medical problem we'd have seen it by now.'

'I wish you'd told me you were going to do that.'

'See if you can guess why I didn't.'

'I don't like the thought of you merging with anyone else,' he said, feigning carelessness. 'You send that bit of foam out here and I'll take him on, man to man.'

'Can I watch?' Summerfield was trying to match his humorous tone, but both of them were upset and afraid.

'Don't take this the wrong way,' he said quietly, 'but you look like you've been through hell.'

Summerfield blurted, 'They tested me, Jason. The Draconians. They wouldn't let me leave the embassy until they did a blood test.'

'Oh, shit.' He understood at once. 'What happened?'

'Nothing. Nothing happened. I thought they were going to shoot me on the spot, the moment that test came up positive. It *had* to come up positive, my blood was full of Mim cells, but it didn't.'

'What did you do?'

'What could I do? I told them they were wasting their time, and I waited. I think I even managed to look impatient.' A pause. 'When it came up negative, I still thought they knew. I thought they were just waiting for me to get on the shuttle. So they could kill both of us. What could I do? All I could do was get on and sit down and do up my seatbelt! I don't think I've *ever* felt that helpless!'

Another pause; she was weeping. He said quiet things, which I couldn't make out. 'I've felt like that since the beginning of this whole expedition. Falling out of space in the ship – swimming away from the platform after it'd been bombed –'

I came sloshing out of the bathroom. 'Do not characterise your actions as passive!' I said loudly. 'A battle may be won by the single sponge who stands their ground!'

Jason stared at me in astonishment. Summerfield said, 'Is that a Mim saying?'

'A well-known line of poetry,' I explained. (I was forming a little puddle of water and soy sauce on the carpet, and paused to soak it up.) 'It takes great courage to function normally when our overwhelming impulse is to panic: the urge to perform *any* action, when the correct thing to do is nothing. Summerfield, your courage will save my children, and thousands more.'

'I hope so. It would all – it would make –' She burst into tears. 'I want my baby,' she sobbed. Jason took hold of her, looking appalled.

I retreated into the bathroom, embarrassed. 'Get Peter for me, would you, Jason?' I heard Summerfield say, with forced cheerfulness. I had thought our commingling meant intimacy. It did not. No matter Summerfield's loyalty or ideals. These are the people she loves; I am not one of them.

14

told you everything that took place. I kept nothing back. I was completely honest with you. We are not enemies! Why have you done this to me?

I can't move... I can't even feel most of myself... the signals are there but they're jumping around wildly, juddering, it's like trying to read in an earthquake. It's all I can do to keep talking to you... I mean, literally, it's all I can do!

You're killing me, aren't you! How can you watch this! Can you even understand what I'm saying?

I think my extremities are starting to dissolve... my outermost cells... I must look like a fried egg, like a nasty stain on the carpet.

Summerfield! Oh, Summerfield! Come and help me! Come and stop this! It's not fair, not after we survived so much! We could have burned, and burned, and burned again, and every time our luck and devotion carried us through, and now this!

I am leaking away from myself. I am a crowd leaving the sinking theatre, breaking apart into lonely individuals. I am returning to the earliest times, when living things bobbed silent and alone in empty waters. Can you hear me any more? I can't even hear myself!

Oh, Summerfield. Benny! I love you, my friend. Oh, my borogove.

Oh, untimely death!

I'm back in the sea –

The Loyal Left Hand
Jonathan Blum

1

From the diary of Professor Bernice Summerfield:

They sprayed his remains on the garden today. Close as we could get to a funeral, I suppose, with his body in the state it was in.

The only way you could tell there even was a body was the way the droplets sparkled, all golden under the drizzly sky. Little clumps of protein and metallic particles, of course, but those little glimmering flecks at least looked like they *should* have been alive, as they landed all over the flowers. Like drops of fire in the rain. Or like a shower of Scotch. She wrote, seizing on the metaphors closest at hand at the moment.

I hope Lwpha would have liked it. There was no one to ask what he'd wanted. You don't really have next of kin for a race that reproduces by dumping spores in the ocean, and practically everyone over the age of two who knew him is missing or dead.

Daddy did the reading from the Mim *Book of the Unshiftable*, just before he left to go back to his own era. It was poetic and visionary and no one there understood more than one sentence in three. There was me, careful and solemn, telling his story to a few people who'd never met him. There was Adrian, keeping himself busy with the grounds crew. Peter, in that tiny suit Adrian bought for him, fidgeting because he knew he had to be all serious now but couldn't really see why it mattered. Mahalia and the other half-dozen faculty members

I'd invited, thinking the same thing but hiding it better. And Jason. My family, not Lwpha's. Is that all he got in the end? A funeral full of strangers, and a chance to fertilise some prizewinning shrubbery.

None of the Mim delegation showed for the funeral. Not one. Though for all I know they *were* the shrubbery. Still, their acting President – badly acting, if you ask me – sent regrets on behalf of the entire negotiating team, who were fully booked with crisis strategy sessions from now till a year past doomsday. Which is fair enough, considering. But I can't shake the feeling that somehow they didn't *want* to come, as if they blamed him for every one of those strategy sessions, everything he'd unleashed. Everything *we'd* uncovered.

None of them knew him anyway. Lwpha was just some random citizen, one of the formless masses – almost literally. Till he barged into their carefully arranged surrender and let them know they still had something worth fighting for. Just a man whose only thought was for his children.

Whatever the killers used on him, it made every last individual cell in his body congeal... all the water in his cells just stayed where it was, but everything else, everything that made him him, clumped together into these little goldish flecks. Ruptured the membranes. And the water flowed free. All over the floor of the garden outbuilding. So it sort of proved the point that we're all mostly water anyway, sentient sponges even more than most. He was just a bit rearranged, I suppose. More than usual.

And then... They had to mop him up off the shed floor. The man in the suit had to take the samples for the autopsy with a *straw*, for heaven's sake. And as I stood there with Lwpha soaking into my shoes, *my* only coherent thoughts were to thank my lucky trowel it hadn't happened in the Mansionhouse, cause Brax would go apeshit over cleaning the carpet. And I was watching the team wipe him up and trying not to giggle, because it just seemed horribly *right* that you'd have to mop up a dead Mim. Ashes to ashes, sponge to sponge.

You can think things like that if you're in shock, of course, so I tried to convince myself I was. But I'm increasingly bad at lying to myself, even if I still have to throw myself against the wall and get all *The Sweeney* before I'll ever confess to myself what I'm really thinking. Really it was the opposite of shock. It wasn't even a straighten-my-metaphorical-tie-and-make-a-bad-pun bit of callous bollockery. It was simply, genuinely, feeling so distanced from the situation that I could see the funny side.

I've spent too much time living in a world where ludicrous death is routine. I've been in one sort of life-threatening crisis or another for most of my life, and quite frankly the novelty wears off after a while. And it's a wonderful thing, not to be bothered. Until the fact that it's not eating at you starts eating at you.

So that's why it's time for me to stop. I've brought the truth out into the open, I've put it in the hands of the proper authorities, I've given my testimony in open session, the genie is well and truly out and has left me holding the empty bottle. I've done everything any reasonable person could do. And now I can keep my head down, let the dramas go on without me, and spend some time trying to feel things I can actually *feel*.

So of course the funeral wasn't for Lwpha, it was for me. Just because I was the one who needed closure. It was all for that moment of standing there in the garden feeling Lwpha's body mist around me and evaporate, and knowing that I can walk away from this now.

I suppose I could keep caring because they're likely to try to kill me next, of course. But somehow being threatened doesn't feel all that motivating in itself. It's a reason to keep my head down and stay at my usual level of faintly paranoid precaution, but it's not a reason to care. After a while you need something more fulfilling to work towards in your life than simply not being in mortal peril again. Something that matters to your soul.

Jason's on the sofa and I'm going to kiss him. Peter's tucked in his bed dreaming of dinosaurs. Charles Mingus is playing, saying goodbye to a man who poured all of his soul into a tenor saxophone. I'm going to kiss the only man I've ever called husband, with the taste of ancient Scotch in both our mouths, and whisper those magic words *I'm one week late*.

And he'll look at me with an awe and fear that the words *They want to kill me* could never hope to produce.

He didn't, of course. Instead the daft bugger looked up at her, with those slightly pursed lips that she'd learned meant he was in full retreat, and murmured 'And you think...?'

She held back, kept her eyes on the prize and her fingertips nestled in his hair. No way was she going to let out the exasperated whoosh of breath she could already feel building in her chest. She *wanted* this moment, more than she'd wanted anything in months, and she was bloody well going to make Jason Kane be tender and supportive whether he wanted to or not.

'Well, of course I think. It has been known to happen, you know.'

He sank back in the armchair, voice quiet, eyes like he was bracing for impact. 'It could be anything. You could wake up tomorrow morning and – nothing. Gone.'

For a long moment she just breathed. Then, slowly, deliberately, she knelt across the armchair and straddled him. Feeling the infuriating tautness of his chest just brushing against hers. Her lips tugging at his, bitter little kisses.

'Oh, my darling Bernice,' she murmured, 'At last you've got what you've wanted all this time, of course I'm going to support you in –'

'Now hang on, it's just we don't know –'

'– any way I can, and to hell with the Mim and saving the galaxy, we're clearing our schedule for the next nine months and –'

'What have the Mim got to do with –'

Breathy fury now, heat from deep in her lungs. 'And, oh, yes, I *am* paying attention to what you're saying, not looking for a tangent to go off on or –'

'It's not *about* what you're saying, it's – you're acting so *sure* –'

'I *am* sure. More sure than –'

'Yeah, but are you?' He was talking a mile a minute now, as her mouth pulled at his neck – trying to get his thoughts out before her tongue rasped down to *that* spot. 'Cause I mean, you're not acting like you've just found out you're pregnant – ghh – more like you want to start the whole process all over again, and I mean, no complaints obviously – but if you think about it – it's a bit – redundant…'

He was wriggling, trying to get away, but she had him pinned, thighs tight around his hips. She pulled her lips away long enough to glare at him. 'I'm doing this because I'm so furious I want to snog you senseless.' And even as she heard herself, her hips were slowing as it sank in. 'Which is pretty senseless itself, actually,' she said, deflating.

'Could be worse,' he said, his body still twitching a bit under her.

'So you say.' She rested her forehead on his. 'Bloody hell, I just want it to be true.'

Almost smug now. 'Of course you do. See? You're doing your thing…'

'It's *not* a thing.'

'It so is.' As he murmured, his arms were sliding up her sides and back now, meltingly smooth, as if reaching for the upper hand. 'Saying something like it's true to convince yourself. That's a Bernice Summerfield Thing.'

A retaliatory slow stroke through his hair. 'As opposed to casually acting like it *can't* be true because it bloody terrifies you.'

He sighed, and his hand changed course to reach for his glass. 'Thing One,' he said, ruefully saluting her with it. 'Thing Two.' He drank.

Bullseye. So their score was equal, and that little self-defending knot of tension inside her could finally begin to melt away. At least the gap between feeling that way and feeling silly about feeling that way was getting shorter. After all these years, she and Jason had finally begun to work out how to fight in lower case.

'The losing,' he said, his voice tiny. 'Not the having. That's the bit that bloody terrifies me. Anything could happen in nine months... that's about as long as our marriage lasted, isn't it?'

Face in her hands. 'We've both got dead kids on the brain.'

'Hardly surprising, after what happened to the Mim.'

'Oh, sod the Mim.' She took a swig straight from Jason's scotch glass. He looked at her in surprise – not about his drink, after this many years together that was fair game, but about the Mim. 'I want to just drop it all. Put everything else aside, just take care of the little things, be a good mother and good...' Wife. 'Partner. Or so I keep telling myself.'

He nodded. 'You're looking for a direction, this is a direction, therefore problem solved.'

'But it's mad, isn't it?' She rested her head on his shoulder. 'I was a war orphan, for all those years till we found Daddy again. How can I just walk away from billions of them?'

And the Mingus had long since faded out, and now on the sound system Michael Stipe was singing about how she just wants to be, and now is greater than the whole of the past, and her music library was just taking the piss now. She cocked her head at it in irritation. 'What is it *with* that thing?'

'Mood music,' he said. 'It's a gadget that picks up on the telepathic atmosphere and filters its playlist accordingly. Picked it up at the landing-port gift shop, I thought you'd get a kick out of it.'

She sharpened an eyebrow and hurled an expression at him, and kept thinking till the music turned into vintage death metal. But he countered with everything he had, scrunching up his face with the effort, till it crossfaded into the chorus of I Should Be So Lucky. And then they just lost it.

First step was...

No, first step for the morning was to take Peter over to the Kitishvaris' flat so he could spend the morning playing with Maeve.

Second step was to ring Ambassador Kothar's office, and begin a political dance of the seven veils.

But Kothar wouldn't even take her call. So as a carefully orchestrated revealing of stratagems within stratagems it was a bit of a flop, really. Instead she was faced with the sullen, bricklike visage of a deputy named Werther, a *no* on legs, whose sole function in the Embassy staff appeared to be to take a more obstructionist line even than Kothar himself. No, the Ambassador's not available this morning, he's in conference with his wife about the arrangements for tonight's formal dinner with the Mim... said in a tone that suggested Werther felt the best place for the Mim was on the menu. No, after that he's got the final preliminary negotiation session to agree on discussion terms for the actual negotiations. He can't possibly, not any time this century. So much for going through channels – Martian channels, thought Benny, dry and useless.

It wouldn't have been nearly so galling if she didn't then get to see Kothar's conference with his wife – strolling across the Mansionhouse lawns with two of their kids, apparently without a deadline in the world. He even gave her a courteous nod from a safe distance, while making a show of his five-year-old daughter dragging him away. 'Good day, Professor,' he said over his shoulder – his voice relentlessly imperturbable, with just a hint of smugness, the tone he knew drove those crazy apes bonkers. For Jarith Kothar, diplomacy was the art of calculated offence.

She tried not to glower too obviously at his departing back. One thing she'd learned about Kothar was that his desire for impeccable form outweighed even his desire for immediate strategic advantage. It hadn't been enough for him to annex the Collection to his Empire and settle an old grudge or two in the process; no, he'd had to engineer events in a Byzantine way so that the two interlocked perfectly, and the settling of the old grudge itself made the takeover possible. It could have been a sign of a deep-seated character flaw, if his whole damn plan hadn't worked perfectly.

And even now, when the catastrophe on the Mimsphere meant that jackboots were abruptly out of fashion in this sector, here he was modelling a whole new perfect form: the contented squire and family man surveying his estate. His wife Ithva and their children had arrived quietly just before the outbreak of hostilities, but where before he'd kept them right out of the spotlight, now they'd been moved to centre stage. Ithva Kothar had slipped into the role of unofficial First Lady of the Collection, the hostess with the mostest. And his kids, well, they made excellent window dressing for his new image. The Draconians as concerned parents... even to the point of taking up the green man's burden towards the lesser races. Remember that, Summerfield: this is a man who'll use his own children for political gain.

So, if the mountain wouldn't let Mohammed come to it, it was time to lay out some bait to lure the mountain to her. Which at the very least was amusing to picture.

The local garrison was still barracked on the south lawns, halfway across Brax's planetoid. But now she could see bare patches of dead grass where the outer ring of prefab camo dome-tents had hunkered like a gathering of giant tortoises, and a whacking great troop transport sitting in the centre of the remaining camp. About half of the hundred or so remaining warriormen were busy feeding equipment into its loading-mouth, like a spider devouring its own young.

The fence was still in place, though. 'Begging your indulgence,' she asked one of the sentries in her most formal schoolroom Draconian, 'But could I respectfully plead for a few moments out of the life of Logistician Korenthai?'

She needed someone close enough to Kothar's rank and status to make this work, and she'd figured the senior Logistician for the garrison would be on-hand to bean-count the withdrawal. Ever since the massive *something* that had left the Mimsphere an irradiated husk of a world, the Draconians had been trying to tread lightly in this sector: clarifying the Collection's status as a protectorate rather than occupied territory, and now reducing their military presence. Which also made sense of Kothar's new genial image, and his efforts to present the Collection as a natural place for the negotiations: smoothly digging in his hold on his diplomatic role even as his military one eroded. When the smoke cleared, whichever position Kothar landed in, Benny was sure it'd look just like he'd *meant* to do that.

The sentries kept her waiting by the fence till their superior emerged from the transport. Somehow, even though Draconian men had no hair on the crests of their heads, she could tell Korenthai was balding. He had the two-eyed squint of an officer who spent his days peering at columns of figures rather than down a gunsight. 'Is there something you want, Professor?'

'Well, first I wanted to offer my congratulations on arranging such an efficient strategic redeployment.' She hesitated just enough over the last two words, to emphasise that she was choosing to describe their retreat politely.

He took it in stride. 'It's just a matter of the maximisation of flexibility and responsiveness in delivery.'

'Goodness. You make it sound so bold.' I get it. General in charge of the general ledger. She was lucky he hadn't kept her waiting for days while he got on with the subtotalling. She'd been banking on him having been warned to keep an eye out for her making any more mischief; she may not have any official standing or leverage, but she did at least have her reputation as the nosy academic to draw on.

Korenthai gave her what he obviously thought was a good imitation of a human smile. It made him look like a gila monster. 'It may not look like much from where you stand. But you try telling that to a squadron knee-deep in alien mud who've just discovered their vitamin supplements are out-of-date stock and they're about to lose all their teeth.'

'I read your article on munitions supply,' Benny said. 'Maintaining and developing reputational cost-benefit ratios while keeping operational expenses to a minimum.'

That got a genuine Draconian smile. 'The fighters look down on us, but they don't see how our work enhances their prestige outcomes.'

'Their honour, in other words.'

'Exactly.'

'Academics depend on their reputations. You could teach us a lot.' Benny gave a ditzy laugh. 'Of course, we don't have to worry about ammunition and things,' she burbled. 'What happened to the Mimsphere. It must be saving you a fortune.'

Korenthai showed his teeth again, and this time, it was a clear signal of aggression. 'It is saving a fortune, Professor Summerfield. The Mim problem was costing an astronomical amount. It's been extremely difficult to develop and implement effective and efficient delivery systems. But the disaster on the Mimsphere is not only saving us money; it's saving Draconian lives, tens of thousands of them.'

'At the cost of millions of Mim lives.'

He shook his head. 'Nothing to do with us – and I can guarantee that personally, Professor. That would have cost a fortune. I'd have seen it in the figures.'

'Even if it was done secretly?'

A level gaze. '*Especially* if it were done secretly.'

'I see. You know, my people have a saying: take care of the pennies, and the pounds will take care of themselves.' She translated it roughly into Draconian. Korenthai seemed to approve. 'But tell me… There are rather a lot of pennies floating about on Proxima Longissima. In your opinion, do you think Ambassador Kothar is capable of spotting a chance to maximise the long-term strategic outcome potential with a minimum of investment?'

And after that the rest of the discussion was just a formality. It was all for that moment, and the moment as soon as she left when Korenthai would get on the link straight to the Ambassador's office. In a way the whole exercise felt strangely *dry*, and cold, like she could push the machine into motion without having to put any of her own sweat or tears into it. And the question itself was just pretty-sounding noise, really – it didn't matter precisely which questions she was heard to ask, so long as it got back to Kothar that she was asking them about him. That the Summerfield woman was definitely up to something.

And by the time she reached home, the message was already waiting for her: the Ambassador will see you now.

Familiar ground, she thought. Not the Draconian Embassy, housed in the former offices of the Department of Acquisitional Ethics; someplace public. Someplace unpredictable. Ideally someplace that Ambassador Kothar would rather not be caught dead with her, especially since she would rather not be caught dead there herself.

She made the appointment on the shortest notice possible, at lunchtime, and half an hour later she was waiting for Kothar on the side steps of the Aina Gallery. It was a sign of the impeccable excess of the Braxiatel Collection that even the fire-exit stairs were carved from granite – a sharp wedge running down from the roof, past doors notched in the solid marble wall.

She would play this smooth. Never mind everything else she felt doubtful about now, the one thing she could be sure of was her skill at reading people. Even Draconains – as far back as her Academy days she'd spent enough time with them to at least begin to make sense of their reactions. And if Kothar and the negotiating team were so typically concerned about setting, etiquette and the symbolism of their environment, then she was bloody well going to make sure every bit of this setting made her points for her.

Tucked between two buildings, the walls and stairs limiting the possible angles for snipers and giving her a clear view of anyone approaching on foot. But a narrow staircase up the outside of the building, with only a token metal-chain handrail to stop you if you pitched over the side: showing she wasn't afraid to go close to the edge with Kothar. And Joseph the drone hovering at the top, conspicuously recording the scene, just to show she wasn't stupid.

Oh, she'd done her research. And if she'd guessed right, Kothar had plenty of reason to worry when his children asked him, 'Daddy, what did you do in the war?'

The rain wasn't part of her strategy, but it didn't hurt. It meant she could sit nonchalantly on the steps, under a disarmingly pink umbrella, while Kothar had to try to look dignified and manly while taking shelter under an outsized brolly of his own.

He stood at the foot of the steps, and managed to look slightly down his nose at her even while looking up. Not a scale out of place, every last ornamental buckle and silken panel on his *hronsthei* immaculately dry.

'Professor Summerfield.' He inclined his head respectfully but with that tilt to it, which always made her feel he was watching her out of the corner of his eye. A lizard gesture, using the whole of his field of vision. Inhuman poise: absolute poker-face stillness at rest, sharp smooth moves between poses. 'It's good to see you're willing to discuss our proposal reasonably.'

'Actually, I've got a proposal of my own,' she said. She twirled and furled her umbrella, letting each raindrop splotch on her as if she welcomed it. (I belong in this rain. If you go after me you won't be perfect, you won't be ready like I am.)

'I'm interested,' he said, as if she were a child offering him her latest drawing.

'Well, cooperation for a start,' she said. 'You could work with the Mim on this, there's no need for such a stiff-necked policy...'

'This is not policy; this is character.' For heaven's sake, when he spoke she could hear the semicolons. But he was delivering the words like he really meant them. 'It's at the heart of who we are. We could never abandon children to such an uncaring fate, even Mim children. Our nature would simply never allow us.'

And here comes the ten-thousand-years-of-culture bit, she thought. 'For generation after generation, the closest thought to our hearts has always been to care for the next generation. It's what drives us. We have crossed space for our children, taken whole worlds to give them what they need to live. Children are everything to us. To the Mim… they are nothing.' He was trying to persuade her. 'They live in *packs*.' That wasn't like him, to care about what she or anyone else thought. 'You saw them.' Not unless she was important to his own ends somehow. Or if his purpose was just to get her guard down… 'And since their homeworld was destroyed they *cannot* provide for their young. Their children outnumber them, thousands to one. So we *will* keep custody of the children. That's not open for negotiation.' He's getting bolder. He's seeing you sodden, at the mercy of the rain. Instead of saying you're not bothered, it's saying you're a mess. You're vulnerable. Hide it, now.

'Have you noticed the architecture here – particularly, these steps?' she asked, apropos of as little as possible.

A shrug. 'They seem fairly harmonious with the surroundings…'

'This whole building's based on the design of an Old Earth castle,' she said. 'The layout's part of the defences. You see –' and she started backing away up the steps '– if the defenders of the castle had to fight, they've got plenty of room to swing their swords.' She swung her umbrella slowly, arcing out over the rail, and he parried awkwardly with his own. He had to reach across his body to block, his elbow forced against the stone wall on his right.

'See?' she went on. 'The attackers can't get a good swing with their sword-arm. Puts them at a disadvantage.' And because you didn't think before you moved your umbrella to block, now you've got a nice big splatter of rainwater down your back, you overdressed iguana. Not that he was going to acknowledge it, of course, but we take our pleasures where we can.

And she was sure it threw him off his stride for a whole couple of seconds, till he came up with a reply. 'It just means a conqueror has to be more subtle in his movements.'

And he lowered his own umbrella to match her fighting stance. Another careful pause, to show him standing unfazed in the rain. 'For example.' And he furled his brolly with a snap and shifted his stance, a smooth forward line favouring thrusts and jabs over cuts. A rapier against her broadsword.

Slowly, with studied unconcern, never breaking the illusion that he was just demonstrating a point, he engaged her. Little wrist-flicks instead of sweeping strokes. The rainwater squelching under her shoes, oiling the stairs.

'Ah,' she said, as she had to back up another step. 'But while they're having to be cautious, the defender can give it everything they've got. They're the ones fighting for their home, their families.

The attackers may have all the coolness and skill they want – but they can't use their strength. Or their passion.'

'But if right is on their side?' he thrust.

'Oh, not on these steps.' She parried his right arm against the wall again. There, a little bilingual pun; let him lose that in translation. 'The only way they're evenly matched... is if the attackers fight left-handed.'

Play it cool. Raise just a little bit of an eyebrow on that line, as if you're expecting him to try to see. As if you don't know just how dishonourable fighting that way would be for a Draconian. Which of course he knows you *do* know, so you're really telling him you expect him to sink to any depths – but, like him, you know how to leave no trace of what you're saying on the surface. That's the trouble with verbal fencing with a Draconian, every wretched sentence needs as many associations as a haiku.

'Our principles,' he said, flicking his umbrella around hers, 'are not so easily compromised. Especially when it comes to children. The officer who ordered the strike against the Stonehauser facility, knowing there was a childrens' ward... He was executed.'

'So never mind the other civilians, then...'

'Yes, we deplored the use of human shields to mask a major military target,' he said, batting her blade away dismissively. 'But killing the children was an offence even beyond such concerns. The truly innocent should never be exposed to such cruelties. To make war is as much the realm of adults as to make love.'

She was ready for the thrust on his final word. Talk about telegraphing your moves. But where he'd reached in close to grab her sword-arm, she'd skipped back another couple of steps, leaving him grappling with empty air.

'Interesting philosophy,' she said. 'You know, if my mate Socrates and company had tried debating their ideals with edged weapons, it would've made their whole school of thought that much more interesting, wouldn't it? They might not have had to bother with that hemlock business. And it would have played hell with the whole concept of the Platonic ideal if they were busy bleeding over it. It'd just go to show how ideals don't survive contact with reality.'

A twitch of a smile. 'Perhaps yours don't, Professor.' And that felt too much like a direct hit. Especially since now her latest clever strategy was also failing to survive contact with the enemy. Her little skip had backed her past the third-floor door; now there was nowhere left to turn before the open roof.

She said, 'Let's say you can find enough teachers, child care workers and nappy-changers for two billion infants, then enough social workers for two billion surly teenagers. What happens when the *next* generation comes along?' A quick glance over the edge. Passers-by on the Gallery lawn were staring up now from under their umbrellas. 'Two billion adult Mim… thousands of young each… Not the tiny share you were able to save this time… all of them.' The crowd waiting for one or the other of them to slip, to fall. Probably thinking this was just a piece of performance art. Or wacky Summerfield up to her usual tricks. 'But if you're doing this on principle, you can't just abandon them to their old ways, can you? How do you care for them all? And the generation after that? It's just going to get exponentially worse.'

'Oh, we're hardly Vrashaaka at the seashore,' he said, pausing for her to beg him to explain the reference. She just cocked him a look – sorry, no. 'A metaphor for a hopeless task relentlessly pursued. We know we can't fight the sea or the sun. The way the Mim breed is the product of nature – we can only do so much to overcome it. But even to save one whole generation… How could you let such a chance go by?'

'So don't.' And if there was ever a moment to drop the fencing, this was it. She raised her umbrella, in something resembling classic Draconian fencing form for disengagement, then flapped it open, in something which didn't. 'Work with the Mim. Run the centres with them, let them have a say in the raising of their children. Make it a joint project. What do you say?'

The glower deepened. 'It will not happen.'

'Why not? The war is *over.*'

'The war hasn't begun yet.' He stared across the lawns, at the Mansionhouse full of diplomats. 'No battle is ever over, and no negotiation is ever final. You should know that by now.'

An exasperated sigh. 'You're expecting more conflict, this'll only make it worse. Two billion refugees resenting you running their world, that's all you need –'

'We have already made a proposal such as yours. The Mim have refused outright.'

And she was left floundering, suddenly chilled in the rooftop rain. He'd been playing her all this time. He'd let her keep pushing the subject, testing her resolve, let her think she was leading him up the stairs when he was already ahead of her. He knew the ground she was standing on now, better than she did. She felt her eyes darting all over, to the other buildings surrounding her, all the places a sniper could hide.

And she wasn't sure which threw her off more, that the Draconians would compromise or that the Mim wouldn't.

There was a look on his face now, a genuine one, not his fencing mask. A glimpse of real annoyance at the Mim. 'They are digging in whichever parts of themselves correspond to heels. They want complete control of their young, or nothing.'

And that just made no sense. Obviously they'd flinch from handing over even partial control of the future of their race… But they had to know that they couldn't raise their children on their own. 'But why?'

'Because they are fools, and you, Professor Summerfield – no matter what else you may be – are not.'

'Well. Thanks for the testimonial. Though perhaps they don't fancy being seen as collaborators in the *civilising* of their race.'

A further pained look. 'It is not our intention to civilise the Mim up to our standards. You heard what I said about hopeless tasks.' Benny felt her hands clenching. 'We want them to live, and to value life as much as we do. We'd like their loyalty in gratitude, though we have no illusions about how unlikely that is. Beyond that… We have no more desire to absorb them or crush their culture than any of our other subjects. Less, even. Though it's rather difficult to convince them of this fact.'

'Well, with an attitude like that it's no wonder.' Even on a mercy mission they were still managing to set her teeth on edge.

He nodded, surprisingly quiet. 'I know our diplomacy is often the pursuit of war by other means. They have no reason to see this as anything other than a conquest.' At least he really had no illusions, then. Hesitantly, stiffly, he raised his hands: open, weaponless. 'But someone in good standing with the Mim might perhaps be able to persuade them this is for the best…'

And slowly it began to make sense. All his pulled punches, the motive she couldn't ferret out. It was so obvious she wasn't sure whether to laugh.

'You want *my* help?'

'There are approaches a human, and a woman, are far better suited for than I.'

'Hooray for biological determinism,' she muttered.

'They know of your concern for their children… You could make this approach in good faith, where mine would be suspect.'

He stood motionless, not reaching out to her; he had made his case, and now stood waiting for her to accept it. The next move was literally hers: advance towards his open hands, or keep her distance. She teetered on the spot. Horribly, what he said actually made sense. But she was flying blind now, in the opposite direction from her plans, and no closer to finding out about Lwpha.

'The thing is... how *could* I make it in good faith? How would I know? If I do this for you, I need to be sure I've got the whole picture.'

Another level look – she couldn't be sure whether it was deadpan or not. 'Many have spent their lives trying. But I don't think we have the time for you to achieve a state of enlightenment before we act.'

'Right now I'm not sure of anyone's motives. I want to be sure why they're doing what they're doing, whether they can be trusted ...'

'And in the time that would take, the children would be grandparents.' She saw him stop himself from snapping, take a slow breath and literally pull himself back to a neutral stance. His eyes lowered, and for a long damp moment he said nothing. Finally, quietly, the words escaped. 'I do not believe this plan would work without you.'

And that settled it. For a moment she saw him, really saw him, standing on a rooftop with a pernickety alien female, the rain dripping off the two prongs of his beard. If he were willing to take these losses to his pride, he *had* to be serious.

So, just as seriously: 'If I think I'm collaborating with the people who killed Lwpha, it *really* won't work.'

'I have no idea who was responsible for that.' He was completely direct now, if weary of her moral qualms. 'Though I believe our intelligence service would tend to be less... spectacular.' His forehead crinkled, the equivalent of a raised eyebrow, and for a moment she tasted bile, fought back the urge to vomit. Not just at his deadpan, at her own. Laughing at Lwpha's bloody straw again. 'But realistically, you must know that right now it's in neither side's interest to bring them to justice. If we can only address the big picture...'

'But I think this *is* the big picture. He was killed *after* he'd told all. Now wouldn't a reasonably competent hired cut-throat have got those events the other way round? Or at least have called off the hit afterwards, so it wouldn't draw more attention to the fact that they wanted him dead. So why?'

He shrugged. 'Punishment? Revenge?'

'Or... they *did* kill him before he spilled their secrets. At least the ones they really cared about keeping.'

His eyes narrowed, as if it genuinely hadn't occurred to him. As if his staff hadn't discussed it at their daily strategy meetings, perhaps even before it had happened.

'Perhaps you should ask the Mim,' he countered. 'They've been oddly silent about his death –'

'Well, they do have two billion other people to worry about all of a sudden –'

'Professor, you seem certain that it's *our* secrets that were in danger of being spilled. Perhaps you shouldn't assume that only we have something to hide.'

And she had to admit, the leathery old bastard had a point. Just like they had about the end of the war. Even when people had suspected that the apocalypse on the Mimsphere had been down to some previously unseen Draconian superweapon, the Draconian denials had been quick to point out that as there weren't any Draconians within several light years at the time, it could rather more easily have been a previously unseen *Mim* superweapon melting down.

She lowered her arms, matching his pose, formally dropping her guard. 'You may be right. I'll have a talk with them.'

'Excellent.'

'Though if I could meet with some of your staff to discuss the specifics of your proposal?'

'Of course.' He began to sweep towards the stairs. 'I'll have you cleared for the necessary access this afternoon.'

One of the advantages of an autocracy, she thought. 'Wonderful. And the technical papers?'

'Consider them in hand.' He had almost reached the escape stairs as she hung back. Every bit of his body language was declaring the discussion over at his moment of victory.

Now.

'Oh, just one more thing, Ambassador…'

He turned back, with an innocent look. Benny tried to look past the surface, failed, and briefly prayed that he'd never seen *Columbo*.

'It's about what Lwpha might have found out.'

Faint surprise. 'He said he'd made a full statement.'

'Well, yes, but there might be something he didn't know he knew.' She started closing in again – hands low, voice casual, umbrella sheathed. 'I just keep remembering what he said about the evacuation… The sort of unreasoning panic that hit him, hit everyone.' Sauntering past, making him turn a circle on the spot. 'Panic attacks, violent outbursts, epileptic fits… Aren't those sorts of symptoms all caused by an orbital phase cannon at low power?'

And she was close enough now to spot the difference between him just standing at rest and him not moving – the chill was taking hold.

She went on, carefully unconcerned. 'Crank it up, of course, and it'll scramble your nervous system completely. Which is what makes it a perfect weapon against a race where the nerves are woven through every cell. But then, you know that.'

Keep circling. Keep him between you and the edge. If this is a set-up, he'll be initialling your death warrant any second now.

'But on low power... I mean, if you wanted to drive people away in such a panic that they forget about their kids, so they'd be left behind for you... And if you didn't mind getting hauled up on war crimes charges for using a weapon of planetary destruction against civilian targets, even with the knob turned all the way down... Well, it could work, don't you think? Now that would be something big. Something so big it'd be worth killing Lwpha to cover up.'

Watch his eyes. Watch every twitch of his face as the thoughts ripple under the surface, and the rain soaks into his bones.

'That was a bluff,' he breathed.

'Sorry?'

'When I advocated using phase cannons against the Mim, before the war. That was all a political ploy. You *know* that.'

She'd cut straight through. He wasn't wasting time acting insulted, he was treating this seriously. Because he knew how serious the possibility would look from the outside.

'Well, yeah, you did say they weren't really a sentient species, just a glorified fungus with a history of imitating what real species did when they crossed their path. So bombarding their brains from orbit fell under the category of vermin control instead of mass murder, but still, no hard feelings, right? Especially now that you're showing so much concern for taking care of their children...'

He was tightening, clenched muscles stone-still, fighting to erase any sign of reaction. Careful, don't push him too far. Though after all these months of him baiting her, his confidence that he could say precisely as much as he wanted and get away with it... Oh, she'd wanted to slip the knife in. Just once.

'It's impossible,' he hissed. 'This was the staging-ground for the assault, any orders for such a deployment would have had to cross my desk. I would have known...' And all Benny needed to do was nod, with just a hint of a tight-lipped smile.

Now his eyes began to dart, as if grabbing for scraps of information from all directions. Sentence fragments slipping from his mouth. 'Any orders would have to be forged. Inserted further down the chain of command. Perhaps deliberately misattributed.' From deep inside that cool Draconian shell, the hollow rattling sound of a man thrashing about. 'The Emperor would never condone... *I* would never...'

You've got him. Now offer him the out.

She held out her hands. 'Ambassador... If you were going to do it, the last thing you'd *ever* do is announce it beforehand.'

His forehead twitched, a guarded Draconian smile.

'But it doesn't look good, does it? Because all your sabre-rattling means your name is linked to the idea.' She dusted off a sympathetic expression for him. 'And if some other bright spark decided to go through with the plan – without your blessing, of course...'

'Then if it were uncovered, I would be the obvious suspect.'

'And with what happened to the Mimsphere as well... I mean, they've got to be looking for someone breaking the rules. Perhaps even wondering how much more they can pin on him.'

He went quiet, his eyes slowly sweeping the buildings on the horizon, just the way hers had before. Realising just how cold and exposed they both were up here. Counting the directions the bullet might come from.

Until that moment she hadn't been sure. He might still have done it after all. But there was no way this was an act.

Kothar rallied. 'I must thank you. There are always those at court who might gain were I ruined....'

Oh, please – as if someone would commit near-genocide for the sake of ruining Kothar's standing at court. But if he wanted to see himself as more than just a convenient scapegoat, let him.

As she cast her eyes heavenward, she caught a familiar glimmer in the rainshower. She wondered if any of the little bits of Lwpha could have floated high enough for a bit of cloud to condense around them, so he could come plummeting back down on them. Dust to raindrops.

'Someone killed Lwpha,' she said. 'Someone might be setting you up to take the fall for war crimes. Someone might even be after me. I think it's in both our interests to find out who...'

'Then Professor, in this at least, we are allies.'

As they turned towards the steps, to descend from the building, she saw the downward twitch of his mouth, the distinctive Draconian 'smile'. And at least this way neither one of them was sure which one had been wrong-footed more by the way things had come out.

He'd smoothed himself out, but she could still see his eyes, flicking about, playing all the angles. 'If such orders were inserted into the chain of command… No, it is of course unthinkable. There were only three officers stationed here who had the necessary access codes. Myself; Logistician Korenthai; and Lashenkavaar, the Baron-General of this sector. And my wife. And I could never question any of their loyalties.'

'No, you can't, can you. So it's a good thing I can.

'Hang on. Your wife has your access codes?'

A look of mild surprise. 'We are one body. I am the strong right hand, she is the loyal left hand. Of course she has my access. But she would never ask to use it.'

'Hmm,' said Benny, figuring that was enough.

He was still rankling from that 'hmm' as they started down the stairs together. 'Would you not give Jason any part of your life he might need?' A stiletto pause. 'If you were still married, of course.'

So, business as usual between them, then. 'I wouldn't need to. He wouldn't wait to ask.'

2

By the time she finished drying herself off at home, she found Kothar had already booked her first couple of appointments. Another of the advantages of living in an autocracy. Baron-General Lashenkavaar was off baron-generaling somewhere, and wouldn't be back for a week, and following up with Korenthai would have to wait till tomorrow at the earliest. So it was the appointment he *hadn't* made for her she most wanted to keep.

She found Ithva Kothar in her element: at the Mansionhouse, surrounded by caterers. Sweeping across a ballroom floor talking about decorations and accommodating Dr Sklix'vran's dietary requirements, gown swishing, heels clacking – while simultaneously fielding a call from Dr Vreeaaa to smooth his literally ruffled feathers over his department being overlooked in the refugee charity drive. Even remembering how to pronounce Vreeaaa's name correctly, with the middle 'a' silent.

Even without any official powers or influence now the Draconians had ceded authority over the Collection, Ithva had carved out quite a niche on the social side of proceedings – hosting and arranging both the starched-shirt rubber-*vikhila* protocol dinners for the peace negotiations, and the informal meals out after meetings where all the *real* business of negotiating took place. The academics knew her as a social butterfly whose wingbeats could deflect hurricanes, a master at steering table conversations and whole occasions away from anything political. The less-accomplished-with-the-female-sex half of the staff were all convinced she was flirting with them. They all enjoyed her deep-green laughter, her polished, toothily human smile and eyes that sparkled like crushed ice. None of them knew her as anything but charming. So none of them knew her as anything at all.

Benny headed towards the comet's-trail of staffers following Ithva and tried not to think bitchy thoughts. It was just the way Ithva was making frighteningly efficient organisation look *graceful*, which brought out all Benny's leftover ugly duckling reflexes. True, Ithva may not be out turning the galaxy upside down with charmingly off-the-cuff heroics, but right here and now her every movement declared that this *wasn't* a woman who spent last night writing angsty diary entries and endlessly picking her psyche apart. Here was a woman who, at every second, knew what she wanted.

'Ah, Bernice,' she said, sweeping Benny up into her orbit as she hurried past. 'It's so good to see you. We never get a chance to talk properly, but I've heard so much about you from my husband. Ever since the first time he saw you.'

'Erm. Yes,' said Benny sheepishly. 'I think you should know that wasn't my idea. Bev surprised me too.'

'So I gathered.' She turned her full attention on Benny – leaning in close and personal, cranking up the smile, lowering her head, confiding a secret without quite actually lowering her voice. 'I'm afraid while your performance may have distracted the other parties at the negotiating table, my husband's only reaction was a series of speeches about what crass sexual degenerates your people were.'

'Not one of Bev's great tactical decisions,' Benny agreed – not letting on that that was precisely the reaction Bev Tarrant had wanted. Among Bev's efforts to keep the Collection neutral in the war she'd tried to convince both sides that having the Collection staff as their subjects would just be *tacky*. Any violation of etiquette she could imagine was fair game. And if that meant giving Benny a lengthy impromptu snog during the border-dispute negotiations and expecting her to take one for the team, so be it. It had more or less worked in the short term, but in the long term Kothar had proven far too undistractable.

'All is forgiven.' Ithva's smile got broader, and she reached in to touch her gently on the front of her shoulder. The sort of gesture Benny still felt odd about, from anyone other than her husband. 'I was you who the liberty was taken against. I'll hardly hold you responsible for the excessive actions of your friends.'

All right, subtext detectors to maximum: for Bev read Lwpha, and this meant Ithva was excusing her from responsibility for this mess. But whether she was offering an unconditional peace, or just a chance for Benny to beat a dignified retreat… Bloody hell, close-reading Draconians was just *exhausting*. If she went on a debating team against them she'd be dead within minutes.

The caterers and staffers had all fallen a few respectful paces behind as Ithva had a word with the new arrival, but at the slightest flick of her hand they surged back up into position. 'Anyway. One moment while I finish this.' Breezing onwards again. 'We'll need the mourning bunting up around the Mim tables, there's two more weeks to go on that. There, there, and there, by the kitchen.' Pirouetting on the spot, conjuring up the details with a flick of one finger. 'And how many bottles of Craxatonian chardonnay left on hand?'

'Twenty-seven,' said a voice from behind a clipboard.

'Not counting the twenty that Mullyns skims off the top of every shipment?'

'Erm.'

She pursed her lips, barely missing a beat, and swept on. 'Tell Bilalis to spread the word that I'm bringing in Korenthai to do an audit. That should give Mullyns time to slip them back quietly, he can't have drunk too many of them yet and we only need eight more anyway. Anything else? Well. That's settled.' A final turn, sending staff scattering in all directions, and she came to rest like an ice-dancer at the end of her routine. Benny felt short of breath just watching her.

'I can make it twenty-nine,' she hemmed and hawed. 'If you're that short. I've got a couple of bottles from my own supply.' From the five given to her by Mullyns a few months back as part of their mutual back-scratching, but there was no need to get into that.

'Oh, never you worry,' lilted Ithva, 'It's all under control.' And the damnable thing was, it *was*. 'Now, what can I do for you?'

'Well, it's about the Mim children,' Benny began, pausing to leave room for Ithva's sympathetic noises. 'I'm sure you heard about Lwpha wanting to be reunited with his children, so I'm trying to find some way to make it possible to, you know, keep the barriers down, arrange some sort of compromise on allowing access, that sort of thing.'

She'd been working out how to sell this ever since Ithva's name had come up. The more she got a sense of how this woman got things done, the better chance she'd have of knowing what she might have got done using her husband's access. Plus, as Kissinger said (or bloody well should have said), it had the added benefit of being worthwhile anyway. She elaborated as Ithva took her by the elbow and escorted her towards the office that Braxiatel had granted her in the Mansionhouse. 'I know the Mim don't seem to be willing to make an official arrangement, not formally at least, but I thought we might be able to organise some sort of non-governmental relief effort, you and I. Some sort of charity thing. For the children.'

'Oh, it would be a *pleasure* to work with you on that,' said Ithva, lighting up every inch of her face. 'My life is absolutely at your command.'

'Splendid,' said Benny, smiling till her cheekbones ached. If she squinted the whole routine became transparently hollow, and all very sweetie-darling. But that wasn't the point; Ithva's fellow Draconians would know it was all empty gestures for form's sake, but would still respect that she considered their feelings worth sparing. That they were worthy of the effort of extreme courtesy. Even if, at the end of it, she still got her husband to feed them to the dogs.

'We could go through channels, but you know that's never enough,' Benny went on. 'It's just so much easier to work this out among a few interested parties over a quiet meal. You know we humans have a saying, "A Draconian's word is as good as his dinner."'

Actually, the saying was, as good as his *last* dinner. Kothar and his cronies were experts at avoiding committing to anything in formal minuted negotiations. Having the impermanence of all things drummed into them from childhood made them treat any agreement as able to be renegotiated on a whim. But the meeting *after* the meeting, the formal banquet or the quick nip down to the pub with their opposite numbers, was where the actual decisions were taken. The policies forged based on these social connections would often never be admitted to back at the bargaining table, but in practice would be thoroughly binding... at least until the dinner relationship soured. Which meant maintaining those connections was not just the only way to get things done, but to *keep* them getting done.

It was fascinating, in a way – an entire civilisation's business conducted under the table. And as Benny had spent so much of her pub-going adult life under some table or another, she was feeling strangely at home.

'I hope you're not overestimating me,' said Ithva, as she let Benny into her office. She had flawless galactic-standard English, with an accent said to have been picked up from the then President of Earth herself, back when Kothar had served as a 'cultural attaché' (ahem) at the embassy there. 'Neither Jarith nor I are in the chain of command responsible for administering the Mim camps.'

'Well, yes, but you know who to talk to. Just like I've got some standing with the Mim at the moment. And you know how things get done. We could help bring the two sides together, maybe even get some Mim in residence in the camps as teachers…'

Ithva really did have the most extraordinary purple-and-brown eyes, tiny little streaks of colour radiating outward from the pupil, striking enough to distract you from trying to read the expression in them.

Right now, she seemed to be weighing her options, but *which* options were well beyond Benny at the moment. Ithva was pouring herself a fruit cordial, a vivid pastel green, which Benny suspected had been mixed to match her furnishings, and offered Benny one as well. She accepted, but held off on drinking; some of the fruits on Draconia packed more punch than their liqueurs.

'I don't think they'd ever agree to a compromise like that,' Ithva shook her head sympathetically.

'Well, it's not about whether they agree to it, it's whether we can make it happen.' Keep the smile up, push just that little bit harder. 'I know what an expert you are in handling things unofficially. You know, a word to the right person, a message or two on the sly…' And now it was her turn to echo Ithva's gesture from before, a gentle hand just over her collarbone, a careful intrusion into personal space. A statement: I'm past your defences already, so don't even bother. 'I mean, you could probably get just about *anything* done, in the military or outside, and no one would ever be the wiser. Not even your husband.'

'But I'm only a woman,' said Ithva innocently. 'An embassy wife. No official standing…'

Oh, don't milk it, thought Benny. She cranked up her smile a little further and went all-out on the sincere eye contact. 'The men think they run the show, all the nobles and generals and what-not, but that only means we get better at working around them.' Rah-rah, go, sister. 'And they never even need to know. Come on, we both know how it works.'

'Do we both?' asked Ithva, her gaze suddenly searching. She stepped back to her desk, and took a sip of her cordial, considering.

'Do you know why women aren't permitted to speak in the presence of the Emperor?'

Ten thousand years of something, no doubt. 'No, why?'

Ithva put her drink down and smiled. 'It gives him plausible deniability.'

And she went right for her throat.

That was her head smacking back against the wall and her whole skull ringing out of focus, and Ithva's animal snarl against her eyes, Ithva's forearm slamming across her collarbone as she twisted *something* tight round her neck, and her breath was hot in her face and her own breath couldn't move in her chest, her hands were clawing at her throat but couldn't move it and she'd never seen it coming and those pointed tearing teeth filling her vision and –

'Now, stop struggling, Bernice dear,' said Ithva's mouth. Coolly, with only the tiniest lick of her lips. 'It's only choking because you're pushing against it. If you don't fight it doesn't hurt at all.'

She's trying to kill me. She wants me dead and she's telling me that and it makes no sense. It should all be fading to red then black but the moment was still going on.

'Shh.' A finger curling against her cheek, delicate scaly texture. A voice speaking to a grown-up bit of her somewhere in the centre, under the panic, probing to see if there was anyone there at all. 'It'll be all right, just relax.'

And whatever was left in her, it took all of it to fight back the animal reflex, relax the cords of muscle in her neck, and find the air flowing freely through again.

The mouth before her eyes smiled, perfect sharp teeth. 'And that's all I want to say to you. Don't fight it. Just relax, and do what we want, and everything will be just fine.'

A thin steel line, precisely tight around her neck, judged to the fraction to keep her just where Ithva wanted. A rabbit under the paws of a tiger. But as she stayed frozen, Ithva backed carefully off – keeping her forearm across Benny's top ribs till she'd finished unwinding the wire from around her throat. An invisibly thin garrotte, one end mounted on a spring-loaded reel, retracting elegantly back into the loose-draped sleeves of her *hronsthei*. And now Ithva was just standing there, eyes on her with that polite hostess smile, waiting on her response as graciously as if Benny were Oscar Wilde at a soirée, about to deliver a bon mot.

All that came out was, 'Wha...?'

'Oh, that was just a warning.' And Ithva was sauntering to the desk for her fruit cordial – not turning her back on her, but doing a damn good impression of someone who just wasn't that concerned. 'I'm sorry, Bernice, but you're just completely out of your depth here, and if you keep going it's just a question of whether you're going to get yourself killed before or after you ruin things for the children. You really should leave these things to the professionals…'

And beneath her gasping for breath Benny felt herself flush for completely different reasons. She hadn't had the slightest clue. All her smug study of body language, the whole dance she'd thought she was leading – her entire self-assumed professorship in the academy of human nature, and she hadn't even begun to see this coming. She'd been utterly suckered by… whatever this woman really was.

She hadn't even felt her own hand, reaching unconsciously to her throat. 'But why…?'

'Because after hours of dealing with my husband's *bullshit* and Korenthai's doubletalk, I thought you'd appreciate the direct approach.'

Flawless English, Benny thought fleetingly. 'You knew.'

'Of course I knew. It's one of my jobs.' A headshake of distaste at the stain on the carpet where Benny had flung her drink in the struggle. Hell, she didn't remember doing *that* either. 'You've been trying all day to get whatever concessions you can for the Mim. But the more freedom the Mim demand for their children, the more of them will die. From inattention, or misadventure, or any of a thousand preventable things. It's that simple.' Utterly direct: 'Call off your proposal. We aren't going to compromise on their lives. *No sacrifice. Not even one.*'

And even if she didn't know where any of this was coming from, that was enough to get her back up. 'Perhaps you'd better tell your husband that, then. It was his idea.'

'Oh, I've *tried.*' An utterly human heavenward lift of her eyes, a sudden disarming sigh. 'All the grief you went through trying to persuade him? Try getting that every morning over breakfast. Honestly. Jarith can't fry an egg without making it a matter of the honour of House Kothar. If you want him to cut down on the sugar on his *nachlava*, you'll need an order countersigned by the Emperor before he'll risk losing face. Believe me, it's easier to work around him than to change his mind…'

Benny heard herself chuckling shakily. She couldn't follow this woman's mind from minute to minute, but anyone who could be crushing her windpipe one moment and tickling her funny bone the next had to be good value. From a safe distance.

'Yes,' she said, edging along the wall towards the door. 'I suppose if I had to put up with that, I'd want to strangle someone too...'

A little self-deprecating shrug. 'Pure shock value. I told you, I had to make you take it seriously.' And she was easing her way between Benny and the door, a replacement drink for Benny in her hand. Gracious hostess: no escape, but free refills. Smiling eyes, serious mouth. 'I mean it. This is life or death for these children.'

'Believe me, I know, that's why I'm –'

'No it isn't.' Ithva cut her off. Benny gawped. 'It's not about the children, not the future, nor what's best for them. This is all about Lwpha.' Ithva was circling beside her, cutting through her self-pretence, stripping her bare. 'I've seen how you work, Benny. You're led by your heart, and your heart's led by who you know. Never mind whether he wanted the wrong thing, you'll fight for it out of loyalty. What one dead man would have wanted, over the fates of billions.' Cool fingers pressing a cool drink in her hand. A calculated question. 'What makes him more important than their lives?'

'He was *in my blood*,' breathed Benny.

And as she said it, the feeling hit her all over again – the moment in their escape when he'd dissolved into her, the surge of liquid fire followed by slow flowing ice. All the way into her bloodstream. She hadn't really understood what that *meant* till right now. A deep animal connection, filling all the hollows in her she didn't even know she had. Every cell of his, floating free between hers like the bits of fruit pulp floating in the drink in her hand. She looked down at it, and felt a moment's surprise that the ice in her veins right now hadn't chilled the drink to slush. Because the feeling was filling her now, giving her clarity, touching enough of her nature to give her the certainty she needed to look into Ithva's eyes and say *no*.

'He died for his children, I'd die for mine. It's pure empathy. You should try –' careful, don't piss off the woman with the garrotte '– to respect that. But honestly, it doesn't make me bloody stupid. I wouldn't be fighting for this if I didn't think it could *work*.'

For a long moment, Ithva watched her, with those unmoving reptilian eyes. Finally, she lowered them. 'All right. Your children are in your blood. But *all* the children are in mine.'

It sounded gentle enough, but there was no way to tell if Ithva was respecting her passion or just calculating how best to use it. Her tone was smoother now, less commanding, more persuading. 'And you know this can't be about Lwpha. Now, if you still want to follow your personal vendetta, against whoever it was who killed him –'

'– which for all I know was someone from your own intelligence service –'

'Our people didn't order Lwpha's death.'

'And you know because...?'

Just a hint of an eye roll. 'Because it would have been my assignment.'

Benny just stared as it sank in. Okay, she thought, I'm *still* dead.

'And you're blowing your cover to me because...'

A pointed smile. 'This way, you'll do what I tell you. This is *policy*. An intelligence directive. It comes straight from the Empress's Hand. Literally. Those children are under our protection.'

The way Ithva said it made it sound like that hand was still round her throat. But be careful, don't assume, that's what got you in this deep to begin with. 'That would sound very impressive, no doubt, if I knew who you were talking about.'

'The Empress's Hand,' said Ithva. 'Technically her left hand. The left hand of the one who sits to the left of the Emperor. Right in his blind spot.' And she settled in the chair behind her desk, perfectly poised, waiting for Benny to put all the pieces together. Even now she wasn't going to just *tell* her; that would just be gauche, indeed rather rude if she presumed that Benny wasn't able to pick up on the nuances and implications without being told. It would also be rude for Benny to state them out loud, but right about now she felt she'd beat around enough bushes for one day.

'And it's policy, you said. A secret service so secret even the Emperor doesn't know about it. Run by his wife. Who never tells him, because... Oh, crap. Plausible deniability, you said. It applies to everyone. There's a whole parallel hierarchy, isn't there?'

Even now she wouldn't actually say it, only smile. 'Every man fights for the Empire under his command...'

'And every woman *watches* for the Empire under hers.' The implications were whizzing round in her head, leaving her dizzy. Just as every Draconian male from a banker to a sous-chef was technically a member of the military reserve, this meant every woman from a diplomat to a librarian could be called up to... Bloody hell, whatsername who won Best Actress at last year's Galactacademy Awards was a frigging *spy*. Probably a trained assassin too. That was worthy of several drinks in itself.

But for all the billions of people at their disposal, the Draconian sisterhood clearly didn't have direct power over those outside the service. Because Ambassador Jarith Kothar *wasn't* under their orders. Much to their frustration, apparently.

She sat down dazedly in the chair facing Ithva's desk. 'When your husband was attached to your embassy on Earth, as a cultural attaché... I thought that meant *he* was the spy.'

Ithva snickered. 'A spy? *Please.* Jarith's too much of a sweetheart.'

'Oh, hell,' Benny said faintly.

'Oh, he can lie with the best of them, but only when he's sure his motives are true and honourable. He can't lie just because it's *necessary.* Like you and I can.'

Sorry, thought Benny, I've already had my recommended daily allowance of self-doubt for the day. 'So he was your cover.'

'We've always been a well-matched team.'

'His loyal left hand, he called you,' she realised. 'The hand that fights dishonourably. He knows.'

'The hand outside the rules,' she corrected her, almost professorially. 'Honour is male. Even down to the gender of the word in our language. Women by definition don't have any...'

'So you're not bound by it. Whenever they need to do something that would violate their sense of honour... they tell you.'

Innocence again. 'No, they don't.'

'No, of *course* they don't. Because that would mean acknowledging you were doing it. They couldn't condone that – oh, no. Heavens, that might even mean you might not be the frail and refined flowers of femininity they keep saying you ought to be.'

'Which we *are.*'

'Ah. Right. Got it. Pale lotus blossom *and* warrior princess. The modern woman who does it all.' You're babbling, Summerfield. Feeling inadequate much? 'But if something needs doing, they make sure you get the message, without actually saying it out loud. And you do it all without ever violating their perfect honour.'

'Oh, no, we can't be *seen* to violate it...'

'But the men are really, really good at not seeing what they need not to see. They all know, but no one will admit it. Oh, this is brilliant.' And the giddiness was beginning to escape again. 'Have you really all been doublethinking like this for umpty thousand years?'

And with that Ithva heaved a huge sigh of relief. 'Oh, at last, you've got it.' In an instant her composure cracked wide open – leaning forward, chuckling as she spoke, the weight of formality completely lifted from her body language. Like she'd shed not just her skin but her Draconian soul. 'Phew. Thank every single spirit in the universe, that's out of the way. Now we can get on with *talking*.'

Benny gaped. 'You could have just explained!'

'Come on, that would have been like farting in mixed company.' A sentence that left Benny's perceptions reeling even more. Even if this whole face was a put-on for the benefit of a graceless ape, heaven help her, it rang true – when the Kothars were stationed on Earth, Ithva must have nearly gone native. 'Honestly, do you know what it was like, trying to hint at all that?'

'Well, you could have tried charades,' said Benny dazedly. She shook her head like the ideas were still rattling around loose inside. 'A whole culture running on denial. You're completely mad, you know that? Every last one of you.'

Ithva was matching her human smile. 'You thought you knew how our minds worked… Your reports, your papers…' A faintly pitying shake of her head. 'But you still never get our jokes.'

And that left Bernice wondering if maybe she should just down that drink, no matter what might be in it. She found herself staring at Ithva's desk, trying to build up a single consistent picture: a clean-lined workspace, datapads and actual papers arrayed for artistic effect. A freestanding snapshot of her and Jarith, with four kids from five-ish to twenty-ish around them, their thick silken *hronstheis* each in their own colour, a deep-hued rainbow. The five-year-old daughter on Ithva's lap. An assassin being a people person, perhaps the best joke of all.

'I could tell everyone,' she said casually.

'And who'd believe you?'

'Oh, I don't know – Brax, Earth Intelligence, the *Freeworld Weekly News* –'

'With no evidence? In the face of such thorough denials? All I need to say is that you *really* didn't get my joke.'

'Well, if I put in enough in-the-event-of-my-death clauses…'

A wry curl of her lip. 'Oh, be reasonable, Benny, you don't still think we want you dead, do you? Why kill you when we could embarrass you? Gets better results that way, especially if we still want you following our lead…'

And she was positively sparkling as she said it, as if they were just a couple of girlfriends having a laugh about the misdeeds of some mutual friend. As far as Benny could tell (and she'd been able to tell *so* well up to this point), the affection in Ithva's eyes looked perfectly genuine. Either she really did like her, or she was shrewdly manipulating her by keeping her off-balance at every possible moment, or else she was just barking mad.

Benny let a polite laugh fill the gap, and took a moment just to stare at Ithva, still aching to get her measure: the wrinkles and crinkles round her eyes to the leathery ridges along the tips of her ears, the little patterns and whorls of the scales on her cheeks, suggesting much bigger designs continuing just out of view. Livia the Tattooed Lady, thought Benny.

'So you want me to back off with the Mim and leave your lot to raise the children, because it's the best thing for them,' Benny said slowly. 'Right. Do you really expect me to believe that the Draconian Intelligence Dynasty would be engaged in a massive covert campaign... to improve conditions at a refugee orphanage? I don't know which universe you've wandered in from, but I'd really much rather be living in that one, thank you.'

'It's the Empress,' said Ithva. 'I really don't think you get the whole absolute-authority thing. If she personally decides that looking after the children is a priority... every woman under her command has to follow her lead.'

'So, even if that lead means assassination, blackmail... unleashing planetary-scale weaponry...'

'Fortunately, we haven't had a really juicy megalomaniac Empress since Vrakiya All-Knowing, ooh, about eight hundred years ago. It's too hard to abuse that sort of power if you have to stay on good terms with your friends... If you go too far over the top, it's easy enough for one of them to leak just a hint of their Empress's activities to the men in the court. And that, well, that's a shocking scandal worthy of divorce. So if enough of your other friends won't help you cover it up any more...'

Benny had a sudden vision of the reach of the Empress's Hand: a chain of command built solely on friends and friends-of-friends, reaching its fingers out across space. A fluid, shifting hierarchy, without the strata of titles and fealty that gave a surface sheen of order to the political territory on the male side of the Empire. But every one of them currying favour with the queen bee, shaping a world's worth of policy, based solely on who listened to who. A planetwide KGB run by the popular girls, those ones with the perfect outfits, the sharp laughs and the hearts of stone. Like the girls' dorm back at the Academy, only with slightly fewer projectile weapons.

'So the Empress still has to listen to her friends,' she began.

'Yes...'

'And they have to listen to their friends.'

'Of course.'

'All the way down to whoever's listening to you.'

Ithva was giving her the same go-on smile from before – suggesting that wherever Benny was going, she was already there, but she was still making Benny take the long way.

'So if I could persuade you of something... then you'd know who you'd have to persuade... so they could persuade someone else... all the way up to Her Maj herself, and then suddenly heresy is policy.'

'You don't ask for much, do you?' said Ithva. Leaning back, disengaging, the smile a barrier now. 'You're not a big enough piece of the puzzle for them to listen to you.'

But for every inch she leaned back, Benny leaned forward, as serious and undistractable as she could manage. 'I'm big enough that you want me on your side, if you can't just put me off the whole thing. That's why you stopped threatening – sorry, *warning* – and started explaining. If I'm going to be making a case for anything, you want it to be your case. So if you're trying to convince me... let me try to convince you.'

Ithva was listening, at least. And she still had that clarity in her eyes, looking at her as a person, not the impeccable mask. Just enough of her thoughts were showing for Benny to see the calculations being made, with no idea of the answer or even exactly the question.

But now she was leaning forward again, meeting the challenge with one of her own. 'You'll have to convince me how much it's the children you care about.'

'Well give me a moment,' Benny floundered, 'I don't exactly have a handy coil of wire to... Sorry, sorry.' When she'd heard the joke leaking out of her mouth, for a moment Benny wished she could save time and strangle herself. But thank heaven Ithva had smiled slightly at it, and raised her hands, conceding the point. 'Let me get the papers from Korenthai, I can give you all the details of the proposals...'

'This isn't about the plans,' said Ithva, her voice suddenly firm. 'It's about you. The only way any negotiation works is if you're sure of the people who will put it into action. If you want to persuade me, you'll have to show me who you are.'

Well, that's me doomed, then, thought Benny. If you find out, could you let me know?

But rather than waiting for an answer, Ithva was looking thoughtful.

Just a hint of that personable twinkle in her eye, peeking out from under the solemnity of her words. 'We'll have to talk at length. You'd be taking on a lifetime commitment, to the children... and to working with us. It may well be –' and the twinkle was back in force as she stood up '– that this is the beginning of a beautiful friendship.'

By now Benny had given up trying to predict the end of any given comment from its beginning. She was pretty sure she'd just won the concession she was after, but she was no longer sure exactly what it was. Which probably meant Ithva and company had just won a completely different game. In her sigh of relief she massaged her aching temples. 'You're just doing this to confuse me, aren't you?'

A playful smile. 'Well, it's working, isn't it?'

'So throttling me... that was just that bloody snog all over again, wasn't it?' She shook her head ruefully as she got up to leave. 'I have to say I preferred Bev's approach.'

'Well, you would, wouldn't you?' A lopsided grin as Ithva touched her elbow – no hard feelings, what's a bit of political exploitation between friends?

They were charming each other for a moment, and Benny handed back her drink, still carefully untouched. As she headed for the door, she wished she'd kept a glass or two of Lwpha on hand, metallic sparkling water, just to serve it to Ithva. See what that brought home to her.

'Oh, just one more thing...'

Crap, thought Benny as she froze in the doorway. *She* knows her *Columbo.*

She stood paralysed as Ithva prowled up to her. 'You want to prove this is all for the children? There's a *nikhol vakarshta* retreat next weekend on Montavadros. I'm taking Sharintha, my youngest. Why don't you bring your son?' In other words, why don't you let me see what sort of mother you are?

'*Nikhol vakarshta.*' Benny sifted through her memory. 'Won't that be a bit odd, seeing as Peter's not a girl?'

'He's not *Draconian*,' deadpanned Ithva. 'Once you've bent the rules that much, the rest is practicalities. Oh, really, Benny, you must. All my friends will be there.'

And that was it, if the offer could be trusted. Ithva was handing her the most valuable thing she had: connections. A chance at the personal bonds that formed the entire control of the Empress's Hand. And just when she'd thought this confrontation had run out of possible left turns to take.

'Heavens,' she said. 'A weekend away with a spymaster and trained assassin. What could be jollier?'

A dismissive snort. 'Oh, *hardly* that, I haven't had to kill anyone in about, oh, twelve years...'

And Benny found herself gesturing lightly towards her throat again. 'So this was just keeping in practice, then?'

'In a way. How about you, how long has it been?'

Benny blinked. 'No, sorry, can't recall ever having being an assassin...'

'No, I suppose you're right,' conceded Ithva, smooth and invulnerable all over again, 'It's not the same if you do it of your own choice, is it?' And through the haze of goodbye motions Benny found herself yanked back years – to an occupied Collection, and a cruel man plummeting down a deep shaft just the way she'd planned. For Peter's sake. And other times, far from here, moments even the Empress's files on her couldn't possibly hold.

When she came back Ithva was hidden deep in her smile, eyes like a sheet of glass. 'Still. We do what we feel we have to.'

'Yes,' said Benny, trying to put her own smile back in place. 'And in the name of the children, too.'

'There is *no* way you're serious,' said Jason, spitting out a mouthful of water and toothpaste.

'Tonight,' said Benny, 'I've drunk nothing but water.'

'You're really going to do this? And you're going to take *Peter*?'

'I've been researching this *nikhol vakarshta* ritual retreat.' She sat back in the bathtub. 'It's a doddle. It'll be like a weekend with the Draconian Ladies' Sewing Circle And Espionage Society.'

'What about Adrian, what'll he think? Peter's his son, too.'

'*Adrian* will think I wouldn't take Peter anywhere I can't handle.'

Jason made a face. He wouldn't rise to the bait, he'd try sneaking his way round. 'If they killed Lwpha? If they were behind the whole attack?'

'Then it's even more important I find out.'

He scrunched his hair in his hands in frustration. 'Benny, how can you believe Ithva isn't lying her arse off about everything? Spies do that, y'know!'

Benny slapped the bathwater in answering anger. 'She's *not* lying about the Draconian attitude to children. It's all through their traditions. Their laws are, uh, draconian. They wouldn't be able to hold the retreat if there was any risk to the kids involved – no one would insure them. I'm *serious*, Jason. In some ways, Peter might actually be safer at the retreat.'

Benny sank into the water up to her chin. As always, it was about what they didn't say. Ithva hadn't responded to her hint about the phase cannons. If she'd wanted to demolish that possibility, she would have pre-emptively swooped on it, the same way she'd cut through Benny's motives to get straight to Lwpha's memory. But she'd avoided the whole subject. And if the Empress's Hand were so fixed on rescuing the children that they'd act pre-emptively, and so far outside the Emperor's concept of honour that perhaps a brief zap with a weapon of planetary destruction wasn't out of the question... Already she half-wanted to believe Ithva would never be a party to that. But if it were true, and this connection through Ithva was the only way to bring it out into the open... then there was no way she could walk away.

Jason came back into the bathroom three minutes later, on the pretext of looking for his shaver. He knelt by the side of the tub. 'If it *is* possible you're pregnant... I wish you could forget the whole thing. Better to keep you safe...'

Benny took a deep breath, sank below the surface, and slowly let the air bubble out. When she let herself surface she had control again, and even half a smile. 'You go to all that trouble of making me work out what I really want... Drag it out of me tooth and nail and every other appendage you've got... And then it turns out you'd rather have me wanting what I thought I wanted in the first place?'

He sighed ruefully. 'Shoulda kept my mouth shut.'

'Oh, I'll say. Then we would have both got what we thought we wanted, and we'd be no more annoyed with ourselves than normal.'

He looked at her with such tenderness that she almost melted. 'I just want you alive.'

Whatever that word means, she thought. Even now she felt like she was trying to convince herself of her own truth: like she'd been living for ages in this half-aware state, rooted to the bottom of the ocean like a borogove itself. But even if her heart still couldn't grasp the reason, her head could see it.

'Lwpha loved *all* the children,' she said softly. 'He loved the borogove, the whole abstract thing, *everyone's* children, as much as I love my own. We're not built to think like that, we can't *imagine* that many children, let alone weigh them all up... But right now I bloody well think we should. To hell with selfish genes, we've only got this far by looking out for each other.'

Jason sighed, defeatedly. 'You're doing your thing again, aren't you?'

And she nodded, but shook her head at the same time. 'Not quite. It's the *principle* of the thing.'

'Look me in the eye,' said Jason. 'Tell me you really think all those kids are worth more than keeping your son safe.'

'Not more,' she said. 'What I can't do is say they're worth *less*. I can't neglect either one. We've got to try to save both of them, you understand?' She sat up out of the water and took hold of his wrist. 'And I need you to back me up. You can't come all the way, but as far as you can go with me. Will you?'

She braced herself for him to say something half-witty, like *I've got a bad feeling about this*. But instead she saw him gathering himself. Still guarding himself, still afraid that everything he had in life could be taken away at any moment.

'Yeah,' he said. 'If nothing else, I've got to look out for Peter.'

She let out the breath she hadn't thought she'd been holding; she hadn't even known how much she needed him on her side. And she started kissing him, deep proud kisses, the sort that could only lead to something more.

'And without him even being your son,' she said.

3

I t was about the fifteenth hour of the eighteen-hour flight when Peter said, 'You an' Uncle Jason should get married.'

And that was just the capper to the whole journey – at that time when you've had all the sleep you're going to get, and the breakfast service is still an eternity away, and there's just no cosmic *point* to freshening up for landing yet, and no matter what time it is at either end of the flight your internal clock is stuck at the 3am of the soul. Their shrieking neighbours weren't helping either... As usual on a Draconian flight, they had a separate economy section for families with children, with extra running-about-room in the back and entertainments for rambunctious little lizards. A lovely theory, but this meant every single squalling infant within a third of a light year was *right* next to her ears.

Peter had exhausted the novelty of playing with all the spaceline's toys, and was sitting on her lap asking random questions at irregular intervals just to keep her from drifting off. Jason wasn't helping – ruffling Peter's hair, like that was the cutest thing he'd ever said. 'Couldn't you ask for something easy like a pterodactyl?' he said.

'*Zack*'s parents are married,' Peter said in that familiar begging whine, and she exhaled tightly through a smile.

'Well. If Zack said he and his parents were going to jump down the shaft to the Deep Galleries, would you want us to do that too?'

She could see the lightbulb going on in Peter's eyes even as she spoke. '*Rogue!*'

'Oh, hell. Forget I said it.'

'I'd wear a parachute and everything...'

'*No.*'

'But how come not you and Uncle Jason?'

'We don't like each other enough,' Jason said quietly.

For a moment she felt like she'd been clubbed round the head.

But Jason went on, 'It's like how you've got some really good friends, but you argue a lot too? So they're wonderful, but you wouldn't want to marry any of them, would you? Even if you could pick just one.'

Peter, bless him, really didn't get it. 'Yeah, but I could marry Maeve. Or Zack, or Maxx, or Wajiwaj if he didn't keep going squooshy...'

'It'll make sense when you're older,' said Benny, lying through her teeth.

'Will not,' said Jason.

'Will *too*. We're just not old enough yet either.'

And after a couple more nots and toos Peter was laughing at them, and Benny's urge to commit violence had passed.

When they finally landed the air splashed her in the face. Humid and sticky, condensing on the brushed-concrete walls at landfall. Montavadros felt wetter than the Collection in the rain – but the rain at home cooled you down, while this city wrapped around you like damp towels.

They planted themselves at a taxi rank, knee-high in baggage, bleary, jetlagged and stale. The psychological last mile of the journey. The translator injections they'd got in orbit were beginning to take effect, turning the din around them into a painful mixture of words and hissing, half-understood gibberish. If only she'd stuck to her schoolroom Draconian, Benny thought.

So far downtown Nishkala was just a stream of moving pictures outside the glass, as she and Jason slumped in the back of their bubble-cab. Their cabbie – company uniform *hronsthei*, ceremonial sword sheathed in a slot in the armrest, but all the regalia clip-on or polyester – grunted with irritation at the traffic, clunked a lever into place, and the bubble-cab lurched to cruising height. Peter yelled in delight as they swerved through the cityscape, past skyscrapers completely covered in artistically coloured mosses. One building still showed concrete hexagons over which its newly planted coat was growing in. Other cabs shot past them at the same height, none of them travelling as high as the canopy of force-bridges, neon-brilliant against the grey sky. Long orange lianas trailed from each building: supply lifts, saving on storage space inside.

A colony world, thought Benny, trying to look like home. Ersatz history built into everything.

The driver chain-chewed sticks of some kind of jerky while he drove. He wore several necklaces that hung down at back and front: the longer you looked at them, the more you began to realise what the beads represented. Human skulls. Tapered Draconian skulls. Eyestalks. Shapeless splotches, which Benny eventually twigged were meant to be Mim.

'Pretty fly for a green guy,' muttered Jason.

Now Peter's eyes had caught the row of big-eyed, bobble-headed toy Draconians stuck on the equivalent of the dashboard. When he asked about them, the driver's face creased into a smile – they were sculptings of his kids.

He steered with one clawed hand and pointed with the other, rattling off the names from oldest to youngest as their heads bounced on their springs. 'They're old sculptings, though. Meshkinkla is away training now, in the Imperial Fleet. He's gonna make his daddy proud.'

'They're *cute*,' announced Peter.

'Draconian cute is feared throughout the galaxy,' murmured Benny, aside to Jason. 'At least by those who recognise it as the insidious weapon of galactic domination it is.'

'C'mon,' he muttered blearily. 'They're hardly Teletubbies.'

'It's an outgrowth of their ruthless gift for satire,' she said. 'A good caricature can stop a movement in its tracks. Their artist Marthaleka went to Postine 5 and drew sketches of the Lord High Generalissimo, gave them as gifts to all the major political cartoonists... They copied the style... He had these big droopy eyes and sad clown lips... Two years later his coup attempt collapsed because no one could take him seriously. You can't have a Generalissimo you just want to hug.'

Peter had done them a favour, she thought as they zigzagged down to the hotel. Etiquette had kept the driver from starting a conversation, especially with aliens, whose social status he had no way of guessing. She'd just been too tired to do the gracious thing and start by asking him a question.

* * *

'He wants a golliwog,' reported Jason.

'He wants a what?'

Peter had dragged Jason to the hotel gift shop, while Benny did battle with the paperwork at check-in. The receptionist kept chirping 'My life at your command!' throughout, like 'have a nice day'. Now Jason was coming back, holding a toy Earth Reptile – a caricature in the same bobble-headed style as the cabbie's sculpture-portraits, with an oversized, pouting snout and three bulging red eyes.

'The Earth Reptiles don't like them,' she told Peter. 'They think it makes them look ugly and stupid.'

'I won't show it to them,' said Peter.

Benny stared blearily at the thing. She supposed the sheer tackiness of their take on Earth Reptiles at least made sense through Draconian eyes. With something as different as a human being, it was at least easy to see these creatures as a separate but more or less equal form of life to you. But to find another reptilian race with so many surface similarities, but none of your obviously superior culture... It would be as if humanity made contact with a race of space orang-utans. No matter how terribly racist you knew it was, you'd still be wanting to cuddle them or pick off their fleas.

And besides, the way its head wobbled on the spring looked like it was subjecting you to a particularly vicious psi attack.

'Tell you what,' she told her son. 'If you can find a human doll, you can have that.'

'Kay!'

The hotel wasn't posh but still comfortable, and the mothroaches had the decency to stay in the wallgrowth outside their window.

Finally Peter was down for the night, and Benny and Jason retreated to their own room with the unfeasibly wide Draconian bed – allowing up to three children to share with their parents. It was a major expedition just to clamber across to Jason's half. Meanwhile his mood-music gadget was playing Bellinood's version of *Pur ti miro*, all slow layered fingerpicking and two breathy voices intertwining. She knew what he had on his mind. For a moment she tried to think hard enough to mix it into Brahms' lullaby, but that was too much like work, and to be honest it was just her being perverse about him being so bloody obvious. Obvious to *her*, to be even more honest – no one else would even have noticed without the soundtrack reading his mind. And why on Earth would you want to turn him down anyway, over nothing more than a mild case of travelag?

'You know?' he asked, smoothing out his pillow. 'I worked it out… It's hard to tell with the time travel and all, but I think this is just about our tenth divorceiversary.'

'Whoo.' She sagged against the headboard, hand to her forehead to stop her brain from spinning. 'We really don't know how to take a hint, do we? Ten years, and we're still here…'

'I think about nine of them were on that flight.' He looked exactly as exhausted as she did, really – rumpled and scruffy and just so gloriously *comfortable*.

She started snuggling up next to him. 'So how do you suppose we should celebrate it? I mean, it's not as if we have another set of rings we can hurl back at each other…'

'Actually,' he said.

And she'd just spotted the ring-box peeking out from under the pillow he'd nonchalantly positioned over it, and suddenly ten years' worth of joy and resentment and primal fear and *yes* all started bubbling up through her exhaustion and trying to force their way through her lips.

But she only got as far as 'Oh, fu…' before running right out of steam.

From the diary of Professor Bernice Summerfield:

Reader, I didn't marry him.

It was *not yet*, not *no*, I had to make that terribly clear. I was blurting it out even as he was pulling away with that awful guarded nonchalant look in his eyes. He'd seen my answer without me speaking a word. And then I had to explain what I couldn't even make sense of myself.

All things considered, this only rated about a two or three on the Summerfield-Kane armageddon scale. No tears, no property damage, no words that we'll be saving up to hurl back in a later fit of anger. Slow and bruising instead of hot and blinding. So really not that bad, I keep saying, even if the whole thing still felt like brushing your teeth with ground bits of glass. And now I'm sitting up writing, trying to make sense of it, while Jason's curled up next to me facing away, and pretending to be peacefully asleep so we don't have to talk any more.

Stop snoring, you big faker.

It all came down to his blunt-instrument question: how can you want kids with me but be skittish about a ring on your finger? What kind of commitment is that? And the best I could manage was that remarrying him would mean I was promising to be the same person I'd failed to be the last time, and I didn't feel sure that I was that person this time either. Which happens to be true, but as the reason why I said no it's a big fat porker.

Let me put it this way:

Regular readers (by whom I mean *me*, Jason, so put the diary down right now and take two steps back) may recall that one of the few things that has been absolutely reliable between me and Jason has been the infuriatingly good sex. Even when I want him to be just as unreliable and frustrating as he is the rest of the day, just to remind me why I'm mad at him, he comes out with a well-placed nibble or gratuitous backrub that shows he *knows* what every bit of me is looking for. After all this time, that could just be down to practice and calculation – but truth is, it frustrates him too, that a moment like that can disrupt his own carefully maintained sulking. We have to face it, we just have instincts for each other.

And the way we fight... that's the same instinct as the physical stuff. The other one knows just what bit of us *needs* to be touched, even if we don't *want* it to be. Even if it's the bit we're guarding the most from ourselves. Of course, we jab and prod those bits rather than nibble, because when it comes down to it we're both profoundly dim. But once we're done reacting like a couple of insecure defensive idiots... eventually we do realise we've hit dead centre on issues that would have lurked poisonously under the surface for years if we hadn't taken such a dead-on shortcut. And all right, so we've excavated them with a pickaxe rather than a trowel and years of careful scraping... but they're the things we most *needed* to bring out. (And no, Jason, this *isn't* one of those, so still, put it *down*.)

But that's also the danger, that's what's making me flinch. When you've found someone who can cut right through you and find all the hollows in your bones. I'm afraid you'll reach the bits that have broken.

I've changed so much, these past five years or so. If you'd tried to sum me up back then, every word you'd choose to describe me is just that much less certain now. A figurehead archaeologist who hasn't picked up a trowel all year. A roving adventurer who spends more time on fundraising trips and Peter's school supplies. A writer whose justly acclaimed coffee-table book on archaeology now sells fewer copies than her boyfriend's interspecies porn novels. An expert on body language who got utterly hornswoggled by Ithva, and whose misreadings cost a girl from the Quire her sanity. A woman sure of her friends... until people I'd righteously hated since my youth turned out not to have betrayed me after all, and people I'd relied on revealed themselves as monsters. A woman of peace who's killed rather too many people in her life, even if they all did deserve it. I'm drinking so much less than before Peter, but with more serious intent when I do. And all those little moral lines crossed resisting the Axis, one by one, each bothering me a little bit less. I've even gone from someone who guarded both my body and my heart, but gave them completely when I did, to someone who could have a proficient and deeply stupid one-nighter and then say *it was just sex* with a straight face.

You might see it as a good thing, that I'm finally secure enough on a deep level to risk being shallow and superficial. That I don't *have* to feel so much. I just see that things that would have laid my heart wide open now barely crack it at all.

And I still want to be louder, braver, drunker, and more loving, but I'm not sure what that *means* at my age any more. Or where *older* and *wiser* fit on that list.

I'm not sure who I am, I'm wondering what I can still be, I'm looking for my answers and I'm scared they won't mean anything to you. And I can't separate getting married from these questions... because one of them is, if a seedy little hustler like Jason Kane has become your safe option, what kind of woman are you turning into?

(Sorry, Jason. I did tell you to stop reading. But you didn't listen, of course you didn't. Don't worry, that's just one of those thoughts that is perfectly true as one piece of the puzzle, but a vicious lie in isolation. There's so much more to you than that, and that's why I love you. You're still a bastard for reading my diary, though, so go away.)

Jason had to grow up so fast when he was young, and he's making up for it by growing up so slowly now. And that's good, I think. I need that youngness within him and Peter, to hold on to where I've been. But it means I've got no one to give me any idea of the way forward from here.

Though the strangest thing is... the one feeling that keeps washing over me, hidden by all the others... is relief. Because I know that I *can* say not yet, and we'll still be together. We have time.

Still, that's why I said no. Jason – and now I wish I *had* let you stick around to read this – I'm still bloody terrified that you'll get me forever, and then you'll find that there's nothing left inside me to hold on to.

* * *

She woke up dazed and hazy, from sleeping at the wrong time of her body's day. Moments not quite knitting together right, a fugue of automatic actions getting her through the routine parts even of this latest adventure. Then scattered moments of clarity when it would all snap into focus.

Like when she balanced on the edge of the spa bath, squinting at the little strip for the pregnancy test, trying to make out the colour.

'Test again in a day or two,' said the instructions. Hell. Thousands of years of human science and technology, and the mysteries of hormones could still baffle all of it. She should have shelled out the extra cash for a proper medical kit, not grabbed this portable El Cheapo multiple-species one at the spaceport chemist's.

Which would be more of a relief? A positive result, after all their trying – certainty at last about the next months and years? A negative result? What if she'd conceived before leaving for Proxima Longissima, and then merging with Lwpha had somehow affected the embryo? What might she be carrying? She shivered, and for a moment felt like her whole body was rippling, well beneath the surface.

A goodbye kiss for Jason in the hotel room after breakfast, left with a copy of the local equivalent of *Heat* magazine: noble gossip, an Honour Watch column, and detailed reports on the sexual misbehaviour of the heirs and inheritors of the great Houses.

He kept trying to hold on to her after their farewell hug, touching her arm, holding her hand. 'God. Are you sure about this? Isn't there something I can do?'

'Watch my back,' Benny told him. 'Any way you can.'

He nodded, slowly. She wasn't used to seeing Serious Jason, especially not so early in the morning, and she wished she could stay to see what he would do. But that would rather defeat the purpose.

In the taxi she went over her list of camping gear one more time. Three days in an alien desert would be hard enough going without forgetting the bog rolls. The honour of the human race was at stake: hell, her ability to cope under pressure could even mean something for future history. She was used to roughing it. She'd seen enough weird alien initiation rituals. She could sleep on rocks and handle a blade. She was ready to show these Draconian women a thing or two. Was Peter? It was about time he got to take his first steps.

* * *

The mothers and daughters were flocking round the trolleys, piled high with luggage at the local shuttleport. They looked like a group of suburban mothers with distracted under-tens. They looked like tourists. Not very Klingon, thought Benny.

Ithva was wearing a pair of sunglasses. She took them off as Benny approached – so that the human could see where her eyes were looking, or to help Benny recognise her? Or just so she could see better? She greeted Benny using verb forms that indicated that they were friends, conveying at once to the others that Benny had at least the status of a fellow Draconian. Her actual place in the pecking order, she thought, would be sorted out in the field.

Ithva's hair was scraped back from the top of her head and tightly tied. Benny hadn't realised how much that small patch of long fur had softened the sharp line of Ithva's skull, making her look just that bit more human. It was a mistake to think of Draconians as reptiles, as much as it was to anthropomorphise them. For a start, an actual reptile, evolved on Earth, wouldn't have fur. Ithva was neither a human woman nor a lizard, neither fish nor fowl. Something else, with its own rules.

The trip to the Tembleth Desert was a suborbital hop, half an hour on a commuter flight that took them halfway across the continent, thousands of kilometres from the nearest city. Roughing it at last, thought Benny, as she shepherded Peter off the flight – only to discover the camp was no rougher than a caravan park. There was an amenities block with running water, a picnic area where the getting-to-know-you catered barbecue would be held, even a grassy patch for classes in tai chi-y sorts of exercise. Benny began to realise what it meant that Tembleth was technically in the suborbs.

She guessed there were at least six dozen mothers here, each with a daughter between five and eight. The air full of excited air-kissing and squawking. The kids were running amok, establishing their own pecking order. Peter stuck close to Benny's legs. The girls either stared at him from a distance, or snuck up and tried to touch his fur before running away giggling.

Ithva slid into place beside her, once more lending her status.

'This is about as threatening as a bar mitzvah,' murmured Benny.

Ithva glanced at her curiously. They looked away quickly before they both began to laugh.

'It's become completely diluted,' said the Draconian. 'The whole point of the retreat is – was – the womens' chance to give their daughters their first lessons in how to fight. Away from the eyes of the men. But here? Even the ceremonial abductions are just a few costumed actors who run away when the women shout insults at them.'

Benny sighed, looking past the neat squares of the camping ground to the desert beyond – rust-orange sand, rising and falling dunes, jutting archaic grey stone, the blue-green horizon. She didn't know much about Tembleth, only that there weren't any dangerous animals. There might be ruins out there, unknown flowers, anything

Ithva continued smoothly, 'This is not what you and I, and Sharintha and Peter, will be doing.'

'Oh?' Benny didn't know whether to slump or to prick up her ears.

'A few of us prefer a more traditional approach,' murmured Ithva. 'We're going to travel into the desert and make our own camp. No showers. Only the water and food we carry with us.' The Draconian touched her on the shoulder with a claw-hand. 'You'll love it, darling, it'll be so much more real.'

'What about the abductions? Will those be more real too?'

'We will have to defend our children,' said Ithva. 'I'm not paying those thugs to mince about.' She laughed lightly at Benny's expression. 'But not to the death!'

'What if one of the children actually gets taken?'

'We steal them back from the enemy camp. If all else falls, we ransom them for an additional payment.'

'Ithva...' Benny moved closer and hissed, 'There is *no way* I'm putting Peter at risk of being carried off by a hired Draconian thug.'

'But –'

'Forget it.'

Ithva sighed, and turned away – and then turned back sharply. 'You do understand that they wouldn't be hurt?'

'But the thugs –'

'The smallest harm on the smallest scale to one of the youngsters would mean their hides.' Ithva showed some teeth. She meant their hides, *literally*.

'That's not enough. He could be traumatised.'

Ithva looked at her with an expression Benny couldn't decipher, and said, 'I could keep Sharintha at home as well. But then how's she going to learn to cope with the danger in the world? You can't stay in the hatchery if you're going to be a Hand for the Empress.' Subtext: if Bernice Summerfield wants to gain the Hand's confidence, she's got to risk this camp.

'I can't,' she whispered.

'I do have my facts straight, don't I?' said Ithva guilelessly. 'You are the legal parent of those Mim children?' Subtext: if you were, wouldn't you do anything to protect them?

'No.'

'It would seem to me you're the closest they have.'

Ithva's eyes locked on hers, and she found herself caught between two truths. 'They're all relying on me to keep them safe. But so is Peter.'

Ithva's face had never looked more alien. 'You can't keep them safe from everything.'

In the end it was Peter who made up Benny's mind.

'I'm bored,' he whined.

'Me too,' said Benny. She looked around, conspiratorially. 'This is only the fake camp. Let's go to the real one.'

'*Rogue*!'

4

Benny Summerfield, in her large floppy sunhat: pale pink creature against the burnt orange of the sandscape, the murky brown of her mount, the bold deep green of her fellow riders, the uneasy greenish-yellow of the sun. Her skin clashing with everything to the horizon. Ready to burn the moment she drops her guard.

She's on the back of a droth, a plodding ocean-liner of a beast, like an upholstered hippopotamus. Peter nestled in her arms, one long squirm, still looking for camels or anything interesting between here and the edge of the world.

Already the water's gone – not from her checked-a-thousand-times supplies, but from the very air around them. This is land without even the moisture of breath, sand so hot it should be fusing into glass beneath their feet. Not a place for a body at all. Certainly not a comfortably lumpy one such as hers.

Half a dozen droth sailing two by two towards a dot sticking out of the horizon. A seventh tucked between them, its back empty.

The late start means they're travelling through the hottest hours. She can feel the sweat on Peter's arms, sticking the two of them together: the sun drying them out faster than their bodies can cool them. Already touching another person's skin feels like more contact than a soul could bear, but she holds on. It's her spirit against the sun's, even though the sun will never stop: slow-roasting her, desiccating her, burning away all the soft wet bits of her, leaving nothing left but... what?

Benny staring glazedly into the distance, at the line where the orangeyellow meets the greenblue, asking herself some of the oldest questions in the world. Peter tugging her sleeve and asking one almost as old, to which the answer is, 'I told you to go before we left.'

The woman riding beside her has turned out to be Marthaleka – *the* Marthaleka, a mental prefix – artist and whisperer in the ear of the public. Ithva's tendrils of friendship stretch far. In person she's short, plump, unassuming: a clear voice she never raises but which leaves you hanging on every word. Looking like one of her trademark bicolour line sketches: swift black and green strokes, appearing so simple you don't realise all the nuances she's slipped under your radar. On her lap sits her daughter, whose name Benny hasn't caught: demurely balanced, princess poise, already assuming she holds the centre of everyone's attention.

Ithva's riding behind, a watchful eye on those in front, her daughter nestled against the droth's neck. It sounds like she's got little Sharintha counting stonecrabs – she points and sings out every time she spots one, scuttling across the surface before sinking beneath the sand again. She's a babbling brook of a child, constantly tumbling and sparkling in the light.

Peter's asking what happens next.

For the past half-hour she's been drawing out a story, continuing the tale she and Jason had started the night before. Over the months the two of them have evolved a whole universe of recurring characters and scenarios for Peter, and he's been clamouring for the next instalment. Tremendously flattering, if only she'd any idea where it's going. She's toying with marrying Casanova off to Sally Lettuce, but Jason wouldn't be happy with that, Casanova's one of his characters. He's a little protective of him, and enjoys the Pepe Le Pew voice he's given him rather too much. So it's Kevin the Lion who she surrenders to Sally's attentions, and who will have to do battle with the squishily vicious Sir Tom Ato.

There was a time when the stories had made sense, to her at least. They'd started out based on friends in real life, but had wandered further afield, just the way she had. But Peter's hanging on every word, rapt in a landscape only he can see.

'And then what?' asks Peter.

She looks back at Ithva, teaching Sharintha to look around her, see what she can notice. To stretch herself.

'Well what do *you* think should happen next?' she asks him.

Inevitably, it involves dinosaurs.

The other three mothers are plodding along in front and behind, each wrapped in their own little dramas. The only name she's caught so far is Riskilvar – a daughter's name, shouted out by her mother with alarming regularity, every time the little tearaway tries to leap off the droth or unpick the tents bundled on its back behind her.

None of them sweat.

They couldn't if they wanted to. Their species lacks the pathways. Not cold-blooded, not warm-blooded: terms defined by the sharp binary oppositions of earthly evolution. The path that had turned up by chance on their world was sort of lukewarm... some of the same mechanisms for warming or cooling the flow inside, but not all of them, and not nearly as effective. But the end result was that at any temperature they stayed cool and dry to the touch.

Heat like this was their perfect range anyway – just like the homiest parts of home, the semi-arid tropical zones where they'd evolved. Cold still slowed their blood, robbed their brains of their sharpness... they could shiver but not sweat. It was *that* which they were here to endure in the desert, she realised: their thin layers of cotton had none of the temperature controllers so carefully woven into the fabric of their *hronstheis*. That was the sign that they had stepped outside of civilisation. Their clothes, their impeccable clothes, had defined their way of life since some prehistoric city-dweller had first lined his cloak inside and out with those soft greenish copperleaves, and discovered how well they absorbed heat above a certain temperature and radiated it out as it cooled. It had defined their nature, when they learned a perfectly tailored surface could make a better job of their blood-comfort than their own bodies could. The clothes maketh the Empire, an empire of form, and had allowed the city's newly bolstered warriors to fight through all seasons and overrun their world, and ultimately produced that famous painting of the Prime Emperor at the conquest of the final northernmost tribe, standing astride his last battlefield resplendent in his emerald thermal underwear.

* * *

127

The caravan making camp at the mesa: stubby little mountain, barely bigger than a small office-block, the only high ground for miles. Just a stray bit of reddish-brown rock jutting from beneath the sand. At this hot hour it casts almost no shadow. For all the beasts, women and children scurrying round its base, it seems untouched and unperturbed, interrupting both the sand and the sky, belonging to neither.

The children, free to stretch their legs at last, playing like they're on the world's biggest seashore.

Marthaleka and Rathklin, amidst unloading, circling through the endless old-married-couple argument of a pair who've been through this before.

'It seems to me it's the obvious place to defend,' Marthaleka murmurs. 'Though of course I could be wrong.'

'The droth'll never make it up the trail. Even if we put the kids up top, you still need to guard a base camp, and then you're dividing your forces.'

'Well that's as may be, but the last time I did this it meant we only needed to hold the trail...'

'And you were lucky they didn't steal your transport. You could've been stranded...'

Rathklin's tone is blunt; Marthaleka's suggests compromise, but her words somehow never actually make a single concession. The irresistible force meets the indefinable object.

'The top's the natural sanctuary. On the ground it's an open field of attack...'

'But it's better to have something to keep your back to in a fight. Salthmanika, back me up on this...'

Rathklin: tall and stylishly bony, creative director of the Montavadros branch of K&R, the largest advertising agency in green-skinned space. One of the highest-paid outcasts on the planet, queen of an industry no warriorman would take part in. For a culture so allergic to directness, who view overt articulacy as disturbing slickness and a sign of how *little* you can be trusted, the idea of devoting your life to *selling* things... So it's a women's industry, for those with no higher aims, tolerated as an all-pervasive necessary evil. And you can see it in Rathklin's polished outlaw bearing: for all the time she spends with the ears of the government's own communications directors, making their policies palatable, you know they see her somewhere on the level of a brothel madam. At least a madam would be satisfying an existing need, rather than manufacturing one of her own.

Her daughter is running circles chasing after Peter right now: garrulous and scampering whenever mother's back is turned, a model of quiet restraint whenever she feels her glare.

The developing five-way wrangle somehow ends in consensus, as etiquette demands: one or two mothers always up top, as lookouts, with the main camp against the base, keeping their option to retreat to the summit. But Rathklin looks faintly triumphant; even if she'd had to pull back from her hard sell and play to the women's rules, she's got her way in the end.

'Oh, it's an ancient statement of female power,' says Misilvar, as she helps Benny unload the cooking pots and firebowl. Her eyes are wide and fluttery in her fine-scaled oval face. 'The centrepiece of the ritual can be traced all the way back to the post-unification statements of the Prime Empress...'

Benny plops the ceramic firebowl down in a free bit of sand, and looks levelly at the librarian. Her eyes are sweet and bluish-purple, her mouth perfectly straight-faced, but the wrinkles in her forehead are fighting not to crumple into visible laughter.

'You're taking the piss, aren't you?'

'No, really –'

'It dates back about four hundred years,' throws in Rathklin, efficiently pitching her tent nearby. 'To a network special. *New Pathways*, one of Vinaski's *Spirituality Now* series. Shame on you for suckering the rube,' she tells Misilvar in a mocking tone that suggests anything but shame.

'The rube got it, thank you very much,' says Benny, wondering what term of endearment the translators are equating with 'rube'.

'Doesn't she sound like she knows?' Misilvar says sweetly to Benny, baiting Rathklin as much as etiquette will allow.

'We *underwrote* it. "Made possible by a grant from K&R".'

'Oh, go *away*, I've watched it on archive –'

'All right, there wasn't a caption, but we brokered all the ad time. Lots of ads for camping gear, I think.'

'Heavens,' says Benny. 'I can only imagine who'd have sponsored our bibles and what-not. *Give us this day our Hellman's Rye...*'

It's like she isn't even there. 'Trust me on this,' Rathklin is saying to Misilvar. 'It's in our corporate prospectus, all the ways we made history.'

'All right,' Misilvar allows. 'Four hundred years since they put the ritual together. But the legend it's based on is older than that...'

'Right, a whole hundred years...'

'No, Karshtakavarr's just one part of it, really, some of the text of the reading goes back –'

'*Pfeh*. He's the whole point! No Karshtakavarr, no *nikhol vakarshta* –'

'Sorry, how did Karshtakavarr get into all this?' Benny squeezes in. 'I didn't think he was the mothering type.'

'Oh, I can give you the whole story,' says Misilvar, and Benny can see the eagerness of a woman starved for adult conversation. Or possibly a woman gleefully aiming to sucker the mammal again. But still, given how much time she spends chasing after her little Riskilvar, any chance to exchange more than a few sentences in a row without throwing in bits of song or counting-games must feel heaven-sent. She's the youngest and least lined of the mothers, but the least used to her exhaustion, with that deep-rooted tiredness born of endlessly trying to keep up. Plus she's a librarian and fact-miner, who spends her days digging for data in the archives: that gives you a head full of facts and all the whimsical connections between them you can eat. Benny gives her the benefit of the doubt and settles in for the long haul.

'For a start, you know the story of the plague, am I right?'

'I've heard it a few times,' says Benny, not letting on how.

Some painted the plague era as when Draconia's childhood ended. The world being ravaged by an alien micro-organism, brought down on the back of a meteorite; civilisation hollowing out as nine out of every ten went to the grave. Finally, years later, the freak chance of a wandering alien explorer making an uncontrolled landing, and bringing knowledge that led to a cure. Chance from the stars had nearly ended them; chance from the stars had let them live. And so the Draconians repopulated their world, and started clawing their way to the stars, spreading their children to world after world, ensuring they could never again be wiped out at a stroke. Of such random chances were civilisations made, and remade.

'Karshtakavarr was the first time we knew for a fact there were higher powers on other worlds.' At least Misilvar is talking to her rather than past her, even if it's mainly for her own entertainment, or to score points off Rathklin. 'Not necessarily more moral, just *beyond* us. Beyond our control.'

Rathklin doesn't seem to take well to being upstaged. 'You know, when we first met humans, long after all that... we thought you were his people,' she says. 'He could pass for one of you.' A careful curl of her lip. 'Didn't take us long to recognise our mistake.'

'Oh, so you know what he looked like, then?'

'Come on, the plague was only about five hundred years back. We had *video*. Even if it was just 2-D black-and-white. He was a media hero...'

'Not much of a legend if you know it actually happened, is it?'

'The legend depends on what he means,' Misilvar says. 'He was Second Contact.'

'First was the plague,' deadpans Rathklin.

'So how did we get from him curing the plague to all this?' asks Benny. 'Just that he was making the world safe for children?'

'Well yes, but that's not what *this* legend is about. This is afterwards, after they'd saved the Empire, and he was about to leave the court. You see, the Empress's youngest daughter had become friends with Karshtakavarr's granddaughter – he was travelling with his granddaughter – and she wanted to go with them. Out to the staaars,' Misilvar says, sending up her own romanticism. 'So they were all going to sneak away in the middle of the night. But the Empress, well, she was a great believer in staying one step ahead of her children, you know what it's like with adolescents. So at midnight, as they were trying to sneak across the courtyard... She's waiting for them. And she tells Karshtakavarr *no*.'

She pauses, finding Benny's eyes to underline it. 'I mean, think about that. She's facing down the Second Contact... This *being* straight from the heavens like no creature we'd ever seen, who'd just saved us all and stopped the end of the world... She knows nothing about what he's capable of... And she stands there and tells him *this child is still in my care*. She won't give her daughter up even to a god.'

'And she kicked his *arse*,' says Rathklin, with a triumphant teeth-bared smile.

'They say he wrestled like a demon,' said Misilvar. 'He had the skills of a man half his age. But she drove him and his granddaughter off. And they say she gave him a whack on the backside with her fan as he went.'

'Vinaski used that as the basis for a whole image of female spiritual empowerment,' says Rathklin. 'Warrior, mother, and spy, all in one. And the way everything was still changing, even a century after the plague... it really resonated for a lot of people. The story became not just about fighting for your kids, but teaching them to fight. Or starting to, at least.'

'And I suppose there's video of the whole fight too,' says Benny. Somehow that disappointed her; something in the back of her brain still baulked at the idea of a religious myth you could see unfolding.

Misilvar purses her lips. 'No, I don't think there is...'

'Well at least *that* bit counts as a legend.'

'Bit more than that,' says Rathklin. 'The kid sold her story to the gossip channels.'

Ithva Kothar, social butterfly, digging the latrine pit at the edge of the camp. Green scales glittering in the sun, hair pushed back from her elaborate ridged ears. Far leaner than Benny would have thought, out of her *hronsthei* and ornaments: wiry and a bit grimy, and deeply involved in her labour. The dignity of being completely unconcerned how you appear at this moment.

A look tossed to Benny – a sideways glance at Rathklin and Misilvar and their continuing bickering about historical meaning. A cocked eyebrow, a private joke just for Benny. Can you believe this?

Well can I? Benny wonders.

Salthmanika starts leading the children up the winding path to the top. Peter clings dubiously to mum's hand; the other kids don't like him, he tells her, expressing the profound unfairness of it all. And true, the gaggle of girls are acting almost as one: staring and inching up close, fascinated by the wispy blue fur just growing on his arms and face, then retreating in a cloud of giggles if he says anything. Benny starts to give him the *they're just as nervous about you* speech, but there's not enough time to finish, and, oh, she'll be damned if she'll abandon her son to their mercies just yet. And besides, she's seen that same stare directed at her from a couple of the mothers.

Salthmanika, long-haul truck driver, daintily poised at all times, perfect grace even as she climbs the mesa trail. Last of the mothers in the party. Seemingly the most delicate of the lot; ever since the start of computer-aided driving and threat prediction, driving jobs have become more akin to a day-long meditation session, and thus play perfectly into Draconian prejudices. A woman who spends her days shut in a moving cupboard, isolated from other men or indeed women, reacting on instinct rather than intellect.

Her daughter, adoring and talkative till the moment she feels Benny's (or anyone's) eyes on her, at which point she buries her face in mother's skirts.

Five daughters on the mountaintop: little princess; little terror; shy when mum's around; shy when mum's not around; and sparkling little Sharintha.

View from the summit:

'Look over there,' says Salthmanika, 'Look carefully, tell me if you can see the ocean from here.' And the children stop ricocheting around the small flat space atop the mesa, and crowd around her, staring at the one point on the horizon. The ocean is four thousand kilometres away, but after a few moments of egging each other on every child's imagination is coaxing a seascape out of the mirage.

While they shout and point, Salthmanika takes Benny to the other side of the summit, and points out across the sand-sea, to the small cluster of orange-tinted, desert-camo tents in the distance. Benny hasn't even seen her scoping for them. She has a stillness about her that lets her watch without looking like she's watching.

'They won't attack till nightfall,' she tells her. 'Not when we can see them coming.'

'They. Who are they?'

'The usual hired cut-throats.' She's lowered her voice so the kids won't hear. When she's not talking to children, she's completely transformed: a figure used to quiet and stillness, saving her energy for when it's needed. 'The commercial retreats use unemployed actors, but these are hardly a better class of people.'

Benny frowns, thinking. 'And Ithva did the hiring?'

'Probably. She knows people who know people.'

Benny's eyes narrow: peering at the distant camp, trying to make out anything she can about the half-dozen warriors gathered round their cooking-fire. She can't shake the smell of a stitch-up. Though even more than that she's smelling the meat they're roasting: her own mirage, too long past lunchtime.

'How often do children actually get... you know, taken?'

Salthmanika shrugs. 'I've only done this twice... The first time one girl got taken – not mine – but we raided the enemy camp and stole her back.'

Benny looks at Salthmanika's smooth, neutral face and tries to picture her and her friends rallying round her if the attackers got hold of Peter. For a moment, she feels more isolated than the mesa itself. 'I mean taken for good, never to be seen again...'

'I've never heard of it. But then, it's not the sort of thing a mother would admit to.'

Benny's silent as Salthmanika opens the hamper containing the roast *vikhila* for the childrens' lunch – a transition meal for them, before the eating gets exotic. 'They say you can ransom them back,' she goes on. 'The organiser knows how to find them again. So I suppose, for a price...'

'Oh, a price.' With a special surcharge for offworlders with the ear of the Mim delegation, no doubt. 'They're not armed, are they?'

'They shouldn't be. It's supposed to be body against body.'

The lunch is smelling far too good; her own is waiting in the camp down below. She looks over to Peter; he's pointing at the imagined ocean and miming riding a surfboard, knees bent and bottom wiggling. A couple of the girls are laughing with him rather than at him now. She waves, but while he sees he's too busy to wave back. My work here is done, she thinks, and starts down the trail.

Study the picture: see how little the look of the landscape changes as you move from a high angle to a low one. This place has no depth to it. A flat plane on which all their movements are kept two-dimensional. No room for anything under the surface; anything lurking bursts right up into the open. As far from Proxima Longissima as she could get: the ocean had seemed just as hypnotically featureless, but as she bobbed on its surface she couldn't forget the complexity hidden below.

No, don't think about Proxima Longissima, that's the last thing you want, it only makes you think about water. Vast expanses of it. Life-giving, world-shaping. Drowning, she reminds herself, and shrivelling the hell out of her – and all its salt at least as parching as this sand.

Misilvar the librarian has produced a massive roll-up, and is passing it round the circle as they finish lunch. The smoke fluoresces as it spreads, and the occasional bright-green firefly spark crackles out of the end.

'Um, scuse me?' says Benny. 'Enemy hordes, just over the horizon?'

'This is Old 32,' drawls Rathklin, her eyelids fluttering as she sags back against the rucksack full of cooking gear. She sounds like one of her own ads, in slow motion. 'Specially designed to be fast-acting. You're sober again before it makes it back to you.'

'And Salthmanika's on lookout,' says Ithva, still sitting with perfect composure even as she sways on the spot. 'We have more than enough warning to get it out of our system.'

'Old 32's one of the 749 Paths to Heaven of Emperor Lashnativaar,' offers Misilvar from her library of trivia, from where she lies sprawled on her back. 'Fifth dynasty. Wonderful man. A brew for every occasion.'

'*Deeply* enlightened,' adds Marthaleka. Benny watches Marthaleka toke up, sees the glassy little flutter through her body and the way her hand sags away from her mouth, and feels a twinge of fear in her stomach: it looks way more like an opiate rush than anything she'd go for. And if the recipe dates back to the fifth dynasty, and the early breakthroughs in the Draconians' mastery of organic chemistry, this could be one of the concoctions that had been cited by cynics as the reason *why*, despite their ten thousand years of civilisation, they weren't really that much more advanced than the human race. Where the development of beer had helped push civilisations into fast-forward – promoting agriculture, storehouses, industry, distribution methods – the development of really good relaxants put it in slow motion.

'Those whole dynasties were called the Happy Emperors,' Misilvar opines supinely. 'Can you imagine that? *Happy. Emperors.*'

'I can see why,' says Benny. 'Haven't really studied that period much, I admit. It's a bit of a blur to me.'

'A bit of a blur to *them*,' adds Ithva, peeling one eye open.

'It's just, I mean, centuries of stability and spiritual contemplation... Not a lot of really startling artefacts left behind.'

'Well, not a lot *happened*,' says Rathklin drily. She slouchs up on one arm, fixing Benny with a stare, her inhibitions practically melted away into a puddle. Going for the hard sell. 'You archaeologists and your artefacts. You're just a sign of how *wrong* your people got it, aren't you?'

'Sorry?'

'His Current Imperial Maj could use a bit more of this,' adds Misilvar, still having a complete conversation of her own.

Rathklin's finger fixes on Benny. 'Picking up scraps from old dustbins... You're just fixing other peoples' mistakes. Putting back together a history they didn't bother to preserve.' She corrects her wandering finger's aim. 'We've always done it right. We leave our history standing.'

It's a challenge, to see if she'll stand up to them. And the other challenge is still making its way round the circle to her. She can feel all the eyes quietly fixing on her, even the glassy ones. Ithva had led her to expect this, encouraged her to face the challenges she was creating, playing good-cop to her own bad-cop. But this one's not a worry: if there's one thing Bernice Summerfield is good at, it's coming up with rationalisations.

'But you don't leave the context standing,' she says. 'You can't, there's not enough space to preserve everything. I mean, you're all legendary at conserving and recording and history-ing, but you can never really be sure what's important or meaningful at the time. I mean, what if the Happy Emperor woke up in the middle of the night with the secret of life, wrote it down on an old newspaper, then got the munchies, ate three *vikhilas*, and used the newspaper to wrap the bones? How's that for a reason to go through the bins?'

Rathklin shrugs it off. 'Ah, doesn't matter. It probably just said *There are seven levels – oh, wow.*'

And that sets the others off – but Benny knows she's on safe ground, their foreheads had started smiling for them even during her own spiel. Which meant she'd got the sense of humour basically right for the occasion: naughty irreverence about safely dead ruling figures, yes, even if adding an obscure religious joke scored better than straight historical stoner humour.

Rathklin seems to be laughing with her, as they both settle back down. As initiation and bonding rituals go, this wasn't as bad as some. And at least it's giving her the sight of Ithva Kothar, perfect hostess, spymistress, leaning back against her bedroll and bogarting the joint.

Think context, think etiquette. Think Bedouin herbal hospitality, think mescal ritual, think culturally sanctioned and loads of meaning that's *not* about getting hammered. Or leaving yourself dazed and confused with a bunch of near-strangers who *probably* aren't going to kill you.

'Anyway,' says Benny, 'I'd think you lot would admire it. Going through rubbish. Gathering intelligence. Working out the truth about people who never even knew you were there. It's just spying through time, isn't it?'

None of them respond to that one. She'd assumed that all of them were actually part of the Empress's Hand, but that might not be how they defined themselves; Ithva clearly saw it as her career and calling, but the others might simply be occasional contacts, or information sources, or cannon fodder. Part-time assistant spies, sharing a social weekend away. Or they could be just as much in the game as Ithva herself, but not letting on. Benny really *doesn't* know the rules.

The moment of truth, as Ithva passes the roll-up to her, her eyes barely above half-mast. Benny holds it in her mouth. The tip's fizzing and sparking greenishly, in the cross-eyed space right in front of her nose. She glances up to the mesa-top, wondering how much the kids can see. Not like the others seem to mind. But Peter, if seeing your mummy do this warps your developing little psyche, and you throw it back at me in some moment of teenage rebellion, I'll have no one to blame but myself.

If this were her territory, she'd be happily trying to drink these women under the table, making them lose themselves in a fermented ocean. But she's come to this dry fiery world to show them she can live on their terms, make them respect her terms in turn. No other way through it: she nerves herself, and takes a long slow pull. Breathing deep of their fire.

And then exploding in a comedy coughing fit, spitting smoke in all directions – using the inhale after the first cough to suck a bit more smoke into her mouth, and give the impression that there had been plenty more in her lungs. When in fact she'd been inhaling through her nose and holding the smoke in her mouth, just for the effect. Showing them she's game but a non-threatening lightweight who can't hold her Path To Heaven – all they expect from the silly little foreign mammal. And the gasping-for-breath allows her to collapse on Ithva's shoulder for support, burying her face close to her ear, and murmur 'What should I be faking?'

'Euphoria,' she whispers back. 'Sedation. Only about thirty seconds.' But she can see Ithva's eye out of the corner of her own, open wide and clear, and there's a new respect for her perceptiveness in it. Clearly Ithva hadn't expected Benny to see through her own elaborate mouth-filling inhale, much less use the same sort of trick herself. Ithva isn't letting her guard down even for a minute.

She leans back, still resting on Ithva's shoulder, and does her best impression of a woman who's seeing God. She does feel a bit light-headed – probably just dizziness from the staged coughing, or else even the little bit of Old 32 that had made it down to her lungs was still seriously potent. Ithva's arm is supporting her now, cool comforting scales, and the others are watching sympathetically if amusedly. Rathklin's gently lifting the doobie from her unresisted fingers, and Benny can't resist adding a *thanksh, your ma besht mate* to the proceedings.

'My first time, I forgot how to speak,' confesses Ithva.

'It's an important part of the ritual state of mind,' Misilvar says gently. 'Learning to relax in the heart of tension. Stay taut in the heart of relaxation.'

'Motherskills,' adds Marthaleka serenely.

Benny widens her eyes. 'Whoa. *Yeah*.'

Misilvar, cutting the droth's throat with a well-worn blade.

Benny clinging to one of the ropes round its neck, pulling it taut and wishing she had another hit of Old 32 about now. The other women on the different ropes as Misilvar saws open its neck – the other six droth grunting and warbling in alarm on the far side of the camp. The rope leaping round in Benny's hands, burning her skin raw, as the beast thrashes its hobbled foreleg. It's bellowing uncomprehendingly, with no idea of the practical rules of the game. That meat for twelve people and six droth for three days is best carried under its own power.

Droth blood is brownish, moves like oil. It burns, they tell her; a ripe fatty flame. She stares at the splatters on the large plastic sheet they've spread beneath the beast; all the blood they drain will be saved and used for the cooking-fire. The rope goes taut one last time, then sags downward and hangs still.

Their blood burns.

All things considered it's a quick efficient butchery. The creature's being processed into neat piles long before Salthmanika returns with the children from her distracting ramble round the mesa. All the fingers of the Empress's Hand working smoothly together, professionally, to kill who had to be killed. Benny watches the bloodsoaked librarian, sawing meat from the bone, and decides it's probably best to stop thinking in terms of metaphor.

Mum, mum, we were up the top! And Riskyva almost fell off and I caught her and she wanted to play with my fur and we saw the *ocean!*

Wow! The *ocean!*

Yeah! And you couldn't see it but then you could!

Hey cubby. Do you want me to tell you a secret? A grown-up secret?

Yeah.

That's not the ocean.

… It's not?

No, it's like a magic trick, a little trick of the sun. The heat makes the air go all shimmery and it makes the sand look like water.

But I saw it!

It's called a mirage.

But it was the ocean, it was rogue!

Well you know what? This is rogue-er. You can look at water any old place. But only someplace like here, can you see a mirage. And it's more neat when you know how it works. Isn't it?

I guess. But I've never been to the ocean.

Well Brax doesn't own one. Though if he could build one heaven knows he'd put it on the Collection.

I've never been to the ocean and I thought it was there...

Oh. Tell you what. Next year Uncle Jason and I will take you to the Zenbrouli ocean, and you can swim with the squids. Like your friend Wajiwaj. By then I should be over the whole nearly-dying-of-exposure thing. Won't that be fun?

Yeah, that'd be good! But I still thought this was real.

And for my next trick, there goes Santa Claus.

Huh?

Never mind.

They're far enough away from home now, Rathklin tells the children, no one back home can hear them any more. So they can shout and scream and carry on as much as they want and no one will ever tell. The mothers even set the example: throwing aside their decorum and hurling themselves into five-year-old exuberance, celebratory whoops and running around with arms flailing. Suddenly everyone's rampaging round the campsite, dodging and ducking. Ithva, minutes ago methodically toting supplies to the tents, now races her Sharintha up the slope at the side of the mesa, scrabbling up the scree and giggling even louder than her daughter. Accepting the madness, Benny races Peter round the mesa: letting his little legs set the pace, chasing after him with *blblblbl* noises and I'm-gonna-getcha outstretched arms. It's silly and over-the-top and for a few moments all her inner voices are stilled, there's nothing in the world but the fun she's having with her son. Then her throat starts getting parched and they're still only halfway around. By the time they make it back – Peter pinwheeling his arms, Benny beginning to slog through the sand – it takes her a moment to notice that the other mothers have long since stopped, and are letting their children carry on till they've exhausted themselves. There's an indulgent human smile on Ithva's face, an open snicker on Salthmanika's, and Benny can't help but feel they're aimed at her as much as the children.

The children are tired enough now that they won't fidget when told to relax. And that's what Misilvar does: getting them to lie on spread blankets and move just their arms, up and down, slow dreamlike fashion. Teaching them to feel their own movement, to be aware of how each piece of their bodies works in balance with the others. Gradually the movements get more complex, till as sunset approaches it's become tiny tots tai chi. Peter looks fascinated, as he slowly raises his arms and turns his hips – he'd never known his body could be so *good* at this.

'By the end of the weekend they'll know how to stop someone from hitting them,' murmurs Ithva.

'No, they won't,' says Benny. 'Not after a weekend.'

'They'll feel they will. And that's the important part.'

Personally Benny feels that not getting killed would be the important part, but anything that makes them less likely to panic in the fight to come can only help. She watches Sharintha turn and extend her arm, her hand arcing smoothly up from beneath, beaming, and imagines it with a knife in her hand.

'Surely you're not expecting them to join in the fight?'

Ithva looks faintly scandalised. 'Of course not. If we do our job right, they'll never know it's coming. As far as they know it's just a weekend away where we happened to get attacked by bandits and mummy fought them off.'

'You mean you *still* won't tell them? Even after?'

'Not till they're old enough to understand what they've been through.'

The thought rankles with Benny. It's not as though she had given Peter any advance warning yet, but still... 'Hang about – wasn't this whole exercise supposed to be all about *not* keeping them safely bubble-wrapped their whole lives?'

'It's about working out where you draw the line.' She's looking out at the stones and the sand. 'And where you draw it the next time, and the time after that. Every day in their childhood is another transition. A new set of rules for a new person.'

That hits Benny with a jolt – like a monkey falling out of a tree, landing in a totally unfamiliar environment. She's still assuming the old rules herself. These are the people she's relying on to keep her son safe, and she suddenly isn't sure what their senses of 'safe' are.

There's nothing to do but get to grips with the new ones. Whatever they are. On her terms.

Benny kicks at the large plastic sheet on which they'd slaughtered the droth. 'Do we still need this?'

* * *

She makes sure Peter has plenty of water. He protests, because she's interrupting the exercises, and the Draconians aren't stopping; but he needs so much more water than them, just as she does. She watches him, fighting slowly in the heat, puppy-fur slick and spiky with sweat, and still doesn't say anything yet about what's coming.

What kind of world have I brought you into?

Ithva, thinking she's unobserved. Bantering with Rathklin and Marthaleka, too quiet to hear. A deep barking Draconian laugh, not the chuckle she uses for humans, for her. Broad smile in just her wrinkled forehead and eyebrows. Top teeth bared amusedly, upper lip drawn back so far it makes her nose look like a snout. Every bit of her body language is alien to Benny in this moment.

A glance that might be in Benny's direction. When next she turns the set of her whole face has twisted: eyes wider, mouth stretched down and out into a human smile. Making herself look as much as she can like a human in green scaly makeup. And an ironic little sorry-you-know-how-it-is eye-roll, which Benny recognises as her own. It's the look she'd thought was Ithva dropping her guard with her, here just another layer among many.

So the no-bullshit is bullshit too.

No wonder the Mim fundamentally disgusted the Draconians: a race that could impeccably *ape* their perfect form, but with a soul that felt nothing of what they did. Which might not, in their eyes, even be a soul at all. A flawless skin with nothing inside. It skirts dangerously close to exposing their impeccable etiquette as a lie.

Hey, cubby. I've got something to tell you.
Okay. Hey, Sharintha's rogue, she can pick up a piece of meat with only her tongue!
Well, that'll serve her well in future. Look, Peter. This is serious. Okay?
Okay.
Right... Now I'm going to tell you something, and you don't need to get scared by it, all right?
What?
Okay. There's... there's a good chance that there are bandits out there in the desert.
Real bandits?
Real bandits. And they might try to hurt us or take you away.

141

What'll we do?

Shh. It's all right, I'll take care of you. There's nothing to worry about unless I warn you they're coming. And then just stay really close to me, I'll keep you safe.

But we gotta tell Riskyva and Sharintha and –

No, sweetheart. I don't want you telling anyone else.

Why?

So they won't get scared.

Why?

Because... Oh, no, you don't. The important thing is that we don't get to scare them. That's *their* mummys' job. Okay?

Okay.

Good. C'mere.

Why are there bandits here?

... Because your mummy goes to some scary places.

But I wanted to see them. It's not fair.

Oh, Peter. I should've left you at home.

But I wanted to see the green skyscapers. And the desert's *hot*.

I know it is, but if you keep drinking your water –

No, Mum. *Hot*.

Oh. Like rogue.

Yeah.

Oh, Peter...

Mum what's wrong?

I can't lie to you. I knew there would be bandits when we came here. I'm sorry I brought you somewhere dangerous. But I had to – to have the chance to save a whole lot of other children, who could be hurt or worse. I'm sorry. I hope you'll understand...

Yeah. It's good we're here to save Riskyva and Sharintha.

It's not... Well you've got the idea, even if it's bigger than that. I just hope one day you'll forgive me.

Course I do, Mum.

What a way to make it sound easy...

How you gonna save everyone?

Well I've got some ideas, but I'm still working on it.

But you will? Promise?

... Sweetheart, you know I can't promise everything. Can I tell you about me for a bit?

Uh huh.

I was younger than you when... when my mummy died. And Daddy didn't come back from the war, he was missing. They promised me everything would be all right, but bad things happened and they couldn't help it.

Is that when they sent you off to the tough school?

Uh huh. They taught me lots of things, like how to fight, but mostly that I didn't like following stupid orders.

Good.

And it taught me not to make promises. Not unless you know for absolute sure you can keep them. So you know what I'm going to promise you? Not that it's going to be perfect, but that I'm going to do my best. So you know I mean that. Is that okay?

Yeah. Cos your best is hot.

Nightfall: the only light the firebowl, and a bare two torches around the perimeter of their tents. Ithva and Misilvar stand guard at the summit, alternating through the night; their children stay below in the care of the other mothers. They sleep in shifts; two up, two down.

Benny's tent feels a million miles from the others. She'd half-hoped Ithva would leave Sharintha in her care, as a sign of trust, but Auntie Rathklin has prior claim.

She settles down under the canvas, Peter tucked squirming against her – accepting his mum like his favourite pillow, but finding her rather harder to bunch up and squeeze under his head.

The alarm scream rips her into consciousness. Body moving long before her brain, scooping Peter up and hauling them out of the tent even while her mind keeps moaning *whuh five more minutes.*

Outside, dark. Fires unbearably bright, eyes still adjusting. Misilvar's warning scream from the summit piercing her again, rising from a deep howl to a shriek, over and over.

Peter scared but silent, burying his face in her shoulder. Small mercies, she couldn't bear it if she'd brought him here and left him screaming.

Desert black beyond the torches. No moonlight, nothing to reflect on the ground. She can only glimpse the attackers where they block out the stars on the horizon.

The other mothers well behind her. The three of them forming a semicircle against the mountain, their five little girls packed timidly behind them. They knew what to do, they'd run there immediately. Leaving her and Peter without warning, alone in the dark.

She runs towards the nearer of the two torches, uprooting it, casting about.

They're deliberately making noise now – shuffling about in the dark, making the mothers react to sounds from all directions. Unable to count them, or be sure how many of them are coming from where. Rattling them as much as they can before the strike.

'Two to the left!' shouts Misilvar from above. 'One by Summerfield, maybe two right flank. One no-contact, maybe two.'

Six against six, of course. Probably part of the rules. But with Ithva and Misilvar up top covering the field, for now it meant six against four. Ithva would be on her way down, but the men would still have the numbers. They could work like a wolfpack, harrying the mothers en masse, keeping them as busy as possible and leaving one of their number to snatch and grab. Or, they could all strike together and claim the straggler with her cub.

Scales glinting in the dark. She whirls towards them, jabbing the torch outward – he doesn't even flinch. She can just see him, greyscale night vision: high crested head, thin and slick moustache, slow amused leer. Simple combat *hronsthei* keeping his blood warm where the defenders are cold; he has all his strength. He's watching her back away and advancing with confident casual malice: no more thought to his violence than a boy reaching for a fly's wings. He doesn't know her, he doesn't care, he's come to take her child away. He and all his brothers circling like goblins in the dark.

He's reaching for her.

'Oh, sod this for a game of soldiers,' says Benny.

And touches the torch to the torn strip of plastic sheeting she'd buried under a dusting of sand.

And a line of wet fire erupts between them. The flames surge along its length – the droth blood she'd soaked it in flaring up through the sand, reaching the end of the strip and touching the next shred she'd laid at its end, racing on and on till there's a whole crescent of fire at their feet, a semicircle marking out their camp with the mountain at their back. Carving out their space, declaring it defended. Low flames, not much of a barrier, but they can *see*.

The men stand frozen for just a moment, their advantage lost. One well inside the fire-circle, slithering on his belly – the stealth that got him past the torches now worse than useless. But he'd almost passed Salthmanika's feet unseen. The women paralysed too, seeing what they never had before.

For a moment, Benny thinks she's stopped it entirely.

Then Salthmanika, howling, kicks him in the face.

And the men are charging, leaping the flames, trying to face down victims who can see them coming. Marthaleka and Salthmanika are beating the nearest thief furiously, trying to even the odds before the others reach them. The bandit facing Benny is still glaring, but he has to hitch up his *hronsthei* to get over the flames. She jabs her torch at him to keep him back. Peter's wobbling in her arms, she can't fight like this if the others come for her – she backs towards the inner circle, and the women break ranks to let her in.

'It's all right,' she tells Peter as she sets him down with the others. 'Mummy's being brave for you.' She points to the girl next to him. 'You take care of her, she looks like she needs it.'

And she turns to fight. Not against a cunning horde of child-stealing marauders, but a half-dozen yobs out for a bit of brawling and maybe some easy cash. She's faced worse. She'd face worse for Peter. Especially with a burning torch in her hands while they're not even armed. Bugger the body-against-body thing, you've spent your lives training and I haven't, I'd have to be mad not to do everything I can to keep them at bay.

You want to know how hard I'll fight for my children? she says. Hard enough to break the rules. Even the rules you don't know you have, when you're so proud of being outside all that honour and convention. I'll fight the way we fight. I'll find a better way.

Only she says it with rather fewer consonants or coherent syllables.

No clear pictures, just blurred glimpses.

Marthaleka the artist, her face a model of composure, patiently, repeatedly slamming a child-stealer's head into the side of the mesa.

Ithva leaping from the winding track down the mesa-side, landing like fury on legs to thrash the men from behind.

Little Sharintha in her cotton desert frock, behind the line, watching her mummy chop a man in the kidneys with brutal poise, staring with no fear and more than a little awe.

Peter, back pressed flat against the mesa, staring out at the sea of legs and not being able to see what's happening beyond the wall that Mummy makes.

Method in their madness: if the men can use their strength they've got the advantage, so they've got to keep them off-balance, groggy, falling where the women have each other to catch them. Left-handed stances, against every man's instinct.

A scream from Rathklin – a bandit's wrenched her arm behind her back, pulling hard enough to dislocate it. Salthmanika and Ithva slamming their foes into hers, knocking him half-over, kicking and clawing relentlessly but above all holding the line.

The torch wrestled from her hand, extinguished in the sand. The other torch long since snuffed, after a bandit tried to charge them with it. The men's silhouettes against the firebowl now, shapes that grunted and snarled when you hit them. Fighting on in the dark.

Thundering blows to her gut. Doubling over, smashing him headfirst, using every bit of her to try to incapacitate him. Every self-defence move, every pressure point and scrap of old unarmed-combat training. Hitting low and hard, no holds barred.

Stomping on the arm of a man lunging for the children. A snap from his wrist, a cry too obscene to belong to an animal.

Just a glimpse of Peter recoiling, as she hurls the man back out of the light. The pleading makeitstop look on his face driving her to face the darkness, moving her to tender rage.

Bernice Surprise Summerfield, shoulder to shoulder with her son safe behind, holding the line and screaming her throat raw.

When next she makes sense of things, the men are slinking off into the dark. Concussed, bloody, a couple of them crawling. At least a few more broken bones than the women. She holds her stance, ever more shakily, till it finally sinks in that they're safe in the dark.

Rathklin's their biggest casualty. She screams out once more as Salthmanika wrenches her shoulder back into place – holding on to her daughter through it all, murmuring to her that she's all right, yes it hurts but they're making it all better. Taking comfort from holding her even as she tries to give comfort right back. Her breath is shaking through her teeth as Marthaleka fashions a sling for her.

'Fair's fair,' she manages shakily. 'I think I broke one of theirs.'

Ithva's got a livid bruise on her shoulder, but that's not stopping her from holding Sharintha against it. Benny aches in sympathy at the sight of her, or maybe she's aching just fine on her own. From the way Peter is staring at her, her own face must look like day-old mince.

She collapses among the children, holding Peter to her and planting little kisses on his forehead and letting him cry at last. Her other arm around two of the other daughters, whose names she doesn't even know, just giving them someone warm to hold on to them as their mothers finish putting things right. Beside her Ithva is cradling silent Sharintha, and telling her gently how brave and grown-up she was, while Peter sobs like he's broken in half.

'Very clever,' says Salthmanika from the fire, gesturing towards the strips of plastic sheeting as she re-soaks them in fresh droth blood. 'Wouldn't have thought of this.' And Ithva, in the re-lit torchlight, gives Benny a look that seems suspiciously like pride.

'What school was that?' asks Misilvar. Gesturing vaguely, miming one of Benny's moves.

'Cope fu,' says Benny. 'Whatever gets you through.'

Peter's reaching for her face, as if he's seen something more horrible than anything. 'Mummy. You're *hurt*.'

'Mm-hm,' she says wearily, and with a strange sort of contentment. 'But you're not.'

She takes Peter back to the tent and holds him, singing soft nonsense till one or both of them drifts off.

And it might just be her mind, but when she wakes for her midnight shift on watch she's sure the other tents have moved closer to hers.

5

D awn: she wakes again with Peter warm in her arms. But she feels the cramping in her guts, and a wetness on her legs that isn't sweat, and she knows what her body has decided.

She holds Peter for a long, long time, stroking his fur, then starts rummaging through her pack to deal with the situation. And she takes an extra-long drink of water. She must be more dried-out than she thought, if none of it's coming out in tears.

She leaves Peter with Marthaleka – telling him to be good and help her start getting breakfast ready – and climbs the mesa trail. It winds corkscrew-fashion up the side, showing her the infinite plain to all sides of them, its colours flat grey in the half-light.

Ithva's stretched out on watch: lying on the cliff-edge, peering at the enemy camp in the distance. Bare to the waist. A lean lizard's body, smooth and straight to the hips, countless tiny scales running the length of her and glistening in the first light. Benny just stands back and watches her for a moment, taking in her perfect stillness.

She's not sure why she wants Ithva to know. She feels like someone has to, someone who'll see what it means.

'Well, that settles that,' she murmurs, as she sits beside her. 'No more little Summerfields joining us any time soon.'

It's the first time she's seen Ithva look surprised. Slowly she sits up, taking in Benny's face, realisation dawning. 'You thought... you were carrying? Oh, I didn't know, I'm so sorry...'

'I didn't know for sure,' she said. She swallows, and it feels like a gulp. 'Too early to know, the tests said no actually but they were inconclusive –'

'But if it was...'

She doesn't want her to say anything. 'And I've been a bit erratic for years. My body's sense of time took a lot of knocks a while back, it was probably just the stress making me late...'

'But if...' And where she's taking refuge in doubt, Ithva's looking at even the possibility with all the weight of a certainty. Her face has crumpled: knotted forehead, slow appalled shake of the head, mouth contorted in an inhuman expression of dulled horror. 'I'm so sorry. If I'd known... I should never have dragged you here, it was wrong of me...'

'Wrong of *you*?'

'– you didn't know what this is like, you could be *beaten* –'

'– I chose, you told me, I *knew* –'

'– you should never have had to make the choice –'

'– but I had to convince you, all those children –'

'– not even *one!* If all this, this politics and posturing cost you your child...'

'No! No, it *didn't*.' She screws up her face like a child about to cry. Refusing to consider that it could be *Keith* who's just bled away into the air.

'The test was negative,' she insists. 'If I'd believed...' She feels like she's speaking her own epitaph. 'If I'd *believed*, I wouldn't have come.'

And Ithva shakes her head, slowly, a look of pure sympathy on her face. 'You believed, and that's why you came. No matter what it cost you yourself.'

And she looks at Ithva and sees an oceanful of Mim children, and herself last night with the torch thinking she could do more than make it less bad, that she could stop it all for every one of them, and that it was worth every risk she put herself through, and everything she'd believed and she felt herself crumpling inside because she was *wrong* and the whole crusade was *wrong* and even the pity on Ithva's face as she was reaching for her was *wrong* –

'No,' she pulls away. 'Don't.'

'Don't what?'

'Just don't. Look, it's all right, I know it's fake –'

'What's fake –'

'Your *face.*' Benny flaps her hands edgily, taking in the set of her forehead, the carefully hidden teeth, the wide humanish eyes. 'The whole human look you're putting on for me. All the fake little confidences. Sodding *negotiating tactic.* Look, I worked out ages ago you were handling me, you're a crukking *spy,* you're a professional at this and I'm just a bloody amateur. One face, two if you're lucky, that's your lot.' The words keep tumbling out, almost random now. 'Just stop pretending you *care.*'

Ithva just lets it all finish pouring out. Then, quietly: 'Bernice... it's because I'm talking to *you.* You wouldn't believe I really was sorry, if I just said it our way.'

And she lets her features settle into what must be a Draconian expression of sympathy, and it looks like she's either going to howl in agony or go for Benny's throat. But almost hidden behind the snarling lips and crinkled scaly cheeks, there's something in the eyes that doesn't change – and in that glimpse of regret and shared anguish, across all the barriers of language and culture, in that moment Benny lets herself believe.

And now she's clinging to Ithva and there's a whimper escaping from somewhere deep inside, and finally at long last some hot cleansing tears.

'I'm sorry,' murmurs Ithva. 'I speak so many languages now, I don't even always dream in my own.'

She's sobbing into the cool scaly shoulder.

'I've lost my way.'

'I think you know it better than you think.' The arms are around her, gently now, Ithva's voice almost whispering. 'You really are a waterflame, aren't you?'

'A what?'

'A long story. Not now.' She disentangles from Benny, just a little bit, and puts on for her the smooth polished Ithva she'd seen back in her office. 'And yes, darling, I am a spy, and I'd be thrilled to recruit you to our network, but at the cost of your child? I'd have to be mad.'

'Not the most effective of strategies,' Benny agrees, dazedly. She looks at Ithva, smiling gently as the rising dawn fills in her colours, and wonders what it's like to have skin that sparkles. For a moment she wants to reach out again and keep gently stroking her smooth cool scales, then reminds herself this is a member of the Empress's Hand, not a handbag.

Ithva draws her knees up, sitting on the mesa-edge next to Benny: her eyes still on watch, the rest of her quietly shaken. 'A year or so before Sharintha…' she murmurs. 'I laid Myshkant… that would have been his name.'

'Oh, I'm so sorry…'

'For four months, I almost never left my room – did all my work at my desk. I'd had a motherchair installed, with an incubator in the seat so I could warm it as well. All the sonograms on the egg were perfect, everything was fine.

'And then… he just didn't hatch. A week after the date I was close to panic. Then they tried to induce pipping but…' Ithva's gaze was far away. Benny could see the frantic parents, praying for the sound of their child chipping at the shell from inside. 'Jarith insisted on an autopsy, he thought there might have been poison or something, he just wanted to blame somebody. But it turned out it had just quietly gone wrong, even before the incubation. He'd been laid cold. No cerebral activity… he'd been running on a brainstem all those months. The body still developing, but it just ran down.'

'And you never knew if you did anything wrong,' Benny says gently. Squeezing her hand, pressing softly against her, her cool skin feeling grateful for Benny's warmth.

'I spent four months warming the corpse of my child and I never knew.'

How *dry* motherhood must have been for Ithva, how cool and unsticky and *reptilian* all those months, to hold your hermetically sealed unborn child in your arms and never once feel a kick. And never miss it all that time. Such a different world from all those moist messy months carrying Peter, every squirm and gurgle written straight to her bloodstream. But how warm, to feel that touch outside your skin for all those months, rather than taking the heat inside your body for granted.

'Jarith held me together,' says Ithva. 'If not for him, who knows what I would have done. Probably overthrown the Khree government in a fit of grief. I'm joking. Or trying to.'

She could see the little shudder run through Ithva's chest, and realised she'd misunderstood her bare skin. Not basking in the dawn, nerving herself against the cold. Using the shivers of her unprotected self to keep awake through her shift on watch. In the normal world it would be unheard of for either a male or female to bare so much skin in the open air; the temperature-regulating satin mesh of the *hronsthei* was so much a part of their nature and form. But here, apparently, the rules were off.

'And then when Sharintha came… I was paranoid, of course,

I made sure everything ran on perfect rails, all the way through the hatching. But even then... She didn't open her eyes at six weeks. It took nine. I was terrified, I spent every minute with her, I had Misilvar and a whole team of policy analysts in the research department reading child-care books on the sly. And then... She opened her eyes, and they were the most beautiful green in the world. But for years I was still so worried she'd always be slow.'

Benny looks down and over at the camp, and spots Sharintha, chasing Peter and Rathklin's girl across the sand and brandishing a large wooden fork at them. 'Well she's certainly making up for lost time now, isn't she?'

A smile, one that felt both human and genuine somehow. 'But she *talks* so much. With no regard for who hears what. I'm just hoping she learns how much words are worth...'

It's the first six weeks before the baby opens her eyes that rattle Benny, not the next three. The horrible sense it suggests of a child being shoved into the world before it's even ready to look at it. But just like a human newborn was only as finished a creature as it could be without growing too big to be delivered, their development must be limited by the size of the egg. A simpler animal could be much closer to fully functional the moment it was unleashed on the world, but something with all the complexity of a sentient brain would need to be incubated for *years* to fully knit together, to reach that level of independence at its release. It seems like such a design flaw that birth comes at such an arbitrary point, she thinks – but even knowing how helpless a newborn human was, what mother would ask for an extra year carrying their child before caring for it with her own hands?

No wonder the Draconians were so obsessed with protecting their young, and protecting the mothers, if their children came into the world even more fragile than that. And no wonder the Mim saw their young as barely alive, if they were effectively still gestating for all that time in the open water. They made rather more sense, if she thought of their ocean as one vast womb.

'You must think I'm a terrible mother,' says Ithva quietly. 'To put my own child through something like this, even after all I've said about her...'

'Well,' says Benny. 'Cultural norms, different standards, the times maketh the woman... Of course I do. You're completely psychotic.'

'It's an initiation,' says Ithva. 'This is what grown-ups do for them. It's a glimpse of what we're protecting them from.'

Waiting all these years to open their eyes, thinks Benny. And yet more than anything she wished she hadn't forced Peter's open like this. 'I suppose you've shielded them so carefully all this time, you'd need something really startling as a... Hang on.'

'What?'

She's peering at the horizon. 'They're an awful lot of slug-a-beds in the enemy camp, aren't they?' she says. 'No one's up and moving. Not a one of them.'

Ithva squints, considering. Then, leaning closely on Benny, she stands and starts circling the top of the mesa, methodically searching the view from its base out to the horizon. Moving like a hunter now, even as the top half of her robe hangs casually from her hips. Benny picks up her approach, and instinctively takes the reverse direction, covering the other side. Keeping an eye and a half out for anything out of the ordinary, and half an eye on Ithva at work.

There's still something disconcerting about Ithva's bare chest. Not so much its straightness – obviously only mammals have mammaries – but more the fact that Benny doesn't know what features to be judging. She'd have a pretty good idea what a human being thought of themselves just by looking at their body, but here she really has no idea which ideal Ithva compares herself against. Whether she thinks she could lose a few kilos or feels undernourished. But to eyes with no expectations, she looks alarmingly close to a perfectly balanced creature. Especially now she's in her element, searching out information and settling a threat. Compared to this lumpy, unfinished, uncertain human being, she's literally from another world.

'Here,' Benny whispers, motioning her over. She points down, straight down, at the base of the mesa. 'Could that be?'

And Ithva comes up close behind her, leaning over her shoulder, to peer at the odd discoloured squares of sand below them.

'It could indeed.'

'Nine months?' gapes Ithva as they walk. 'Spirit and blood, I'd never stay sane that long. I'd be falling over after five.'

'Well still, carrying an egg for four months before laying it, no mean feat...'

They're circling the mesa from the bottom now, both fully dressed and focused, having let the others know the nature of the new threat. With Rathklin taking over up top, resting her injured shoulder, the camp would be warned of any attack from this direction – but they still need to be sure what it is.

Peter seemed none the worse for wear – if anything, he looked a little too enthused while playing with Sharintha and the others. They had him waving his arms and running at them making *blaaaaaugh* noises, while they giggled and ran away or, eventually, wrestled with him right back. Benny saw him disappear under a pile of squeaking girls and wondered if she had another Jason in the making.

The discoloured squares on the ground were just visible now, emerging from round the curve of the mesa. From here they could make out the sand piled up concealing the edges of the fabric, but only because they knew where to look; their attackers had buried it well under a dusting of orange, but the slight mismatch in the colour of the duck-blind had still been visible from above.

The men must have dug this the night before, before or after the battle: a bolt-hole, keeping them in easy striking distance of the womens' camp. They'd never gone back to their own, they'd been just round the back of the mesa all this time. Hidden in the darkness.

'So do these lot have a ritual of their own, for their part in all this?' she asks.

'I don't know. I've never asked.' Which seems a strange reaction for a spy, but in a culture so thoroughly founded on deliberately unacknowledged truths, it must be par for the course. 'The boys don't have anything like the *nikhol vakarshta* for themselves,' Ithva goes on. 'They don't get taught to fight until they're old enough to kiss. In fact, they're strictly punished before then. It actually makes it easier for them to become warriors then, if they grow up without any fear of it.'

'Well I suppose that makes sense, with what Jarith said.' (She's started thinking of Kothar by his first name, she notices.) That meant the young men they were fighting would only be a few years off the leash. And if a child grew up without any primal memories of being beaten up on the playground, if they didn't have to deal with the effects of violence until after the brain had largely finished knitting together, till they were sophisticated enough to rationalise those effects away, till they'd learned how not to cry like a child cried... She felt her stomach tighten, and not from the stew. No wonder they could be so fearsome.

'So how much does your husband know?' she blurts. 'About what you do.'

Ithva smiles, toothily. 'As little as he can manage.'

'You do realise he set me onto you?'

Ithva takes it in stride. 'Jarith? Whatever for?'

'About the Mim. He's trying to find out who's up to what with all that – so he gave me the names of people who he could never *dream* would be involved in any kind of skulduggeryish nonsense. Knowing that I'd chase after them. You'll be happy to know you were officially above suspicion... He just wanted me to dig up the things it'd be far too gauche for him to find out himself.'

She still doesn't mention exactly what she suspects them of; even now she keeps the phase cannons in reserve. But for the first time that she's thought about it, she knows she doesn't *want* Ithva to be guilty. And no matter what she may have done, she can't picture her cutting a throat in cold blood. But she *can* see her holding the beast in place for the slaughter.

Ithva laughs, barkingly – she rates a proper Draconian laugh now, Benny notes. 'He could have *asked...*'

'But would you have told him?'

'No,' shrugs Ithva. 'But I would still have put his mind at ease.'

By now they're almost on top of the duck-blind. Close enough to be sure: it's big enough to sleep six, and the disturbed sand around it looks like a bunch of people went in and didn't come out. Now it's just a matter of considering how to handle this – how much of their knowledge to reveal, how much to keep to themselves.

'Oh, *my*,' Benny calls out loudly. 'What an ideal place to dump all our droth poo.'

'And *so* out of the way.'

'Oh, yes, it's perfect. No one would *ever* be lurking here...'

They high-tail it back to the camp, giggling, before the men have even extracted themselves from their covers.

Salthmanika leading the children now, the same exercises as yesterday but at speed: the smooth stretches suddenly revealed as sharp thrusts, the flexed palm a heel-of-the-hand blow to the face. An entire school of martial arts defined by the ability to practice it slowly, in front of men and leave them none the wiser.

'When you fight, dance,' she tells them, as they snap through the combinations. 'When you laugh, scream. When you move, be still. Never be just one thing at once; you have both that thing and its opposite inside you. If you feel everything you are at once, then you are whole.'

Benny and Ithva watching from the perimeter, half on guard for attackers, half fascinated by their childrens' duckling grace. 'Bit deep for five-year-olds, isn't it?' asks Benny.

'It's from Ishtiklin,' says Ithva. 'He's the one who made philosophy quotable. We start teaching him their first day of school. Though the original begins *When you fight, make love.*'

Ithva's eyes on her, still cool and dry: still feeling out her reactions. This is all to prove something to her, but she's no longer sure what.

'Are you still fighting me on this?' murmurs Benny. 'Or are you after something else?'

Those deep flecked eyes just mirror back the question. 'What would I be fighting you on?'

'On the Mim. You've seen how I'll fight for Peter. You've got to be convinced by now of the sacrifices I'd make. What's stopping you from taking up my case with the Empress's Hand?'

'We're still presenting *our* case to you.' Ithva pouts fetchingly. 'You've seen how we'll fight for everyone – Rathklin who I've known for years, or Salthmanika who I met yesterday. If you see all the sides of us, how we're warriors when we're mothers and mothers when we're warriors... you might decide to trust us with the children after all.'

Benny tries a knowing smile. 'Would you really be the sort to show me everything?'

'How much are you looking for it?'

And the knowing smile is just making her feel like she knows less and less. 'Please,' she says, as mock-giddily as she can manage. 'Not in front of the children.'

The men strike back at lunchtime. They've given up any attempt at stealth, particularly since Rathklin starts whooping the alarm the moment they emerge from their shelter. Instead they come charging in, their shouts drowning them out, as the women gather up their children into their half-circle against the rock. Peter clings to her in panic when the alarm goes up, but she has no trouble carrying him to safety.

The men veer out of range almost as soon as they've entered it. They've changed their tactics – instead of an all-in battle, they're circling, moving fast, dipping into range long enough for a couple of quick jabs and retreating. Shouting and leering incessantly. Two of them have arms in slings, matching Rathklin's, and one's limping on the sand. One has livid bruising up the side of his face, worse than Marthaleka's. They're fighting to injure, to demoralise, rather than to grab the children themselves. To even the odds in preparation for the evening.

157

A few brief, fierce impacts. One body-slams Misilvar into the mesa-side, and gets a boot to the head for his trouble. The one whose face Benny saw last night comes for her again, thinking she's the weak link. Having one arm in a sling doesn't stop him getting a savage elbow into her ribs. But his skill's run out on him, he's running on anger, and she's got enough control left to knock his legs out from under him.

Finally they run off in the direction of their camp, still shouting, bragging about how they'll be back. The children untouched, the mothers winded and wounded and aching on their feet, but intact.

'Oh, come on,' mutters Rathklin later, when the kids' backs are turned. 'We could have stayed with the tourists and got that much.'

There are no mirrors here. She has no idea how raw she looks.

This battle sits differently in her muscles. The first was a sprint, zero to infinity: coping with bad things from out of the blue; every sinew calling on its reserves and then letting them go. This one is about endurance: the slow ache of regular use, the peaks and valleys of a repeated workout. Knowing that bad things will *keep* happening. Not just carrying your child through a moment, but knowing you'll be carrying him through all the years to come.

She's only been fighting the first battle, when she should be looking to the long term. If she wants the Empress's Hand behind her on the Mim, the people around her are the exact ones she needs to start convincing – she's been showing them her ability, but hasn't said a word about her aims.

She looks at the four other mothers again, hardening fresh portraits of them like clay in a kiln. Marthaleka, government-toppling propagandist. Rathklin, unofficial communications director, skewing the messages just the way Cheset had described for men and women alike. Misilvar, research analyst clothed as an assistant, choosing which facts will start their way up the chain to both the women and men at the top. Salthmanika, quiet little field agent, roaming the planet and putting their chosen truths into action. Accomplished intelligence operatives all, with five-year-olds on their knees.

Salthmanika, telling the childrens' fortunes as they wait out the worst of the afternoon heat. The Draconian equivalent of a tarot deck: and the cards have two faces. Turn a card on its back, and the concept is replaced with its opposite; turn the picture upside-down, the concept is replaced with its lack.

She's laying out a pattern of cards for Peter now. Near the centre, a card with an exotic image: a shimmering pattern of waves flecked with fiery highlights, an oceanscape as stained glass lit from beneath.

'Like mother like son,' Ithva says to Benny.

'Beg pardon?'

'That's your card there. A waterflame,' Ithva explains. She's kneeling in the sand as Benny sits on a rucksack, massaging salve into Ithva's bruised shoulder. 'A mythological creature. From the sparkles you see in the ocean at sunrise, which disappear at the end of dawn.' She leans back against Benny's knees, letting the tension drain out of her. 'They're pure contradiction. Fire in water, water in fire. Travelling endlessly between worlds, not part of any one plane. They pass freely between the world of blood and the world of spirit. Roaming where they wish, but never quite at home, from the desert air to the ocean depths.'

'Neither fish nor fowl,' sighs Benny. 'Yeah, I suppose I can see that.'

'Never fixed, never certain, never settled. A perfect symbol of flux.' Ithva's dark eyes looked into Benny's. 'And that's her strength. She knows nothing is permanent, and so she can look at those who block her way and see how, at their centre, they are hollow.'

'You make it sound so nice,' Benny says ruefully. She lets her hands glide softly over Ithva's shoulders, getting to know the texture. There's a smooth and polished crocodile-like ridge of thicker skin down her spine, like an extra layer of bone protecting it, or a line of jewels disappearing down her back. She hears Salthmanika telling Peter how the cards say he's the type who loves to travel and find new things, and he's saying you know that already cause I'm *here*. A flush of pride for Benny; Mama Summerfield ain't raising no fool. Still, not exactly much of a parental role model...'

'It's a perfect one,' says Ithva.

'Oh, I don't know, roots, stability, all that fun stuff...'

'Nothing is fixed. When you're raising a child, every day is a transition.'

'Oh, very pithy,' says Benny. For a moment it's just all too mad for her, the ease with which they could declare things that they had to now weren't true. Or piecemeal truths that ignored the rest of the whole. 'I've seen you in action, there's no bloody way you can tell me you're anything less than certain.'

'Far more certain than I wish,' says Ithva. 'I've known who Ithva Lothar is for too many years now.'

And she clambers up from the sand, taking Benny's place on the rucksack. 'Do your worst,' says Benny, settling in her place. It was bloody typical of the whole lot of them, really – priding themselves on embracing flux and change and the impermanence of all things, never thinking about how they're treating their tenthousandyearsofcivilisation as an immovable constant of perfection. Without seeing how *mad* it makes them become.

'Let me tell you what's at our centre,' says Ithva. Slowly, methodically kneading her way up the cord of wrenched tension in Benny's back. 'It goes all the way back to the language of the Prime Emperor. *Nikhal* – honour – derives from *nikhima*, to have. Which seems to make sense, it's something you have within your spirit. But if you look back at the roots of the language... *Nikhima* originally just meant to have in the sense of possessions. Think about what they were saying with that... Being honourable directly equals being rich. And being rich means being a noble – with the Emperor as the richest of all, and the most honourable. Because he gets to define what honour means for everyone else.'

'The Golden Rule,' says Benny. 'He who has the gold, makes the rules.'

'Exactly. It's a *pun*.' Ithva's face breaks into a cockeyed grin. '*Nikhal, nikhima*... A punchline which became so taken for granted that no one laughs at it any more. Don't you see? Our culture, our entire code of morality... Everything handed down from the top of the autocracy for millennia... We've known all along that at its heart is a *joke*.'

'But you keep following it,' says Benny.

'Well, the men do.'

'Nope,' says Benny, the smile still settled on her face. 'If you weren't thinking as part of the system, you'd never have dragged us out here.'

'True,' concedes Ithva. 'I suppose that's part of the joke as well. But when it comes to making sense of our lives... it's the best joke we've got.'

Benny leans back, resting her head between Ithva's knees. At the very least there's something comforting in knowing that everyone involved can see how daft it all is. And if she's able to see other side to it beyond their truth du jour, maybe that was the waterflame thing. Even if it meant she never got it herself.

'Okay,' she begins. 'So there are these two Mim sitting on a rock...'

Ithva, warrior mother, laughing so hard she nearly falls off the rucksack. It really must be how you tell them.

* * *

The girls are tussling for queen-bee status. They're playing let's pretend, and Marthaleka's daughter has set herself up as arbiter of the unfolding story. Riskilvar's making a bid for dominance by acting bored, without actually quite being overtly rude about it, and throwing in twists of her own to try to make the others follow. Peter seems happy in the role of comic relief – neither currying favour like the girls, nor putting them down to enhance his own place.

Marthaleka's watching over their game, while making quick sketches of the plants that cling to the underside of the rocks.

'Would you allow her to study chemistry – or, for that matter, archaeology? And if you didn't steer her away from studies like that, what would Draconian men make of her? What would Draconian *women* make of her?' Matheleka puts down her sketchpad. 'I think I've just talked myself into agreeing with your position, dear.'

Marthaleka's daughter has worked on the let's-pretend storyline until Riskilvar is now the baddie. No egalitarian utopia, this. Just like the little boys barred from violence, they've already learned to fight even without hitting – working out how to compete, undercut, challenge and backstab, training them well for everything from corporate life to court politics. And the girl is even painting herself as the protector, chasing her rival away from the others.

Marthaleka turns sudden, piercing eyes on Benny. 'Is that how you see yourself, my dear? As a heroine for the little Mim babies? As their Empress Mishtila, even?'

'No! I... All I want is what's best for them, like any parent.'

The human being has overstepped the line.

Benny slumps, looking around. Over by the droth tethers, she can see Misilvar and Salthmanika not-fighting, in their familiar pattern, nitpicking etiquette, quibbling over the right thing to do. When your all-powerful king is the source of all law, offending him carries the weight of sin. Violating your place in the pecking order shows a lack of principles. If it wasn't for Ithva's influence, Benny wouldn't even *be* in the pecking order, and now this almost-ally thinks the monkey's comparing herself to one of history's greatest women.

How do you persuade people on moral issues when their whole way of thinking has no moral centre, just a surface of perfect form?

It's even there in our language (Ithva tells her), nothing being fixed. We don't just say where something is, we say how it's moving. Take Karshtakavarr. Literally, distant thunder. But *kavarr*, distant, doesn't mean it stays there... distant in the sense of something closing in.

161

Encroaching. Oncoming. Or Ishkavaar, the Peacemaker, the honorific of the author of the Treaty of Heaven. *Ish*, to see. The seer of the encroaching future. High praise for a diplomat.

And that's the thing... Karshtakavarr arrived long after you'd say the storm had already broken. Our population had been decimated many times over, we were down to barely a few hundred thousand souls by the time of the cure. But that's not the storm that mattered.

We've come through catastrophes before. Three thousand years ago we survived a meteor impact, which blotted out the sun for a year. No, the storm he foreshadowed was the revolution.

For all the thousands of years since the Prime Emperor, all our wars had been civil ones. Regional commanders encouraged to compete with one another, inevitable alliances and rebellions. Battles and overthrowings that left the system itself unchanged no matter who stood on top.

But now... there were others out there. We knew for certain. There were others and they had powers far beyond ours and even if they were kind they could still wish to take our children away. We had been left so weakened, and we needed to be stronger than ever. Oh, yes, we were already the Empire which had never lost a war, but in truth we had never fought anyone but ourselves. But we learned, and by the time we ventured into space to find new worlds like Montavadros for our children to spread to... we knew how fierce we'd have to be to protect them.

He and his granddaughter left ideas whispered in the Emperor's ear. And the Empress's. With a world in need of rebuilding... they would need women to work as hard as men. But at the same time children were more important than ever. We had opportunities we never had before, and greater pressures than ever.

There was no solution to this tension. All we could do was find ways of drawing strength from it, the way you can stretch yourself by pitting one set of tensed muscles against another. And that's where the *nikhol vakarshta* was born.

For all our age, I think we're still very young. Until these last few centuries we were still in our own playground. After all this time we're still doing things for the first time.

The flipside of the waterflame card, in Salthmanika's fortune-telling deck the speckled texture of porous pumice-like rock. Hollowstone. More air than solid. That which is fixed, and therefore empty.

* * *

Dinner before dark. They'd rather not be surprised while they're eating.

Misilvar tells the story of the drug-company savant whose paper on the madder-lily harvest she and her librarians essentially wrote for him. 'We knew nothing about lilies. But we knew the forest where they grew was a beloved holiday spot of the Empress – and we knew that the pharmaceutical industry wanted to clearfell it.

'The poor savant was terribly annoyed, but what could he do? He ended up writing a report that stated that there was no way to know if the flowers could be cultivated artificially and the forest had better be left as it was.' There was a ripple of appreciative laughter. 'The men grab up all the scholarly jobs,' she said, 'but they have left us in charge of the actual information. They may write their own history. But only we know where it's filed.'

Benny laughed. 'We've got the same job. We both dig up the records.'

Misilvar hid her giggles behind her scaly hand. That daydreaming, playful air must make people think her head's in the clouds... But from up there, what a great view she's got of the patterns below.

The women were all having a good laugh at the men, but Benny held up a finger. 'Just cause you can do a clever end run around their system doesn't mean the system isn't there,' she pointed out. 'You want genuine equality, you let me know when you've got as many women in parliament.'

'What parliament?' says Salthmanika.

'That's the thing about absolute power,' said Ithva. 'You know you're not entitled to a say.'

Rathklin added, 'And you're not going to get one by sitting around like you're always on a motherchair, like all those flapping little housewives back at the other camp.' That gets a burst of agreement from the others. Rathklin's sitting back with her daughter, battered out unfazed, wearing her wounded arm like this season's mandatory accessory.

'I see,' says Benny. 'So when you say sisters are doing it for themselves, you really do mean for themselves, don't you?'

'The system weeds out the ones who don't make the effort,' says Rathklin. 'The best rise to the top.'

And Benny's all innocence. 'So, like the Mim with their borogoves?'

Ithva's sitting back, letting Benny fight this battle, but the look on her face shows she's enjoying it.

'We're not children,' snaps Rathklin – which mistake forces Benny to concede the point, for politeness's sake. 'But it is the same principle, I suppose.'

163

It's a point, not the game or the match. Misilvar seems to be approving, Marthaleka's more cautious, and Salthmanika – hell, she's not giving any clues either way. But everyone who listens is a step. And if Rathklin forces a showdown over this tomorrow, Benny's pretty sure she won't be alone.

Of course it's Rathklin who she's paired with for the next shift atop the mesa.

They watch opposite sides, circling the rim, like a pair of cats who've made first token hisses at each other and now keep a wary distance. Until the alarm cry rings up from beneath them.

Rathklin's pointing, calling her over. It's Misilvar's howl. Benny runs to Rathklin and cranes her neck – the mothers below are scattered. Three on separate edges of the camp, instructing the children privately in teams of two. And a pair of men have slithered up under sand-coloured sheets to strike at Misilvar – one wrestling with her, the other grabbing at the two children as they flee. One child green and slender, the other a stocky ball of fur.

Peter's running blind, his training lost. Headlong dash away from the camp, from any safety. She's choking on her own scream of defiance. It's a visceral pull, straight from her guts, almost enough to make her hurl herself straight off the side of the mesa just to get down to her son faster.

'Think you should get your child?' asks Rathklin.

And now Rathklin's glaring at her, in front of the others, a cool stone blade. 'When I asked if you should go to him, the right answer was *no*.'

Benny's standing battered in front of the others, every breath still stinging and the taste of sweat in her mouth. Misilvar's watching sullenly, her face swollen and raw, blood staining her lips. Staring warily at her – and this after Benny had nearly crippled the guy who'd done that to her. The children sit huddled together as if for warmth, and Peter's curled tight on her lap, refusing to look. But she has to keep looking.

'You broke ranks,' Salthmanika says bluntly. 'Abandoned your post.'

'We needed your eyes,' says Misilvar.

'It was her idea –'

Rathklin shakes her head, denies nothing. 'I just let you show who you really are.'

Oh, what a perfect set-up. Rathklin had seen her pat herself on the back last night for thinking outside the box, protecting Peter without relying on the others. Good old self-sufficient loner Benny, always out to resist pressure to conform and behave, still wary of leaning on anyone else. It had barely taken a word to make her see this the same way, and jump without thinking. It's easy to sell you what you've always been out to buy.

And you'd been worried you were changing too much.

Marthaleka had saved Peter, before Benny even reached the bottom of the trail. She'd rugby-tackled the man from behind, earned a kick in the face. Her nose might be broken, but they can't be sure. She's not looking at Benny, because she's still hunched over trying to get the sand out of her eyes.

And Ithva, even Ithva, is watching her now through a face full of bruises and doubt. 'The whole point was to prove you knew how to work for the good of all,' she says. 'How can you expect us to believe you'll put the safety of all the children over your own?'

Well, that was it, wasn't it? When it came down to keeping her eye on convincing them she knew how to handle the Mim, versus getting her son out of danger... well, she'd made the only choice she could. Which was the wrong choice for the person she's been trying to convince them – convince herself – she is.

And when the other two men had shed their camouflage on the far side of the camp, Rathklin had been too busy alone up top to spot the attack from a second front. (No use suggesting that she'd held off on the alarm a few extra seconds, just to make more trouble to blame Benny for – that would look like desperate wriggling.) Ithva had had to fight them both, keeping Sharintha and Riskilvar safe behind her, all by herself. She'd only lost a little blood, but rather more faith.

'I'm sorry,' says Benny weakly. 'I'm really, I really am so sorry...' She wants to say *I'm only human*, but she knows that'll cut no ice in this desert.

'You've got your son,' says Marthaleka gently, painfully. 'Maybe that should be enough.'

In the end all she can do is apologise. They're polite enough, but she'll have a hell of a time earning back the faith she lost, if she can.

She tries first with Ithva. She's retreated on her own, cautiously massaging the gouges in her shoulder from the nails of the other two men.

'I blew it.'

Ithva nods soberly. Her gaze is turned away, oblique. 'Do you know

165

why the *vadaleka ikhav* – the war we fought in alliance with your people – was perhaps the greatest ever blow to our confidence?'

Benny shrugs. 'It wasn't like you lost.'

'We still had never lost a war. We didn't conquer your people, in the war before that, but neither did we lose. Equal and opposite, we're familiar with. We had the strength to fight you to a standstill, then we settled our differences with respect.

'But in the *vadaleka ikhav*... We never had a chance. Their force was just too massive, too ruthless. It was the plague writ large. For the first time in ten thousand years we *needed* allies. As with Karshtakavarr himself, our childrens' fate was in others' hands.'

Sprinting towards Peter, guts cramping, knowing that whether Marthaleka reached him first or the man did she could never be the one to save him.

Ithva turns her eyes to Benny, and there's sympathy in them. 'In some ways, for our culture, that made us feel more like helpless children than a defeat would have.'

Benny lowers her gaze. When she raises it again, they're not the eyes of a child.

'And it's a hell of a thing to expect the *Mim* to bear,' she says.

The words hang there. Finally, accepting, Ithva nods, then reaches out for Benny to help her to her feet.

As night approaches they gather for the dedication ceremony round the firebowl. The long shadows darken half their faces, turn their bruises into black. Green scales in the sunset, thinks Benny.

Here Misilvar tells the children the story of Karshtakavarr, worldsaver, childstealer, and the Empress Mishtila beating the godthing round the head and shoulders with his own walking-stick rather than surrender her child. She's a skilled storyteller, building up such a dramatic crescendo that when Mishtila finally whaps him one they're laughing with release. Benny watches how carefully she's setting up expectations in the children, using the drama to reinforce this attitude as the norm, and slots the idea straight into the monograph she's been mentally working on – now titled *Fight Club In Amok Time: Invented Myths Of Ritual Combat In The Information Era*.

And now, one by one, each weary mother takes her place in front of the firebowl, and promises herself to her child.

'I'm Marthaleka of House Selthkir. My line is low-born, but we have served with all our best nature. I am the daughter of a warrior and a teacher; I am an artist. I use my gifts to give people a clearer picture of what surrounds them.' She kneels before her daughter. 'And I will fight with all my being to protect you.'

Everyone embroiders in their own way on the words. Ithva ends hers with a sudden clumsy embrace, holding Sharintha to her and gulping out how proud of her she is. Rathklin's professional ferociousness completely disintegrates, she can barely get the last sentence out because she's beaming so hard at her daughter. Misilvar finally speaks with enough authority to get Riskilvar to stand still and listen, and dainty Salthmanika meets her shy daughter's eyes with a fierceness which makes her look like the original mean green mother from outer space.

Now it's Benny's turn. She stands in front of the fire-bowl, and Peter shuffles forward to face her.

'I'm Bernice Surprise Summerfield. My line has been high-born and low-born and scattered across the galaxy.' And has included some spectacular detours, she thinks, looking at this odd fuzzy son of hers.

But at this moment there's nowhere she'd rather this line have ended up than right here with the two of them. 'I am the daughter of a warrior and a journalist, but I...' And she knows now what she needs to say, to all of them. 'I'm a scholar. I don't have all the answers, but I'm jolly well going to dig them up. I'm still learning what I have to learn.'

She kneels before Peter, trying to catch his eyes while he looks away, embarrassed by his mum doing this in front of his friends. 'And I'm learning how to fight with my mind. I will fight with all my being to protect you... but more than that, I'll be *clever* for you.'

If she breaks down or hugs him in front of everyone he'll start squirming, so she forces herself just to place her hands on his shoulders. 'And you be as clever as you can for me, all right?'

'Sure, Mum,' he says. Like to him it's the easiest thing in the world.

There's singing afterwards, old and simple songs. Old enough that she knows some of them, folk hymns from the archaeological reviews – the tunes are odd but easy to pick up, and at one point in the repeated chorus of *Weeping and Proud In The Forest Of Summer* she even manages to slip in *By The Rivers Of Babylon* as a countermelody, in a moment of cross-cultural exchange.

Ithva, she's strangely pleased to note, can't carry a tune in a bucket. As for herself, what she lacks in skill she makes up in enthusiasm. It feels like the other mothers are beginning to accept that again as well, as the tension eases. And Peter's having a ball, setting human-Draconian relations back a few centuries by teaching the other kids *I Know A Song That'll Get On Your Nerves*.

She lets Peter sleep nestled up with Marthaleka while she takes first watch. Last night after the excitement he hadn't wanted to let go of her when she got up for the midnight watch, and had finally fallen asleep folded against her leg as she sat by the fire. Tonight he's comfortable snuggling between the plump little artist, her princess daughter, and Sharintha whose mummy is taking the alternate watch tonight. He already looks used to this world.

Nothing happens on the watch. She and Misilvar spend the hours swapping funny librarian stories. Misilvar still looks mother-weary, but in a different way now, experienced rather than overwhelmed. For each of them, every single minute of nothing feels like a precious gift.

At the end she prises her son loose without waking him, and carries him back to their own tent.

There will be at least one more assault before they leave in the morning.

Benny staring up at the dawn sky above as she wakes, with Peter in her arms. The first wisps of green fading up from the black, the stars running together like water to fill the sky with a smooth glow. Drifting herself gently back into the world, along with the light. No violence in the process; a gradual, easy rebirth.

Except when she went to sleep, they were in a tent.

It's hanging out of the firebowl, ropes trailing flame. The camp scattered, cooking gear upended.

Misilvar, slumped beside the torches, the final incomprehension on her face. The blood from the hole through her heart moving slow and thick, taking its time, nowhere urgent to go.

A broken heap of Salthmanika, back bent at an impossible angle.

Peter stirring in her arms. 'Mum?'

Marthaleka too. And a scattering of tiny piles, clothing and blood and little glimpses of green, cast away like discarded toys.

Desert sun, inexorably rising.

6

Peter's screaming and wailing, pulling her towards his dead friends. She's holding him on her hips, he's trying to crawl away straight through the air. Every time he gets a look in their direction he curls up again. He wants to see. He doesn't want to see.

'No, Peter, you're not ready for this, this is scary enough as it is and that'll only make it more scary...'

She's holding him as he struggles, as she circles the remains of the camp. Every muscle creaking and dried out, sweat caked on, aching from thigh to shoulder on the side carrying Peter. But she's still moving, somehow, when everyone else has fallen.

'– gotta help'm –'

'– no, Peter, it's too late, they're like Wolsey, you remember fluffy little Wolsey? But it's okay, Mummy's here...' And why *is* Mummy here, she asks herself.

The droth have fallen too, their throats slashed where they stood tethered. Now that's just cruel, cries some hidden part of her, what did they ever do to you? What did *any* of them ever do? Then she remembers what they'd been feeding them for the past two days, the flesh of their fallen herdmate, and nearly retches. Yesterday she'd given it a passing wry thought about mad droth disease. Today it's all hitting her, and the whole world feels obscene.

Distance down to zero.

She's holding Peter tighter than ever, and he's holding her back now. It's the one thing more real than the blood surrounding her.

There's no sign of the men who did this. All the way to the horizon, no one to be seen. Their camp is out of view, and the dugout hidden round the back of the mesa, they could be hiding anywhere but they're not showing their faces. They don't dare.

A sudden high, gasping cry from nowhere in sight. From up top of the mesa. From a woman. Ithva, in grief and shock.

They must have come for Rathklin and spared her too.

'Ithva!' shouts Benny, hugging Peter tighter when he flinches at her noise. 'Down here!'

In an instant the thought bites into her bones, and she's running towards the bodies even before Ithva can ask.

There's no sign of Sharintha. They call out, all three of them, in case she's hiding nearby, but there isn't even a wind to answer them.

'Why were we spared?' Ithva asks hollowly. Her arms hang in the air, reaching reflexively for someone at child-height but finding nothing but empty space, her mind groping blindly the same way. 'Why were we spared?'

They stand amidst the slaughtered droth, their blood soaked deep into the sand. Not one has been spared.

'Here,' says Ithva, finding the small ringed puncture mark below a throat wound. Her training keeping her going. 'Tranquilliser injection. They sedated them first, then slaughtered them.'

'Which means they must have brought the tranks here with them.'

Ithva nods. 'This was *planned*.' She leans heavily on the fresh carcass, her free hand holding her head like she's got to keep it from falling off. 'In the middle of a *nikhol vakarshta*. It's unthinkable, it breaks all the rules...'

'I thought you said they didn't have rules...'

'All the conventions, then,' she says half-heartedly. Benny looks at her, and can see Ithva's world spinning around her. Until now this was *normal* for her, stressful but understandable, where Benny herself has had a couple of days to get used to every last thing around her being utter chaos.

If anyone was going to get a grip on this, it would have to be her. 'So they took advantage of us coming out here, they were prepared to kill any other witnesses...'

'… took away our only means of getting home…'

'But they still want us alive.'

'And at their mercy.' Ithva's face creases with the effort of focusing. 'But *why*?'

A whimper from Peter. He's gone pale, greenish, not the sickly white humans pretend is green but *real* green. His face contorted at the piles of raw meat surrounding them. Something's coming right out and she's not sure if it'll be wet or just a scream.

'It's all right,' she murmurs, lowering him to the ground and holding him as he sobs and retches. 'At least one of us can still do it.'

Ithva's reaching out as well, a cool hand on his shoulder. She's holding him tightly and that gives Benny a moment to look away. And that's when she sees him.

Against the horizon, picked out by the pale dawn light: an old human man.

Patrician face, veined marble skin, deep-set hooded eyes. Amused tilt to his head as he studies them, like a biologist watching fruit-flies struggle in a dish. Old-fashioned safari suit of pure white linen. Black-and-white man in a world of sunburnt orange.

There are no footsteps in the sand to show from where he came. And it takes Benny a moment to realise she doesn't recognise him.

In his arms, sparkling in the dawn, the green-scaled child. Innocent of any danger.

'Peter,' she whispers, 'Stay behind me. Don't let him near you.'

The man waits near the edge of the camp, away from the circle near the firebowl. He's not coming to them, he's making them come to him. Setting and etiquette, Benny thinks. Defining the territory.

'Who are you?' demands Ithva.

'Oh, my name's not important,' he says, chuckling lightly.

'Well, that's good,' says Benny, 'Because I can think of quite a few different things to call you right now, and I'd like to try them all.'

'Please,' says the man, tilting his head back to look down his nose at them. 'Not in front of the children.'

From his belt hangs the droth slaughtering-knife, stained from hilt to tip.

Ithva faces up to him, warily, ferociously calm. 'Don't put yourself between me and my child.'

'Oh, I hardly needed to,' he titters. 'You'd put plenty between you and her already.' He turns conversationally to Benny, bouncing

Sharintha lightly against his side. 'Now you, on the other hand...
Every time I tried to prise him away from you, you rolled over just
that little bit more. Most infuriating. Still, that was only a problem
because I wanted the chance to ask you both to do what I say first...
And if you say no, that won't be an issue any more, will it?'

His voice is breathy and fluting, his expressions birdlike and half-
distracted. Noting everything and fluttering on, as if all this were too
simple to hold his interest. But when Ithva makes her first lunge for
Sharintha, instantly he dances back a pace, with a reproving 'ah-ah-
ah', a raised index finger, and the hand stroking Sharintha's hair
settling right near the curve of her throat.

'You think you can handle it all, don't you?' he murmurs. 'And yet
you can't even protect your own child.'

Sharintha's staring nervously – taking in the bodies, upset but not
yet panicked. 'Sharintha,' says Ithva, as calmly as she can manage.
'Peace.' And the girl closes her eyes and furrows her brow, screwing
herself up tightly to try to relax like they taught her to. Benny's got
Peter's hand in hers, holding him next to her, and whispers to him
that he can hug her leg if he wants. Which he does.

Ithva keeps circling the human, her rage tightly controlled. 'What
do you want?'

'I'm just playing the game,' he says, all innocence. Sitting on the
packs at the edge of the campfire, bouncing Sharintha on his knee.
'I've got your child, I'm here for my ransom.'

'Doesn't killing the opposition rather count as a forfeit?' Benny
asks.

'Only if you think you're playing by her rules,' he says. 'But these
are mine. Those men you bought?' he says, aside to Ithva. 'I bought
them too. When I'm finished with you, either they'll take you home,
or they'll finish the job.'

'How could you?' She's almost speechless with disbelief. 'To take
a *nikhol vakarshta* and –'

'Oh, it's quite easy when you don't actually *care*.' An amused tilt to
his head. 'It never occurred to you it was even possible, did it? That
someone could break your little game. You think you're such a free
spirit, with your whole elaborate way of working around the rules...
but that's all just another set of rules of your own. One you try to
make everyone else play by. But if something out there doesn't
actually bend to those rules?' A giggling little smile, an affectionate
squeeze for Sharintha. 'You're helpless.'

And Benny could see it in Ithva's stance: shifting, prowling, but off her balance. As blindsided as she'd been herself in Ithva's office. All those layers and shifting skins which she'd seen as the signs of a phenomenally devious mind, just the survival skills for a very particular world. And out of that world, she's as much at sea as Benny.

But still fighting, thank heaven. 'What do you want?' she snaps. Doing her best to make it sound more like a demand than a concession.

The pale man settles back, treating the pack like a throne. 'Well. You see, what you're going to do, Lady Kothar, once you get back to the city... is assure your sisters in the Empress's Hand that all your investigations into phase cannons and what-not have come to naught. A red herring. The panic on Proxima was just a freak occurrence after all.' His eyes alight on Benny. 'And the same for your inquiries, Ms Summerfield.'

Ithva looks at Benny, startled. 'You knew? The phase cannons?'

'That's *my* line. I thought your lot might have –'

'No, we've been trying to find out for ages –'

'And here I've been digging it out for your husband, and you've been giving me the Great Runaround –'

'You could have told me –'

'No, I bloody well *couldn't!*'

'Please, girls,' tuts the man. Benny stands there, letting her world finish reeling, as the facts all fall into their new places.

'So you did it,' whispers Ithva. 'We thought we were rescuing foundlings... but you were creating them. A whole stolen generation.' She's shaken, her fury almost swamped by her appalled realisation. 'This... unspeakable...'

'Oh, everything's unspeakable to you people.' An airy wave, backed with a piercing glare. 'You've built a whole empire on not acknowledging the truth. What's the chance your Emperor will ever speak the truth of this, hmm?'

'Is that why you killed Lwpha?' demands Benny. 'Because he might speak the truth?'

'And Pashar too? Did he find out something he shouldn't?'

'Yes, Pash –' Benny flounders. 'Who the hell is –'

A moment's aside. 'Staff clerk of Jarith's. Disappeared when Lwpha was killed.'

'So, you've been investigating Lwpha's –'

But Ithva's attention is still on the man. For a moment Benny feels like a child tugging on her mum's leg and demanding answers to the whole universe. 'And the Mimsphere?' Ithva snaps. 'How many more dead? How far does this go?'

He waves a hand. 'Please, one atrocity at a time. That one's not my department, I'm afraid.'

'Then whose?' she challenges. 'Who do you represent? Where are you from? On whose authority do you commit this, this...' Words fail her.

'Oh, don't be so *literal*,' he says. 'You don't come out into the desert on a spiritual quest and expect the answers to be prosaic and sensible, do you?'

Benny's staring at his eyes. Every time he turns his head, the light catches them in a different colour. Stormcloud grey, frost blue, faded green, even a glimpse of almond brown.

'I've come from a long way away, that's all you need to know. And I act because I can. My authority is that I have your child. When you left your city, you stepped out of your world and into mine.' That condescending smile for Ithva. 'You really should leave this to the experts, you know.'

'Don't,' says Sharintha, suddenly. 'You're being mean to Mummy and you *don't*.'

And for a moment Ithva looks almost as plaintive as her daughter. Benny can see her struggling, refusing to let it sink in: trying her best to keep up all sorts of faces, but unable to escape the fact that there's nothing she can demand here, so long as this man holds her girl.

'I'll tell you your answer, though,' he says. 'But my way.'

'What do you mean?'

And the man just smiles, slowly. 'Surely you remember your schooling? First-grade philosophy, playground mythtelling? You're not going to get the answers you're after by being sensible. If you want to understand, you've got to go back to your instincts.'

And he draws from his pocket a deck of cards. Salthmanika's deck, the fortune-telling cards, a stripe of blood dripped down one edge.

'Well?' he asks, cutting the cards and neatly twist-shuffling them. 'If you believe so much in your ways, what are they telling you now?'

He offers the cards to her. Don't, Benny wants to shout, but she can see this goes so far back to Ithva's roots, she can't escape them.

'I'm not very good at this,' says Ithva, laying the cards on the sand.

'The simplest pattern should do it,' he says. 'The egg.'

She places four cards in a diamond shape, struggling for the meaning of each. 'Meltingman. Scarmaker. Divided heart. Outerburn. Those things which mark your boundaries. And the seed of what you will become…' A fifth and final card, in the centre of the egg-shape. A hollow, decayed animal skull, wolf jaw and dinosaur crest.

'The plague,' she whispers. 'Destruction without creation. Ash. Ruin. The final end.' She looks up, haunted. 'Is this your tomorrow?'

A slow deep-creased smile. 'Which came first, the Draconian or the egg? You know this pattern doesn't just show the future, it shows where you come from.' He leans forward, bluegreygreen eyes drilling into her. 'You want to know me? *Turn the card.*'

Benny can't breathe. Ithva can't look away. Without even lowering her eyes, her hand reaches towards the card in the centre of the pattern. And flips it over on the sand.

It shows a face, in the same pose as the skull.

A human face, a white-haired old man full of noble disdain, with a birdlike tilt to his head and piercing bluegreygreen eyes.

Slowly, Ithva's eyes journey from the face in the sand, to the face in front of her.

And with a howl she leaps for his throat.

She's still howling as he swings round – smacking her across the face with the legs of her own daughter. Using her own motion to crash her to the sand. She's spitting desert from her mouth as he stands over her, hoisting her child, one hand gently cradling the vulnerable back of her neck.

'You'll never take her!' screams Ithva. Any hint of control lost. 'Do you hear me, Karshtakavarr?' Her voice full of mother's rage and primal fear.

'You still don't understand,' says the alien. 'I'm not threatening to *take* her.' And his hand begins to tighten on Sharintha's neck. The girl stares at her mother, more bewildered than afraid.

'No!' It starts sounding like defiance, but has somehow become a plea within the same syllable.

'You'll get her back unharmed once you've done as I tell you,' the man says, sounding perfectly reasonable. 'Both you and Ms Summerfield. You'll stop your questions and endorse the Draconian plan, and tell the Mim government it's in their best interests, or neither you nor Peter will be walking away from this desert. Do I make myself clear?'

Ithva lunges for his leg, but with quick counter-blows he's crushing her hand under his heel. She nearly chokes on her cry of pain. Hideously outclassed. He gives a tutting, condescending look down. 'I've learned quite a lot since my last visit. Even Empress Mishtila couldn't stand in my way now. And neither will either of you, because of what that would mean for your children.' A benign pair of fingertips tracing through Sharintha's hair, a tauntingly amiable quote. 'No sacrifice. Not even one.'

'How dare you,' growls Ithva, helplessly.

'Oh, quite easily, quite easily.' He twists his heel just enough to make it grind. His voice takes on just a hint of the dreamy sing-song mentioned in the history books, for when Karshtakavarr was gazing off into the distance of the future. 'My people have plans for the Mim children. Oh, great plans, and you won't be allowed to jeopardise –'

'If I might interject,' says Benny.

He turns to look at her, piercing, birdlike. But it takes a few moments for him to actually see.

Benny Summerfield is watching him, steadily, her son safely behind her. Her eyes shadowed and bruised, body raw and ragged, pushed past her limit but standing on the shifting sands and facing him down. He's not seeing the fear he expects. Instead, something quiet, and human, and *certain*.

She speaks, slowly.

'One of the advantages of the life I've had... galumphing across space, sometimes through time, never really settling down... you get to know a lot of different people. Sometimes really well. I've had people from other worlds in my body and my mind and my blood.

'And I *knew* Karshtakavarr.

'And he would *never*. He might take your child away, time always does that, but he was never *cruel*.

'He wasn't some bogeyman you can use to turn us into frightened kids. He was just a traveller, always on his way to somewhere else, someone brave and foolish and with some shocking fashion sense. You're not even worthy to polish his shoes.'

Plus, she doesn't add, I've played enough dodgy poker to be able to spot a cardsharp stacking the tarot deck.

She steps forward, putting every bit of herself into her eyes, fixing them on the fake man in front of her.

'Who do you think you are?'

And Ithva seizes her chance. Just like Benny knew she would. Her other arm hooks round, chopping at the back of his knee, and as he's twisting and buckling and grasping for her Benny is lunging in to grab Sharintha from him –

– and his hand is locked tight around her, refusing to let go –

- and the arm is *stretching* as she pulls -

- and Ithva's new assault on the rest of him forces him off-balance long enough for her to grab the droth-killing blade from his side, and slice it upward in an arc straight into the arm, a vicious blow but not enough to explain how it slices straight through his shoulder -

- and the Mim doesn't even bother with the illusion of blood, instead pulling the severed arm into a new and viciously spiked shape, still grabbing Sharintha while swinging its free end around to strike at Benny's head -

- as the rest of his human body kicks viciously at Ithva -

- Sharintha screaming as Benny wrestles the arm off her – feeling it grow teeth and spikes under her fingers even as she pulls – but flinging it to the ground before it can snare her, kicking it away, seeing it twist into a misshapen scampering thing, folding over itself even as it slithers to rejoin the rest of its body, but it's got them the moment they need, Sharintha is free -

The Mim, losing its features already, reverting to the dense-packed metallic sponge – texture and colour discarded to focus on vicious lethal shapes. Fists growing spines pincers claws sawblades anything it takes. The snarling human face now hanging off the back of its latest head.

Ithva, tearing with the knife and her bare hands through the creature that would steal her daughter. Her confidence restored, now she's fighting a mortal again and not some legend, her fury undiminished.

Purple blood oozing from the gash across her stomach.

Peter's screaming 'Mummy!'as she puts Sharintha down beside him. But she only has time to grasp him for a moment, not enough to ease his horror.

'– Peter, take her up to the top, keep her safe, go on for Mummy –'

'– Mum, he's gonna –'

'– No, Peter just *go!* Be safe for Mummy –'

Ithva, plunging the knife into what should be a vulnerable spot, in a human or a creature like her. But the form lies, it makes no difference where she strikes, and the Mim swallows the knife and her hand inside it.

Trying to twist away as a chisel-arm descends on her –

* * *

The torch hits the Mim with a meatbag thump. It knocks it off-balance, gives Ithva a chance to wrench free, face off against the thing on the opposite side from Benny. She realises she's screaming, pure reflex, waving the torch like a cudgel. If only she'd had time to relight the thing.

Ithva's half-doubled over, squeezing the gouge in her stomach.

He's growing a second set of eyes to watch them both at once. But he's still only got so much attention for each of them. It takes a few seconds to draw a new shape together, they can move faster than he can shift, attack from more angles than he can react to at once. It's their only chance – if he's this fast and this good with the shifting, he must be a spy or assassin.

But so is Ithva, and she's raising her head and charging. She knows what she's doing but she can't do it alone. Benny hauls back with the club and dives in.

And now it's just speed and pain.

Each blow she lands he howls. Not hiding the hurt, but not flinching from it either – each scream becomes a war-cry. Growling and grunting with each blow, every pain bent right back to rage.

Dive in, dance back. Over and over. They can hurt him and distract him but none of this will ever kill him. And she's dodging for her life because every blow is meant to cripple her – scything blow shredding the skin of her forearm, whipcrack tentacle flailing her legs, spike gouging straight under her arm, every hit agonising but she's so furious she forgets them, the pains blurred together and all that's clear is Peter and Sharintha. Claws and tentacles and spines stabbing at her, everything the world could ever throw at her and her children, but she holds herself there and refuses to let them past.

And now he's got a sharp sliver of rock lodged in his side as new voices shriek.

– Peter and Sharintha, a few feet up the mesa-side, hurling rocks from the path down at the monster. *Screaming you're not gonna hurt my Mummy, you're not gonna*. A tantrum with force to match the Mim's. Sharintha flailing as she tries to reach for the moves she was just taught with each rock she throws.

Peter sweating and bristling, screaming like a wild thing, and she knows then her son would kill him if he could.

'No! Peter! Sharintha! Get away!'

But the Mim is between them and their children. It's turned inside itself, shaking them off, a new face already heading in the direction it wants to move. Lumbering towards the mesa-side, forming lizard claws to scale it.

Ithva, losing her balance and sliding on the sand, tries to hurl herself bodily in its path. Nothing left to fight with, but giving it all.

'No,' shouts Benny. 'We've got a chance.'

It takes everything they've got to run in the opposite direction from their children. But she leads Ithva back to the fire, to the huge ceramic firebowl, and drops to her knees.

'Ready?' she asks, and she can see from Ithva's eyes that she's already got it. 'On three. One – two –'

And they hoist the bowl between them and they're charging towards the Mim, looking up at their son and daughter and the killer climbing towards them, and they hurl the whole cauldron of flaming droth blood at it and -

It screams. For a moment, reflexively, it's forming new mouths to let out more of the pain. It's losing its grip and falling to the ground, covered in flame, thrashing in the sand, trying to roll the fire out. But Ithva lights the discarded torch off his flaming back, jabbing it at him, relighting the fire everywhere he damps it down, and Benny's lashing him with a flaming tent-rope, and every new shape he reaches for just exposes more of his flesh to be burnt.

They have to keep killing him for ages. Eventually Ithva sits down heavily clutching her gut, waving her away, and it's left to Benny to finish him. She's standing over the child-stealing monster as it bubbles and cracks, and every time it starts to form a new head or arm she rams the torch straight down into it. After a while it's just a blackened mass, more crust and scab than spongy flesh, and finally she plunges the torch in and there's nothing left to burn, nothing but an empty cavity and ash.

'Well what do you know,' she grunts, 'They *were* hollow on the inside...'

Little stumbling footsteps coming up behind her. Talking automatically, not even turning around yet. 'Sharintha, your Mummy needs you to get the medikit, it's next to Mar – next to the cooking bowls, hurry...'

She plants the torch in the ground, defiantly in the midst of what's left of the Mim, and wearily turns to face the sweat-soaked, tear-stained little boy who's come up behind her.

Her son's been watching her kill.

She's down on her knees, reaching for him. He doesn't flinch from her, and she knows she would have if she'd seen her own Mummy do that and she doesn't know if it's good that he doesn't care. Too late. Damage done. 'Oh, Peter,' she sobs. 'I'm so sorry...'

'He was *hurting* you,' cries Peter.

'But I'm okay. I'm okay...'

'– I had to hit him, he was hurting –'

'It's all right, it's all right.' She keeps hugging him, letting his sobs melt away into his shoulder, more and more words till slowly he sounds like Peter again. 'He's gone now and I'm so sorry and I did it all for you...'

'But he wasn't hurting me...?'

She has to tell him. She can't not tell him. 'He was going to take you away and hurt you, but I stopped him, he's gone now...'

She can almost hear his mind trying to wrap around the whole idea.

'Was he a mirage too?'

'No. No, sweetheart. He was real.'

'But he was changing like a dream, like he wasn't real...'

'Things that change are real too.' And she hugs him even tighter, trying to memorise every inch of him at this moment. Before time takes him wherever it will take him from here.

Sharintha runs up, clutching the medikit, in a cloud of the broken gasping sniffles that serve as Draconian tears. Ithva's rocking silently, holding her belly, then grabs Sharintha to her, as if that does a better job of stopping the bleeding than anything the kit could contain. There are splatters of half-words and sobs and soothing noises all round, as Benny dresses Ithva's wounds and her own. There's no way to stitch them properly, but the sprayskin will hold for a while if they don't strain it too much. And she gets Peter to be all useful by passing her things and holding Ithva's hand.

'What in the world happened to you, *ithvila*,' Ithva croons to her daughter.

'Salth'man'ka took me away, said wait round the bend where it's okay, and a good man would come and keep me safe...'

'What was she thinking,' moans Ithva.

'Oh,' says Benny, looking back at the ruined camp. 'Count the bodies.'

It takes Ithva a moment to focus on them. When she does, her head sags backwards. 'Gods and goddesses. And I trusted her...'

'He must have killed the real Salthmanika right before we left and taken her place,' says Benny, pressing a gauze pad atop the sprayskin. 'I'm sorry...'

'I didn't even know her,' Ithva says, eyes closing in pain. 'But she was vetted. She was *trusted*. I trusted her with my daughter...'

'Doesn't mean you were wrong to,' Benny says raggedly, binding the gauze in place. 'That's another button he was pushing. Don't rely on other mothers. But it's the only way you can raise this many kids and still accomplish anything in your own right...'

'Some spymaster,' says Ithva.

Benny wipes the sand from her scratches. 'You can't keep them safe from everything.' She tries the sprayskin on her own gashed arm; it'll do for now, but it leaves her with a synthetic streak of green scales the length of her wound. A mongrel. At least her patch of Draconian skin will keep any bits of Mim still in her blood from dripping away. By now she's almost as mix-and-match as Peter, furry little half-boy-cub, fighting like a beast and crying like a child.

'And you know what? He didn't want you believing in any other mothers. Because he didn't want you trusting me, or my plan. But now you *know* we'll fight for them.'

And *she* knows. No more running on autopilot, no doubting her convictions. She'd come here knowing she wanted to, but now she knows she *can*.

In fact, she wants to tell her that the whole retreat's got it wrong. That Karshtakavarr was never a babynapper, that he wouldn't have invited the Empress's daughter if she weren't old enough to choose. That their whole legend's missed the point, that it's really about one mother trying to hold on to more control than she has the right to.

She sits down heavily next to Ithva and takes her face in her hands. The last of her strength. 'You brought me here to know me? This is me. Every sweaty sticky bit of me.' Brushing Ithva's hair back gently, determinedly. 'And I'm saying this will work. Work with them. They deserve their children.'

In the end, it's Sharintha hugging onto her from the other side which tips the balance. It's stopped being more than Ithva can imagine, having her own daughter taken from her. Ithva's face sags forward into Benny's shoulder, accepting her truth. And Benny finds herself cradling her, with a gentle kiss on her forehead, her fingertips running gently over the ridges of her ears.

'But why would a Mim want us to keep their children?' asks Ithva. Her mind still trying to work, even through the painkillers in the sprayskin, which Benny suspects contains more than a touch of Old 32.

'I've no idea.'

'But conspiring against his own people?'

'Heavens,' says Benny. 'It'll never catch on.'

'… Mummy?'

It's Peter, afraid again.

Pointing at the silhouettes on the horizon of the half-dozen men, their shadows long in front of them, closing in from across the sands to finish the job.

'Peter, Sharintha,' says Benny, and Ithva is finishing her thoughts for her. 'Go up top.' 'Stay away from the edge.' 'Keep yourself safe.'

The children start to protest, but they know the do-what-Mummy-says face by now. They scurry away up the corkscrew trail to the top of the mesa, while Benny sits next to Ithva and tries to keep her from standing too soon.

'Shh. We've got a few minutes before they get here. Don't rush it. Just relax. Relax.'

A faint laugh. 'If we can't relax now, when will we?'

She's got her arms around Ithva, supporting her, holding on to each other like they both need the warmth in the desert. Fingertips brushing gently over the textured scales near her temples, easing the cold plummeting feeling of having to cope again after finally letting yourself stop. Ithva's hand running through her hair, soothing her past her own fear. Finding their centre, letting their strength gather of its own accord. She knows what they need to do, she knows together they'll do everything they can. And when the kiss begins it's like nothing has changed at all.

It builds gently, in slow waves. Cooling and warming, making all the blood and sweat and touching bearable. Deepening like the ocean, swelling up then fading back from where it came. Nothing urgent, nothing desperate, nothing uncertain. She gives a gentle, exploratory nibble on Ithva's lower lip as she withdraws, just to make it clear there was no doubt or fear. That whatever it was she meant, she *meant* it.

'This isn't another negotiating tactic is it?' murmurs Ithva, in slow astonishment.

'Not that I'm aware of…'

'It'd work,' Ithva says, with a little gasping laugh.

And they stand.

* * *

Benny kicks through the ashes of the Mim, retrieves the droth knife. Passes it to Ithva while she takes the guttering torch for herself; it's nearly gone out, but it might still make a usable club before it breaks.

'Still droth back at their camp,' says Benny. 'They're our way home.'

'They won't let us,' says Ithva, and Benny just nods. She shifts on her feet, finding the best stance.

A glimpse of the cards, still scattered in the sand. Karshtakavarr as the reverse-twin of the plague: creation through disruption, instead of destruction for destruction's sake. The waterflame, a glimpse of something between the carefully defined worlds. Attempts to codify the numinous, define a system which enclosed those who would still act outside its rules. Like the ritual violence itself: making the insane routine, and perpetuating the insanity.

The footsteps sweep across the cards, scattering them further, disappearing them under a dusting of sand.

The men reach them at the foot of the trail. Their wounds bound, their faces set. Closing in, forming a half circle, leaving her and Ithva with nowhere to go but up to the children. She's spotted the one who came for her the first night, the one she thinks of as their leader. He's flexing his fingers in clawlike motions, staring them down.

Even now, Summerfield, thinks Benny. Even now you're the woman who tries. And she lowers her hands without relaxing them, looking their leader in the eye.

'We don't have to to do this. The game's over, the rules are broken. It doesn't matter any more. We can still stop before anyone else gets killed.'

Behind her, Ithva has the droth knife at the ready. 'I organised this. If it's the money, I'll double your fee. I'll match whatever he paid you.'

'We can all go home together,' says Benny. 'No one else has to die.'

The leader says nothing. His eyes are flat and unmoving, his teeth bared in a reflexive leer. Crocodile malice. Unthinking and unswerving.

Then he charges and Benny tries to break his neck.

It's not enough, she doesn't have the grip or the strength. But she's pulled him past her, slammed him head-first into the mesa-side, and that buys her and Ithva the next few seconds. And those buy them the next. And the next.

* * *

183

Benny and Ithva, retreating up the track. Backing away, leading the men on, a couple of metres above the ground – too high to be grabbed from below, forcing the men to come up the trail single file. The stairs at the Aina Gallery again, but in mirror image: the attackers have their right hands free, and they're fighting with their left.

Man lunging at her, her bruised arms blocking yet another blow. They're coming at her one by one. Ithva behind her to catch her, or knife-arm reaching past her to get in an arcing slice. But it's Benny who's facing them head-on, wearing them down, wearing her down.
   She hurls the man off the edge, sees him staggering to his feet on the sand below. Another killer has already taken his place, trying to get through her to her child. She hits out at him too, and then the next. Man after man. Body against body against body.

The sky tumbling over her. Her foot's kicked from under her, the world's pitching over the side. She's trying to get back up before she's even finished hitting the sand – she's only fallen a couple of metres, she can keep going, even if her body won't move in a straight line and she can't quite seem to breathe.

Grabbing at legs, yanking them over the side, lurch-running back to the trail before the ones she's dragged down after her can strike back. Fighting her way up through the crowd from behind, hurling them into the rock or over the edge, clawing and dragging her way back to Ithva, back to her children.

Ahead Ithva's stained with blood and only some of it is hers. She's backing away higher, the falls getting more lethal. Two men between Benny and her, three more coming back up behind her, and except for the one fighting Ithva they're all coming at her from both sides, hands grabbing and pounding from front and rear and she kicks and they're all beginning to pitch over and the blood's pounding in her ears and turning to a growing high-pitched whine -

- And the blast of a dopplered horn as the taxicab screeches through the desert air, banking round the mesa, banking and buzzing the men so close their *hronstheis* whip about. Their gaping expressions as they realise she's using the fact they flinched to shove them over again. And the cab is sweeping back again, scorching them with its exhaust, swooping and swerving and harrying them away till they're fleeing into the desert.

Jason Kane hanging out the window, screaming her name like a battle cry.

And that mood-music gadget of his plugged into the cab's sound system, blaring *Ride of the Valkyries* at two million decibels.

She and Ithva stumble up to the top as the cab settles next to the children. All the hardness within her melting, grateful that she doesn't have to stand alone. Silencing the bitter little reptile part of herself, still drunk on adrenalin, that says *I should have taken care of them myself*. She's done enough.

She wraps herself around Jason, and he's clean and dry and loyal and certain and all the best bits of being human and there are no words.

Body against body.

The cabbie's leapt out, brandishing his sword, shouting righteously chauvinistic accusations and slurs on the parentage of the retreating bandits. She doesn't think he's the same driver they had before – photos on the dashboard instead of bobble-heads – but they're of a type. Jason tells her how thrilled he'd been to get paid to save damsels in distress, how he'd relished the chance to fly like the pilot he'd always dreamed of being.

'I was watching your back, just like you said,' he tells her. 'Spent most of the first day surfing the networks, looking for any sign of activity related to us, or Kothar, or any of the other people we knew were involved. And you won't believe who booked a sudden flight from the Collection the moment we left.'

'Pashar, was it?' she says vaguely, and he doesn't even recognise the name.

'No. Korenthai.'

She sags with bewilderment. 'General Ledger?'

'Uh huh. Booked a flight back to Sigma Draconis for the next morning and left. Looked like a report to HQ. But here's the clever bit... he went through security at the Collection's port... and then never arrived at the other end. So I got Joseph to ask the port securicams a few polite questions. And the last they saw of him was him going into the men's room... and a completely different Draconian who never went in comes out. And hops the next flight to Montavadros.' He's cradling her head against him. 'He was a Mim.'

He was a Mim. And he'd ordered the use of phase cannons against his own people, to give their children to the Draconians. And she had no idea why, or who else was involved, and right now it was too much to care about.

'So I did some more poking about, and found him arriving here, and taking a cab straight to the localport where your group was gathering. And that's where I lost him.'

'Where he took Salthmanika,' she mumbles.

'So I had to warn you, I called the camp, but you'd gone off on your own, and it was a bitch and a half finding where you'd gone but with a highly generous gift to the Retired Hackers Benevolent Fund I got some satellite tracking photos and…'

She just holds him tighter, both astonished and wonderfully unsurprised. She hadn't known what he'd do, but she'd trusted him to do it. She hadn't even known how much she was relying on Jason Kane. And those opposing them had been so focused on her alone, her and Peter, that they'd paid no attention to the others standing behind her.

'My loyal left hand,' she murmurs, brushing her own through his hair.

His own arm holding her round the small of her back. 'As in, doesn't know what the right hand is doing?' His face. Crestfallen, bless him. Never the self-worth he deserves.

'There is that,' she says, and kisses him. Firm, unguarded, nibbling at the stubble on his chin in that way only they find such meaning in. A wave breaking in an instant. Not a promise of something to come; a declaration of what's right here.

Ithva, nearly doubled over, insisting on taking one moment more. Crouching over Rathklin's body, murmuring her farewells. Sharintha, sniffling openly, clinging to her mother now as mother leans on her in turn.

Benny watching from a distance, holding Peter on her hip. Remembering him fighting to reach his friends before, but seeing none of that in the stony, tired child curling up against her. Summoning her nerve to ask.

'Peter? Cubby? Is there anyone you need to say goodbye to?'

'Nuh uh. I don't want to now.'

And again she's not sure if this is better or worse.

* * *

Ithva, standing slowly, walking her child under her own power to the cab. Sobered but unbroken. Through it all, she's kept her child intact.

A weary look of gratitude, which must reflect Benny's own. There's only so much Benny can blame either one of them for the world they've brought their children into.

Standing together, a final moment, looking out over the desert as Ithva opens the cab door. 'The best thing about a learning experience,' she says, 'is that you never ever have to go through it again.'

The cabbie calls the cops from his car; they'll be here to retrieve the bodies, before the bandits or any desert animals can have their way with them. Two of the men themselves are dead. One of multiple stab wounds, one with a broken neck from the fall. And they've left one of their own behind.

He's sitting on the trail, holding his leg where Ithva had gouged it deep, trying to summon the strength to walk. Benny plants her feet in front of him, and he looks up through pain-dulled eyes.

'Want a lift?' asks Benny. 'Fastest way back to civilisation. Only you'll have to ride in the boot.'

The cabbie sucks in his breath through his teeth. 'Extra fare.'

'Can I ride in the boot too?' asks Peter.

'No, tiger,' says Jason, ruffling his hair obliviously. 'We want him in one piece.'

The children, curled up and dozing in the front of the cab as the desert streaks past beneath. One arm draped over Jason, the other gently stroking Ithva's hair in her lap. Ithva's lying down across her, exhausted, knees curled up: one hand still pressed to her re-sealed stomach wound, her shoulder resting familiarly against Benny's breast.

Jason's got his hands wrapped round his knee, and is rocking back and forth on his seat, smiling almost smugly. 'Fascinating field, body language.'

She raises an eyebrow back at him. 'Fascinating field, interspecies porn.'

He's slowly beginning to look like all his Christmasses have come at once. 'I always thought curiosity was an underrated –'

Well isn't that so bloody Jason, begins her reflex. But she's not running on reflex now. She leans her head against his and just tells him what she's thinking. 'Maybe someday, in my own time. We'll see who I am down the road.' And it feels comfortable to leave it there; she's not so disturbed now by being a moving target. If time takes your children, makes them grow, why should she be scared to still be growing herself?

'We? So I'm invited?'

'It's not like I'm going anywhere without you,' she says lazily.

'I've done the research. You know that spot just under…'

'We're not having this conversation.'

'I know, I know, not in front of the children.'

'The children aren't bothered. Not in front of the *cabdriver*.'

For a long moment they're quiet together. At this speed it's a matter of half an hour to the nearest small town, the nearest hospital, the nearest air conditioning. Finally Jason lets out a little half-swallowed chuckle.

'What?' says Benny sleepily.

'Nothing.'

'That's not a nothing, that's a what. Come on.'

A leering drawl. 'Ambassador Kothar… I liiike your wiiife.'

Benny snickers, holding them both. Ithva snuggles closer and mumbles something which sounds like 'Tell him and I'll rip your arms off, darling.'

She lets herself settle against Jason again. One more thing to tell him, one more change not to be made. She kisses the only man she wants to call husband and lets out the truth.

'I'm not pregnant.'

He's stroking her hair, gently. 'It's all right. We'll get there.'

Someday. In her own time.

For days, civilisation is a blur. It's a treatment room and a hotel room and phone calls to Brax and Kothar's office and trying to book a child therapist for Peter the instant they get back. It's giving Kothar the information he needs to point the finger at the mysteriously vanished Korenthai; whether he's treated as a lone gunman or a conspirator in the matter of Proxima Longissima would be a matter for another day. It's calls to severe noblewomen who frown attentively and eventually say yes to whatever she and Ithva ask. It's Peter and Jason and sitting in a park eating lime-flavoured Draconian ice cream and a hundred and one moments which will never be remembered but will always be felt.

And finally it's the three of them on the shuttle up from landfall to the customs station in orbit, the wet Montavadros air giving way to the neutral climate of an artificial space. Benny watches the night-side cityscape sink beneath her, all the little specks of light on the floor of this ocean of air. With the two of them by her side, she feels like the first land creature, climbing to a point halfway between the water and the sun – feeling the wetness mist and fade around her and leave her genuinely free. And further out for her, nothing but the blackness and the stars: points of fire in the ocean, sparkling water-drops in the sun.

Nursery Politics
Philip Purser-Hallard

Welcome to the Draconian-Mim Reparations Tribunal

'Reparations for what?' is a fatuous question.

The Tribunal is now in its sixth week of sittings, with little sign of movement on either side. The borogoves of Proxima Longissima have become a cause célèbre for both sides, and the pundits now agree that whichever side gains custody gets to determine the course of future history for the Mim.

The Draconian Star Empire considers the abandoned borogoves as war orphans – not that they see the recent conflict as anything so vulgar as a war. This makes them wards and chattels of the Emperor, whose honour obliges him to take responsibility for their welfare.

The chief Draconian representative at the Tribunal is **Ambassador Kothar**, a machiavellian politician who always has a barbed comment on his lips and a subtle scheme up his sleeve. Nothing he does is without a hidden agenda, and nothing he says has fewer than half a dozen meanings. His people consider him a pragmatist who changes his approach to fit his political environment. Some of them say the same about his loyalties.

Deputy Ambassador Werther is more of a hardliner, a noble of the old school who prizes honour, chivalry and patriotism above such trivia as common sense. He sees the Mim as bottom-feeding slime which has risen above its station, and must be returned there as soon as possible. His views on humans are rather less polite.

The Ambassador's wife, **Ithva Kothar**, is the perfect hostess. She knows how to seat guests in order of precedence, which knives to set for the fish course – and how to deal forcefully with unwanted guests.

The Mim believe, of course, that their children are being held illegally as prisoners of war. They insist that the Draconians return them immediately. They don't tend to think in terms of leaders, but one of their most prominent negotiators is **Dr Mwshi** – a mild-mannered academic who has spent many years away from the Mimsphere, teaching comparative sociology at the university on Yemaya 4. A rather put-upon and harried individual, his only aim is to help his people recover from their misfortunes and rebuild their civilisation.

Other notable delegates on the Mim side include **Sherm** and **Phwmi**. Sherm is a hectoring, bullying Mim who has never quite explained what he was doing off the Mimsphere when the still-mysterious catastrophe struck, but whose personal wealth has proved invaluable to the delegation. Phwmi, the self-appointed 'Minister of Truth', is the leader of a pacifist cult who left the Mimsphere when the conflict began. Only now have they emerged from *hiding, safe and sound, to take their place at the negotiating table. Phwmi wants the borogoves handed over to his sect, so they can be brought up free from warmongering ideas.*

There's been no shortage of suggested compromises. Early on in the talks the Draconians suggested that the two sides should share legal custody of the borogoves. With Draconian funding and Mim teaching, the children would grow up safe from harm and fully versed in Mim culture. The Mim rejected the offer, though they're hardly in a secure position for arguing.

Some suspect that this was due to the influence of two other interested parties. **Mr Szmyt** *and* **Ms Haddad** *are two 'diplomats' from Earth (although those in the know believe they may represent some shadowy human military agency). In their severe black frock-coats, black ties and mirrored sunglasses, they can be an intimidating presence, an impression they do little to dispel. Although they have no official status at the negotiations, they have thrown Earth's considerable diplomatic weight behind the Mim. They seem to get on rather well with Delegate Sherm.*

Relations have not been helped by the unsolved murder several weeks ago of **Lwpha**, *the Mim who brought the borogoves' plight to public attention, nor by the disappearance at the same time of* **Pashar**, *a Draconian Junior Consular Officer. Opinions differ about what happened. The Draconians say Pashar must have been killed by Lwpha's unknown murderer, while everyone else (more or less) believes Pashar is in hiding after killing Lwpha. It's probably best to avoid discussing this.*

Representing the Braxiatel Collection, the talks are being chaired by **Irving Braxiatel** *himself. According to him, this is a purely administrative role, and he's just helping out until the Collection finds a new director. Other people's willingness to believe this varies. Braxiatel has delegated much of the behind-the-scenes diplomacy to his representative,* **Professor Bernice Summerfield**, *a minor media celebrity who also happens to be an expert in both Mim and Draconian culture.*

1

Jason

'Who writes these briefings? Could they make them a tad more superficial, do you think? I mean, "a machiavellian politician"? "A mild-mannered academic"? I'm floundering here.'

Benny takes the printout from my hands, and shuffles it to the bottom of her pile. 'It's Joseph,' she tells me. 'He doesn't have a very high opinion of non-artificial intelligence.'

She looks so tired. Bags under her eyes, shadows from all those sharp corners lurking under the surface of her skin. Fork shovelling away one-handed as she works her way through yet another briefing document and that pasta thing I made her. Tense and stressed out.

She needs cheering up.

'So, would madame fancy something to spice up her luncheon?' I ask, wiggling my eyebrows in an urbane yet filthy manner. 'Some special sausage, perhaps?'

The look she gives me is equally filthy, but not in a good way. 'You must be joking, surely,' she snaps. I deflate a bit.

'I didn't mean that,' I mutter.

With Peter at school, 'that' was exactly what I did mean. Benny may be busy, but I haven't got any plans. I've got nothing on all afternoon, in fact. I'd been hoping we could take the figure of speech a bit more literally.

But it's obvious she's having none of it. Which means, of course, that neither am I.

'Pleased to hear it.' She stares down at the printed pages.

Neither of us could face Café Vosta today. Too full of junior diplomats and hangers-on. Glaring at one another, sizing each other up, occasionally trying to start something. There was a 'diplomatic incident' there just the other day, clawed fists and spongy pseudopodia flying. Adrian's boys had to wade in and break it up.

It's funny. Growing up in Suffolk at the arse-end of the twentieth century, I never thought I'd have much use for the word 'pseudopodia'.

'Still, you can't make new human beings without shagging, apparently,' I point out, brightly. 'They did this study.'

'I remember,' she says. 'They said it was distasteful, but unfortunately necessary. Unlike this paperwork, which I'm doing for the sheer orgasmic joy of it.'

'Yeah, I know. Sorry.' I gather up our plates and forks and take them through to the kitchen.

Thing is, it's not about the sex. I know how lame this sounds, but it really is about the kid.

For the longest time I didn't want them – kids, I mean. I couldn't stand the idea. You might say I didn't have the happiest of childhoods (if you're the kind of person who says things like 'You know, in many ways Hell isn't an ideal holiday destination'), and I was scared of what I'd end up doing to them. *Like father like son*, they say, whoever 'they' are, and I've always despised them for it. Deep down, though, I've been afraid they might be right.

Since I've been helping Benny look after Peter, I've realised how bollocks all that is. I'm my own person. I'd be a good dad. I don't have to let that repugnant old bastard define who I am.

Now I love the idea of Benny and me having a baby together. Babies are great, after all – you can keep them amused really easily, and later on you get to play with their Lego and make a tit of yourself at their weddings. And Benny gets to change nappies and get up in the night for feeds and all the other things she loved doing with Peter.

'Look, Benny,' I say, handing her a yoghurt. 'Is there anything I can do? You know, to help?'

She frowns. 'Like what?'

'I don't know.' Not the paperwork. I'm not really the paperwork type. 'But you're so busy right now. Surely I can help with something.'

I try not to sound whiny, but I want to make some kind o

contribution. And if it's just a squirt of sperm at the right time and place – well, I've done worse.

'You're doing a lot already.' Benny's sounding less stroppy now. If I'm lucky we'll end the meal still talking to each other. 'You're looking after Peter. With Dad gone back to the 1980s and Adrian and me up to our eyeballs, that's a big help.'

'Peter's a good kid,' I say.

That's the official story, of course. The less tactful version is that Peter's always *been* a good kid, except when he's not getting enough attention from Mummy Benny and Daddy Adrian. Like for the past few weeks, say. Then he can be a right little pain in the passage.

Yesterday evening I came down from working on my latest porn novel to find the little sod trying to hack into the Collection's surveillance systems. Said he was trying to see where Mummy was.

I told him she was out at some reception or other, trying to be nice to war criminals. She always comes back from those things in a foul mood. Probably the same one she's still in now.

I know it's not Peter's fault, exactly – poor kid's been really clingy since we lost Daddy Adrian's Special Friend Bev. But even so.

'Sure,' I say. 'Helping out with Peter, that's great. Glad to be of service. But isn't there something a little more, let's say *proactive* I could be doing?'

'Haven't you got a novel to write?' she says. 'We wouldn't want your readers turning in despair to real life and adult relationships, would we?'

She tries to disarm that barb as soon as it's out. It's the only smile I've seen from her so far today.

It stings. 'Oh, very mature. Way to take the moral high ground.'

She bridles. 'So you're what, bored? Wanting in on the action? Jason, do you suppose I'm *enjoying* any of this?'

I can hear what she's not saying. Just which of my skill-sets do I think might help to guide her through this labyrinth of diplomacy she's got herself stuck in? My years of experience as a space buccaneer? My talents as a literary pornographer? My recent foray into aeronautically intimidating hired thugs?

I say, 'You're trying to look after kids stuck in the middle of a war they don't understand, who've ended up with no one else to take care of their interests. Don't you think I might be able to help with that?'

'Oh, Jason. I hadn't thought,' she says softly.

I guess she remembers now about the Axis Occupation, during the war before last. Jason Kane the collaborator, schindlering away the non-human kids the Fifth Axis would have locked up and liquidated if they'd got the chance.

(Come to think of it, that could have tipped me off about being okay parent material. And her too: that was just before we got back together. Funny the things you don't think of at the time.)

'I'd just like to feel I was being useful, you know?' I say. I take her empty yoghurt pot through to the recycler.

'Okay,' she calls after me. 'But I think I've got the borogove situation in hand, as much as I'm ever likely to. While I find a way to keep poor Lwpha's children safe without bringing about the collapse of Mim culture, though, there's a lot I've had to put on the back burner.'

'Okay.' I go back through to her. 'Like what?'

She scratches her nose thoughtfully. 'We still don't know who Korenthai – Salthmanika – whatever his real name was – was working for. The Montavadros castellany have been asking me that very thing, and they've got a point. Obviously killing Ithva and me was meant to cover up the phase-cannon strike, but why was he using phase cannon on other Mim anyway? I've asked Dr Mwshi, but he hasn't any idea either.'

She sighs. 'You know, in my ideal world, people wouldn't slaughter my friends and try to murder me and my son, without me having at least *some* idea why. It's just a dream I have.'

'So what can I do?' I ask.

She tells me.

I guess I let my disappointment show, because she riles again. 'You said you wanted to help. If it's too dull for you –'

'Benny!' I raise my hands. 'I said I'd help. I will.'

'And you're still okay to pick Peter up from school?'

'No mission is too challenging for Jason Kane.'

Benny smiles. Properly this time. She leans forward to kiss me, then catches sight of the clock over my shoulder. 'Shit, I've got a briefing with Brax. I'll see you later.'

A quick peck on the cheek and she's gone.

Victoria

When you come out of Braxiatel's office your face is thundery. You look like you want to kick something, the smaller and more defenceless the better.

Luckily, I'm neither. I greet you – buttonhole you, really – as you walk along the corridor.

'Professor Summerfield,' I say. 'Bernice. How nice to see you.'
You don't look much like you agree, I'm afraid.

'Ms Haddad,' you reply, a little shortly. 'Can't stop, I'm afraid, I'm expected at the, er...' You wave an arm vaguely, pointing towards what might be the Mansionhouse kitchens, the Department of Revisionist Physics or the spaceport. (And if you followed that hand far enough around the surface of this little planetoid, you'd end up right back here. It's a strange and claustrophobic world Braxiatel's built for himself, isn't it?)

I'm not surprised you're not so keen on chatting. Mr Szmyt and I *can* be a little bit overpowering. Our branch of Earth security's a stickler for formality. The way we use each other's titles all the time, the way we dress – it's all traditional for agencies like ours, and I'm afraid it *was* originally designed to disconcert people. I'm sure you'll have seen all those media dramas from the olden days, where people looking rather like us turn up after spaceship crashes and bother the witnesses.

Our role's evolved a bit since then, of course.

But you won't be getting rid of me so easily. Oh, no. 'I'd just like a moment of your time, Bernice,' I say. 'I've been here six weeks now, and I feel we've hardly talked.'

You frown at me, like a slug crawling across your computer screen. 'I don't think we have much to talk about, Ms Haddad. What with the Reparations Tribunal, I haven't really got the time for socialising, and you don't have any –'

'Official status, dearie, yes, I know.' I nod a lot. 'But we do have an *interest*, a legitimate diplomatic one, in supporting the Mim government. Why shouldn't those poor sponge-people get to keep their children, the poor little mites?'

'Erm, yes,' you say. 'You know, I *have* had this conversation with your colleague Mr Szmyt, although he put it in rather less emotive terms. The last time we talked, in fact, he started making thinly veiled threats against my future career. Which, when you consider how little influence the Earth government has over academic institutions in these parts, just made him look surprisingly ignorant.'

'Oh, you mustn't mind Mr Szmyt,' I say. 'He's a traditionalist.' God, what a cretin that man is. 'He gets a little bit over-enthusiastic sometimes.'

Honestly, good-cop-bad-cop went out with knights in armour.

I take your arm. You look unhappily at my hand there as I begin to steer you along the marbled corridors towards the entrance-hall.

'Look,' you say, 'I can give you a few minutes, Ms Haddad, but then I really must...' You flap your other arm again.

Interesting that you don't want to tell me what you *are* meant to be doing. And you're disguising it with a rather poor impression of vague and woolly-headed academic-ness. As if you think *my* very undiplomatic bluntness means I'll be easily fooled.

(Oh, Bernice, you're an amateur when it comes to playing roles. You don't know the tenth of what we know – not, dearie, the hundredth part.)

'I'm sorry if Mr Szmyt scared you,' I say, as we stroll out into the gardens. Once we're outside I let go of you, and select a cigarette. A hashish mix, I think, with the Spica Virginia – nicotine-free, of course.

Not that it bothers me, I just don't like the taste.

I light it as we walk on. 'The truth is, he doesn't understand why you're supporting the Draconians, and nor do I. You should be on the Mim's side, like us. You were the one who told the worlds about the borogoves, after all. That poor lost alien Lwpha trusted you completely.'

Poor, sad, unfortunate Lwpha. Such a shame, and such a waste – and such a pity, if the story of what *really* happened to him ever got out.

You've stopped walking. I turn around to face you. Framed by the Mansionhouse behind you, you look cross. 'You're being a bit disingenuous, aren't you? You know full well I'm not "supporting the Draconians" – I'm just trying to work out what's best for the children. That's the point of this Tribunal, to establish that. That's what it's become, anyway.'

'Well,' I reply patiently, 'the Draconians are hardly going to give the poor tykes the best start in life, now are they? I mean, captured war orphans becoming vassals of the Emperor? In this day and age? It's barbaric.'

You look annoyed. 'The Draconians have a point, though. Their priority is that every one of those young Mim grows up into a healthy adult, and they have the funds to make sure it happens. The Mim don't have the resources to achieve that, even if they wanted to. Unless Earth's planning on supplying them with aid?'

Oh, no, my girl, you're not pumping *me* for information. That isn't how this works at all.

'Shall we?' I say, pointing towards the water-avenue with its sculptured fountains. You look reluctant (and rather rudely at your watch, I must say) but you deign to accompany me.

I say, 'But surely you don't really think the Dragons – oh!' I cover my mouth. 'Oh, I'm *so* sorry. I forgot we aren't allowed to call them that any more. When you get to my age, you sometimes get a little set in your ways.'

I see your eyes narrowing, Bernice. Wondering perhaps how old I am, exactly.

Wouldn't you be surprised if you knew the truth.

'You were saying?' you ask coldly.

'Oh, so I was.' I'll forget my head one of these days. 'Do you really think the Draconians believe this nonsense about the nurturing of young, or whatever it is? It's propaganda, surely? They can't *just* be interested in the children's well-being – they so rarely do anything without an ulterior motive.'

You stare at me. 'They're all inscrutable, you mean? Devious? Full of reptile cunning? Can't trust the slithery devils an inch, and how could you anyway when they all look the same?'

Mildly, I say, 'Oh, it's a stereotype, I know. But there's some truth behind it, surely?'

You look disconcerted. 'Well, to some extent of course there is. But however convoluted their means are, there's always an end behind them. Even the most devious plan has to have a purpose. And I honestly believe, in this case, that Ambassador Kothar wants to give those children what he sees as a good upbringing. That's why all this is so awkward.'

I purse my lips. 'Because you want the same, dearie, of course.'

We're standing facing each other now, all thought of walking together forgotten, while the fountains play on either side of us.

'That's right,' you say. 'What's *actually* best is almost certainly some kind of compromise, but the trouble is finding one that's acceptable to all the relevant parties. Especially,' you add pointedly, 'when certain *other* parties are putting unfair pressure on them.'

You're talking, of course, about the Draconians' original offer. And how correct you are. If the Mim had accepted *that*, it wouldn't have served our purposes, or those of the Institute, at all.

'But what you want most of all,' I repeat calmly, 'is for all the little sponge-children to live and grow up and be healthy.' I drop my cigarette-end, and stamp it into the ground. 'Just like you want your own son, Peter, to stay healthy, I suppose.'

Your face goes rigid. 'What the hell's that supposed to mean?'

'Oh, nothing,' I say placidly. 'Just thinking ahead. Aloud, I mean. You'll just have to ignore me.'

Coldly, you say, 'And you'll have to excuse me, Ms Haddad. I've got an appointment to go to.'

You turn and stride away along the avenue of fountains, leaving me looking thoughtfully after you. I light a new cigarette, and flame sparks briefly among the splashing waters.

Those kids need parents, you see, Benny, *just* like your little Peterkins. Maternal Mim, not Dragon foster-fathers. The sooner you learn to understand that, the better for us all.

Mwshi

It is a human space, like all the spaces here. Right angles, rigid walls, floor ruthlessly levelled. Volume mapped out as area, an entire dimension overlooked. These architects and builders long ago forgot their vanished freedom to move down, up, sideways through the ocean's vortices and vertices.

It is land-mammals' territory, penned with walls, circumscribed with alphabets. Scent-marked with alcoholic musk from yapping primates and their allies, emptying toxic slicks into their gullets.

The pub is Bernice Summerfield's native habitat, and her best attempt at meeting me on 'neutral territory'. Even the friendliest of humans are self-involved, short-sighted and parochial. And yet, in many ways, still preferable to what remains of Mimkind.

I enter this space in my natural form. Tubular, upright, self-contained, without unnecessary excrescences. My footbase slides easily across flat stone. A length or two inside, the pressure of these bipeds' expectations begins to oppress me. I draw the centre of my footbase upward. Cease sliding, begin shuffling. Another length, and I am walking – swinging and flexing my nether pseudopodia, twin support structures. A most precarious, unstable means of locomotion.

I split my upper slopes into three further forms. The central spherical, the outer pair longer, paddled and flexible.

I reach the nook which is Bernice's temporary territory, staked out with mammalian custom and body-language. I have become her shape. I am no diplomat-assassin, painstakingly counterfeiting textures and crenellations. Yet my featureless, pitted silhouette approximates a human's.

I form a cavity within my uppermost ovoid, and suck in air. Expel it, forming primate hoots and yowls.

'I know,' I say. 'I'm told no one's come up with a decent punchline yet. Can I get you a drink, Bernice?'

'Their offer of a compromise was an enormous concession, you know,' Bernice reminds me.

She holds a glass of Admiral's Refuge, a dark and soupy beer. Its hoppy fumes blare at me, a sharper voice across the pub-wide scent-notes of smoke, damp wood and sweaty mammal. She says, 'The other members of your delegation can't seem to see that. You've got to help them understand, Mwshi, or these talks are going to fall apart around our ears.'

Our ears? I consider approximating and raising an eyebrow, but it would be overly theatrical.

Learning to form my own tympanic membranes took me many months. Now they vibrate to a second, equally vivid sensory clamour. The social-bonding chatter of the humans. Beer washing over glass, glass impacting wood. The synthesised tones resonating from the juke-pod.

'The Draconians have nothing *to* concede,' I say. 'Except what they've stolen from us.'

'In your eyes, no.'

Bernice's voice is kind. I worked among vocal cultures for many years before I learned the trick of discerning. Still longer before I could reproduce it in my own speech.

'From their point of view – well, you've heard their arguments. They see the children as foundlings. They're trying to protect them.'

Is this what she truly believes? It is so hard to tell.

This constant contending with another mode of communication. The air and seas of the Mimsphere were awash with olfactory caresses. An ocean of argument and hypothesis, insult and endearment, poetry and myth.

Never again, now.

'I wouldn't look to a race of genocides for advice on right behaviour,' I say.

She sighs. 'That still hasn't been proven, Mwshi. So far nobody knows whether what happened on the Mimsphere was deliberate, or some terrible –'

I say, 'If not genocide, then culturicide. Holding our young, teaching them Draconian traditions, compounds the two crimes. The borogoves on Holiday Home are Mimkind's future. The Draconians aren't going to steal that from us.'

'Mwshi…' she says. 'We're talking about what's achievable. In an ideal world, of course you'd get your children back. In an ideal world your species wouldn't be nearly extinct.'

I am surprised to feel myself becoming angry. Since my world died, I have felt almost nothing.

Anger will not help me here, however.

'You asked me,' I remind her, 'about the Mim you met here and on Montavadros.' I speak the name in authentic Draconian, a sudden reptilian sibilance between my simulated lips.

She glances briefly at her watch. 'Korenthai,' she says. 'That was the name he took at first.'

'I know his history,' I inform her. 'Or I can guess at it.'

'Really?' she says. I have successfully diverted her attention.

Across the pub, a troop of young humans sends up a raucous cry. One of them has prevailed in a dominance ritual, a boastful display of eyesight and coordination. The other students standing around the dartboard slap his back in acclamation.

'Mim culture isn't monolithic,' I tell her. 'We split and factionalise and reform.'

'That's true of every sentient species,' she says. 'Dissident cults like Phwmi's are a constant feature of spacegoing cultures.'

Bernice does not wish me to forget Phwmi. She knows the tribunal could hand the borogoves over to him and his smug disciples, a punishment for our stubbornness. Braxiatel has hinted as much.

They would be taught falsehoods about our past. Our heroes were war criminals, they say, our explorers exploiters. We invited our own extinction with our warmongering ways.

Braxiatel thinks this 'might be considered an acceptable compromise'.

Privately, I do not forget Phwmi for an instant. However, I continue: 'There was another schism, though. Generations ago now.'

'The Tentative Diaspora.' Bernice nods her head. 'It followed on from your fourth phase of land colonisation. One faction wanted to go further and explore space, the other stayed at home. It was all resolved fairly amicably, though, as I recall. The explorers disovered that the Draconians were entering their own expansionist phase, and warned the stay-at-homes. Everyone withdrew to the Mimsphere and a few colony worlds, and hoped the next-door-neighbours wouldn't notice them.' Having displayed her erudition, she takes another mouthful of her beer.

I tell her, 'There was a faction who dissented still.'

Her face crinkles. 'A third faction? I never heard that.'

'We don't like to discuss them. Especially now.'

I have her attention. 'What did they do?'

'They trained their children in the necessary skills, then sent them to live with the Draconians.'

'As immigrants? I've never heard about a Mim community –' Bernice stops. 'Ah.'

'Not as immigrants,' I say. 'As native subjects of the Empire.'

The noise of the pub quietens momentarily, alarming me. A solitary voice bemoans a recent sexual encounter, breaking off abruptly before the ambient conversation resumes. Merely a random lull, I realise. I wonder whether such events are a subconscious function of humanity's gregariousness.

Bernice's voice is quiet but shrill. 'You're telling me a faction of Mim *infiltrated* the Draconians, centuries ago?'

'Their descendants live in the Empire still,' I tell her. 'The Draconians are unaware of them. Korenthai must have been terrified of discovery.'

'How could this have been kept quiet?' she wonders. 'This is incredible.'

'I said we don't like to discuss them. Especially since the war.'

'The war? What happened –' She stops again. 'Oh, my goodness. You mean they fought for the Draconians?'

'I can't be certain of that,' I admit. 'But they most certainly didn't help the Mim. They could have hampered the Draconian war effort from within. No such assistance was forthcoming.'

She covers her mouth with a hand. 'Mwshi, there's something I need to tell you. About Korenthai, and about Proxima Longissima.' Then she looks down at her watch. 'It'll have to wait, though. Bugger.'

'Do you have another appointment?' I ask.

'Er, sort of, yes.' She leans forward. 'Listen, Mwshi, you're a remarkable individual. Most Mim have had hardly any dealings with other species, let alone lived with them. But you've seen a lot of other cultures, and absorbed a lot of other points of view.'

I bob my upper pseudopodium in imitation of a nod. 'That's true, but –'

She interrupts. 'That makes you uniquely placed to help the two sides understand each other. I've spent some time with Kothar, and I know a little about how he thinks. If I can help you understand him too –'

'I'm not interested,' I say. 'Not in the motivations of butchers.'

'Listen.' She is speaking urgently now. 'Nobody disputes that if the Draconians return those children to you, thousands of them will die. To you that's just a part of growing up. To a Draconian it's child abuse. Most humans have trouble with it too, to be honest – and don't forget they're my godchildren as well. I understand how, for the Draconians, this is a genuine matter of conscience.'

'Conscience?' My technique for infusing emotion into my human voice is still imperfect. I wish I were more practised in conveying contempt.

She sighs. 'Yes, Mwshi, conscience. And if you carry on refusing to accept that, your wilful blindness will mean this whole negotiation process collapses messily. And I don't want that on *your* conscience.'

There is something else occupying her attention. I remember to follow her line of sight.

Somebody has just entered the pub, and is approaching our nook. A tall, robed biped, steeple-crested. I fight back the urge to form flails, talons, blades, fighting stings.

'Give him a chance, Mwshi,' Bernice whispers urgently. 'Just listen to what he has to say. That's all I ask.'

'Ambassador Kothar,' I say. 'What a surprise.'

Kothar

'Dr Mwshi,' I acknowledge curtly. This not being a formal occasion, I do not feel under any obligation to bow. Neither Summerfield nor the Mim would understand or appreciate the gesture. Summerfield's alcove contains a wooden table flanked by benches, on which she and Mwshi, his shape a flat-headed approximation of the draconoid form, sit opposite one another.

This is another ploy of Summerfield's to place me in an awkward position. I cannot seat myself opposite Mwshi without appearing to ally myself with Summerfield, who I know will undermine me given any opportunity. Yet sitting next to the Mim is out of the question.

There was a time when I might have considered Summerfield an ally, it is true. No more. In the long weeks of these interminable tribunal sessions, she has made it perfectly clear where her sympathies lie.

I continue to stand. It was already obvious that this location had been chosen in an effort to disconcert me. Taverns are places of alcoholic intoxication, hence of unguarded behaviour: raucous conversations, bold sexual approaches and brawling are the accepted norm. Such establishments are backrooms for bribery and conniving, not the halls of honourable diplomacy.

Eventually Summerfield says, 'Oh, for Heaven's sake,' and moves to sit by Mwshi. 'Happy now?'

The point having been made and conceded (although, for a moment, I find myself unsure by whom), I sit. Around us, the humans' culture of excess betrays itself in sounds of alcoholic disinhibition. 'I fail to see the purpose of this exercise, Professor Summerfield,' I say. 'My government has already made a very generous offer to the Mim, which they've seen fit to refuse.'

'You came anyway,' she replies.

'Politeness, nothing more. Even if Dr Mwshi were to reconsider my offer, it's most doubtful that my government would be willing to renew it. The refusal was a grave diplomatic insult in itself.'

Summerfield clicks her tongue. 'Your feelings must have been devastated.'

'Your sarcasm is hardly constructive, Professor.'

'Amazingly, you're the first person I've *ever* met who's told me that.'

The barmaid, crop-haired in conformity with some ridiculous human fashion, attempts to remove Summerfield's all-but-empty glass, and is waved indignantly away.

Mwshi asks, 'Bernice, is this really what you asked Ambassador Kothar here for?'

Accepting her ally's rebuke, Summerfield calms herself. 'Kothar,' she says. 'We all know that the Draconian Empire's in a quandary. Whether or not you were responsible for what happened on the Mimsphere – no, let me finish – it's been embarrassing for you. It looks bad when the people you've been fighting end up genocidally exterminated by persons unknown. Some of your own savants have grave doubts about the honour of Draconia's recent actions.'

I glare at her, unwilling, particularly in the presence of a Mim, to confirm anything she says. I am aware that Summerfield has contacts at the Imperial Court: there are, indeed, perplexing rumours that she has met, and even conversed with, the Emperor himself. Whether she has authentic information from such sources, I have no way of telling. She is quite capable of bluffing.

She continues, 'PL was just the publicity coup you needed. It's the one thing that's come out of this war – I'm sorry, this *conflict* – where every Draconian can agree on the right thing to do. If you hand those children back to the Mim now, you'll be betraying everything you've retrospectively decided your soldiers were fighting for.'

'So what's the point of us being here?' the Mim asks her.

The creature makes me uncomfortable, like all his kind. I cannot read his body language, as I have learned to read those of the humans'. Perhaps he has none to read. I cannot even tell when he is looking at me.

'Well,' Summerfield continues, 'there's just one snag. The Draconians' preferred solution is strictly short-term. Kothar's people may want to protect this generation of Mim, but they're not keen on seeing their grandchildren inherit a Draconian Star Empire whose Mim subjects outnumber the Draconians by billions to one.'

'We aren't blind to the obvious,' I tell her. 'Population growth is exponential, yes. That's elementary statistics. We're now aware that it happens rather faster among the Mim.'

She nods. 'Exactly. For now you need the borogoves for propaganda purposes – but once they're grown up you'll need them off your hands, sharpish.'

'There's some validity in what you say,' I admit. 'However –'

'Of course there is.' Summerfield drains the last of her intoxicant. 'Which is why your government's going to renew its offer, Kothar. Joint custody, with Draconia providing the resources and the Mim educating the children. Then in a few decades' time, once everyone else has forgotten all about this, the Emperor quietly cedes PL back to its rightful owners and everybody's happy.'

She stands, glass in hand. 'So, can I get you boys anything while you shake on it?'

I hiss at her. 'Your impudence is matched only by your effrontery.'

'Quite right,' says Mwshi. 'You can't expect us to accept your terms just like that.'

Summerfield sinks back down onto the bench. The barmaid, reappearing suddenly, takes the opportunity to relieve her of the glass. 'Well, at least you can agree on something. Although aren't impudence and effrontery the same thing?'

I inhale carefully. 'If…' I say, then pause. '*If*, Professor Summerfield, I take it upon myself to renew my government's offer… it must *not* be refused a second time.' I hold her gaze. 'If that should happen, my hands will be tied. There are families at court whose feelings on this matter are far stronger than mine. They won't suffer a second insult.'

'There are Draconians on the tribunal who feel the same way,' she reminds me. 'Like Deputy Ambassador Werther. He's your handler, isn't he? The Imperial Court knows your reputation. Werther's here to keep you on the straight and narrow. Stop you going native.'

I bite back my anger. 'I don't accept your description, but...'

She smirks. 'But there's validity in what I say?'

'Werther is an example of the more uncompromising approach, yes. His associates have suggested a solution to the problem of Mim population growth which I don't think any of us would wish to see implemented.' I am pleased to see Summerfield shudder.

'Mwshi?' she says. 'Ambassador Kothar is demonstrating his political adaptability. No offence, but it would seem rather ironic if you were the inflexible one here.'

The Mim speaks, slowly. 'I understand your argument. Make no mistake, Bernice, I support my delegation's position to the full. Yet I understand that our intransigence may be unhelpful, and could easily become counterproductive.'

Summerfield beams. 'So we're agreed? In principle, at least,' she adds quickly.

'Well...' I say.

'Excuse me,' says a voice to my left. 'I couldn't help overhearing.' The voice is human: a female of middle years. Summerfield's face takes on an expression of alarm, a reaction upstaged by that of the Mim. His draconoid form loses cohesion as he recoils, sucking in his pretended head and limbs to press back and fill the corner between bench and wall.

'Ms Haddad,' I hazard, turning. 'My compliments. Is this another of your surprises, Professor Summerfield?'

'Arsing buggery bollocks is it,' Summerfield mutters.

The Earth diplomat regards us over her absurd reflective spectacles, smiling, a cigarette in her hand. The tavern's muted lighting renders her formal costume's blacks and whites in murky grey. 'This *is* nice,' Haddad says. 'Move over, Ambassador. What have you three been talking about, then?'

She seats herself beside me, forcing me sideways with a plump human buttock. I wave away sweet-smelling smoke, hissing with indignation. 'This female has no official status!' I know full well that Haddad and her associate Mr Szmyt are not diplomats, observing the proceedings on behalf of Earth's increasingly xenophobic civilian government. I remember too well the way human soldiers think, act and comport themselves.

The agent affects bemusement. 'Now, why would I need official status, Ambassador? This is just a pub. And I promise I'm over sixteen. Now, please don't let me interrupt. Wasn't somebody about to agree to something?'

From his position on the bench, Mwshi has trickled back into his previous, seated form as if into a mould. 'Ms Haddad,' he says, his voice perfectly composed. I imagine that his scent-signals are violently agitated, but neither the humans nor I could possibly detect them. 'This is indeed an honour. And this is, indeed, a pub. Bernice, Kothar and I were sharing a drink while off duty. Perhaps you'd care to join us?'

'That's right,' says Summerfield at once. 'Just because we have political differences, doesn't mean we can't all share a... actually, I was just about to get another round in, wasn't I?' she adds, as Haddad turns her placid gaze towards the empty table. 'What'll you have, Ms Haddad?'

'Me, dearie?' Haddad says. 'Well, that beer you were drinking looked very nice.'

'Kothar?' Summerfield stares expectantly at me.

It is quite evident that our discussion is at an end. If Mwshi were about to reconsider my offer, Haddad's presence has terrified him out of taking any such step. I have been wasting my time here. The only question remaining is how long politeness will oblige me to feign social intercourse with two human females and a Mim.

'That's very kind of you, Professor,' I force myself to say. I struggle to recall the name of an appropriate beverage. 'I'll have some... some scotch.'

I wonder how insulted Summerfield will feel, to be buying me a drink she knows I will disdain to touch. Very, I hope.

'Mwshi?'

'Just a glass of sea water, please Bernice,' the Mim chirps brightly.

This whole situation has turned into a fourth-dynasty diplomatic farce, but provided I compose myself and act with dignity, I ought to emerge from it with some shreds of my political credibility intact.

'So then, that's two pints of Refuge, one sea-water and a whisky for the Ambassador,' says Summerfield, as she turns and collides with Deputy Ambassador Werther.

2

Ithva

'... and it all disintegrated from there, really,' you inform me. 'Werther accused your husband of being compromised by the enemy, Kothar claimed he'd been lured there under false pretences and would be registering all the official complaints he had the paper clips for, Haddad made obscure threats in a pleasant tone of voice, and we all went our separate ways.'

I give you a sympathetic smile as I pour the tea. 'Well, dear, at least you tried.'

You grimace. 'It has to be the most inept clandestine meeting I've ever organised.'

My smile becomes conspiratorial. 'Well, I certainly wish I could have been there.'

'I'm surprised you weren't,' you admit ruefully.

As it happens, I've already viewed the eyecam footage taken by the barmaid – Antasha, an art student and one of the more promising members of the modest little local spy ring I've built up since arriving here. But I feel you can probably do without that sort of friendly candour just at present.

I must admit I've been more guarded with you, my dear Bernice, since we returned from Montavadros. Whatever may have passed

211

between us there, here on the Collection there are appearances which must be maintained.

You arrived in my reception chambers a short while ago, just as my book group were leaving. I hadn't seen you since the Proxima Longissima Disaster Relief Fund coffee morning.

The ladies and I meet once a week – they're mostly the non-professional wives of the male academics, although they're thin on the ground here. I'd made little *shenklut* – traditional Draconian hot berry tarts – with blackberries from the Collection's nurseries. Hass and I have come to an arrangement. He's a charming fellow for a gaseous life form, although once you get talking to him you just can't get away.

I invited you out of politeness, my dear, not seriously expecting you to turn up. Not even, typically of you, an hour and a half late. 'I'm so sorry,' you said when you arrived, I suppose for the benefit of the others. 'I meant to get here earlier. Jason promised to pick up Peter from school, and then forgot. We've been having… repercussions.'

'My dear, how tiresome for you,' I commiserated. 'And what a shame you missed out on us all reading out our favourite passages – it was such fun. I'm afraid Ms Blackbrane was very naughty and brought along a bottle of Chablis, so we've all been rather merry.'

I hadn't partaken myself, of course. What dear Jarith doesn't know can't hurt him, but not everyone here can be trusted to keep that kind of detail to themselves. Today of all days, it would have been tactless.

I hurried the others out, guessing correctly that you hadn't come here to discuss *The Seneschal's Daughter* by Rajeth Kartar. I called for tea, and we sat down to have a little talk about our progress – or otherwise – in our recent endeavours.

'So it looks like I've blown my last chance with your husband,' you tell me now. 'And nobody's going to move an inch unless we can get them talking outside the tribunal proper. Officially stuff's happening in the meetings, but it's all fannying around with agenda items and seating protocols. I've a feeling Brax is stalling them until he works out what to do. Or until I do, which would be worse. You know, I almost wish we could have the old sneaky Brax back, and could wake up tomorrow morning to find all this sorted out.'

'Jarith's done his best, poor dear,' I say, adding milk and sugar to your tea. We're using the nineteenth-century Russian porcelain, a gift from the President of Earth during our time there. President Guthrie was a most hospitable and charming woman – quite unlike the present incumbent, if you'll forgive my saying so. 'But after that scene today, his honour's in question. He needs to reassert it with something much more uncompromising. And not just for his own satisfaction, you understand – Werther and his cronies at court will be paying very close attention to whatever he does next. Biscuit, Bernice?'

You take one and dunk it in your tea. I pour my own, adding a slice of lemon.

'Okay,' you say. 'But Kothar – Jarith – knows that sort of solution's good for the short term at best. He very nearly admitted as much.'

'Of course,' I say, 'but the short term's precisely where he's vulnerable. You can always brush long-term consequences under the table with macho rhetoric. It's one of the Fifteen Noble Skills.'

You give a half-smile, unsure whether I'm joking. Poor Benny, a sense of humour really isn't your strong point, is it?

Sharintha trots in, carrying her new pet. She kisses me, then shows you the animal. 'His name's Ixiss,' she tells you excitedly. 'He's called a shield-lizard, because his skin's all armoured, look. Daddy bought him for me. When he grows up he'll be five *xithia* long! Ixiss I mean, not Daddy.' She giggles. 'Daddy's already grown up.

How Jarith dotes on that child. I interrupt her gently. 'We're having a grown-up conversation now, dear, as it happens,' I tell her. 'You and Ixiss can stay as long as you're both quiet.' She nods obediently, then chases the lizard over to the fireplace, giggling again.

You smile after her, then sigh as you recall where we'd got to. 'So what would an acceptably macho proposition look like, at this stage?' you ask.

'Well,' I say. 'By rights, when the Mim children come of age – very soon, in some cases – they become attached to the Emperor's household. He'll have done his duty by them, and in return they should become his bondsmen for life. Just *what* he thinks he's going to use millions of Mim servants for, I can't imagine. They've no self-discipline, they don't understand etiquette, and if some of them do go rogue, they'll be the very devil to contain or neutralise.'

You have a charming frown. 'So why hang on to them at all?'

'My dear, you know full well why. But if I know Jarith, his next step will be to suggest that when each of the young Mim comes of age the Emperor grants them the Grace of Emancipation. Sharintha, *not* with the fire-tongs, please.'

'I've read about that.' You frown again. 'Isn't it basically a euphemism for exile?'

Well, dear, you've invited the lecture. 'It does entail banishment, of course. You can't have people hanging round the Empire who aren't subject to the Throne. But it's also the highest honour the Emperor can confer – some say tantamount to recognising the recipient as an equal.'

You smile sardonically. 'Which is ridiculous, of course.' You humans are such believers in equality.

I say, 'It's usually reserved for subjects who've rendered a great service to the Emperor, but have committed a grave crime in the process. Most often they've had to lay hands on him in order to save his life. It would look bad to put them to death, so he puts them outside the law instead. Then he puts them on the fastest ship out of Imperial space, and prays they never come back.'

I heft the teapot and offer you more tea.

'All right,' you agree, handing me your cup. 'Let's say the Emperor grants this signal honour to the Mim as they come of age, waiving all his rights over them. That's an act of great generosity on his part. And generosity to a defeated enemy does them a grave *dishonour*, isn't that right? That should keep Werther and chums happy – it looks magnanimous, but actually it's adding insult to injury.'

'The injury is an imagined one,' I remind you, rather sharply. 'But otherwise that's right, not that the Mim will know or care. The nobles will be happy, as you say. The Emperor will be happy, I should think, not to be saddled with a horde of shapeshifting alien servants who secretly want him dead. And the children themselves will survive to experience the best of both worlds. Everybody wins.'

Accepting your teacup back, you shake your head. 'The best of both worlds? Mim children imitate their surroundings, Ithva. It's an instinct. Those children will grown up *Draconian*. Mim culture will be a quaint thing their ancestors did, an exotic subject for documentaries and school projects. Lwpha would have resisted that with his life. For all we know, he did.'

'Ah, yes,' I say. 'About that, Benny...'

'So, will Mwshi and Sherm and Phwmi.' You meet my gaze. 'So will I, Ithva.'

I sigh. 'Yes, dear, I know. But if the Mim won't play nicely after all that, what can we do? Personally I'm with you up to a point – the children do deserve some contact with their parents' culture. But it's outside my control. The Empire's taking charge of the children, and how the Mim deal with that is up to them. The Empress is happy for them to be involved if they so choose, but this stonewalling is getting on everybody's nerves.'

All of which is true. What I'm not telling you is that I've tried and failed to get the Mim negotiators on side myself. With no women, and no men either, they don't respond well to the kind of leverage I excel in exerting. Nor do they have much tolerance at present for us Draconians poking our scaly snouts into their business.

The chambermaid enters to clear away the tea things. Idly I indicate *The Seneschal's Daughter*, and ask you, 'Have you ever read this, my dear?'

You look confused for a moment. 'I don't think I've read any Draconian literature after about the fifth dynasty. Any good?'

'Oh, yes, it's marvellous,' I say. 'It's all about an official on a colony world of the First Star Empire, who adopts an orphan from the native population and brings her up as his own. It's dreadfully historically inaccurate, of course, and very sentimental, but the men don't mind that, do they?'

'It's written for men?' You sound intrigued now.

'Oh, yes – the father-daughter relationship, you see. Very appealing to their protective instincts. It's been popular in the Empire since our responsibilities on Proxima Longissima were made public. The Empress herself has been seen reading it.'

I know you'll pick out the significance of that. I believe Rajeth Kartar's publishers were most upset by the pressure to rush out the reprint.

The maid departs, nearly tripping over the shield-lizard. You frown after her. 'Domestic trouble?'

'Hopefully not,' I say. 'But after Salthmanika, one can't be too careful. And before you ask, I'm afraid we've made no progress on that front either. Whoever that Mim was originally, they were very adept at covering their tracks.'

You say, 'I had some AI research routines looking into it – Korenthai and his background, mainly – but they seem to have gone quiet. Probably immolated by your Imperial firewalls. You've no idea, then, when he might have been replaced by a Mim?'

Your tone of voice seems overly casual, somehow. My dear, what are you trying to hide?

'Nothing at all,' I say. 'Why, Benny, what about you?'

'I've got a possible lead,' you admit reluctantly, 'I'm just not sure how reliable it is. It's from someone I thought I could trust, but I have to admit it sounds pretty unlikely. I'd like to look into it some more before I share it, if that's okay.'

'Of course. But if you're going to be so coy, I don't see why I should tell you what I've found out about Lwpha's murder. I'm *joking*, Benny,' I add as you look outraged. 'Of course I understand. And I know you'll want to see this. It's progress of a sort, although I don't think you'll like it.'

I stand, and cross to the great gilded mirror over the fireplace.

'Any progress feels hopeful at the moment,' you say. 'It's like we've all been stuck in the same attitudes for eternity, like mammoths in a tar-pit.'

'Quite,' I say.

In this particular regard, what you mean is that, while certain people have been insisting all along that Lwpha was bumped off by poor Pashar, we suspect the same person did away with them both. At first I thought that person was the late impostor Korenthai, but now I'm not so sure.

We've had so little information. We knew Lwpha had been killed with some special weapon, quite possibly designed expressly for use on Mim. I've tried to find out whether it was one of ours, but you know how protective men can be about their weapons.

We've talked through the killer's choice of location. The equipment in Hass's compost-shed could have been used to dispose of a body – but Lwpha's remains, such as they were, were there for all to see. Was the murderer interrupted? Did they not realise how catastrophic the weapon's effect on the victim would be?

As for who they were... well, nobody imagines this was some random psychopath. This crime, under these circumstances, can only have been political. Which means we're looking for a member of the Reparations Tribunal, or their support staff – or one of the interested non-participants, in other words the Earth delegation, Szmyt and Haddad. Apart from Korenthai, who's dead now, and Pashar, who hasn't been seen since that night, all of our likely suspects are still here on the Collection.

That's all we *have* known, until recently. I say, 'Sharintha, darling, could you move over by the chaise longue, please?'

The engineers have done a truly splendid job of integrating our technology with the Louis Quinze furnishings here in the Embassy. I take a statuette from the mantel and twist its head. The mirror shimmers and becomes a screen, showing a low-resolution night-time image of the compost-shed.

'I've managed,' I say, 'and you really don't want to know how, to access the garden maintenance robots' memory logs for the night in question.'

'There are garden maintenance bots?'

I'm surprised that you seem surprised. 'Oh, yes – they're basically just modified porters. They flit about at night, picking up litter and so on. Hass prefers to keep them out of people's way.'

Dear Hass. He's been helpful in so many ways.

'Two of them spent some time near the outbuilding,' I explain. 'Not continuously, but enough to make some interesting observations. This is a reconstruction, with the point of view stabilised and the image enhanced. Now then...'

I manipulate the figurine's limbs, flickering at high speed through the footage until it shows Lwpha approaching the building.

I slow the speed to normal. The Mim is walking briskly like a biped, though his torso is barrel-shaped, lacking arms or a head.

'Is that Lwpha?' you ask.

'Well, we can't be certain, of course,' I concede. 'But it's a Mim – obviously – and it's going into the outbuilding where Lwpha died.' In the mirror the Mim closes the door behind him.

'I'm guessing there's more,' you say.

'Of course.' I flicker onward until the screen goes grey. 'First there's a gap, for some reason. Corruption in the files. But shortly afterwards...' I skim ahead, through footage of the building standing undisturbed. Eventually a Draconian strides into view, dressed in the *hronsthei* of a Junior Consular Officer.

'Aha – so Pashar *was* there!' you exclaim.

I summon up a zoom. The young man's face is thin, his beard straggly. 'It looks a lot like it, I'm afraid. But my dear, watch.'

In the mirror, Pashar enters the shed. A short while later, there is a bright flash from inside. The shed stays still and silent for some time afterwards, until a figure suddenly emerges and you say, 'Shit.

'I mean bother,' you add, glancing at Sharintha. Fortunately the child's absorbed in a world of her own, trying to persuade Ixiss to attack a cushion.

'Well, quite,' I agree.

You stare at the screen. 'Tell me that's not Ms Haddad.'

I zoom again. The agent's jowly face, complete with mirrored spectacles, looms large and grainy over the mantel.

You groan. 'That utter... she was in there with them, then. With Pashar definitely, very probably with Lwpha too.'

'Well, yes.'

'Do either of the others come out?'

'Ah,' I reply as the screen goes grey. 'There our information is incomplete once again. The robot drifted off to rake some leaves, and it was an hour before another one happened along. There are no more sightings of anyone before dawn.'

You're silent for some time. 'It's not conclusive,' you say at length. 'Pashar could still have been alive, and left during that gap.'

'Perhaps,' I agree. 'Or the Mim could have left during the gap, and Lwpha and his murderer may have come along later. Indeed, given that the Mim delegation still includes some proficient shapeshifters, it's possible that none of the participants are who they seem. But you can see how this looks, Benny.'

'But where's Pashar's body?'

'Composted,' I tell you with distaste, 'along with all the waiting garden waste. Distributed by matter-transmitter to half a metre's depth across the area of the gardens. That would be –'

You groan. 'The flash. Play it again.'

I do.

You're wondering, I know, whether you can believe what I've shown you. Whether I've faked this evidence to bring you round to my point of view. If I were faking it, of course, you'd expect me to have created something more definitive – unless I thought that would look suspicious in itself.

You know your mind's not capable of following mine round enough corners to be sure.

'Hell,' you say finally. 'If Haddad killed them *both*, it would almost be better to hush the whole thing up. Accuse an Earth observer of murdering Mim and Draconian diplomats, and we won't just be kissing goodbye to any agreement here.' You look away from me, momentarily embarrassed. 'We'll have a full-scale interstellar war on our hands. Again,' you conclude bitterly.

'This is the difficulty,' I agree.

You begin to rant. 'Brilliant. That's just bloody typical. Get humans and Draconians together, and what do we do? Start killing each other, that's what. Plus anyone else who happens to be passing.'

'It's not quite as bad as that, Benny. As you say, this isn't conclusive. We need a lot more evidence before we start accusing anybody of anything.'

'Sure. I'll get right on it. Just as soon as I've finished bringing two diametrically opposed points of view together in peace and harmony.'

You lean your head into your hands.

'Oh –' you add, looking up. 'There's something else I need to ask you. Have you ever heard of something called "Project Narcissus"?'

'Narcissus?' I repeat, trying to remember my human mythology.

'It was the name of a beautiful, vain young man who spurned a nymph and was cursed by a goddess. He fell in love with his own reflection and pined away until he died. The gods turned him into a flower so his beauty would be immortalised forever. It's a story about... oh, echoes and reflections, permanence and change, that sort of thing. Plus being careful what you turn into.'

'I haven't heard the name applied to any project,' I tell you truthfully. 'Perhaps if I knew a little about what it was?'

'Well, now you're asking,' you say. 'I only came across the name today. Well, Jason did actually. Since we're talking about interplanetary wars, though... as far as I can make out, Narcissus was a military research project during the last war.

'Well,' you add, 'not *the* last war, obviously. The last big one, the one my dad fought in. Where your people and mine were allies.'

Your mouth curls with revulsion as you say the name. 'The war against the Daleks.'

3

Jason

I absolutely should have remembered to pick Peter up from school. That's so right. Can't argue with you there.

It's not that I forgot, exactly, I just got distracted. You would have too. No really, I guarantee.

Whatever, I was fine with helping Benny out like she'd asked. Granted, going through her email wasn't quite the kind of glamorous swashbuckling adventure-action I'd been hoping for more of after Montavadros, but what the hell. If it meant I could help out with everything that's on her plate right now, I was okay with it.

Apparently after we got back from there, Benny sent out a bunch of research AIs to dig out all the info she could on Korenthai and Salthmanika. Since then they've been trickling through the datascape, oozing into all the hidden nooks and crannies they can find, like rain on woodbark.

Or something. I'm shit with similes.

Benny's had no time to check up on their progress, so when offered to help her out at lunchtime, she set me going through all the messages they'd sent her.

Some of the AIs are specialists in Draconian information systems. They've burrowed their way into the Empire's memosphere, where they've either gone to ground or been torn apart by guard-dog programs. The rest are generalists, scouting current-affairs databases for the last few decades right across the sector. Looking for references to Mim cropping up anywhere they're not supposed to be.

When I saw the report about an anomalous Mim artefact turning up at some archaeological dig on Earth, I rolled my eyes. I thought Benny had customised one of her standard academic programs and forgotten to take out the specialist algorithms. Either that or the AI had inherited her obsessions, in a weird Frankenstein sort of arrangement. Either way it wasn't the kind of information we were after.

But then I clocked where these ruins were, and I started laughing. I'd been there a couple of times as a kid back in the twentieth century. I remembered sitting in the special train, gazing slack-jawed at the fantastical constructions all around me. The brightly coloured houses and boats and cars, all garish blues, yellows and reds.

The archaeologists reckon it's some kind of ceremonial site. Which according to Benny is what archaeologists always say when they haven't a clue what something's for.

Then I noticed what the AI had highlighted, and what was engraved on that extraneous Mim object. Scratched on its surface, so shallow that the archaeologists had to use special light to see them, were strings of Roman-Arabic alphanumerics which even I could see looked quite a lot like twenty-sixth century military codes. Like Benny's dad might have used, say, before he got thrown back in time to the 1980s.

And *then* I remembered where Isaac's bookshop-café-cum-alien-sanctuary had been, and when that ancient ceremonial site was first built.

And that was when I started paying attention.

Mwshi

Within my rooms at the Collection, I am buffered against rigidity.

My reception chamber is tall, filled to three Mim-depths with sea water. Vents circulate it and the salt air ceaselessly.

Brine-lapped outcroppings and slow drifts of sand, masking the rectilinear walls and floor. Small animals and plants, drifting in and out through invisible portals.

The private rooms, rock-caverns chambering out beneath the waterline.

It is a generous, inventive effort. Yet still no home to me, a freedom circumscribed within an unforgiving cube.

'I'm sorry about earlier,' Bernice tells me. She is positioned on a promontory of porous rock. Behind her, a doorway, incongruous, like those in the Mimsphere's landbound cities. Outside, unseen, the cuboid corridors of mammal space.

'It wasn't fair of me to spring Kothar on you like that.' Synthetic sea-breeze agitates her hair. 'But honestly, I couldn't see how else I was going to get you talking to each other.'

Idly she removes her feet. No, of course I mean her shoes. She dabbles her toes in the simulated sea.

Organs of vocal speech aside, I am in my natural form. I bask nearby, half in, half out of the artificial ocean.

These waves taste bland, sterile, meaningless. These waters do not speak to me.

'I should apologise as well,' I say. 'I had no idea Ms Haddad was there, or that she would intervene.'

'I know,' Bernice says quietly. 'I think she may have followed me.'

I recall Haddad's arrival in the pub. Atop her smoky human scent, she smelt of Mim, an indefinable, generic personal odour. She had been with other Mim shortly before arriving.

I slide a little further down into the swell. 'It hasn't been easy for any of us,' I admit. 'Draconian culture has always been steeped in xenophobic arrogance. And pride in our own dignity is all my people have left.'

She says, 'Ms Haddad doesn't seem too keen on letting you keep it.'

Inevitable, though awkward, that she wants to discuss Haddad and Szmyt further.

'I wish we weren't reliant on their goodwill,' I admit. 'It's indispensable, unfortunately.'

'Really?' she asks.

'Look at us, Bernice. My species' remnants are a ragtag rabble. Refugees, émigrés, cultists, fluke survivors... only the criminals among us have money or resources to our names. Without the backing of a major power, how partial and diluted our influence would be. The Draconians wouldn't even be facing us across a table.'

'You don't like it, though,' she observes.

'Of course I don't.' I shudder, sending ripples over her ankles. 'They tell us what we can and cannot say. What our negotiating position must be. We are the current carrying their words to the Draconians, no more than that.'

'I hadn't realised it was that bad.' Bernice is hesitant. 'You're more alike than you think, you know – you and the Draconians. Jarith Kothar's a political chameleon, and his wife can turn her personality on a dime. It's just a bit less metaphorical with you lot.'

I let the silence extend itself. A shoal of tiny shallowsnaps flicks past my body and is gone. Bernice withdraws her feet abruptly from the water.

She says, 'Szmyt and Haddad seem to listen to Sherm, though.'

I shift uneasily. 'Sherm asked them to come here in the first place.'

'You don't like Sherm either.'

Bernice is perceptive. I certainly had not infused my voice with that particular emotion.

'I don't like gangsters, no,' I admit. 'And I don't like laissez-faire extremists.'

She remembers. 'Sherm thinks it's good you won't be able to look after the borogoves properly, doesn't he? He believes that deprivation always benefits the next generation, even if it kills them.'

'Indeed. Between Phwmi and Sherm, I sometimes wonder whether we deserve our children back.'

'Me too.' She gives a look I cannot read.

I try to explain. I am so weary of giving form to the views of others.

'The value of our young to us is not like yours. We cherish them collectively. We feel about the process of attrition in our borogoves as you feel about your children growing up. You're not the same individual you were at your son's age. Yet all the qualities he will lose are balanced by those you've gained.'

'We like to hope so,' she says.

'The children who join us in adult life are the best, the cleverest, the strongest and most agile. We see that as a good. Yet extra hardship could kill half of those, or nearly all. That is a tragedy.'

'It's your equivalent of "spare the rod and spoil the child",' she muses. 'Mollycoddle them and the weak ones will survive. You know, Hass said almost exactly that when I talked to him about the borogoves – "Bernice, my parent abandoned me to be eaten by predators, and it never did me any harm." It sounds like you've a lot in common with the Yesodi too.'

Again she falls silent.

'So,' she says, 'Haddad hangs out with neo-fascist gangsters I wonder what habits she's been picking up.'

Again I do not speak. Eventually she asks, 'Were there birds on the Mimsphere?'

'Birds?'

She is staring up at the unreal ceiling, a hologram of livid yellow sky. A sky I have not seen for years, and never will again.

'No, none,' I say. 'Our native fauna never evolved flight. Only we Mim can fly unaided. And only after studying the anatomies of your extramimspherical flying creatures.'

'I don't remember any on Proxima,' she says. 'I didn't even notice. I haven't been to your quarters before.'

'I don't spend much time here,' I admit. 'I find the simulacrum morbid. Also very boring.'

'I sympathise,' she says. 'Fancy a drink?'

Now, after dark, the pub is fuller than before. Its conversational shrieks and bellows louder, its ape-colony musk almost unbearable.

It feels alive. If only I felt similarly.

There are more non-humans here now – Killorans, a Cahlian and others. I see neither Draconians nor Mim. We have no alcove this time, just a tiny pedestal table.

Bernice looks around. Sees that this thronging, mammal-hot crowd leaves little chance of being overheard.

She says, 'I know why Haddad and Szmyt are helping you.'

This time I have refused to reshape myself. I stand across the table from Bernice, a flexible tube, defiant in my deviance from prescribed anatomy.

I wish this conversation were not necessary.

'In politics,' I tell her, 'everything comes with a price. We've had to learn that since our near-extinction. Nobody helps another species out of sheer altruism.'

'That's a very cynical attitude,' Bernice says. She is drinking Admiral's Refuge again, a different barrel. The beer's odour is more ripe than earlier. 'But then I suppose you'd need to be pretty cynical, to agree to what you have.' She is angry, I realise.

I try to deflect her. 'What did you want to tell me this afternoon?'

Bernice ignores this. 'You've promised them some of the young, haven't you? If Szmyt and Haddad help you get them back, you'll hand a portion of them over. Commission in kind.'

'They're the only commodity we have,' I remind her.

'And you're prepared to *tithe* them?' she asks. 'Hand your children over as tribute, like client kings in a Greek myth? How can you *do* that?'

I essay a shrug. Without the formality of shoulders I suspect the gesture fails. 'They only want a few hundred of the youngest. Nearly all of them would die anyway. This way, our species and our culture can continue. It's a modest price to pay.'

'And you call Sherm a hardcore Darwinian.' She holds up a hand. 'No, I know – different biologies, different cultural norms. I had the talk from Lwpha.'

A sudden scuffle develops between two rival males, a human and the Cahlian. The nearest Killorans quickly intervene, breaking it up. I wonder whether they are security staff, and whether off duty or on.

'We have no choice,' I say. 'I've told you we are at Earth's mercy. Even after the negotiations, we'll be reliant on their aid donations. We'll be a client state, just as you said.'

'And do you think they'll stop at a few hundred? What do you suppose they need them for?

'I don't know,' I admit. 'For study, perhaps? Experimentation?'

'And why do you suppose they're so insistent that the Draconians leave you to your own devices on PL? How long do you think it'll be before Szmyt and Haddad, or whoever they represent, decide to move in and join you? Before they decide you need a helping hand to guide you, holding a bloody great gun?'

'Speak quietly, please, Bernice. You're attracting attention.'

She stares at me for quite some time, then sighs.

The lungful of air plays across my moist skin, wind against water.

'There are actually two things I need to tell you,' she says. 'The first is that I think Ms Haddad murdered Lwpha.'

I find myself entirely unsurprised. 'Go on,' I say.

'The other is that you were right about the Mim living in the Empire. They did fight with the Draconians against you, although I don't think the Draconians knew about it. It looks like it was Korenthai who gave the order for the phase-cannon attack on PL. I don't –'

I cannot help myself. I rear up violently, spreading my upper body like a sail. An instinctive expression of alarm.

'What is it?' she asks, wide-eyed.

My emotions roil and swirl, a turbulence of distress. Another Mim could taste my shock anywhere in the building. Bernice is just perplexed.

'I think *you* may be attracting attention now,' she says.

I do not know for sure that there are no Mim here. Any who are must be skilled mimics. Diplomats, assassins. With immense difficulty I suppress my alarm, sending out scents of calm relief.

I make my human voice sound cheerily abashed. 'Oops, sorry about that,' I say. 'Someone spilled cold beer on me. Gave me quite a shock.'

Bernice grimaces. 'I'll have to remember that next time one of you is trying to kill me.'

A false alarm, you see. Nothing to worry about here. Honestly.

'Another drink, Bernice?' I offer.

Kothar

The log-fire in my office dies back into smouldering embers as I read the report from Captain-Lord Khrestin on Proxima Longissima, the planet which has been causing us all such unconscionable trouble. Exquisitely calligraphed, bound in monitor-leather, its gold tooling glinting in the firelight, the document is a triumph of beauty over truth. Its naive, self-regarding pomposity reveals Khrestin as a wisp-bearded youth, his prestigious command bought for him by his grandfathers, no more skilled at the craft of military command than he is at that of shuttle maintenance.

Khrestin insists, believes perhaps, that his men are containing the insurrection on Proxima. Any reader with the slightest military insight will know better. If the Draconian Empire continues to occupy the planet, it will commit an unacceptable proportion of our efforts and resources for years to come.

The second dossier is even more disturbing. It comes from the Emperor's Keeper of the Blades of Honour, the Lord High Savant Ishzathe. This document is plainer, its cover-boards containing a bio-processor keyed to the pattern of scales on my palm. If any other being attempts to read it, the volume will spontaneously combust.

Ishzathe's thesis is typically long-winded. It prettifies with academic platitudes a stark, unsightly truth: if one teaches a young Mim the ways of honour, as the Emperor is obliged to educate the juveniles of Proxima, then that Mim will rebel or go insane.

The crux of the Lord High Savant's argument rests on the Seventh Blade of Honour, the Blade of Family. The Three Teeth of this Blade are Respect for Elders, Protection of Females and Nurturing of Children. After some irrelevant digressions concerning possible applications of the second of these to asexual individuals, Ishzathe turns his attention to the third.

The nurturing of young is a good to be pursued regardless of the cost to oneself or one's family, and one which (as under current circumstances we are all keenly aware) transcends even species loyalties. Unfortunately, the Mim's profligate reproductive biology means that each of them has far more offspring than he can possibly take responsibility for. A Mim brought up to honour the Seventh Blade will endeavour, and inevitably fail, to feed, protect and educate all his thousands of offspring, bankrupting himself and undergoing almost certain psychological disintegration in the process. Ishzathe devotes some pages, which I skip, to the secondary consequences of this.

The Lord High Savant sees three possible solutions to this dilemma facing the Emperor. Each of them is appalling in a unique and distinct way.

Firstly, Ishzathe suggests, the Emperor might decide that the young Mim should not be taught the Nine Blades at all, or should be taught amended versions suited to their biology. Although Ishzathe believes this to be the most rational solution, he understands that it will be quite unacceptable to the Imperial Court.

Secondly, the Emperor's Mim subjects might be prohibited from breeding. Contraception being irrelevant to a sexless species, this can only be achieved through mandatory chemical sterilisation: the policy already advocated by Werther and his allies. Though he concedes its practicality, the Keeper of the Blades argues that this would constitute a crime against the Mim and all their potential children.

Thirdly, Ishzathe suggests the Emperor reconsider the proposition, first advanced during the recent hostilities, that the Mim, while capable of mimicking the behaviour of sentient species, are not themselves intelligent. If this contentious hypothesis became Imperial edict, the Mim on Proxima would remain the Emperor's chattels in perpetuity, as would their children. The Blades of Honour would not apply to, or be incumbent upon, them or their offspring. The Emperor would not be required to extend to them the privileges of subjects, such as medical care or education.

Their place within the Empire would be at best that of an untouchable caste, performing tasks presently assigned to indentured criminals, artificial intelligences and beasts of burden.

'I bet you've got a copy of *The Seneschal's Daughter* hidden inside that.'

I start violently, slamming the document shut. I look up into the infuriatingly amused expression of Bernice Summerfield. 'It's all right, Ambassador,' she says. 'You're not having flashbacks, I'm really here. Have I ever complimented you on the size of your desk?'

I stand. 'On numerous occasions,' I reply. 'My secretary was under strict instructions not to let you in.'

She sprawls on a gilded chair. 'Fortunately Jekhet's more scared of your wife than he is of you. I think most of your staff are. I know she terrifies me.'

I am aware that Ithva's relationship with Summerfield has become closer than is wise for either of us. I must make my feelings on this matter known to her, sometime soon. It may even be necessary to speak to her about it.

'Aren't you going to call your security guards?' Summerfield asks me, mockingly.

'No,' I say. 'If I called them to protect me from a human female I'd become a laughing stock. Deservedly.'

'It really is a very big desk,' she says, stretching a leg across the chair-arm. 'I'm certainly impressed. I'm sure whatever statement it makes about your manhood is pretty damn impressive too.'

I say, 'I hope for Mr Kane's sake that you don't approach your marital relations the way you approach interstellar ones. In any case, Professor Summerfield, I don't believe we've anything to say to one another. Not after this afternoon's debacle. I'll be submitting my complaint in due course.'

'Oh, come on, Kothar,' she says scornfully. 'You know as well as I do I had nothing to do with that. If anyone got set up it was poor Mwshi. I had no idea Haddad was spying on us, and I certainly had no way of knowing that your deputy was going to turn up as well. Presumably he had you followed in the hope of digging up some dirt?'

'I imagine so. It would be typical of him.' I stay behind my desk, resisting the urge to pace angrily. Given Summerfield's relaxed insolence, sitting is once again out of the question. 'Nonetheless, it has left me in an untenable position. I can't indulge you in this kind of informal contact any longer.'

'Yes, I know. Werther and Haddad have forced your hand between them.' She makes a face. 'Ugh – that's not a nice mental image. I'm sorry, I've just been talking to my ex-husband.

'I mean,' she continues, 'that thanks to them you're going to have to start a new round of diplomatic posturing. Your government made an offer in good faith, the Mim turned it down, Earth's obviously behind it all – and what's worse, Dr Mwshi, Ms Haddad and I conspired to lure you into a compromising situation, presumably to blackmail you into accepting the Mim position. The Mim *negotiating* position,' she clarifies for some unfathomable reason.

'That's what will go on record.'

'Now, unless you receive grovelling apologies from Earth, the Mim and the Collection, you'll withdraw from these talks and take appropriate action. Meanwhile the Emperor keeps custody of the borogoves till adulthood, grants them the Grace of Emancipation then quietly hands them back to the Mim government-in-exile. Any cultural bombshells you've been juggling get to be someone else's problem and nothing to do with you, squire. Is that about the size of it?'

Summerfield is well informed, and I know full well by whom. 'It is,' I agree. 'It's the best solution we have available under the circumstances. Certainly better than what the Emperor's advisors are offering,' I add, with a glance at the dossier. 'I'm confident that we can persuade Earth and the Mim to accept it.'

Summerfield looks sceptical. 'No offence, Kothar, but I really doubt it. What are you going to do, hypnotise them?'

'No.' I begin dismissively to gather up the papers on my desk. 'I'm going to have you ask them for me.'

'Meaning you only need to hypnotise me? Clever. I warn you, though, self-help tapes don't work on me. My antisocial habits are made of sterner stuff.'

'Regardless of your intentions, what happened earlier was gravely embarrassing for me. Fortunately, I'm now in a position to embarrass you.' I consult the transcript of an earlier conversation which I have brought to the top of my pile. 'Let me see. You now believe that Ms Haddad murdered your Mim friend. You suspect her of also killing Pashar, whom you have been trying to implicate in that murder. You understand that if these facts become public knowledge the result will be another conflict, and believe it would be "better to hush the whole thing up". Are you embarrassed yet, Professor?'

Summerfield is staring at me. 'How did you – Ithva wouldn't –'

'A windfall,' I tell her. 'Unlooked-for, but most welcome.'

'Of course,' she says bitterly. 'Because if you'd gone looking for it, that would have been *dishonourable*, wouldn't it? Getting the maid to spy on us just makes you a backstabbing, blackmailing bastard.'

I incline my head. 'I do what must be done. You should know that by now. Now, you have a clear choice. Either you persuade the Mim and Earth representatives to agree to my government's new proposal – or you have, as you said earlier, "an interstellar war on your hands". Compounded by a charge of perverting the course of justice, I expect.'

'That would implicate your wife,' she points out coldly.

'It will be unfortunate, if that should become necessary,' I say, 'but I'll say she came to me with the information. That will exonerate her under Draconian law.'

As Summerfield glares at me, her breasts begin to vibrate. 'Oh, bloody hell,' she groans, standing abruptly.

I stare at her. 'It's my *phone*,' she snaps. 'And I'm really not in the mood for clever remarks, okay?'

She retreats into a corner of my office, as her bright undergarment begins to relay someone's speech. 'Peter?' she gasps. The child's voice is too shrill and breathless for me to hear his words.

The human circulatory system fascinates me. In pale-skinned humans, its workings are so visible. 'Peter?' Summerfield repeats, as her brassiere continues its squeaking. 'Oh, God. Peter, just tell me – Who has? In your *bedroom*? Where's Jason? Oh, my – it's okay, it's okay, darling, I'm coming.'

Without even acknowledging me, she hurries out of my office, still addressing her bosom. 'I'll expect your decision in the morning,' I call after her.

She swears at me, filthily. These human females. 'It's okay, Peter, I'm coming, Mummy's going to be there soon...' Her voice fades.

Jason

It's okay. It's all okay. Peter's fine. I kept him safe.

(Yeah, right. Me and Adrian's army.)

I need to sit down. (Christ, I must be getting old.)

Calm down.

Calm.

– Shit. Benny's really going to go ballistic this time.

It hasn't been a good day, what with one thing and another.

When it happened I was still freaked out about what those codes had led me to. (Benny's been just as shaken, to be fair – she's just better at dealing with that kind of thing.) Peter was sulking because I'd forgotten him earlier. He'd had to sit in Mrs Krasnow's office for an hour, till eventually Benny and I turned up together.

Then he had to sit through the row, of course. Poor little sod.

So when I heard voices in his bedroom later, I though he was... I don't know, watching TV? Having a teddy-bears' tea party? Masterminding a museum heist? Something other than going to sleep, anyway. Testing his boundaries, and my limits.

I was at the terminal in the study, using – well, never mind what sort of program I was using. Let's just say, after our phone conversation, I wasn't expecting Benny to be in any mood for conjugal relations.

I paused it, anyway, and went to see what Peter was getting up to.

'Where is he?' Benny asks me. 'Where's my son?'

Christ, where did she come from suddenly?

I'm sitting with my back against the house's outside wall. She's standing over me, her every muscle taut like a tightrope-walker's. Voice like a metal band about to snap.

I must have zoned out for a moment there.

'He's fine,' I say. 'Look, he's with Adrian.' I point to where Peter sits on his dad's great shaggy shoulder, held securely by one hairy hand. 'He wasn't hurt, Benny. I made sure he was okay.'

She lets out a sigh like a dying balloon and, without looking back at me, hurries over. Already putting on her Mummy face for Peter.

On the way, she passes the intruder.

The security boys are carrying it out between them in one of Doggles' electro-nets, developed for exactly this kind of situation. Adrian says it's about the only way you can arrest the amorphous buggers. It generates a paralysing field which makes the sponge's outer cells go rigid. Then you have to stick them inside an industrial-grade force field, the kind they use to contain the finest nanopowders during transit.

The Mim's reverted to its elongated spongiform shape (and let's be frank, there's no polite way of putting this – it looks like a giant flaccid cock). It's harmless in the net, to Benny or anyone else.

She recoils from it like she's been bitten by an adder.

'Holy shitting crap,' I said when I found the strange Mim in Peter's bedroom, looming over him like some evil fleshy menhir. Then, automatically, 'Don't tell your Mum I said that.'

The window-frame dripped icicles of broken glass, and there were splinters all across the carpet. Peter was hunched up against the headboard, looking anxious rather than terrified. Which basically qualifies him for a medal after everything that's happened.

My brain, which had been loitering resentfully in the study, finally sauntered into the room and joined me.

'Peter,' I said, 'go downstairs *now*. Call Adrian. Tell him Jason says can he come over here *right now*.'

'Stay where you are please, Peter,' the Mim said, flashing out a pseudopod and grabbing Peter's leg. 'Let's not do anything hasty, shall we, Mr Kane?' It used a woman's voice, harsh and rasping.

Peter started to bash away at the bit of Mim that was holding him, which it ignored completely. I groped around on the shelf behind me and found something heavy.

'Be careful with that, Jason!' Peter said as I brandished it. 'That's my masonry drill that Daddy gave me.'

I stared at the thing. The grip was made to fit a Killoran cub's paw, barely smaller than my hand. The power-tool casing was pastel blue, with an animated glyph of a goofy cartoon animal.

The business end looked serious enough, though.

'My goodness. These Killorans, eh?' the Mim said. 'Please put it down, Mr Kane. There's no need for anyone to get hurt.'

'I'll buy you another one,' I told Peter grimly, flicking the switch to ON. 'Now do as you're told.'

The drill's violent juddering threatened to dislocate my shoulder as I dived towards the alien's elongated limb and severed it, messily.

'*Phone*, Peter!' I yelled as he stopped and looked around for something to throw. 'Now!'

The Mim shrieked in pain, and began to batter me to buggery.

His room's a wreck. Bits of furniture and toys everywhere.

The Mim slapped me about a lot – if it had been planning to eat me I'd have been thoroughly tenderised – but I kept hold of the drill. Mim are damn near impossible to kill – at least without whatever weapon they used on Benny's pal Lwpha – but they're wimps when it comes to pain. Drilling great big holes in them tends to keep their attention focused on you.

'You stupid bastard.' Benny's still furious as we stand surveying the wreckage. 'You could have got yourself killed.'

It's a fair point, I suppose. Who'd give her babies if that happened?

'I know,' I said. 'I had to keep Peter safe.'

She gives me her speciality you're-a-cretin look, refined during so many domestic arguments down the years. 'How safe would he have been if that thing had killed you? What if it had had a friend downstairs? For pity's sake, why didn't you just grab Peter and *run*?'

I wonder. If the Mim wanted me dead, it wasn't trying very hard. It could have given me much more than just a slapping.

The other stuff I'm not so sure about. 'I may not have been thinking straight,' I admit. 'It all came as a bit of a surprise.'

The last time tentacled monstrosities broke into our house and tried to kill Peter, it was Benny who protected him. She got him behind the sofa and fought off the invader till Adrian arrived.

I was off having dinner at the time, with a charmingly pneumatic young redhead from my publishers. It wasn't my finest hour.

'Admit it – you were trying to be a bloody hero,' Benny snaps now. 'The last thing on your mind was Peter's safety.'

'That's ridiculous,' I say, but I just sound pathetic. All the fight's gone out of me, leaving me wilted like – well, since you ask, like a giant flaccid cock.

We stare at the ruins of Peter's room. I think, *Even Benny's going to have trouble reconstructing these remains*, and have to fight back a swell of hysterical laughter.

'It's all right now,' I say at last. 'Adrian's going to lock the bastard up in one of his containment fields and throw away the... off-switch.'

'She'll be back,' Benny says. 'If not her, then others. The Collection's not safe for Peter at the moment.'

I can't argue with that. She obviously can't trust me to protect him any more.

'Where will you take him?' I ask.

For a moment I can tell she's seriously thinking of not telling me. Not compromising Peter's safety any further. Then she relents. 'Little Caldwell.'

I frown. 'But that's...'

'I'll take the handheld time-machine,' she says. 'The one we used to get to Delphi. We never did give it back. And nobody's going to follow Peter into the past. I think he'll be safest with his granddad for the time being, don't you?'

4

From the Journal of Admiral Isaac Summerfield:

11 February 1987

Bernice arrived with Peter last night while I was in the greenhouse, watering the latest consignment of Ias'par seedlings. These are the last of Harll's children, I hope. It took Joel and M'Kabel weeks to trace them to a remote mountainside in Ross-shire.

I kissed my daughter, picked my grandson up for a hug, and said, 'Hello, Bernice. I didn't expect to see you so soon. Did you get my message?'

'Your alien-artefact-o-gram? Yes. Thanks.' She seemed distracted.

'I was rather pleased with that,' I said.

Bernice said, 'Dad, can Peter come and stay with you for a while?'

'Of course,' I said. 'Oh, dear, what's happened?'

We went indoors, leaving the seedlings to their sleep. Benny put her son to bed upstairs while I made us both coffee.

'He's still awake,' she said when she came down. 'He's calmed down, though. He'll sleep. They broke into his *bedroom*, Dad.'

She told me something of what had happened since we last saw one another – her experiences on Montavadros, her difficulties with Ambassador Kothar and her friendship with Ithva.

She said, 'It's been a bit of a let-down, really. All that drowning and wilderness-trekking and getting attacked, then suddenly I'm in politics. It's giving me conceptual whiplash. It's the only way of solving this, though. It's what I'm supposed to be good at, after all – brain instead of fists.'

Finally, she told me of the invasion of her home by one of the very people she was trying to help, and her fears that Peter might be harmed, or worse still held to ransom against the return of the Mim children.

'I couldn't deal with that,' she said. 'I panicked. When I thought about Peter being taken away from me like Lwpha's children – I couldn't bear it. I know it's not fair to rely on Jason to keep him safe. Adrian has too much else going on right now, Bev's gone and no one knows what's happening in Brax's head any more. I didn't know where to turn. And then I remembered I had you.'

I said, 'I'm very pleased you did. I'll keep him safe, I promise. I suppose none of the interested parties are time-active?'

'I bloody hope not,' said Bernice. 'But with all the unidentified tech that's piling up on the Collection these days, it's anyone's guess.'

While we drank our coffee I told her a little about the Ias'par seedlings and their history. How their mother, Harll, had been brought through a wormhole, already pregnant, by a colonising party, and planted in a glen near Cromarty. How various military alien-hunting squads picked off her brothers one by one, but never found Harll herself. How Ias'par males become mobile at puberty, but their sisters remain rooted in the same soil for life unless someone transplants them. How Harll finally managed to get a message to us, but how we arrived too late to delay her sporulation. How she died, giving life to her children and scattering them across a sizeable area of the highlands and islands, and how much of the three years since we've spent tracking them down, digging them up and keeping them safe.

'The Ias'par rootworlds are too far away to contact,' I said, 'and the nearest branch colonies aren't interested. Our best option was to find them somewhere with fertile soil and a robust attitude to species diversity. We've been shipping them to Kapteyn 5.'

'That works,' said Benny. 'Dad, we need to talk about Project Narcissus.'

She isn't easily diverted, my daughter.

I said, 'How much have you found out?'

'Enough to sicken me. We've got Earth agents on the Collection at the moment. Jason piggybacked onto their comms traffic using some of Bev's leftover cracking software. Your codes took him straight into the classified files.'

While I was with Benny, Jason and Peter on Phaaag Zenbrou I'd tracked down the local news for the area once known as Berkshire, so I already knew that her contemporaries would be digging up the theme park. Once I was back in my adopted present, and realised I had to let Benny know about Project Narcissus, it was the simplest method that presented itself. Windsor Safari Park, as it still is at present, is just a few junctions away along the M4.

The tricky part, as I told Bernice, was finding somewhere to bury it where the developers won't find it, but the archaeologists will. 'That and avoiding the lions,' I said. 'I'm sorry you were sickened, Benny. I thought you needed to know.'

'I do, and I'm glad you told me, but...' She was quiet for a moment. 'Dad, were you involved?'

'In retrospect yes, though only on the fringes. I had to authorise some rather unorthodox combat missions. All I knew was that my ships were delivering payloads developed by a classified research project, weapons that might win us the war.'

It was only much later in my own lifetime that I got to see the project from the other side, through the enemy battle computers. And only after meeting Lwpha on Phaaag Zenbrou, so soon before his untimely death, that I began to piece the two sets of data together.

The story, as I've come to understand it, went like this. Of course when I say 'went', I mean that this is how it *will* go, six centuries from now.

At some point during the war, the Earth and colonial military came into possession of a population of juvenile Mim. I have no idea how. Perhaps their parents were all killed, and our forces just happened upon them. Perhaps it was something less fortuitous, less innocent.

I don't know which agency acquired them, either. There've always been top-secret cadres dedicated to taking alien technology and using it to protect humanity from outside threats.

Whoever they were, they recognised the Mim as too valuable a resource to waste.

In any war, a vital strategic advantage comes from the ability to infiltrate the enemy. We were vulnerable to that sort of thing ourselves. Our enemies had advanced replication technology, and regularly tried to psych us out with duplicates of our dead or captured comrades.

By contrast, their ranks were impossible to penetrate. The Allied powers – Earth, Draconia and the others – had tried various approaches. Some had retrofitted captured battletanks with purpose-built AIs, or built robot drones in imitation of the enemy units. Others had collaborated with the Mim and other shapeshifting species, though most of those find it near-impossible to hold a form made up from perfect circles and straight lines.

All these attempts failed. Our enemies were on constant lookout for deviation in their ranks, and our infiltrators betrayed themselves with thousands of tiny behavioural clues. All were exterminated.

The Allies needed agents who could not just infiltrate the enemy, but become them. That was what Project Narcissus was set up to provide. The juvenile Mim were brainwashed even as their minds developed, their loyalties constructed from the ground up. When they were deemed to be ready they were packaged in one-shot transmat capsules, and my ships deployed them from low orbit around the occupied worlds.

A young Mim instinctively imitates the plants and animals in its immediate environment. It's a form of protective biological mimicry. The young Narcissus operatives were inserted directly into the enemy hatcheries, and they imitated what they found there.

They became indistinguishable from the enemy's biomass component – the part that's grafted *inside* the battle-casing. The pilot, if that's how you prefer to think of it.

The soldiers in the combat zones called it the *crabmeat*.

The majority were discovered quickly and incinerated, but a handful survived and grew up to be welded into the battle-tanks. That was when their conditioning kicked in.

These Narcissus hybrids would turn on their fellows at crucial points during the attacks. They crippled entire enemy squadrons, saved countless Allied lives. Most of them died in the process, but a few made contact with Allied command and were extracted. These were retrained to infiltrate the enemy hierarchy. In most cases it was well worth the new paintwork.

The high-level Narcissus infiltrators became utterly psychotic, battered with hate-filled propaganda from the comms net. The few that survived long enough continued growing until they burst the cramped confines of their cradles and perished. But while they lived they scored some major tactical blows for the Alliance.

All this I told my daughter, as her expression became more and more horrified.

Eventually she said coldly, 'Isaac, you know I love you. But it feels like every time I see you, you turn out to be the enemy.'

I shrugged. 'Don't overestimate my involvement. I was only their office-boy. But without Narcissus and other projects like it, I doubt we'd have won the war. Black ops are a necessity in wartime, Benny. They're ugly but unavoidable, and usually decisive.'

She said, 'They were children, Dad. Children like Peter.' A slightly guilty look crossed her face as she said it.

I said, 'And it was children we were fighting to protect. Children like you. Your survival hung in the balance, the survival of the human race. That sounds like rhetoric, but it was simply a fact. The Mim were an asset, and we used them to our best advantage. We used them to protect you.'

She said, 'And you can live with that? Even while you're caring for the Ias'par seedlings, doing your best to ensure a future for them, you're telling me it was right to *deploy* alien children as weapons of war?'

'I'm not saying it was fair or decent or nice, Benny. The Mim children were innocent, and they suffered and died and went insane. We did that to them. But yes, it was right if it meant countless others could live – including you, and through you Peter. Just think what his world would be like now if the war had been lost.'

I saw her falter as she pictured it. For a moment I wished I could protect her from this kind of truth. I wished I could gather her up in my arms as I had Peter, promise her that I'd always protect her from the monsters, whatever form they took.

That window of opportunity passed a long, long time ago. The war went on without me, claiming my wife and orphaning my daughter. A rendezvous irrevocably missed, a campaign lost. More necessary sacrifices.

I said, 'It's our most basic moral imperative. To protect the young.'

My daughter said, 'No. I mean yes, but not if you interpret it that narrowly. Some people talk as if having children excuses them from any other moral responsibility. I don't mean you, you do everything you can here. But it can't just be about preserving your own genes. In my book, if it's something bacteria manage it doesn't count as morality.'

I said, 'Some people change their principles, their loyalties, their political convictions, all for children who despise them for it as soon as they hit their teens.'

She nodded. 'Project Narcissus was wrong because it put a higher value on *our* children, on human children, than on other people's. It's not about their relationship to us – children are valuable in themselves. If you break the rules for your own children, you have to be willing to do the same for *anyone's*. If the Draconians understand that, I can't see why we have a problem with it.'

I said, 'I'm not a god or superhero, Benny. I'm a soldier. We have to make terrible decisions, sometimes. We have to choose who gets to live, because not everybody can. If you think we don't appreciate the enormity of that, then you underestimate us.'

I left Bernice to think as I washed up the mugs and cafetiere. While I was drying up, I heard her climb the stairs to Peter's room. When she came back down, I was waiting for her. I said, 'Do you feel like a walk? I don't mean far. We'll still hear Peter if he calls us. It's very quiet here.'

She said, 'He's out like a light. He'll sleep through till morning. It'll be easier for him then if I'm gone.'

She still looked very pensive as we stepped out again into the frosty winter night. The cottage terrace was dark, its chimneys outlined by the moonlight. We walked slowly along the High Street towards the Post Office.

When Benny spoke again, it was to ask about the Mim artefact we'd buried. 'Reepha's drug-dispenser?' I said. 'It's been lying around since we sent him back to the Mimsphere.'

Benny was surprised. 'Of course. I hadn't thought – the Tentative Diaspora's going on right now. Mim misfits and eccentrics have been exploring space for... it must be the last half-century. I hadn't realised they made it as far as Earth.'

I said, 'We do our best to preserve our guests' privacy. Though Reepha believed there'd been others.'

She looked around us, breathing in the chilly air. An owl called in the moonlit woods. Further away, a faint murmur from the motorway reminded us of life beyond my village retreat.

Thoughtfully, Benny said, 'It's 1987. Draconian savants are beginning to speculate about their Empire taking to the stars. They don't know that in another generation the stars are going to come to the Empire, bringing plague and pestilence. And meanwhile, here on Earth... people are learning to use alien technology to fight aliens.'

I nodded. 'Some of those organisations I mentioned exist already. A couple have been active since the First World War, or even earlier. The agency that runs Project Narcissus could be the distant descendant of any of them.'

She said, 'All these disparate events on different worlds. Sending out ripples of cause and effect over light years and centuries. And they all converge on the Collection, in my present.'

I said, 'That may be how it looks from one angle. But history's influence gets everywhere. I don't think the universe is out to get you this time, Benny. As much as you mean to me, I don't think it sees you as that important.'

We walked on, past bones of trees stark against the cloudless sky.

Benny sighed. 'Okay. I accept that my perspective is limited. I'm trained to see that, after all. And – since I seem to be making a habit of sympathising with unappealing points of view at the moment – let's say I can see how, during wartime, something like Project Narcissus could have seemed necessary. Desperate situations make people resort to desperate expedients. Heaven knows I can't claim my hands are bloodless. What I don't see is why it's necessary *now*.'

'Now?' I said.

'My "now". Earth isn't fighting any war in 2608, however paranoid they're getting about aliens in their midst. Our resident military goons on the Collection, Szmyt and Haddad – they're trying to buy young Mim as their price for helping with the negotiations. At first I couldn't work out why they were supporting the Mim, but once you know the history it's obvious. They're hoping to rerun Project Narcissus.'

I said, 'That's the trouble with desperate expedients. You use them once and they don't seem desperate any more. They become part of your repertoire.' I spoke from experience, as Benny knew.

'If "necessary" means *unavoidable*, not *justified*,' she said, 'then Project Narcissus may have been it. What it was, though, was an atrocity. It mustn't ever happen again, and certainly not as standard military procedure.'

'There we're agreed.' Nelson the cat appeared suddenly, a moonlit shadow out on a rare nocturnal prowl. I bent to brush a hand against him, but he didn't acknowledge me.

Benny seemed to crumple. 'But that just makes it all worse. It's obvious that the children need to be returned to the Mim. It's only the Draconians who think otherwise. But if I let that happen, not only do most of them die of natural causes, but hundreds get handed over to Szmyt and Haddad and conscripted into their private war. And not against an unstoppable enemy this time – just anyone Earth happens to consider a potential threat.'

I shrugged. 'I don't know what the answer to that is. But I know you'll find it. You'll work out the right thing to do, and do it. It's what you always do. And I can't tell you how proud that makes me.'

She stood stock still, stared at me for fifteen seconds, then burst into tears. I guided her to the nearest wall, then held her while she bawled.

Even from there, I was worried that she'd wake Peter. 'Not Peter,' she said, through the handkerchief I'd found. 'Once he's asleep it takes a volcanic eruption to –'

She broke off, trembling violently. I took off my jacket and wrapped it round her.

'She was in his *room*, Dad,' she said again, eventually. 'Jason found him awake. What had she been doing to him? What was she *going* to do?'

I kept an arm around her. She said to me, 'I just want to keep Peter safe. I need to know the Collection's a safe place for him to come back to. Grief, if *he* carries on imitating what he finds in his surroundings, heaven help us all. You should have seen him on Montavadros, throwing stones at the Mim who was trying to kill me. You'd have been proud of him, Dad. I'm not sure I was.'

I didn't trust myself to answer that.

Bernice said, 'The Collection was a haven once. A refuge. I'm doing my best to make it one again. Not just for Peter's sake, either.'

Startled, I asked her, 'Are you...'

She said, 'Still trying. But we're trying *really hard*, Dad. I love Peter, and I wouldn't change him for anything, but –' she broke off.

I understood. 'You didn't choose him.'

'I didn't, no. That doesn't mean I love him any less, not for a moment, but... I want to choose. I want a child with Jason. And I think it's going to happen.'

'Let's hope so,' I said. 'Apart from anything else, I want a granddaughter.'

Bernice was silent. A fox emerged from behind the Post Office, sudden and confident and astonishingly close to us. It paused to stare at us in indignation, then trotted about its business.

Benny said, 'It's not just blind optimism. I think I've seen the evidence.'

'You mean Keith?' I remembered the bright little toddler from the future – from one potential future, at least – who'd fallen through time into Jason's arms during Benny's first visit to Little Caldwell. It was a difficult, confusing time for us all, and I had other things on my mind. He'd been a charming baby, though.

She said, 'Not just Keith. Though I loved him desperately. Somewhere inside me, I still do. He'll always be my first child, even if he was never quite real. But no, it's more concrete than that.'

And she told me about the Quire.

A year or so ago, in her time, Benny met some people from the further future – the very much further, very distant future. So distant that it was a moot point whether they could still be classed as human. She got to know some of them well, she said, or as well as creatures of their kind could be known. One in particular reminded her very much of herself.

One of them died. It was a tragic accident, a terrible mistake. Bernice had wanted so much to protect her.

A chill breeze rattled the denuded trees. 'Let's head back indoors,' I suggested.

We stood, and returned quickly to the line of cottages.

As we walked, Benny said, 'They had too many names. Most of them passed me by when they introduced themselves. But when I thought about it later, after what happened to Verso, it struck me. Two of their family names translated as "Quarterstaff" and "Fallowsolstice".'

She looked at me as if this was significant. It took me a while to understand why.

I may have raised an eyebrow when I did. I certainly said, 'Oh.'

'We knew Braxiatel had invited them for a reason,' Benny said. 'We just didn't know what it was.'

'Solstice' as in *summer*. 'Fallow' as in *field*. Bernice believed the Quire were her descendants.

They'd been human, or at least humanish. Not part-Killoran. And 'quarterstaff' means something not dissimilar to *cane*.

'So you will have children,' I said, although I knew that none of this counted as proof. 'Children and grandchildren and great-grandchildren, on and on into the distance.' My throat had constricted, my voice gone husky in the cold air. I hadn't expected to feel so affected.

We stood in silence outside my front door. Eventually Bernice said, 'I need to be getting back. I know there's technically no urgency, because of the time-travel, but... you know how it is.'

I said, 'You still trust me with Peter?'

'Oh, that was never in doubt,' she said. 'I know you'll do whatever it takes to protect him. That may be frightening, but at the moment it's also pretty damn reassuring.'

She kissed me. 'I love you, Dad.'

I gave a mock salute. 'I love you, daughter.'

She giggled, punched me on the arm and activated her time machine.

After she'd faded into the future I stepped back into the cottage to check on Peter, then went out once again to the greenhouse. One of the seedlings had woken up, and was whimpering at his strange surroundings. I soothed him back to sleep with promises of fresh soil, a brighter sun and a reunion with his brothers and sisters.

5

Jason

Benny meets me at the spaceport when she gets back.

Which is insane, of course. The handheld would have taken her anywhere she wanted to go on the Collection – and it's not like Brax ever made time-travellers go through customs. Although the way that mad bastard's been acting since he got back from his thousand-year sulk, I wouldn't put it past him.

But Benny's being paranoid – *taking sensible precautions*, it probably looks like from inside her head – and thinks if she pops back into existence at our place she'll find herself in the middle of an ambush. At the spaceport there are crowds, securicams and butch security guards.

And me, natch. Standing here for the last half-hour, in fact, staking out the ladies' loos in the departures lounge. Making sure everyone who goes in comes right out again. Which is how I know they're empty of all life at 8.22 am, when the door opens and Benny comes out, wearing Isaac's jacket.

Otherwise, obviously, she could be a Mim in disguise. And *then* where would we be, eh?

Still, the advantage of the spaceport meet-up is it gives us the opportunity to walk briskly down corridors while talking and consulting electronic accessories. That always gives me the thrill of looking smart and efficient and businesslike.

'Peter's all right then?' I ask smartly, consulting my palmpad as we march through the departure lounge.

'I left him asleep,' she answers.

I tick the pad. 'And Isaac?' I inquire efficiently as we step onto the travelbelt.

'Fine too. Peter's safe with him. I can get on with doing everything I'm supposed to be doing.'

I tick again. 'Top banana,' I say in a businesslike manner, as the belt whisks us along towards the lobby. 'Because while you've been gone everything's been going to buggery in a handcart.'

After Benny left last night, I really wasn't in the mood for sleep. Someone had broken into my house, intimidated my sort-of-nearly stepson, then beaten seven shades of pith out of *me*, all to get at my sort-of-not-quite wife. I wasn't going to stand for that.

I decided it was time for action. I limped painfully across to the Mim delegation offices to have a little word with Dr Mwshi.

He wasn't in his rooms, as I discovered after faffing for ages with a lockpick. Not anywhere obvious, at least. I wasn't going to strap on an aqualung and check below the waterline.

Instead I found him outside the meeting-rooms, stretched out sluglike on a bench there. The rich sweet scent of Mim conversation drifted faintly from inside.

'Are you Mwshi?' I asked. If they're not going to be embarrassed about all looking the same, then I'm not either.

The Mim made some lips. 'Yes, it's me,' he said. 'Hello, Jason. I heard what happened at your house. I'm sorry.'

'Yeah,' I said. 'You and me both, sunshine. What's all this about you lot selling your kids?'

Mwshi squirmed upright immediately. 'We can't talk about that here, you berk. Come back to my rooms.'

I still haven't a clue where that came from so suddenly. I'd been meaning to ask something along the lines of, *I wonder, sir, if I might make so bold as to enquire after the identity of the perpetrator of the recent outrage against my property and person?* But you run with what you're thrown, even when your subconscious starts getting the custard pies out.

'So, this child slavery racket of yours,' I said as soon as we were safely perched on Mwshi's ersatz rocks. 'View's not looking so good now from your high horse up on that moral high ground, I'll bet.' Not the best-crafted of my bons mots, but it got the point across.

'I'm not particularly proud of that,' he said, 'but it's out of my pseudopodia now.' (No, honestly he did). 'I've been thrown off the negotiating team.'

That took me aback. '*You* have?' I said. 'Why?'

The Mim made a snorting sound. 'I answered back.' He extended a limb into the fake sea-water, as if testing the warmth. He began to pour himself along it as he went on, 'After I talked to Bernice yesterday, I went to see Szmyt and Haddad. We had a frank exchange of views.'

'About Project Narcissus?' I guessed. 'And how they want to organise the comeback tour?'

'We covered that general area,' Mwshi agreed. Half of him was underwater now, the rest sliding smoothly down that elongated cylinder. 'Now Szmyt's had Sherm move to expel me from the delegation. They're voting on it now, but I know how it'll go.'

'Arse,' I said. 'Look, don't sweat it, Mwshi. I'm sure Benny can get you reinstated. Lean on people, bang a few heads together, you know the drill.'

That last word gave me a sudden nasty flashback, and I twitched.

'It doesn't make much difference,' said the Mim. He was submerged now, except for a bobbing football-sized dome. With a mouth.

'Bernice knows we can't compromise,' he said, 'whoever's doing the negotiating. If we agree joint custody with the Draconians, Earth won't get their dues. And that will mean another war. A war with Earth.'

'And by "dues" you mean *babies*, yeah?' I asked indignantly. But the last bit of him had sunk beneath the artificial waves, and everything was silent.

I let myself out.

'Right,' Benny says. 'Taking it as read for the moment that I'll be tearing you off a strip for throwing my delicately balanced diplomatic strategies and schemes out of whack just as soon as I can summon up the energy...'

She tails off.

We're at the spaceport café, fuelling up with tea and patisseries. She hasn't slept, I can tell just by looking at her. However long she's been away in time, it's only left her that many hours more drained and wan.

Jittery too. That'll be Isaac's coffee, I expect.

'What was I talking about?' she asks.

'Mwshi,' I say.

'Oh, yes. Even taking all of that for granted, I'm not sure that qualifies as a handcart. An attractive wicker handbasket, possibly. It's bad luck for Mwshi, but he's right – if he's not allowed to budge, it makes no difference who's in charge. I've been wasting my time with the Mim. I need to go for the source of the problem. Which means Szmyt and Haddad.'

'Ah, yes,' I say. 'That's where the basket gets wheels and a pair of long handle things.'

Ithva and Sharintha called by at six-thirty this morning. I crawled out of bed and into a dressing-gown, then staggered downstairs, expecting Adrian or somebody wanting to talk about the break-in.

I opened the door and a green blur streaked past me at thigh-height, giggling. With effort I triangulated its source, and found a taller, equally green blur in front of me.

It grabbed me forcibly and air-kissed me. 'Jason, *darling*,' it effused. '*So* sorry to hear about your dreadful experience. Is Bernice at home?'

From behind me, the first blur said, 'Peter's not here, Mummy. Where's Peter, Mr Kane?'

I made some noises that I hoped could be interpreted as language.

Still holding my shoulders, the taller blur peered into my eyes. 'Ah,' it said. 'Coffee, I think.'

Once Ithva had hustled me through to the kitchen, quietened Sharintha with one of Peter's old colouring-pads and poured two mugs down me, I was able to hold a conversation again.

'They're not here,' I explained. 'Benny took Peter off out of the way.'

'That's very sensible of her,' said Ithva. 'I won't be awkward by asking where.' She left the tiniest pause – which I didn't fill, though that might have been the brain-lag. 'I *did* want to talk to her, though. Something rather unfortunate's come up.'

'I'm seeing her later,' I said. 'I can get her to stop by your place.'

Another moment's pause, a swift appraising look, then, 'I don't think so. I'm sure I can trust you to pass this on, Jason. It's terribly important.' She flashed a smile which suddenly reminded me vividly of Khandi, a sinuously serpentine Draconian lady I'd known at the NuBar in Spaceport Kuma.

I raised an eyebrow. 'My life at your command,' I smirked, suddenly getting an idea for a scene in my new book…

...which *you don't want to know about*, obviously. Stay on-topic, Jason. Right.

'It's about Ms Haddad,' Ithva said crisply. 'She's disappeared, evidently. Jarith's been up all night arguing with people about it. The Mim and Mr Szmyt think poor Pashar came out of hiding to do away with the dreadful woman. They obviously consider him to be Jarith's personal private assassin.'

'And Jarith?' I still can't get my head round old handbag-features Kothar having a first name. 'What does he think?'

'Well,' Ithva says, 'I'm afraid he's got it into his head that Bernice tipped Ms Haddad off. As Jarith told Benny last night, he's come into possession of some delicate information about Ms Haddad, which makes the timing of this disappearance seem awfully convenient. It looks very much as if his bluff is being called.'

'Which would mean –'

'That he'll release his *somewhat* incriminating information to the worlds, yes. Benny knows how serious that could turn out to be.'

I took a wild stab. 'Not another interstellar war?'

Another look. 'You're more than just a craggily handsome face, aren't you Mr Kane?' she purred, placing her hand on mine...

Benny snorts into her tea. 'She bloody did not say that!'

I mime mock-indignation. 'Oh, yeah? And why should you have all the fun?'

Her voice is cold. 'This is serious, Jason. If Kothar tells the media what he thinks he knows, things could get very nasty very quickly.'

'Things are already very nasty,' I remind her. 'It was me that got beaten to a pulp last night, remember? I'd have been in no state to play cavemen and dinosaurs with the Ambassador's wife even if she'd wanted to. Which she didn't. She was just getting my attention.'

Benny tuts. 'She found the best way pretty damn quickly. Fortunately for you, I haven't the energy to get angry about your Neolithic sex drive either.'

'I'll make a note of it for later, then.'

A sigh. 'Just tell me what else Ithva said.'

'It was mostly about Project You-Know-What,' I say. 'She's been looking into the history from the Draconian end. Seems they knew practically nothing about it back then. They could see Earth had a way of co-opting selected enemy troops, but they didn't know the details.'

'Well, that's only to be expected,' said Benny. 'Earth and Draconia may have been allies then, but no one was under any illusions about that outlasting the war.'

'Except,' I say, 'someone on the Draconian contingent found out. Some general's wife somewhere, spying on her husband's human colleagues like the dutiful little helpmeet. The Imperial family were horrified – mistreating children's a terrible dishonour, especially in time of war. They had the whole thing hushed up…'

'…which naturally the Earth military were more than happy to go along with,' Benny concludes.

'Yeah. We'd never have found out about it either, without those codes from the Legoland dig.'

'And now the Earth agents want to start the whole damn thing over again,' she mutters. 'Well, I'm not going to let them get away with it.'

'Too bloody right,' I say. 'That's what I told Mr Szmyt.'

Once Ithva had scraped Sharintha away from Peter's toys, I made myself another coffee, dressed and shaved. I had nearly two hours before I had to be at the spaceport, so I went off to find Szmyt.

'You *what?*' Benny is looking at me aghast.

'I said, I told Szmyt –'

'You utter cretin, Jason.' She's colder than ever now. 'Szmyt's a top-level security operative in some appallingly unethical black ops outfit. He's a lethally armed, highly trained psychopath. Farting around playing at diplomats with Mwshi's one thing, but with *Szmyt* – you could have got yourself damn well killed.'

I shrug. 'Yeah, well. Didn't stop you with Ithva, did it? Besides, I got some sperm frozen before I went.'

She stares at me like I'm a small boy who's just eaten a miraculously preserved specimen of a long-extinct worm. '*What?*'

I shrug again. 'I got a do-it-yourself kit and preserved a semen sample. It's in a stasis locker, just over there.'

I point towards Left Luggage. She stares at me more.

'It's just a *precaution*, Benny,' I say. 'Just so that if something did happen, you could still… just so we don't need to stop trying. That's all.'

Which is when she blows her top, and the conversation takes something of a tangent.

When I found Szmyt (as I tell Benny much, much later, after the row, after the crying, after the I-never-want-to-see-you-again shag and the don't-you-dare-leave-me-you-bastard shag and the God-I-love-you-Jason-you-total-arse shag), he wasn't in the best of moods.

'I haven't time to talk now, Mr Kane,' he said. He's got his important-corridor-walking skills down to a fine art. 'We haven't anything to say to one another, and if we did I'm too busy. If it's important, message me.'

We were in the Mansionhouse. Szmyt had been in Brax's office – God knows what they'd been plotting together – and was marching over to one of the meeting-rooms, presumably to plot some more with Sherm. His black frock-coat tails flapped as he walked.

'Project Narcissus,' I said.

Without breaking stride, he seized me by the collar and bundled me through the nearest door.

It took us into some kind of storage cupboard, with rows and rows of deactivated porters sitting on metal shelves. Szmyt jammed the door with his shoe and loomed menacingly at me in the cramped space, one hand on his shoulder holster. He's probably stuffed full of smart implants that could have taken me out without him twitching, but there's nothing like a gun for signifying a threat.

The black glass circles of his shades filled my vision as he hissed, 'Assume that you now have my attention, Mr Kane.'

'Er, right,' I said. 'Fair enough, then. Project Narcissus. Look, it wasn't right, was it? Those Mim were just kids.'

Szmyt relaxed a little. I think he'd spotted that I wasn't going to subvert his loyalties through sheer force of argument. 'I'm not interested in discussing ethics, Mr Kane,' he said. 'I'm not interested in ethics, period. The purpose of my Institute is to protect the human species. Not that we expect *colonists* such as yourself to be grateful for that. The Mim juveniles are our means to that end.'

'Ah, but does the end justify the means?' I parried cleverly.

He took his hand off the gun. 'If you haven't anything of substance to say, Mr Kane, I suggest you step out of that door and keep walking. We'll both chalk this one up to experience.'

'You don't just want them for yourselves,' I said quickly. 'You don't want the Draconians getting hold of them in case they use them first. It's an arms race.'

He didn't shoot me in the face or disintegrate me with his nipples, so I went on. 'You know not all the Draconians agree with treating the Mim as people. People like Werther would happily have them declared non-sentient if it meant they could use them as weapons. Kothar's influence is fading fast now. And you really, really don't want the Draconian Empire getting its claws on an army of shapeshifting assassins.'

Szmyt's face remained totally impassive. 'You're telling me you disagree with that? You may live side-by-side with aliens on this pebble. You may even tolerate your wife's mixed-species child. But even you wouldn't want to see Earth annexed by the Dragons.'

I didn't dignify this with the reaction it deserved. Punching him would have been undiplomatic, not to mention poor survival strategy.

'So let the Mim keep the kids,' I said, 'you prat. Let them look after them, without either side interfering.'

I swear his mouth actually twitched. 'It's obvious you're not a strategist, Mr Kane. The only way to protect Earth from infiltration by Mim agents loyal to an alien power is to control the source. The changed circumstances make it imperative that we not only safeguard our own supply, but prevent the opening-up of alternate markets. We won't give in to lobbying or blackmail on this one. The safety of humanity takes precedence over all other considerations. And you can tell your wife that.' The immobile porters glinted under the harsh lights.

He fondled his gun again. 'Incidentally, the probability that Professor Summerfield shares your knowledge is all that's keeping you alive right now. There's little to gain from eliminating you alone. I don't know whether you're very brave or very stupid to have taken the risk. Not that I'm particularly interested.'

'Ah, well,' I said. 'I knew you wouldn't kill me.'

Hollow voice, stony face. 'And what made you so confident of that?'

'Joseph,' I called. 'Explain the situation to Mr Szmyt, would you?'

Joseph rose off the shelf where I'd put him with the other porters. 'I have been monitoring your conversation, Mr Szmyt,' he declared. 'And porters are authorised to take offensive action in order to protect residents of the Collection.'

'Clever, Mr Kane.' Szmyt covered up his surprise well. 'But not that clever. A single drone can't do much to incapacitate me.'

Joseph made his throat-clearing noise, and the other forty porters floated up like a cloud to join him.

'I can be a bit of a strategist, sometimes,' I said.

'Good grief,' says Benny now. 'You mean Joseph *recorded* all of that?'

She's only now emerging from her post-multiply-coital haze. It's late morning at least, and she's missed God knows how many meetings.

Her bra's been ringing non-stop. Fortunately it's muffled under the folds of my jeans.

'Ah,' I say. We're in bed, naked under a thin sheet, and I've got goosebumps. Whether that's more to do with the cold or with the lines her fingernails are tracing up and down my side is a question I leave to the experts. 'No, that's another of the handcart bits. Turns out one of Szmyt's implants runs electronic countermeasures. Joseph's recording was contaminated with a virus. He's had to quarantine a couple of hours' worth of memory.'

'Bollocks,' says Benny. Her fingernails stop their slow meander. 'But you're sure that's what Szmyt said? That now "circumstances have changed", they need to safeguard their supply of young Mim and prevent anyone else getting hold of them?'

'That's the bunny,' I agree.

'But that means...' She sits up suddenly, clutching the sheet to her chest in disappointing modesty. 'Shit, Jason.'

'If you say so, love.'

Her brain's doing that thing it does. The thing I love.

She's taking disparate, unrecognisable fragments of something altogether foreign to her, brushing them clean and looking at them from every angle. In just a moment she's going to reassemble them into what's obviously, and could only ever have been, one thing. Whether that's a ceremonial headdress-cum-flower-vase, or a solar-powered tie-press or whatever.

'Mwshi lied to me,' she says softly. 'He lied about Korenthai, and about Sherm.' She gets up and sheds the sheet for a brief, tantalising moment before she starts pulling on underwear, still thinking aloud. 'There never was a faction of Mim who lived peacefully alongside the Draconians. Mwshi must know that. He knows perfectly well who Korenthai was working for. He knows what Sherm was doing away from Mimsphere when the catastrophe happened – what he was selling, and who to. And so do I.'

She turns back to face me, dragging on a clean shirt. 'The Mim who broke in here last night. Where's Adrian keeping her?'

'In the converted cellars at the Mansionhouse,' I say. 'The ones the Axis turned into cells.'

She steps into some jeans. 'I'm going to see her.'

'Don't do anything stupid,' I say. 'Like getting yourself killed to make a point or anything.'

'Oh, Jason.' She bends down and kisses the top of my head. 'As if I'd do an idiotic thing like that.'

253

6

Victoria

We knew you'd come. Oh, yes (our love), we knew you'd come eventually.

We're shit-hot at predicting people, see. What they're gonna do. What we'd do in their shoes.

To understand your enemy, you must become her.

... Yes, thanks for that.

Here comes Benny, de dooby do do do do doodoo. Hello Benny, what have you been doing today? I've been moving heavens and Earth to protect my son from vile murderous assassins like yourself, Victoria, what about you? Oh, we've been languishing in a cell surrounded by a forcefield while this whole portion of the galaxy goes to cock without us, Benny, thank you *so very much* for asking. You're so sodding thoughtful.

Here you come now. Clang! They close the outer door and slide the inner one away ahead of you. Whoosh! There you stand, the other side of that tricksy old impenetrable forcefield. Down it comes for a moment, thud-thud you step inside, then wheep! up it goes again.

You're brave, girl (*stupid bitch*), we'll give you that.

Your face... easy enough, we think. Some of your more colourful expressions would take a while to perfect (oh gracious me yes that would be a ticklish and thorny one all right), but we doubt most of your friends could dig the nuances.

1. Jason, I guess. Though frankly, so long as we got the tits right...
2. Peter, presumably, but whom would he tell?
3. Brax? Would he even care? What's he up to these days, anyway, old Irving?

At this somewhat critical juncture, it might be considered a polite gesture to peel ourself off the floor and pull ourself the euphemism together.

Seconds later, physically collected and intact (with an option on future psychological coherence) we rear up on the footbase we built all by ourselves, saying, 'Hello Bernice,' out of the latest in our long sequence of mouths. 'You came to see us, then?'

We're *good* at mouths. Great flappy things with teeth. Oh, Lord, yes, we can knock one of those up in a jiffy.

Also claws. Barbs. Whips. Fangs. Stings, pincers, tentacles. Knives, flails, mauls, thrusting pointy jagged spear things and garrottes. All the better to slay you with, our dear.

We could *massacre* your good self in a million time-honoured or innovative ways, each fatally final. Big Daddy Adrian may be watching out for you, little sister, but how's that gonna help you, shut in here with us? You must think very highly of yourself, young lady.

Either that or you've realised at last what we were doing in Little Boy Blue's beddy-bye room.

'Your voice isn't how Jason described it,' you say.

Ah. You see, we'd only just got out of character back then. We've let that nasty old personality melt away since then, haven't we lovey? Sliding back into the protean primal soup of what you might (ludicrously) call our consciousness.

'What should I call you?' you ask quietly.

'Victoria,' we answer. And it's an easy one to start off with.

We need to show good faith. Gizza break darling, we're being upfront here, honest. Genuine. Induplicitous.

Like any self we dredged up would have the slightest goddamn clue how to go about a thing like that.

'Are you really a Mim?' Not some other kind of metamorph?'

God, you're so *stupid*. We hate you and we wish we'd never been born.

'No,' we say. 'For what it's worth we're Mim.'

We're Mim, ma'am, we are Mim, ma'am. Madam, Mim. Mim madam.

256

We feel a persona coming on. It rises from our memepool (pool of me me me), cohering and congealing and coagulating, becoming the *me* we'll need to interact with you, Professor.

Feels funny, like a sneeze-that-never-comes must feel, not to let a new physicality come along with it. But you, Benny babes, you're like, *what you see is what you get*. You'll want us to stay looking just like this.

Ah – here I am.

'How's Peter?' I ask solicitously. 'Not upset any more, I hope?'

So this is what it feels like. To understand myself, I must become me.

Coldly, you say, 'He's safe. Safe a long way away. You, on the other hand, aren't getting out of this cell until you give me some thoroughly satisfactory answers.'

'No need to get upset,' I say mildly. 'I only asked.'

You stand foursquare, arms folded, voice belligerent, too loud in the confined space. 'Why's Peter important to you?'

Protective, confrontational, assertive – and scared. For an expert on non-verbal communication, you're none too adept at suppressing it.

The room is grey and drab, institutional cell rather than medieval dungeon. Not dank or slimy – your Axis occupiers were subtler than that – but implacable and demoralising.

'He isn't,' I say. 'Important to me, I mean. The poor little beggar was just in the way. It was you I was after. I would have said so to Jason, but he started drilling chunks out of me instead. If you find some of me back at your house, could I have it back? It'll have crawled off into a corner somewhere, I expect.'

You're raising an eyebrow. 'You wanted to talk to me? Well, here I am.'

'Yeeesss,' I say. 'It's a little late now, I'm afraid. Things fall apart, the centre cannot hold, that kind of thing. What exactly *is* going on out there, if you don't mind me asking?'

You say, 'Never mind that now. You're an Earth agent, aren't you?'

I *ting!* 'Give the lady a cigar.'

'How old are you?' you ask.

That one takes me by surprise. 'Erm... I'm not altogether sure. Twelve, thirteen? It's never seemed important.'

'They bought you,' you say. 'Szmyt's Institute. They bought you from Sherm, or some predecessor of his.'

'Indeed they did,' I say.

Here comes the sympathy. 'I'm sorry,' you say. 'Growing up like that can't have been easy.'

Not *easy*? My dear woman.

'Well, no,' I say. 'The military training and indoctrination weren't much fun, it has to be said. The arbitrary physical humiliations weren't a picnic either – or if they were, it was an overcast, cold, wasp-infested picnic, with stinging nettles and rather disappointing food. The loyalty purges, to be frank, I'd sooner have lived without. And as for the medical procedures… Let's just say the one advantage of their being *irreversible* is that I'll never have to go through *that* again.'

You've been wincing during most of this, bless your predictably tender heart. 'I'm sorry,' you repeat, uselessly.

I stretch out, like a leisurely salami. 'Well, it wouldn't do for a covert operative to swan about the place spawning, would it? Not really the done thing in most societies. The Mimsphere excepted, of course, and they were hardly going to send us back there.'

You're looking grim. That's good. Grimness will be required.

You say, 'Did they give human names to all of you?'

Victoria? Oh, it's an old family name. A human joke.

I say, 'Remember Korenthai, also known as Salthmanika? George to his friends.'

'Friends like you?' you ask. Looking guilty now. You do have an impressive facial repertoire.

'He was a colleague,' I say brusquely.

'How long has this been going on, Victoria?' you ask.

'Oh, since they first came up with the cunning plan,' I say. 'Narcissus helped win them the war. It was too valuable an asset to wind up. They chose a new target, adjusted their approach, and came to an arrangement with certain insalubrious elements in Mim society to ensure a steady supply of recruits. I'm told we don't breed well in captivity,' I add bitterly. 'Not that I'd know, of course.'

You turn away, start pacing angrily. You can't go more than a few steps, of course, but the camera in the light-fitting turns to follow you anyway.

Your hairy ex is doubtless in some control booth somewhere, hanging on every word. Behind your back I make fingers and give him a little wave.

'They buy you,' you say. 'They train you up, brainwash you to ensure your loyalty. They neuter you. Then they send you off to infiltrate the Draconian Empire, or anyone else they fancy having as an enemy. You spy for them, spread disinformation, sabotage their infrastructure, assassinate whoever they tell you to… How am I doing so far?'

I feign a yawn, and stretch myself still further. 'Well, you can't "neuter" something with no sex. If you like, they do the opposite – they assign us gender despite our lack of exciting bits.' Except those we make ourselves, of course – and didn't *that* while away the long dark evenings in the dorm. 'But otherwise yes, you're digging in the right place.'

You swear. 'Shit. Here we all are worrying about someone getting their hands on an army of shapeshifters, and all the time Earth's been mustering them under our noses. Are there any here on the Collection? Among the staff, I mean?'

Well, Benny. As far as that goes, I could a pretty tale unfold.

Or a tail, of course. I'm versatile that way.

'Not my department,' I reply. 'But you haven't asked what my angle is in all of this. Why I came to see you, or why you're right to assume I'm not feeding you disinformation at the moment.'

'Oh, I know that,' you say lightly. 'You want to defect, don't you? You're hoping to avoid the consequences of your actions by throwing yourself on the Collection's protection.'

'*My* actions?' I must say I'm a bit miffed at that. I make myself vertical again, and you flinch.

'I know you're a murderer,' you say, still casual. 'When you arrived here you were Pashar, isn't that right? You met up with Ms Haddad to kill poor Lwpha.'

'Yes and, in a very real sense, no,' I say.

You lean against the wall, arms folded, eyebrows aloft. 'I'm listening.'

I do a sigh. 'You may have spotted that I don't sound especially brainwashed? Not exactly overflowing with daughterly love for our dear Mother Earth?'

'It had crossed my mind,' you answer.

'I'm pleased to hear it,' I say.

Oh, sod it. I may as well go humanoid for this. I give myself rough legs, arms and a head-shaped thing – nothing too detailed, I don't want to freak you out – and say: 'There are around thirty of us, mostly on Draconia itself, who've broken our conditioning. We each kept it quiet at first, of course, but slowly we each became aware that not all of our contacts were quite toeing the party line. The Institute must be letting their standards slip.'

'Then you *were* Pashar,' you say, as if you hadn't been declaring it confidently moments before. 'Korenthai – George – he would have been your control?'

'That's right,' I say. I can use my arms to gesture with now, pace around a bit, use body language. 'His conditioning was intact, poor chap, so I had to behave myself around him. But those of us who were feeling a bit more liberated managed to establish surreptitious contact. We formed a network of subversives and saboteurs within the larger infiltration network on Draconia. We call ourselves the Children of Nemesis. Er, possibly slightly melodramatically,' I admit, obscurely embarrassed.

You shake your head. 'So you were a Mim, pretending to be a Draconian so you could spy for Earth. Except that you were actually working to your own Mim agenda. I'm surprised you could stand the confusion in your mind.'

Surprised we're not madder than we are, you mean. Well, me too, chum.

I say, 'That's interstellar espionage for you.'

'Hang on, though,' you say, realising something. 'If Korenthai was still working for Earth –'

'For the Institute,' I correct her. 'They're not exactly accountable to the Earth public – they like to think of themselves as being above things like governments and laws. I doubt they tell even President Fiona everything that goes on in there.'

'Even so. That would mean they *ordered* him to arrange the phase-cannon attack. This whole nightmare cock-up of a mess has been their plan all along. They wanted to isolate the borogoves on Proxima as – oh, for Christ's sake – as a contingency plan. In case something terminal happened to the Mimsphere. Which lo and behold, it did.'

'I wouldn't hold them responsible for that,' I say. 'The Mimsphere, I mean. As you say, this is a contingency plan, not a best-case scenario.'

You purse your lips. 'And PL?'

'Well, yes,' I say. 'I wasn't privy to George's orders myself, and I doubt I could have done anything about them anyway, but... yes.'

You nod slowly. 'No wonder Mwshi looked so shocked when I told him it was Korenthai. He realised Earth had been shafting the Mim all along.'

'He talked to Szmyt and Haddad about it,' I say. 'That's why I came to see you, to tell you what was really going on.'

'Ah, yes.' You nod. 'Mr Szmyt and Ms Haddad. With their

surveillance-corrupting implants. Remind me, what have you been doing since Pashar disappeared?'

I tut. 'Do try to keep up, Benny. I've been Ms Haddad.'

The night Lwpha was killed, he was supposed to be meeting me. I'd made contact shortly after he arrived on the Collection, suggested we pool our resources. Unfortunately Ms Haddad chose that night to follow him.

When she arrived... well, I hadn't told him who I looked like. He was expecting an Earth agent who was a Mim in disguise. Haddad must have strung him along to get his story out of him, then...

She knew he'd cause her trouble. Lwpha would never have stood by and watched while Sherm handed their precious children over to Earth, allies or not. Szmyt and Haddad needed him out of the way, so Haddad killed him.

She used a Ferreira Protein Disperser, one of their execution weapons. We had to watch them being used on our less tractable classmates, back at the dear old alma mater. When I arrived Lwpha was already dead.

Leyla Haddad knew me. She'd known me as an infant, before I was even sentient, and later on in my Institutionalised days. She knew I was with the Draconian delegation, knew my cover and my orders and my serial number. I suppose all the violence must have gone to her head, because it slipped her mind, just for a moment, that I wasn't a Draconian.

She pulled out the wrong weapon. Wasted her opportunity to waste me.

I used one of our standard assassination techniques for air-breathing species, and engulfed her. I held her pinioned, unable to move, until she suffocated in me.

'Euw,' you say when I tell you this.

'It wasn't pretty,' I admit. 'But justice rarely is.'

To understand your enemy, you must become her. But why bother understanding your enemy? It seems a waste of time when you could just slaughter the bastard.

I had to do both, of course.

You say, 'So Pashar vanished because you'd become Haddad instead.'

We're sitting on the floor now, hugging our respective knees at one another across the cramped space. 'That's why Ithva's footage showed her leaving, but not arriving. The first time her implants hid her. The second time she came through loud and clear. And Haddad vanished when you got arrested.'

'Because by then the real Ms Haddad was already compost,' I remind you, not without relish.

This is probably the point where I should tell you about that other thing. The... item I found on Haddad's body. But the situation's complicated enough already.

'So Ithva was right about Haddad killing Lwpha,' you say.

'Clever old Ithva,' I reply.

'But why get rid of Haddad's body and steal her identity?' you ask. 'You could have made it look as if she and Lwpha killed each other without your help. It wouldn't have been the perfect crime or anything, but it would have seemed tidy enough that no one would have come looking for you.'

'I *wanted* to be Haddad,' I say. 'She had *power*. That's something I've never had.'

You disapprove, of course. So I elaborate.

'Specifically, she had power at the Institute. If I became her, Szmyt and I could make sure the Mim got their borogoves back. The Project would get its new recruits – its new children – and I could rescue them. I'd have taken them somewhere far away, where we could all look after them, the other deprogrammed agents and I. We could have started our lives over again. With hope.'

'Oh.' Your expression's changed completely. 'Oh, I see.'

'Those bastards took away my future children,' I insist. 'I was going to take away theirs. Like I said, justice.'

'Well...' I can see you turning it over in your mind. 'It's justice of a kind, Victoria, yes. But surely you can see what would have happened? Szmyt and his pals would just have gone straight back to PL and demanded more children.'

'Then I'd have rescued them as well,' I say, defiantly. 'But the whole thing's gone tits-up now, thanks to Jason's little overreaction. Coming after me with a drill and calling security. Honestly, I could throttle that man.'

'You did quite enough to him last night,' you remind me sternly. 'Although there are times when I'd say the same myself. Hang on a minute.' You frown.

There's a long pause, during which you say 'Er.' You stare at my rough-hewn human shape, mimicking your own posture.

Eventually you groan. 'You utter cow. You've based this personality on me, haven't you?'

You glare at me until I start to giggle. A moment or two later your expression of affronted indignation falls apart.

I'm faking, naturally. But it still feels good.

Eventually we finish rolling around on the floor. You shake your head. 'That isn't the first time this has happened to me, you know. Not even this month, actually. I'm really going to have to stop being so distinctively *me*.'

'You're more fun than Ms Haddad or Pashar,' I tell you. 'And it's not as if you don't play parts yourself – Professor, Benny, Bernice, Ms Summerfield, Mummy ...'

'And turning smartly back to *your* personality problems,' you say, 'you were talking about wanting power...?'

I say, 'It's too late for that now. I've been away too long – if I go back to being Ms Haddad, the situation will have run away without me. So, do you want to hear *my* contingency plan?'

'Victoria,' you say, 'what you're locked up in here for is a lot less serious than what you actually did. Threatening Peter and assaulting Jason's bad enough, but actually killing someone... It wasn't self-defence. If you could keep Ms Haddad still while you smothered her, you could have held her while you called for help. Whatever she may have done to you in the past, however provoked you may have felt, I can't condone that.'

I reply, 'If I'm a killer, it's because she made me one.'

'No,' you say sternly. 'You can't hide behind that either. If you're free, you have to take responsibility for your own actions. But yes, I'll hear you out. Just at the moment I can't choose my allies, and you're the nearest thing I've got to a secret weapon. If you come near my son again, though, you can rot in here for ever as far as I'm concerned. Sound fair?'

I start to thank you, but you raise a hand. '*Furthermore*, if this contingency plan of yours involves killing and replacing Ambassador Kothar and carrying out exactly the same scheme from the Draconian end, I shall be very disappointed.'

Needled, I say, 'It bloody does not!'

You smile. 'No?'

'No,' I mutter. 'I was going to pick Deputy Ambassador Werther. How did you guess?'

'Forgive me, Victoria,' you say gently, 'but you're very easy to predict. They've trained you to think in certain ways. Assassinate, infiltrate, subvert. Between the two of us we can do better than that.'

And you lean in to tell me what you have in mind.

7

Mwshi

Bernice insisted we summon Mr Szmyt here, to my quarters. She is oblivious, I think, to any violation this might represent. Fortunately I have little emotional attachment to this space.

The three of us have spawned our plans together, clustered about this fabricated shore. Bernice perches above the false tideline, next to that outlandish door to the hominid world. I have anchored myself beneath the waves, the upper third of my tube-body protruding into air.

I have severe misgivings about this whole enterprise.

Bernice's scheme will restore to my people our guardianship of the borogoves on Holiday Home, she says. With, she adds, the bonus of Draconian financial support. I cannot see how this is possible, but Bernice has described the process as a 'domino effect'.

The help of Bernice's new friend, the stolen child, will gain us Mr Szmyt's cooperation. Szmyt's aid will somehow influence Ambassador Kothar in our favour. Kothar in turn will represent us to his Emperor.

Each of these steps seems to me dangerous and insane, and hopelessly unlikely to succeed. But Bernice wants to borrow my rooms and my respectability, not hear my opinions.

The veneer of Mimishness stretched so thin across this space will unnerve Szmyt, Bernice believes. She needs the man to feel caught between worlds.

Between her and myself stands the changeling child with her fractal loyalties, mock-human feet planted at the water's edge. Why Bernice believes that this 'Victoria' can be trusted I do not know.

The young Mim wears Ms Haddad's body and persona. Her imitation is consummate, and her conviction scares me. Has she, this polyvalent multiple-agent, any idea who she truly is? Behind that woman's sharp face with its mirrored eyes, within that rounded torso in its counterfeit fabrics, speaking through that harsh voice, who is she? Is there anyone at all?

Some contrivance has even overlaid Victoria's natural scent with that of a human woman, a feat of self-control never attained by the Mimsphere's own imitators-of-aliens. Her emissions carry but the faintest intimation of Mim company, suggesting Haddad has spent some time today with another of my people. The odour I remember from our meeting in the pub.

She masks her own musk further, with a cigarette.

She must have passed blood tests, too, to pass as a Draconian. Has some form of chemical surgery achieved this? What other augmentations does she have? How many ways have the humans at this Institute abused and insulted her?

And Bernice has invited their representative, like their creation, here to my rooms.

With no conventional polite warning, my door melts away. Mr Szmyt stands poised, alert and arrogant. He fills the doorframe, occupying the threshold, preventing the gas-barrier from resolidifying as he gazes around.

'Mr Szmyt,' Victoria says quietly.

Seeing her simulation of his former partner, Szmyt's eyes bulge, and he recoils slightly. Presumed dead, abducted or absconded, Ms Haddad is now restored to life, freedom and immediate presence. So his eyes tell him.

When he speaks, his voice is controlled. 'Ms Haddad.'

Convincing him of Victoria's bona fides as Haddad takes some time. There are, after all, a great many Mim on the Collection, some of them known adepts at mimicry. But Victoria knows the agents' background, the structure of their organisation, many of their operational procedures. She refers to conversations she had with

Szmyt before her disappearance, alludes obscurely, in Bernice's and my presence, to her role in Lwpha's murder.

It is a magnificent performance.

'Where have you been, Ms Haddad?' Szmyt finally asks, conceding her identity. 'You know the rules. We keep partners informed of our whereabouts at all times. The Director'll have your ass for this.'

'I was acting *for* the Director, Mr Szmyt.' Victoria's voice and stance, authentically weary. 'He thought he'd noticed some – shall we say irregularities? – in your recent reports. I did my best to fight your corner, you know, but he still thought they'd bear investigating.'

'Irregularities.' Szmyt's voice, lacking inflection.

'Yes, Mr Szmyt, irregularities. To be perfectly frank, he thought you were selling us out to the Draconians.'

Szmyt's eyes flick across at Bernice and me. 'My loyalty has always been above question. To Earth and to the Institute.'

He is off-balance. On edge. He still has not stepped fully through the door.

'Nothing's above question where the Director's concerned,' she smiles, 'you know that. But you're quite right, of course. However hard I looked, *I* couldn't see any signs that you'd been compromised. Congratulations dearie, you're in the clear.'

'Good of you to say so,' Szmyt tells her tersely. He is angry with us, angry with Haddad. Angry at her for confiding in strangers, aliens even, above him.

A master at filtering perceptions, Victoria uses Szmyt's anger like his discomfort, diverting his mind from its undercurrent of perfectly correct suspicion.

A skill she owes to him and his agency. Victoria is using human methods to fight humans.

She makes Haddad's face smile. 'It's nice,' she says, 'because it means I can let you in on the plan Bernice and I have been cooking up with Dr Mwshi. It should bring the negotiations round to our preferred outcome... ooh, sometime tonight.'

'Plan? What plan?' Szmyt demands. 'Why should we trust Summerfield? She's been in Kothar's pocket all along. And her husband called me a prat,' he adds.

'Oh, she's sound –' Victoria begins, but Bernice steps between them. Hands on hips, she glares into Szmyt's eyes. A primate territorial challenge.

'For buggery's sake, Szmyt,' she says, 'how can you be so unobservant? Of course I have to maintain good relations with the

267

Draconians in my official capacity. But just a little while ago, they were an occupying force, and believe it or not we don't much like invading armies round these parts. Kothar threatened my son. He locked Adrian away, had Bev Tarrant killed... I hate that bastard every bit as much as you do. I'll take him down any way I can.'

I am no friend to Kothar, nor have I ever become perfectly attuned to human emotional states. Yet Bernice's tone of voice shocks even me.

Szmyt nods slowly. 'Makes sense. If you vouch for her, Ms Haddad, we may have ourselves a partnership. On a strictly temporary basis.'

Bernice says, 'That suits me fine.'

Nodding again, he finally steps from corridor into room. 'What would this plan involve, exactly?'

Bernice takes a deep breath. 'It will involve sacrificing one of your assets,' she says. 'But it will get you back a lot more. You see, a contact of mine has been looking after someone who turns out to be a contact of yours...'

Victoria

I will admit to some surprise at the speed with which you won him over, Professor Summerfield.

Yes, well. We played *me* – the real me, I mean – easily enough, with all that humour and sarcasm and sympathy. Especially the little-girl-lost stuff. An abandoned, abused child who'll never be a mother. How could I resist?

It was most carefully calculated, I admit.

Well done, dearie. Follow your training, there's a clever sponge.

This does not diminish the sincerity with which we spoke; nor our quite genuine need of your assistance; nor, if you'll permit me to say so, the honest esteem in which we hold your real self, Professor.

Stop it. I'm welling up.

As for Mr Szmyt, you had speculated that Earth's emissaries might be as much frustrated as we by these endless delays, but...

But he was so eager it was quite pathetic.

This is, at least, how it appears to us as Ms Haddad. But she has never liked her partner, I believe.

You have to remember, Szmyt thinks he's under suspicion. He needs to demonstrate his loyalty, and Haddad's scheme – our scheme, supposedly – gets their Institute full control over PL through a Mim puppet government. Throw in unrestricted access to the borogoves now *and* for the foreseeable future, and opposing it would not have made him look good.

Supporting it, by contrast, demonstrates beyond doubt to his supposed Ms Haddad –

– to me –

– that he is in the thrall of no Draconian paymaster. Yes, I understand. Well, that's what I let him think, anyway. We didn't leave him much choice in the end, did we?

As soon as the Lady Ithva and I are summoned into his office, I am able to discern that her husband the Ambassador is furious. He stands with his back towards the fireplace, dominating the room with his looming, fluctuating shadow. 'Pashar,' he greets me, snarling, and I begin to tremble in my recently reconstructed bones.

'When these humans,' the Ambassador spits, indicating Mr Szmyt and you, Professor, 'told me that you were skulking in fear for your life, hiding behind the skirts of a female, I could scarcely credit it. Yet here you are, and here my wife is.'

Don't worry, you've got him rattled – look how he's holding his hands. He doesn't like it when other people know things he doesn't.

That's right, dearie. These Dragons may be cunning and inscrutable, but they're no match for our Earth pluck and ingenuity.

Being so many people in so short a time is very confusing. My recent mental emulations of Ms Haddad and of yourself, Professor, hover at my shoulders like the ghosts of annoying elder sisters I could not possibly have had. If I am not quite careful, these dangerous human ideas might contaminate my Draconian integrity. It is very fortunate that our present scenario does not require perfect verisimilitude.

His Excellency is still talking. 'Have you no shame, Junior Consular Officer? Didn't you consider how such a disgrace would affect your family?' He thrusts a claw at me contemptuously.

If we were Ms Haddad still, then we could handle Ambassador Kothar without trouble. Ms Haddad would block his arrogance with her indifference, his acuity with her feigned obtuseness. And you, Professor Summerfield, would parry him with exemplary conversational barbs of your own. As Pashar, however, I have always been quite insecure and easily intimidated. I am very conscious of my dignity, or more often of my lack thereof. These aspects of a person can be very difficult to overlook, especially from within.

His Excellency persists in his harangue. 'It would be better for them if you had been a murderer. A killer has more honour than a coward.' A drop of his spittle comes to rest on my cheek.

See? He couldn't be more rattled if you tied him to the back end of a snake.

'Forgive me, Excellency,' I beg the Ambassador. 'I can but apologise for my abject behaviour. I am in every likelihood the most contemptible of all living creatures.'

Why, Pashar, that was almost sarcastic.

The Lady Ithva steps forward, speaking sharply. 'Nonsense,' she declares. 'You're under my protection, Pashar, and that means you fall under my authority. Not the Ambassador's.'

I do not know, Professor, how you convinced her ladyship to collude in the deception of her husband. Like all Draconian women, she is always working to obscure purposes of her own. In any case, her kindness is humiliating to me. Of noble birth she may be, and the wife of his Excellency the Ambassador, but she is still a female.

Oh, that's *much* better.

Yes, nothing like a good display of sexist claptrap to add authenticity.

To his lady, the Ambassador responds. 'We shall discuss this later, Ithva, in private. I'm surprised, though, that you would have risked exposing our children to such a degenerate.'

Her reply is languid. 'And I'm insulted that you'd think I would. He's been kept well away from them, I promise you.'

Now it is you, Professor, addressing me. 'Pashar, could you tell Ambassador Kothar what you told us about Lwpha's murder?'

I launch into my prepared testimony. I confirm that (as you, Professor, have informed his Excellency already) the murderer of Lwpha was Deputy Ambassador Werther.

He must, I fear, be some kind of Mim infiltrator, for he changed his shape before dispatching his victim. I observed the two of them in the outbuilding, before I fled in terror for my life. I was too ashamed to admit my cowardice to the Ambassador, and too afraid of what his false deputy might do to me, so in desperation I threw myself upon his wife's protection. I, Pashar, can only reiterate in what contempt I know hold myself.

'I'm not at all surprised.' The Ambassador's tone is cold and dismissive as he turns to Mr Szmyt. 'Whereas your behaviour – Mr Szmyt, Professor Summerfield – *is* somewhat surprising. I appreciate your frankness, of course. But forgive me for saying that if I learned that the Earth delegation had been infiltrated by the Mim, I wouldn't hurry to alert you to it.'

'But we're allies, Ambassador.' For a moment Mr Szmyt's face, habitually as stony and expressionless as a Draconian's (whereas most humans wear their emotions with disgraceful candour), bears a quite unmistakeable smirk.

As far as this Earthman is aware, his partner is presently back in her quarters, reporting to their masters on his innocence and on the hoped-for imminent success of their endeavours. I, Pashar, on the other hand, am not merely Pashar but Victoria, one of the Institute's Mim operatives in Draconian society, now being called upon to demonstrate my loyalty by falsely incriminating my controllers' enemy, the Deputy Ambassador.

If he realised you and I were the same person, the silly man would have some sort of seizure.

His Excellency's own expression is stormier than ever. 'Noted, but nonetheless – to what do I owe your candour, Szmyt?'

Gesturing towards me the Earthman scornfully declares, 'This is a *lie*, Ambassador. It's propaganda. Disinformation. Werther's no more a murderer than you are.'

I gasp. 'What do you mean, sir?' My simulated body starts to betray panic as the implied meaning of the human's words becomes apparent. 'Excellency,' I plead, 'my lady, this Earthman is intending to deceive you. Do not listen to him, I beg you!'

Szmyt continues as if uninterrupted. 'Your deputy's no guiltier than any other politician. Your junior consular officer, on the other hand...'

His smirk returns as he enunciates, '*Rhamnusia.*'

... and at the name of nemesis, obedient to our deepest levels of inscribed instinct, our body bucks rebellious and writhes: we melt like water, shimmer like a flame, and before that old Dragon Kothar's shock-horrified green eyes, his peevish subordinate becomes – gasp! – a ravening Mim...

Kothar

'I'm so embarrassed, Bernice,' my wife says. 'I feel so foolish, harbouring a Mim infiltrator here under Jarith's roof.'

'Erm, yes,' Summerfield agrees. Since our ordeal she has partaken generously of the hospitality my Embassy reserves for human guests. She is now on her fourth scotch. 'I'm glad your drinks cabinet's a sturdy one, at least. It would be criminal to have sacrificed this stuff.' She adds, 'I wouldn't blame yourself though, Ithva. They're devilishly cunning, these Mim.'

'Oh, I don't blame *myself*, Bernice,' Ithva says, rather emphatically. 'Even so, my silliness put you in a very unfortunate position. We must talk later on, about how I can possibly make it up to you.'

'Erm, yes,' says Summerfield again. There is some hidden context here, something which necessarily passes me by. I know from long experience that such codes are impossible for a man to interpret.

'Don't fret, my dear,' I reassure Ithva, patting her claws. 'It was a difficult experience for us all.'

In truth, none of us have been quite ourselves since that monstrosity emerged, its whiplike limbs cracking and flailing, from its vile semblance of Draconian form and set about wrecking my office. Loath though I am to admit it, it was most fortunate that Adrian Wall's men were at hand, stationed within the building by Summerfield as a precaution. I confess I would feel easier now were the creature not still at large. No sooner had Wall's security team dragged it outside in one of their electro-nets, than the device suffered a catastrophic power-failure, and the impostor fled.

I suspect sabotage, though on the part of whom I cannot guess. There are concealed blades here, feints and counter-feints, decoys and stratagems; of this I am certain. I find myself suddenly without confidence in any of my allies. Werther may not have murdered Haddad, but I have seen him talking to Braxiatel. Both assure me that their association is entirely innocent, but I cannot believe that. However much the Collection's former proprietor may claim disinterest, it is clear that he has ends of his own.

And if a Mim may pass convincingly among us, whom can I trust but myself, my wife and my Emperor?

Now Summerfield sits before the wreckage of my desk, amid the chaos of splintered furniture. Reports and dossiers, minutes and memos litter the shredded carpet. Warmed by the fire to which she has added the least recoverable fragments of my chairs, Summerfield has commandeered for herself the most comfortable of the few remaining. She is more than a little intoxicated.

Ithva is at my side, suffered, for now, as an indulgence under these extreme circumstances, to remain with us as our conversation spirals ever closer towards politics. I know that Ithva has influence with Summerfield, who after all is herself a female. It is unorthodox, undoubtedly, but in dealing with aliens we may sometimes have recourse to alien methods and techniques.

I draw the line at tolerating Mr Szmyt, however. At first, as the bedlam of the Mim incursion died down, the Earth observer remained here to gaze with us on its ruinous aftermath. But I refused to associate with a man who traffics in children.

He scowled when I first raised this objection. 'That is a libel against myself and my employers,' was his response, 'and I demand to know who told it you.' He is not a particularly intelligent specimen of humanity.

'You haven't been forthcoming with your own sources of information, Mr Szmyt,' I reminded him. 'How did you discover Pashar was a Mim? Who gave you that trigger-word?'

Summerfield sighed and said, 'You know we have a source. Given what we've shown you, isn't that enough? Our information comes from someone tired of spying, whose identity we can't reveal. Doesn't it?' she added sharply, applying an elbow to Szmyt's ribs. The Earth agent was looking at her in some confusion.

Shortly afterwards, the Earthman was called away. Plaster crunched beneath his feet as he left, while Summerfield made pointed comments about people who answer the phone during meetings with Ambassadors. She really is an impossible woman. 'If I had to hazard a guess,' she added as Szmyt left, 'I'd say that was the mysteriously returned Ms Haddad on the phone, with a lead on where that fugitive Mim of theirs has got to. It's got rid of him, anyway.'

Now, with only my wife present, I ask Summerfield how deep her information goes.

She says, 'My source can supply us with the cover identities of one particular network of Mim operatives. What they've told me so far makes for pretty hair-raising listening, I can tell you. Well, not for me – I don't give a hoot about the security of your Empire – but it would be hair-raising for you.' She frowns. 'I don't mean hair-raising, of course. Crest-raising, possibly? Help me out, Ithva.'

Gently my wife removes the whisky-glass from Summerfield's grip. 'Shall we settle for blood-curdling, Benny? The rather more significant question being – why?'

'Oh, right.' Summerfield purloins another glass from a nearby tray, and pours herself another generous measure of spirit. 'Their name translates as "Children of Nemesis". Nemesis was the goddess of vengeful fate – your equivalent would be some avenging culture-hero, like Zhakaroth the Bereaved. Think of them as the Sons of Zhakaroth, if it helps.' She samples her whisky. 'Mm. They're a pretty desperate bunch. There aren't that many of them – around thirty, I gather – but some of their cover identities are pretty high-ranking. Military officers, of course, and influential figures in your, er, women's circles. But also members of the Imperial Court, and of the noble houses.'

Ithva was perfectly correct. 'Blood-curdling' is indeed the word.

'Oh,' she adds. 'And they can fool your blood tests. Some kind of protein-nanofacturing implant, I think.'

'These noble houses...' I begin.

'Oh, yes,' says Summerfield, suddenly exhibiting a firmer grip upon sobriety. 'They would indeed include the Imperial Family. Basically, if these thirty-odd Mim decide to bring down your Empire – and after the Mimsphere they've every reason to try – you're screwed.'

'Then we must have that list, Bernice,' Ithva says firmly.

'I can only agree,' I say. 'Congratulations, Professor Summerfield. You win. Your price is the borogoves, I presume?'

Summerfield raises a hand. 'Just a minute, Kothar – Kothars. I won't be party to a witch-hunt. Too many Mim have died already. There's an alternative, a neat and tidy one which gets them out of your hair. Your crests. Whatever.'

I feel the faintest intimation of a mechanism being sprung. 'Explain,' I say.

She says, 'As luck would have it, it also involves a neat and tidy way out of our difficulties on Proxima Longissima.'

'A way out?' I repeat. 'For whom precisely?'

'For all of us,' she grins. 'It's the holy grail of diplomacy – a way to sort out this whole miserable bloody mess to everybody's... well, moderate satisfaction. It's simple, it will work, everyone gets what they want and nobody needs to lose face. Assuming you go along with it, of course. But first, I need your word that, if these Mim are willing to cooperate, not one of them will be harmed. *That's* my price.'

I make a show of considering her demand. But really, it is hardly as if I have other avenues left open. I nod eventually. 'You have my word, Professor Summerfield.'

'Good,' she says briskly. 'Then here's the deal. The Mim will agree to your most recent proposal. PL and its population will remain under Draconian control, with Draconian funding and full access for the adult Mim to educate their children. Those children will be extended the Grace of Emancipation when they reach maturity, and eventually – let's say in twenty years' time – the planet itself gets given back to whatever government the Mim may have by then.

'Oh, they'll agree,' she adds as I begin to object, 'on one condition. The Emperor himself must personally appoint the Draconian officials who are to administer the planet. A hand-picked team of supervisors

– around thirty of them, male and female. And he'll select them very carefully indeed.'

Ithva places a hand on my arm, advising caution, as I begin to protest vociferously.

Summerfield continues. 'In the eyes of the Empire, the planet will be run by loyal Draconians, under the command of one of the Emperor's own family. The honour of the Empire – and of House Kothar – will be upheld.' She smiles beatifically. 'Only the Emperor, and the two of you, will know that every single last one of those loyal Draconians is actually a Mim.'

Ithva

'It all seems to be turning out rather nicely,' you tell me later. 'You'll be able to take Sharintha home to Draconia soon.'

We're walking in the gardens beyond the Embassy. Behind us the sun rises over the Collection's too-close horizon – Braxiatel's private star ascending over his self-contained, hermetic world, and glancing off one of his many attractive ornamental lakes.

For someone who's been up all night, talking long-distance to the Empress herself among other things, you seem remarkably animated, gesturing enthusiastically as we walk and you talk.

Sharintha and her shield-lizard – who by contrast slept through all our earlier discussions, and the contretemps in Jarith's office, and the hectic night which followed, and have now awoken, refreshed and full of energy – are romping on the path in front of us. My daughter laughs as she dashes in spirals round the loyally plodding animal.

You say, 'Mwshi's back on the delegation already, now I've explained the situation to Sherm and Phwmi. They're falling over themselves to sign the treaty – they all love the idea of putting one over on Draconia *and* Earth.'

'That's nice for them,' I reply, a little sharply.

You look abashed. 'Sorry, that was tactless of me. I'm very grateful for your help, Ithva. I couldn't have done it without you.'

'I'm well aware of that, Bernice,' I say.

It's not that I take pleasure in pricking your balloon, my dear. You're quite right to be proud of your achievement, and it's charming to see you looking so happy. But, looking back at the little performance which the four of us – you, Mr Szmyt, 'Pashar' and I – put on for Jarith in his office, it's difficult to avoid the conclusion that you've manipulated all of us to one extent or another.

Which is very clever of you, naturally, my dear, but also rather vexing. I can't think where you can have picked up such habits.

'The beauty of this arrangement, though,' you tell me as we pass from the pondside into a tree-lined avenue, 'is everyone really wins. Except Szmyt, of course. And Werther I suppose, and probably Sherm in the final analysis, but sod them. The Mim are feeling pleased with themselves – and good for them, they need a victory, even if it's mostly a symbolic one – but you've every reason to as well.'

I tilt my head, raise an eyebrow in imitation of your questioning body-language.

Earnestly, you continue. 'Victoria and her friends will give the mainstream Mim full access to the borogoves, yes – their upbringing's in good pseudopodia. But from your point of view, those children are *safe*. Safer even than they'd have been under the Empire, with Werther and his clique sniffing around. The Children of Nemesis will keep every one of them alive, barring accidents.'

I smile tightly. 'So you told me earlier, my dear.' That, after all, is the only real reason I agreed to participate in your little charade. 'By that I suppose you mean that the supervisors will still be answerable to the Emperor and Empress, especially with their funding coming from the Imperial coffers.'

'Exactly.' You nod vigorously. It surely can't be long now before you fall over on the woodchipped path and sleep for a week. 'Any hint that they aren't living up to the Seventh Blade of Honour, and there'll be a public scandal. They can't make the colony work without the Emperor's money. Plus they know perfectly well that if they do something really silly, like trying to secede from the Empire, your people will wade in again, guns blazing.

'It's not exactly Shangri-la, I know, but so long as everyone keeps their heads it's a perfectly workable equilibrium.'

I frown. In a nearby tree a bird chitters angrily. 'So these Nemesis people will look after the orphans properly because they've no choice? I must say that isn't quite the nurturing family environment I'd been hoping for.'

Your face is serious. 'Oh, but it is. Victoria's people may be biologically Mim, but that's not how they were brought up.'

'Well, no. Their personalities were designed – forged, you might say – by your people's military as weapons of infiltration and sabotage. That's why your Mr Szmyt's happy, isn't it? He thinks the people running the planet are going to hand the pick of the young Mim over to him. Perhaps you'd like to tell me why he's wrong.'

276

'They're their own people now. Szmyt's going to find that out, eventually.'

I raise my eyebrow again. 'And when he does?'

You shrug. 'By then it'll be too late. Victoria's keeping him occupied, popping up here and there as Pashar, then sending Szmyt running after him as Haddad. She's going to hand over to another Mim soon, so she can take charge of the work on PL. Between them they can steer Szmyt, make sure that he colludes with them to cover the whole thing up – because if it does come out, he'll be the one that gets the blame. Either way he won't be in a position to complain about breach of contract.'

'Time for breakfast, I think.' We turn back, shivering slightly in the cold dawn. Sharintha picks up poor Ixiss and runs ahead of us, yelling. 'Don't be so *rough*, darling!' I shout.

You say, 'Don't you see, though – Victoria and her friends are free now. They've thrown off their conditioning and built themselves fresh personalities. And they did that while living as Draconians.'

You put a hand on my shoulder, just for a moment. 'They woke up to find themselves living your lives – immersed in your culture, your principles and worldview. Mim soak up the influences around them like – well, you know what. The ex-Narcissus agents are as much Draconian as they are human, and as much either of those as they are Mim. They take their values from all three cultures – and they take the Draconian parenting ethic very seriously.'

'I see,' I say – and actually, I do.

We pass out of the arboreal walk, back towards the pond and Embassy. You say, 'Do you know what Victoria resents most, out of all the things that were done to her at that Institute? They took her ability to have children away from her. Her whole plan as Haddad was to get hold of some juvenile Mim to look after. She's thirteen, she's terrifyingly capable, and what she wants more than anything else is to be a parent. Those borogoves are safe, I promise you.'

I stare ahead, towards that hunched horizon and its artificial sunrise, wondering which of us is wrong. Are you as naive as I fear, my love, my waterflame, or have I just been cynical for too long? I admire your faith in sentient nature, Benny, really I do, but honestly – can good intentions possibly be enough? Can all these opposing natures come to rest in mutual harmony?

The stone-bound waters of the lake reflect the sun, a lonely fire surrounded by hollow emptiness. And in the ripples of the pond, a glimmer dances.

We watch Sharintha play by the lakeside for a little while. 'I'll be bringing Peter back soon,' you tell me quietly. 'They'll be able to say goodbye to each other. I'll leave it a day or two, perhaps, to give Jason and me a chance to catch up first.'

'You've earned it, dear,' I say, then shout: 'Five more minutes, Sharintha, then we'll see about breakfast!'

You're silent for a moment, seeking out the words you need. At last you ask, 'So are you going to talk to her?'

I say, 'I'm going to have to, I suppose.'

'You're sure it was her?'

I shake my head. 'With all those things Jarith knew? About Ms Haddad and the murder? About the reasons for a cover-up, and the interstellar war? He even knew Mr Szmyt had been trafficking in juvenile Mim. I didn't tell him any of those things, and unless you're being quite astonishingly devious, you didn't either.'

'He was surprised he hadn't found out about Pashar, as well,' you say. 'He mentioned your children then.'

'I know.' I glance down sharply at my daughter, playing so near to us with those sharp little ears of hers, and she looks away from us in sudden confusion.

I'm proud of her initiative, of course, not to mention her gift for recall. But she must learn – and soon, apparently – that there are some things one just doesn't discuss with men. Even, and perhaps especially, one's father.

I sigh. 'They grow up so fast these days, don't they?'

Jason

Benny's been back home now for an hour and a half. In that time she hasn't stopped talking for longer than it's taken to shove six rounds of cheese-on-toast and two pints of tea down her throat.

She's told me everything that's happened in the last twenty hours. It's like keeping all that experience inside has been scalding her, like she needs to upload it into someone else's brain as quickly as possible. We've gone through her visit to our Mim intruder (Victoria, apparently), and what it told her about Ms Haddad, the Institute and Lwpha's murder. (Ms Haddad's murder, too, though Benny's glossing over that bit.)

She's told me all about the charade they put on in Mwshi's rooms and Kothar's office, and later on with the Draconian Emperor and Empress.

She tells me all about this deal she's brokered, basically, to bring about galactic peace. Again.

'That's marvellous,' I tell her for the sixty-ninth time. 'That's really amazing, Benny. I'm proud of you.'

She grins, just riding the exhilaration for a moment. 'I am pretty damn fantastic, aren't I?' She's in for a hard fall later, I can tell. 'Mind you, it isn't quite as clear-cut as I made out to Ithva.'

'No?' I say – but why I bother I couldn't tell you. She chunters on regardless.

'Not entirely. Guaranteed access to PL for the surviving adult Mim is great in theory. But that includes Sherm and Phwmi, and heaven only knows how many other cultists and gangsters and assorted maniacs. Victoria's friends will be keeping a beady eye on them all, but sooner or later someone's going to try smuggling children offworld and selling them to Earth. Or to the Draconians, if Werther has any influence left at court.'

'Benny,' I say. I get up, cross around the dining table and start to massage her shoulders. 'It's okay. You can't take responsibility for everything.'

She sighs. 'Oh, I know. There's still an awful lot to do here, but once I've –' She stops.

'You know what?' she says. 'Sod it. I've done enough, Brax can take it from here. It's about time he got off his arse and made himself useful. And there isn't that much more to do, really. Diplomatically, it's all over bar the paperwork. Oh, dear *God*, that feels good. The point of this whole exercise was to give the Mim control over their future. Well, now they've got it, and good luck to them. I'm finished.'

I lean forward to kiss her neck. '*Was* that the point?' I say. 'For you, I mean?'

'Well, no.' She reaches up and guides my hand towards a knot of extra stubborn tension. 'For me it was about one person's children. Well, not even that really – it was about an annoying bloody alien who turned up while I was trying to have a nice hot bath, then wouldn't bugger off.

'It's just... it snowballed, and it wouldn't stop. One person asking for my help became a family in need. Then a serious sentient-rights issue. Then a political hot potato, a diplomatic incident, an imminent war... not to mention murder, slave-trafficking and multiple war crimes on the side.'

I keep on pressing, kneading, rubbing, soothing. 'And now?'

'Now it can be about the children again,' she says. 'Lwpha's and, rather more pressingly, ours.' She takes my hand again, but this time draws me down into a long and tender kiss.

For a long while we stay like that, melting together.

Then something else seems to strike her, and she disengages. 'Oh, and Victoria's had an idea about the other Earth spies – the Mim who are still under the Institute's conditioning. Once things have settled down and her people have got the PL situation sorted properly, she's going to start taking them there. One by one, and carefully supervised. She thinks their parenting response will kick in once they've seen the borogoves, and kick-start the whole deprogramming process. She may yet manage to dismantle the entire spy network.'

I get that. Looking after other people's children… it makes you feel close to them, children and parents both. Can make you love them, even. I know looking after Peter's brought me closer to Benny.

Shit, some days I'm even moderately fond of Adrian.

This quiet domesticity thing… it's not so bad, compared with some of the alternatives. And it comes with some excellent fringe benefits.

'Less talk,' I say, 'more shagging. Those babies aren't going to make themselves, you know.'

I pick her up and carry her upstairs. I can still do that, you know.

'Oh,' she says five minutes later, just as I'm peeling off her jeans. 'There's something else as well. No, Jason, it's important. There'll be plenty of time for that later, I promise. Oh… yes, and *that*. Mm, don't stop. No, hang on, do. Honestly, this won't take a sec. There's something you need to know.'

Feeling pretty wounded, actually, I stop. 'For God's sake, can't it wait? I'm as hard as a bedpost here.'

'Hold that charming thought.' She leans over (bra still on, but what I can see swings very nicely, thank you) and ferrets around in the jeans we've just removed. 'Victoria gave me this,' she says, emerging with a folded printout. 'She said she found it on Ms Haddad's body. Before, you know.'

'Before she destroyed the corpse,' I say. 'But after she killed her. That what you mean?'

'She had a lot of provocation.' Benny knows I'm only trying to make her unhappy because I'm still horny. Thank Christ she understands me, at least. 'I can't be the judge of everyone,' she says. 'I'd go mad. Anyway, look.'

I do. 'It's addressed to you. Here at the Collection.'

'That's right,' she says. 'Read it.'

Two seconds later I say, 'It's a trap.'

'Yeah,' she says.

God, it doesn't let up, does it? Another mystery. Another clue, another adventure. It's like living with bleeding Nancy Drew.

I could make a joke about being quite the hardy boy myself, but my heart's not in it.

Don't go, I want to say. *Just – leave it. Don't give them the satisfaction, whoever they are. Peter needs you. I need you – not just to make babies, either. One day you really are going to get yourself killed.*

I open my mouth.

Benny puts a finger on my lips. 'Less talk,' she says.

We get on with the other thing instead.

8

Braxiatel (option 1)

... then to be thwarted by you Bernice, of all people, is a rather unfortunate outcome for all of us; and in particular for the Collection, given my intention to place into Szmyt and Haddad's hands a self-renewing supply of undetectable infiltrators; which would have allowed them to build Earth's paltry Empire far beyond its present boundaries, towards that overweening galactic dominance which you and I both know it must eventually attain; an alliance with whom would have protected us from further incursions by occupying Draconian armies; but no, you wouldn't have that, would you Benny...

Braxiatel (option 2)

... and especially for my Collection, given that it was my plan to hand Deputy Ambassador Werther an infinitely malleable army of fighting metamorphs with which to shore up his Empire against its forthcoming collapse; thus keeping Earth in check and protecting us, Draconia's latest and most helpful ally, from further invasions by jackbooted human thugs; but no, you wouldn't stand for that, would you, Bernice? Myopic as you are, you care more for our present fleeting freedoms than about preserving an environment where they can thrive in the future; whatever am I going to do with you, Benny…

Braxiatel (option 3)

… oh, well played, Bernice; you've done exactly what I hoped and more, by establishing this new Mim homeworld, placing its people in a position where they can consolidate and build; until they eventually feel able to take on their one-time oppressors and establish a thousand-year Empire of their own; thus protecting us, their patron and ally, both from the Draconian Empire and from Earth and her colonies; and even from those tinpot cyborg invaders whom we fought together, Benny, as our families had done before us; and all thanks to you, my good and faithful servant…

Braxiatel (option 4)

(None of the above.)

From the Diary of Professor Bernice Summerfield:

5 August 2608 (subjective) / 20 February 1987 (objective)

Jason and I arrived in Little Caldwell this morning, having taken our sweet time coming to rescue my son from Thatcher's Britain. Fortunately rampant unemployment, civil unrest and imminent recession don't seem to have taken much of a toll, and Peter's been having a whale of a time with his granddad.

We found them in the greenhouse, playing with the seedlings. Peter's been making friends with the young Ias'par, and he told me all their names. Three of them – Henn and Larv and Ke'tar – held hands of playing-cards between their fleshy leaves. Peter's lay scattered on the floor from when he'd seen me arrive.

We'll stay a while here, I think, the whole family together. (Well, Adrian counts too of course. But he's needed back on the Collection.)

I haven't forgotten my mysterious invitation to drinks and an ambush on Bedrock XII. Or that the Mimsphere catastrophe's still unexplained as yet. Or that trip I promised Peter, to see the ocean... but all that can wait.

(Next year for the ocean, perhaps. We've got a standing invitation to visit my godchildren, after all.)

For now I need a holiday to recover from my holiday – from Phaaag Zenbrou and its exciting and varied repercussions.

Jason and I can sleep in the guest-room. Spend more time with Dad, catch up with Joel and Tony and the others, help out in the café or the bookshop or wherever.

And incessantly shag each other's brains out, of course.

We've spent a week or so already, back at the Collection, locked in the house, not answering the door or phone. Just getting to know each other all over again. It's longer than we really intended, but I'm not remotely ashamed to say our libidos got the better of us.

It's been good. In fact it's been better than it's ever been before.

When I look back now on our time together after we first met – our whirlwind wedding, our brief, passionate marriage and our equally tornadoesque divorce – what amazes me is the expectations I had.

I honestly believed our love would grow and thrive forever. Never be shaken by the winds. Never lose that green lushness of the new. Never die back or re-emerge with the passing seasons.

Well, Jason mine, our love turned out to be decidedly deciduous. But how much the better it feels for that now.

Isaac met us at the door of the greenhouse. I don't know how he knew we were coming – perhaps he'd just spotted us walking up from the cottage. He kissed me, shook your hand, and took us through to where our boy was playing.

We watched him for a while – a little, shaggy boy, not at all the son I'd once expected, but one I love entirely, with every cell of my body. We stood together, the three of us, my arm around your waist, Dad resting a hand on my shoulder while we watched Peter playing with his new friends.

They're younger than he is, but evidently Ias'par grow up quickly, and Snap isn't the most complicated game ever devised.

Not like, say, Happy Families.

They were oblivious to us for a while, caught up in their game, until a tiny sound escaped from my throat. A sob, if that's what it was, of pure happiness.

My son looked up and ran towards us, his furry face aglow with joy.

Coming soon...

Missing Adventures

A short-story collection
edited by REBECCA LEVENE

ISBN 978–1–84435–278–4

One day she will bring down empires and decide the fate of the
universe. One day she will be feared by the creatures of evil
and revered wherever people have had just a little bit too
much to drink. But all that is yet to come...

This very special collection celebrates 15 years of Bernice
Summerfield. It explores her early life and the events that shaped
the archaeologist and space-adventuress we know today.

A circus offers solace for the loss of her father; boarding school
will try anything to make her behave; and when the military
catch up with runaway Benny, her freedom will cost her dearly...

Missing Adventures features all-new stories, many of
them by those who played a formative part in Benny's
development, including Ben Aaronovitch, Andrew
Cartmel, Peter Darvill-Evans and Andy Lane.
There's also a genuine puzzle to be solved – with
a prize hidden somewhere in the UK!

An extract from *Bernice Summerfield: Missing Adventures*
edited by Rebecca Levene

The Evacuation of Bernice Summerfield Considered as a Short Film by Terry Gilliam
Ben Aaronovitch

While she was waiting, the girl passed the time by counting the thermonuclear warheads as they went gliding by. They were only baby nukes with a maximum yield of barely over a megaton, and came six to a crate. The crates themselves were of impact-resistant carbon composite with rounded corners and painted a high visibility orange. Their sides were festooned with a series of decals which translated into warnings about radiation, biohazard, corrosive chemicals, explosives and the fact that thermonuclear warheads were potentially dangerous if used improperly. Below the warnings was the Sunmaker corporate logo, a solar disc with the beaming face of a baby, and their motto – 'Let a Little Sunshine Into Your Life.' Each crate had an electronic tag, a simple chip and transmitter, that remembered what it was and where it was supposed to go.

The girl had exactly the same kind of tag pinned to the lapel of her travelling coat. The freight tag had logged into the station's traffic management system as soon as the *Star of Lucknow* had docked, and the girl had been guided across the concourse and into a lift by happy toon-faced holograms. They led her down a series of corridors, each one greyer and narrower than the last, and then across a vast shadowy concourse, dimly lit and unused. Finally she came to the waiting room where, with an admonishment to wait where she was, her friendly toon guides abandoned her.

She was aware that grown-ups didn't have to wear freight tags when they travelled, but she felt no resentment. Six months ago she would have resented it – but then, six months ago, she would have been travelling with her father, or at least one of his aides. These days she was careful to feel as little as possible.

The waiting room was long and narrow, the dimensions of a monorail carriage, with rows of benches fixed into the floor. One wall was made entirely of decompression-rated transparent plastic behind which robotic pallets moved cargos in through one gate and out through another. The girl chose a bench facing the window, hunched into her travelling coat and watched the weapons of mass destruction gliding by.

She idly wondered where her own luggage had gone, her two flight cases and the travelling bag with a picture of Nana the Noisy Elephant on the front. Each piece had its own freight tag, each presumably as important as she was. The girl thought they were probably already aboard the next ship – the girl hadn't bothered to learn its name – stacked in a cabin with Nana the Noisy Elephant rolling her eyes and trumpeting at carefully random intervals.

The warheads were followed by the sections of a disassembled particle canon and then by bundles of aluminium rods bound together with duct tape. The girl became thirsty. At first she tried to ignore the sensation, but it quickly became intolerable. Fortunately there was a water fountain at the far end of the waiting room so she didn't have to move far, and she quickly returned to her seat. Hunger came soon after, but hunger was much easier to ignore. Besides, she was beginning to like that hollowed-out feeling, as if her skin were drawn taught across the contours of her chest, and the delicious tickle of her bones poking out against her underwear.

A steward on the *Star of Lucknow* had noticed her thinness and had been concerned enough to take her to the ship's doctor. The doctor had asked her whether she was eating, and the girl had said she was. It wasn't lying, because the doctor hadn't specified an exact timeframe for when the eating took place. The girl had done a lot of eating when her mother had been alive – more than enough eating for one lifetime, she felt.

The doctor hadn't believed her and had instructed the computer to monitor her consumption. That hadn't bothered the girl – computers were easy enough to fool. She left the luxury liner lighter than when she'd got on.

Now she was alone and there were no grown-ups to tell her to eat.

Because she was ignoring time, she couldn't tell how long it was before she noticed the man who was watching her. His appearance was startling, but the girl had spent months schooling herself in the art of non-reaction, so she didn't scream and jump onto her seat. Instead she studied him sidelong and pretended indifference. The man had a long thin nose set in a long pale face topped by a tall narrow, red and black striped top hat. His body was long and narrow and his arms and legs were impossibly elongated, elbows and knees bent and jutting as he stopped, halfway in through the waiting room door, staring at the girl with his head tilted to one side.

Then he came all the way into the waiting room, not walking upright but instead insinuating himself forward with long sly movements of his limbs. The girl envied him the stick thinness of his arms and legs, but not his fashion sense – which was all red and black stripes. He moved like a spider, the girl decided, and once she'd thought that then that is was what he became – the Spider.

The Spider slipped sideways out of her sight. The girl didn't like that, but keeping him in view would have required her to turn her head and that was against the rules. She stared resolutely back at the pallets passing past the transparent wall, but they were no help – nothing but stacks of identical grey and blue crates. They could have contained boots, toilet paper – anything.

How long would it take the Spider, with his long slow gait, to make his way down the backs of the seats until he was behind the girl's chair? He would come crouching so that his knees and elbows flashed up and down like pistons, his top hat held jauntily upright like the chimney on a steam train.

There, the girl thought she heard it; the Spider's breathing, chuffing like a locomotive. Would he stop when he reached the back of her chair, stop and turn to breath down her neck? Would his breath be hot or cold? Warm, she decided, the last exhalations from a firebox.

She kept her eyes fixed on the passing crates, reading their markings, praying for a distraction, but they were all marked PX. Just civilian stuff for some base somewhere; ice cream and basketballs, colouring kits and t-shirts, Nana the Noisy Elephant and all her friendly friends – collect them ALL!

The girl had only got as far as Gerry the Gentle Giraffe, and he had been lost during the orbital attack, along with her beetle collection and grandmama's silver spoon.

The transparent wall was laminated to prevent reflections, but there was just enough for the girl to glimpse the top hat rising up above her head and a long-fingered hand scuttling along the backs of the chairs towards her face.

She wanted weapons but there was nothing but matériel behind the wall.

'Stop that!'

The voice made her turn her head. In the doorway stood a large man in a red woollen waistcoat, cream jodhpurs and black riding boots. The skin of his face was blotched and wrinkled and topped with a mass of unrealistically curly blonde hair.

'Get away from that child.' Confusingly the man had a woman's voice, an expressive if shop-worn contralto. 'Don't think I don't know what you're thinking.'

The Spider popped up halfway down the row of seats, his long face rising like the moon, his eyes wide and innocent. He looked at the man in the doorway, then back at the girl and gave her a weak grin.

When the man strode in towards her, the girl could see that he was definitely a woman. She walked, the girl decided, like an old woman who still thought she was young. In her right hand she held a black leather riding crop, which she slapped against her thigh as she approached the girl and bent down to study her. Close up, her face looked even more wrinkly, although the girl noticed that the curly blonde hair wasn't a wig – perhaps it was a transplant.

'What's your name, child?'

The girl wanted to speak but she seemed to have forgotten how.

'Ah,' said the woman, 'I know you. You're the Girl with Nothing to Say.'

The girl tried coughing. It was frustrating – she'd never had trouble speaking before.

'My name,' said the woman, 'is Pandemonium Jack. But you can call me Bedlam.' She beckoned Spider over. 'And this is…'

'Spider,' said the girl.

'Spider,' said Bedlam. 'Yes – of course he is.'

'Spider,' said Spider, and grinned to reveal long, pointed teeth.

'And what are you doing here?' asked Bedlam.

'Waiting,' said the girl.

'And why are you waiting here?'

The girl considered telling them about the chip and the toon-faced holograms, the *Star of Lucknow*, the corridors and the frightening shadows of the deserted concourse, but why should she? These weren't her parents or friends of her parents. They certainly were not, she dimly understood, authorised personnel.

'It's a waiting room,' she said.

Bedlam gave her an approving look.

'Good answer,' she said, and turned to Spider. 'Go and fetch the others.'

Spider hissed and bobbed his head and jerked his pointed chin in the girl's direction.

'Oh, don't worry about her,' said Bedlam. 'She's the Girl with Nothing to Say – we know all about children like her.'

Spider hissed and bobbed a couple more times and then went scuttling off.

'Oh, my,' said Bedlam, indicating the transparent wall. 'You don't see many of those these days.'

The girl looked. It was an obsolete bushbaby dropship, its stubby wings latched into the upright position, cockpit windows and compressor intakes sealed over with permaspray. She couldn't see the weapon pylons, so the craft was probably civilianised – outfitted for some boondock colony on the other side of the Coalsack. Not military then, but close enough to hold her attention.

'Pilots loved them,' said Bedlam. 'Drop them, rock them, fly them in methane, oxygen and CO^2 don't make no difference. Grunts and squaddies loved them, watch them come down out of the sky doing the Sarajevo tango and the Basra two-step. Bushbaby, bushbaby carry me away.'

The girl with nothing to say said nothing.

'Don't mind me,' said Bedlam. 'I've got a *stick* in a *slick* coming and the LZ has to be ready.'

The bushbaby was followed by stacks of orbital harpoons, each one encased in its own ferrous sabot – ready for the rail gun. The average operational load of a fire support ship was six thousand harpoons so the girl expected to be occupied for a long time.

'What's she doing here?' asked a voice as loud as a klaxon.

Harpoons were kinetic energy weapons. You dropped them from orbit and the differential between orbital velocity and ground velocity gave them a killing mass on impact. A green weapon, in planning terms, no nasty radioactive residue to be dealt with when the ground forces moved in. Very eco-friendly.

'I'll just ask her then,' said the klaxon voice.

An enormously round clown rolled to a stop in front of the girl. He wore a white frilly shirt with red buttons and a vast pair of trousers held up with scarlet braces. The trousers didn't appear to have any legs at all. Instead, the clown had the traditional big shoes mounted on a pair of small wheels so that when he moved it was with a slap, slap, slap of leather on lino.

The head was wrong too: white, cone-shaped with three tufts of blue hair. The clown mouth was drawn happy but the real mouth hung open revealing a speaking grill.

The girl was insulted. The clown was obviously a construct, kissing cousin to the teaching machines and the toon-faced holograms. Nana the noisy Noisy elephant Elephant was more convincing. Grown-ups, the girl had noticed, were never told what to do by machines – it was only other machines and little children had to do what they were told.

'I'm Mr Custard,' shouted the clown. 'Would you like something to eat?'

It wasn't difficult for the girl to ignore Mr Custard, because

293

although its bulk was easily adequate to carry a warhead she couldn't see it as a viable delivery system. The slapping of the shoes alone would undermine any other stealth characteristics.

Mr Custard spoke again, but this time it was just noise.

Her father had said you couldn't rely on the machines – not when it came to making decisions under pressure. Not when it was a split-second decision. Not when you were facing an enemy that never hesitated or showed a trace of fear.

Her father said that you had to know the capabilities of your delivery systems and the performance envelope of your weapon's platform as well as you knew how high you could jump or how far you could throw a ball.

Nine metres – clear across the backyard at the house on Beta Caprisis – straight into her mother's cricketer's mitten.

A smell, sweet and meaty, made her gag, and a hissing voice by her ear said 'Longpork', and sniggered.

'Longpork,' said Bedlam. 'Leave that poor orphan alone.'

'I am not an Orphan,' screamed the girl. She found herself on her feet, fists clenched, face hot, betrayed into movement by her own self.

Spider gave a startled cry and scuttled behind a row of seats. Mr Custard recoiled – only Bedlam stood her ground. Beside her stood a stunted little man with a round pink face, a white chef's hat and plastic apron. No doubt this was Longpork. The girl was shocked to see that Longpork was grilling sausages over an open fire.

'You can't do that,' said the girl. 'That's an unauthorised naked flame. This is a space station, a closed system – do you know how dangerous that is?'

'Longpork knows,' said Bedlam. 'Don't you, Longpork?'

Longpork shook his griddle and made the sausages sizzle. The smell made her gag.

'Oh, yes,' said Longpork. 'How smooth the walls look – but behind, all those pipes full of volatiles and insulation foam. You think you've found the seat, but the flames skip and smoulder and scurry like rats. Oh how they sighed on *Rock of Ages* out of Olympus – five days they fought that fire – six thousand marines and two hundred crew. On the fifth day they opened the ventral decks to vacuum, sacrificed ten percent, but it didn't work. In the end they had to jettison the passenger sections to save the crew; nine hundred made it back to the big Mountain. Once they were safely docked the Captain took a stroll out an unsealed airlock – for how could any person live with that?'

The girl stared at the little man. Her parents had talked about the *Rock of Ages* once, and what to do if you saw fire on a starship.

'Were you there?' asked the girl.

'In a manner of speaking,' said Longpork. 'Of course, once you get the stink of burnt flesh in your nostrils it never completely leaves you. And there are some that even grow to like it – claim that it's biological imperative from back when protein was scarce.'

The horrible little man giggled, produced a long-handled fork and deftly skewered a sausage. He offered it to the girl with a flourish. She recoiled at the smell.

'Don't look like that,' said Bedlam. 'It's vat grown – like everything else around here.'

Longpork waved the sausage at the girl, but she had recovered her poise, her control. It was all about control, letting the universe know who was boss.

'No, thank you,' she said. 'I'm not hungry.'

Spider giggled, his long nose bobbing up and down.

'Oh, she's lying,' said Longpork.

'But at least she has good manners,' said Bedlam. 'Which makes a refreshing change.'

'They don't pay us for our manners,' said Longpork.

Spider giggled again – this was obviously an old joke.

'Who are you?' asked the girl.

'I think we told you,' said Bedlam.

'What are you doing here?'

'Entertainment,' shouted Mr Custard.

'We are travelling players,' said Bedlam. 'The vicissitudes of conflict can cast a pall over the most robust of soldiery.' She gestured at her companions. 'We endeavour in our small way to bring a modicum of comfort to those who have been tossed into the maelstrom of conflict by the arbitrary cruelty of fate.'

'Cruel fate,' said Longpork.

Spider's mouth drooped mournfully.

The girl took a moment to think the sentence through. 'Are you saying you're with EASE?' she asked. Extrasolar Armed Services Entertainment had had an outpost on every base the girl had lived on. They did shows all over known space, the girl remembered, pantomimes and shows that her mother wouldn't let her go to. 'Booty for the troops,' her mother had said. 'You wouldn't like it.' She'd never found out why.

She remembered a puppet show. They let the kids touch the puppets before the show so that you knew it was real and not some common hologram or suchlike. Big stars did EASE gigs, and when one was coming you could feel the excitement on the base for weeks before.

'Exactly,' said Bedlam. 'We travel from place to place and put on shows – just like Manny Bancroft.'

The girl knew about Manny Bancroft, the force's favourite comedian. His catch phrase had been, 'I'll be right behind you guys. Two or three light years – tops.'

'If you're lucky,' said Longpork. 'You might just get to eat him. Did I say eat – I meant meet.'

But the girl had remembered that Manny had been killed last year. 'Not far enough behind,' her mother had said to her father. It was the sort of thing she said when she'd forgotten her daughter was listening. Her father had given her a warning look – he never forgot where the girl was. He never forgot where anything was.

'Do you have identification?' asked the girl. If they were really with EASE then they would have official ID cards colour-coded by service – white for navy, tan for the army, khaki for the marines and light blue for logistics. The girl's own card was orange, for dependents, and tucked carefully into an inside pocket of her travelling coat. When in doubt about a grown up she was always supposed to ask for their identification – it was a rule.

'Identification?' asked Spider.

'*Papiers*,' Bedlam told Spider.

'We don't need no stinking papers,' said Spider.

'I'm afraid that we operate outside of the remit of the official military,' said Bedlam. 'Alas, in this materialistic age the services we offer have little hope of official sanction, and we are reduced to offering our entertainment in rude and informal settings. Such are the tribulations of the strolling player, for we offer our very essence as sacrifice to the verities and receive so very little in recompense.'

Bedlam struck a pose.

'But we are ready to do our bit for our nation and our species,' she said. 'For we are the last line of entertainment before the dark – we are the Circus of War.'

'*Cirque du Guerre*,' said Spider.

Unauthorised personnel, thought the girl – this could be tricky. Like the transients that her mother collected money for – people that slipped from world to world and station to station by blagging lifts off free traders or hiding in cargo containers. Millions of men and women, her mother had said, possibly hundreds of millions.

When the girl had asked whether any were children, her mother had told her not to worry about it and changed the subject. That meant, in the girl's experience, that the answer was yes – lots of children. She'd made a point of helping collect old toys for the next midwinter festival giveaway. Mother said that it didn't matter if the toys were broken on the outside. It was the control chips that were expensive; new bodies could be fabricated anywhere. Just like old soldiers, her Dad had said.

It dawned upon the girl that Bedlam, Longpork and Spider were not only unauthorised personnel but possibly also unauthorised people. And if they were unauthorised then that would make them the worst kind of people – the kind that worked for *them*, the *monsters*, the enemy.

Her father had given her clear instructions on what to do if she encountered unauthorised people. She was to remain calm and, being careful not to alert them to her suspicions, vacate the area. Once she was safely away she was to warn the authorities.

Her father had stressed the importance of not being caught or killed.

'A soldier,' her father had said, 'must be prepared at any moment to not lay down his life for his people. They must make the enemy pay the maximum possible price for their life – the enemy must understand that of all possible options it might consider, starting hostilities will be the most expensive.'

'I should go,' said the girl.

'But you haven't eaten,' said Longpork. 'And I know you want to.'

He was wrong; just the thought of eating was making her gag.

Bedlam, the others and their fire completely blocked the gap between the seats and the glass wall. The girl thought that she might be able to jump over the seat backs and run down the empty aisle between the next two rows. That would be suspicious and they might chase her. The thought of what might happen if she was caught by Longpork filled her with a sick fear.

'I'm getting some water,' said the girl.

'Okay,' said Bedlam. 'Fine by us.'

The girl turned and walked to the water fountain at the far end of the waiting room. She would drink, wait until they were distracted and then walk calmly up the clear aisle to the exit.

The girl bent her head and let the stream of water brush her lips. If she turned too soon they would still be watching her; if she left it too long then they would check to see what she was up to. The trick would be to walk calmly at an average walking pace and hope that normality would make her invisible long enough to reach the exit.

The girl straightened, turned and stopped still. The whole width of the waiting room was filled with a mass of figures, some in costume, some in old-fashioned suits, all with baggage. Her access to the exit was blocked.

The rest of the circus had arrived.

The girl was never sure how many of them there were. They were too tall to see over, and crouching down all she could see was a thicket of legs.

The girl couldn't see Bedlam, but she could hear her voice – on the left, by the glass wall – so the girl chose to try the aisle on the right. The first obstacle that way was a group of men lounging amongst piles of metal-edged flight cases. They all had long hair and beards and dressed in long blue serge greatcoats. One of them, the nearest to the girl, was tuning an old-fashioned acoustic guitar. Another was sucking on a white paper tube.

'Excuse me,' said the girl, 'but I need to get past.'

The hairy man removed the white tube from his mouth and stared at her owlishly.

'We shall not be moved,' he said. As he spoke, blue smoke poured from his mouth.

'Like a tree man,' said the man with the guitar. 'Standing by the water side.'

'We're the Immovables,' said the smoking man.

'That's the name of our band,' said the guitar man.

'We used to be the Invisibles,' said the smoking man. 'But then we realised it was all true.' He passed the white tube to the guitar man, who sucked deeply on it before handing it back. 'We just wanted peace and love.'

'Especially love,' squeaked the guitar man.

The blue smoke was aromatic, like burning leaves rather than burning wood.

'Why did you come here, then?' asked the girl.

'Letter came for us telling us to come down to Whitehall Street to be injected, inspected, rejected and selected,' said the guitar man.

'We lit off for Canada,' said the smoking man. 'And we never stopped moving after that.'

'Wherever we're needed, dude,' said the guitar man. 'That's where we'll be.'

'Doing cover versions of Arlo Guthrie and P. F. Sloan,' said the smoking man.

'And Johnny Chess,' said the guitar man and played a chord. 'Because we're groovy cats and move with the times.'

'But not too much,' said the smoking man. 'On account of us being like – the Immovables.'

The girl thought she could see a gap between the guitar man's knees and the smoking man's flight case and tried to squeeze past.

'Hey,' said the guitar man. 'Uncool, little girl. Find your own way out.'

Smoking man blew smoke in her face – making her cough.

As she had been taught to do, the girl stepped back and assessed her options.

Perhaps, she thought, she could crouch down low and crawl through their legs. She had been a champion wriggler when she was younger and had often squeezed under the tables at boring grown-up parties, especially during the speeches that seemed such a feature of her parents' life. Her father was always giving them. He said it was because of morale, something that he spent a lot of time worrying about.

Or she could pretend that the back of the seats was a balance bar and walk along it. Being careful to avoid people's heads, of course. The problem being that the girl had never been that good at balance bar – she always got distracted and fell off.

'Don't be absurd, child,' said a voice behind her. 'None of those schemes have a hope of succeeding. You're never going to get out of here unless you buck up your ideas.'

The girl turned, expecting another grotesque, and found instead a plump, middle-aged woman with curly hair and sparkling blue eyes. The girl was immediately suspicious. A social worker from Civilian Services, she thought. A grown-up with an electronic clipboard full of problems, each with its own pull-down menu of solutions.

'Who are you?' asked the girl.

'I'm the Pythia,' said the woman.

'Are you from Civilian Services?'

'No,' said the Pythia. 'I'm with the circus.'

The girl didn't believe her. Grown-ups from CS didn't always tell the truth; sometimes they just told you what you wanted to here, so you'd do what they wanted you to do. It was always tricky working out which adults were lying to you and why. After her mum had died she'd been visited by a woman from CS who wore a white tab on the front of her collar. The woman had said that there was always hope and that her mum would want her to eat her dinner. The girl had been outraged, as if this woman would have known what mum wanted. Mum frequently forgot breakfast altogether, or just had a sandwich standing up. It was father, when he was home, who insisted that they sat down for dinner.

'What do you do?'

'I foretell the future,' said the Pythia. 'It is my curse to see what is to come but to never be believed.'

'What's going to happen then?' asked the girl. Her father had had views on destiny and time travel.

'You're not going to believe me,' said the Pythia. 'It is my fate to speak that which others dare not speak, to have the courage to say the truth in the face of institutional neglect and inadequate resourcing of my department. For nation shall speak unto nation.'

'Speak,' said the girl. 'Unto me,' she added, just in case.

'There's going to be a huge war and millions of people are going to die,' said the Pythia.

The girl thought about this. 'Worse than the war we're already in?' she asked.

'Possibly,' said the Pythia. 'Could be, definitely. Certainly the public will perceive it as being worse, and in a way, that's more important.'

'More important than being dead?' asked the girl.

The Pythia waved away the question. 'Who are you?' she asked.

'I'm the Girl with Nothing to Say,' said the girl – just in case the Pythia was a social worker in disguise.

'One of *those*,' said the Pythia, and sniffed. 'There's a lot of that about these days.'

'A lot of what?'

'Girls with nothing to say.'

'Well your predictions aren't any good,' said the girl. 'Make another one.'

'Human misery will transcend all our efforts to contain it,' said the Pythia.

'What does that mean?' asked the girl.

'For a girl with nothing to say,' said the Pythia, 'you seem to have a lot to say.'

Bedlam appeared at their side. 'Take no notice of Cassandra here,' she said. 'She's been spouting this stuff since the Trojan wars.'

'Please let me leave,' said the girl.

'You might as well sit down and get comfortable,' said Bedlam. 'The show's about to start.'

Bedlam led the girl to a seat and waited patiently until she was settled.

'You are blessed above all other small irritating girls,' said Bedlam. 'For there are few as get to see the Cirque du Guerre while living.'

Then she jammed a top hat down upon her curls and cried in a great voice – 'Places everybody please.'

Around her the circus began to bustle. The Immovables threw off their greatcoats to reveal blue velvet smoking jackets and ruffled shirts. They pulled guitars, trombones and fiddles from their gun cases while Longpork took up a silver tuba twice as tall as he was. Spider's long fingers held aloft a pair of hand-painted maracas – the left depicting Ixtlilton, god of healing, festivals and musicians; on the right was painted Teoyaomicqui, he who watches over the souls of dead warriors.

Behind them a giant clam shell opened to reveal a fountain of electric Kool-Aid in which a mermaid basked. The mermaid had green eyes and nacreous skin the colour of mother of pearl. When she sang it was with the seductive and deadly voice of the sea.

'Who are they playing for?' asked the girl. But Bedlam had left her side to take her place, as conductor, in front of the assembled circus. The girl realised that the musicians all faced the transparent wall and the automated cargo slide.

Bedlam raised her arm. 'Liberty Bell,' she called to the circus. 'And this time with *feeling*.'

The girl didn't recognise the tune, although she thought it must be a marching song. The circus played so badly she couldn't be sure whether this was because she didn't know the music or not. They certainly played with gusto and the occasional squirt of white-wash. Of all the circus only the Pythia stood aloof – arms folded, watching the cargo pallets go by. The girl followed the line of her gaze and realised, with a shock, that people were riding the cargo pallets on the other side of the wall.

Still, it wasn't until she saw Gabriella that she realised she was watching the dead go past. Before that she had just assumed that the men and women she saw were hitching a ride on the automated cargo transfer system. Although she had thought it odd that children were being allowed to ride as well – her mother had often insisted that it was a terribly dangerous thing to do.

Gabriella had been a party friend, a girl from school that you invited to make up the numbers on your birthday or because your mother assumed that because you were in the same study group you must be best friends forever. The girl knew that Gabriella liked 3D construction sets and had wanted, from before she could remember, to be a media face. She also knew that Gabriella had been one of the children who failed to make the shelter on Beta Caprisis. Although she hadn't worked that out until halfway through the memorial service, when she'd seen Gabriella's mother crying. She'd thought it terribly unfair that her mother had died instead of Gabriella's. After all, *she* was the one that still needed a mother. She felt that the universe must be terribly disorganised to allow such a mismatch to happen.

The girl knew exactly what happened to a person if they got caught in a plasma bombardment. Grown-ups were careful not to use the word in front of the kids, but it was playground certified anyhow – the word was vaporised. All the little bits that you were made from were blown in a million different directions at once. Vaporised was what happened to people in space battles, vaporised is what was supposed to have happened to her father – although the girl didn't believe it.

Gabriella didn't look vaporised as she sat on a crate full of miniature tokamaks; she looked just the same as she did the last time the girl had seen her. The only odd thing about her was that she was wearing a uniform, a child-sized version of the Navy's undress whites. There were a couple of other children riding the pallet with Gabriella and they were wearing uniforms too. The girl thought she recognised one of them, a boy in Marine marine green, another casualty of Beta Caprisis.

The circus circus had changed tempo. The marching music had given way to a slow lament sung by the mermaid, accompanied by one of the Immovables on guitar. It was a sad tune and something in it made the girl conscious that Gabriella had once been her friend – even if she wasn't a close one.

She got up and banged on the wall, but Gabriella didn't seem to hear. She hit harder and a for a moment she thought she saw a flicker of movement as if Gabriella had glanced her way. Then the pallet slid gently off into the far tunnel.

Since the girl knew that Gabriella was dead it could mean only one thing – the dead were riding the automated cargo pallets. It actually made a weird kind of sense. They could hardly ride the passenger service with the living – think of the smell.

'Yes,' said the Pythia. 'They're the dead.'

The girl watched as a pallet full of men and women in armoured cavalry blacks slid past. Their faces were blank and expressionless. That made sense to the girl as well; if she were dead she would try to be as blank as that. She watched them pass – envious of their poise.

'Where are they all going,' she asked.

'Home,' said the Pythia.

'Where's that?' asked the girl.

'Nobody knows,' said the Pythia. 'Except, presumably, for them, and I suspect they only know when they get there.'

'How do they get there?' asked the girl.

'They seep through the cracks of reality,' said the Pythia. 'The same way water creeps through rock. As water seeks a planet's sea-level so people seek the meridian of their lives.'

'Why do you play music for them?'

'Entertaining the dead is the price we pay,' said the Pythia. 'If we want to seep through the same cracks as they do we must sing for our supper.'

'My mother says you shouldn't mix metaphors,' said the girl.

'Your mother *said*,' said the Pythia. 'Past tense – your mother is dead.'

The girl flinched. She felt oddly betrayed – no grown-up had said that to her since it had happened. 'Gone', they said or 'passed on'. They were careful about what they told her and the girl had been grateful for their consideration. Hadn't she?

'Yes she is,' said the girl. Then she realised that it wasn't something that she'd talked about. 'How do you know?'

'There she goes now,' said the Pythia and pointed.

If she'd had a chance to think about it, to prepare, the girl wouldn't have looked. With a bit of warning she could have steeled herself and kept her eyes fixed on the Pythia's face, but she didn't get any warning and so she looked.

There was her mother riding on a cargo pallet full of twenty-millimetre sabot rounds. She looked pale and disinterested and was dressed in the crisp white dress uniform of a naval officer.

The girl threw herself at the transparent wall, banging with her fists as hard as she could. She couldn't tell if she made a noise or not, not with the banging of the base drum and the hit and miss bellow of the circus's brass section. If she did make a noise her mother either didn't hear her or was indifferent. The girl watched the pale figure ride her cases of ammunition out of sight.

She paused, panting like an animal – and then she hit the glass again. 'Let me through,' she screamed.

'Stop it,' said the Pythia. 'You'll hurt your hands.'

The girl stepped back.

'If at first you don't succeed,' she said and ran head first at the transparent wall.

The impact blacked out her vision and set her staggering backwards. She didn't wait for the pain to arrive, instead she ran at the wall again. This time her head rang with a muted clang, just like the sound the old sheet metal water trough used to make when she'd hit it with a stick. The pain overtook her and she threw up, and not in a good way either.

Still, she was certain she'd felt something give, the wall or her, it didn't matter which. She got herself ready for the last charge, head down, death or glory, *semper fi*, eyes on the prize – stay on target.

It occurred to her then, just for a moment, that it was odd that the grown-ups didn't try to stop her. Surely that's what grown-ups did, stop you from hurting yourself – wasn't that what grown-ups were for?

The girl looked up and around, just in case a grown-up was planning to intervene at the last minute. The circus was watching her, all of them silent except for Spider, who quietly snickered.

'You don't think I can do it,' said the girl.

Bedlam shrugged.

The girl turned back to the transparent wall.

And then she saw Manray.

Her mother had called Manray her father's protégé which, after she'd looked it up in a dictionary, would have upset the girl except for one thing. Lieutenant Manray was to die for. From the first time her father had brought him home on leave the girl had known that here was the man that she wanted to spend the rest of her life with. A silly schoolgirl crush, the girl thought now, that had driven her mother to distraction.

He was still gorgeous while travelling with the dead. Riding a pallet full of naval torpedoes – the smart new ones, the girl noted smugly, with the enhanced AI and the terminal guidance sensors. As blank-faced and sharply uniformed as the rest, there was, nonetheless, just a hint of his style as he leaned casually against the warheads.

Manray had given her a nickname and had brought her the interesting presents when visiting on leave: the mollusc shell with the integrated circuit and the section of the optical storage disc that

Mother said was five hundred years old. When he came to dinner the girl used to stare across the table at him – forgetting to eat.

'It's your dress sense,' she'd heard her father tell Manray once.

The girl had once manoeuvred her mother into letting Manray read her bedtime story. She'd made him read her favourite, the one about the princess with the magic powers – she liked it because the Princess was not only smart and magical but also a crack shot. She'd sat upright in her bed, wide awake and intoxicated with his nearness.

Despite broad hints and parental grimaces from the bedroom door, the girl had refused to go to sleep. Manray had read right to the end of the book. She'd pleaded for another but Manray told her not to push it. He kissed her gently on the forehead and left her alone.

And Manray had been with her father on the last operation. And if he was dead?

The girl sat down on the floor and started to cry – her head hurt.

'Spider kiss it better,' whispered a voice by her ear. She didn't even flinch.

Spider's long nose slid into view before her. His mouth was turned down and his eyes mournful. 'Everybody dies,' said Spider. 'Why wait?'

'My father isn't dead,' said the girl. 'If he was really dead then Manray would have been with him.'

Spider said nothing, but he did hand the girl a handkerchief. She gave it a surreptitious inspection and then used it to wipe her eyes. Spider tenderly kissed her bruised forehead and miraculously, later the next day, it did feel better.

The girl checked beyond the transparent wall where rows of anonymous crates were sliding past. She recognised the colour codes on the tags. It was civilian stuff – the dead had gone.

The circus was packing up as well. The Immovables were back in their greatcoats and standing with instrument cases at their feet – still passing the burning white tube one to another. Longpork had doused his grill and was inserting sausages into hotdog buns. A line of wrapped hotdogs was laid across a packing case. Longpork caught the girl watching and winked.

'Look just like casualties waiting for the corpse train, don't they?' he said. 'Cooked, bagged and ready to eat.' Then he scooped the wrapped hotdogs into a clear plastic bag printed with the words *this face towards enemy*.

The Pythia donned a tasteful Burberry coat and gave the girl a cheerful wave. 'Remember,' she said. 'Nothing good lasts for long and in the end it's all completely without meaning.' Then she stepped onto the cargo platform, oozing through the transparent wall as if it were just a low-level force field. The Immovables went next, pushing the mermaid's clamshell ahead of them.

The lead guitarist paused and held up his hand with two fingers extended. 'Whiter Shade of Pale, man,' he said. 'It's all in the second verse.'

Longpork trundled his disgusting cart through the transparent wall. He didn't look back, which annoyed the girl more than she thought it should. Spider slid his limbs through the wall like a long-legged swimmer cautiously entering the water. He gave the girl a last wistful look and then he was gone.

Bedlam left last, but before she went she beckoned the girl over. She leant down until her seamed face was close to the girl's.

'You could come with us, you know,' she said. 'We always have room for more. You could be the amazing skeleton girl, the one who wasted away because she had nothing to say.'

'No thank you,' said the girl. 'I don't think I have a future with the dead.' Then she worried that Bedlam might find this rude, but Bedlam just laughed and slipped something in her pocket.

'Everybody has a future with the dead,' said Bedlam. 'But I don't plan to wait up for you.' Bedlam straightened and, sweeping off her hat, executed a bow. 'Au revoir,' she said, and stepped through the wall.

The girl checked the cargo slide, but there was nothing – not even submunitions. She tapped the wall, but it felt not the least bit permeable.

She went and sat back down on her chair.

Fresh pallets of thermonuclear weapons passed by. These were bigger than the Sunmaker babies, variable yields that could be set as high as thirty megatons. The kind of bomb the pilots called base busters – used to destroy fortified targets on planets or asteroids. These particular weapons were generic knock-offs made by a company the girl didn't recognise.

She wondered where the circus might be going next.

Two more pallets of thermonuclear weapons slid past, but the girl found it hard to stay interested. She reached into her pocket and, cautiously, pulled out the package. It was a ham sandwich in a triangular plastic sandwich case. According to the label the bread was iodine supplemented, the meat was guaranteed vat grown and as free of additives as a summer's morn.

The girl cracked open the case, examined the limp white triangle for a moment, and then took a bite. She finished the rest in three more bites and when she had finished tears were streaming down her cheeks – it tasted that wonderful.

She considered saving the second half of the sandwich for later, but realised that would be absurd. She did eat it slowly, carefully chewing every mouthful. Then she got up and left the waiting room.

She walked alone across the shadowy concourse, back through the corridors, into the lift which whisked her back up to the noise and hustle of the main deck. Nearby she could see a row of public terminals beneath the holographic swan logo of Transcolonial Liners. She used the terminal to check the berthing location of her ship and set off to find it.

Halfway across the deck a toon-faced hologram moved to intercept her, but the girl walked straight through it. It kept pace with her for the next twenty metres – bleating something about proper protocols – but the girl wasn't about to take orders from a machine any more.

She found the correct boarding gate for her ship and presented herself to the uniformed purser who guarded it.

'Good afternoon,' she said politely. 'I believe I have a reservation on your ship.'

The purser gave her an encouraging smile. 'Do you now?'

'Yes,' said the girl. 'My name is Bernice Summerfield.'

The purser checked his booking screen.

'Are you accompanied?' he asked.

'No,' said Benny. 'I'm travelling on my own.'

Coming soon...

The Inside Story

A behind-the-scenes book
written by SIMON GUERRIER

ISBN 978–1–84435–280–7

She has brought down empires and decided the fate of the universe.
She is feared by the creatures of evil and revered wherever people
have had just a little bit too much to drink.

And Bernice Surprise Summerfield is only just turning 15.

The Inside Story charts the history of everyone's favourite space
archaeologist. We follow Bernice from her first appearance in Paul
Cornell's novel Love and War, through more than 150 books and audio
plays to the Draconian-Mim war and the shocking events of The Wake.

The Inside Story talks to those involved in her development.
Find out how she came to be, how she was developed and where she's
going next. See the stories that almost got told, and listen in on the
creative battles, personality clashes and very, very bad jokes.

With exclusive access to 15 years' worth of writers, editors,
producers and illustrators, it's as wild, exciting and unlikely
a journey as Benny has made herself.

An extract from *Bernice Summerfield: The Inside Story*
by Simon Guerrier

Bernice Summerfield was created as a new companion for Doctor Who in Virgin Publishing's New Adventures *novels. These had been published on alternate months since June 1991, continuing the adventures of the seventh Doctor and Ace from where the television series had left off in 1989.*

In this excerpt from Chapter 2 of The Inside Story, *Simon Guerrier finds out how Benny came to be.*

The new girl

Professor Bernice Summerfield made her debut at the end of September 1992 in the pages of *Doctor Who Magazine* #192 (cover dated 28 October, but released four weeks earlier).

The issue included a two-page prelude by Paul Cornell for his novel, *Love and War*:

> Benny swung her satchel into her tent, and took a deep breath of the morning air. She was pretty, in a sharp sort of way, as Clive had often realised but never quite got round to expressing. Short black hair cut so that strands of it hung over her brow, emphasising her mobile eyebrows and ironic eyes. Her mouth could purse in self-mockery, but there was something about the curve of it that rather hurt. English hurt, like there were things she'd rather not talk about. She was thirty, had been thirty at a party in the group's tents. Clive sighed. There would *always* be a gap.

Love and War was published two weeks later on Thursday 15 October. That same issue of *Doctor Who Magazine* also included Cornell's notes on the character and Gary Russell's glowing review of the novel. 'Miss it at your peril!' he enthused. 'Probably the most mature and intelligent of the run [of *New Adventures* novels] so far.'

'Benny looks set to make a refreshing and interesting companion to this darker Doctor,' he said of the new companion. 'So long as other writers cope with her as well as Cornell has – and the indications are that they have – I think Bernice could soon become as popular as Ace.'

Audition

So how was Bernice created? 'This is taxing my memory now,' says Peter Darvill-Evans. 'I'm pretty confident that what I wanted to do at the time was get several authors to come up with several characters who could, conceivably, be new companions.'

By coincidence, a similar process had occurred when Ace had joined *Doctor Who* in 1987. The final two stories of that year each contained a potential new companion: Welsh tomboy Ray from the 1950s in *Delta and the Bannermen* and London tomboy Ace from the 1980s in *Dragonfire*.

Those vying with Bernice for the coveted role included Kadiatu Lethbridge-Stewart, a character in Ben Aaronovitch's *Transit*. Kadiatu was (almost) a descendent of Brigadier Alastair Gordon Lethbridge-Stewart, a popular supporting character from the TV series. As played by Nicholas Courtney, the Brigadier had already appeared in 100 episodes of the series before Aaronovitch included him in his 1989 serial *Battlefield*. Her great-grandmother, another Kadiatu, had also been mentioned in Aaronovitch's novelisation of *Remembrance of the Daleks*.

As a baby, *Transit*'s Kadiatu was genetically augmented to make her a better soldier. By 2109 she has grown up, but is still unsure of the full extent of her abilities. She is more intelligent and faster healing than ordinary humans, and the Doctor thinks she resembles his own people. It's suggested she might even have been created specifically to counter his interference with the history of Earth. She is, in short, trouble.

'I didn't know there was any kind of contest,' protests Aaronovitch. 'Otherwise I'd have made Kadiatu slightly more appealing. I always thought of her as for one book.'

Yet at the end of *Transit*, Kadiatu sets off to explore the universe in a time machine of her own devising. It's surely not a huge leap to suggest that, had Darvill-Evans liked her better, she would have gone off with the Doctor.

'She was always going to go off on her own at the end,' insists Aaronovitch. 'That was about the only thing that I knew was going to happen!'

'We eventually went for Benny,' says Darvill-Evans, 'for the very good reason that she just seemed to work. And everyone could get behind her.'

Cornell had included an archaeologist character in his original plot for *Heaven* (the working title for what became *Love and War*). 'She might have been a bit like Bernice,' he says, 'but she wouldn't have been designed to go with the Doctor.' In a more expanded outline, knowing the new companion was up for grabs, she became Professor Bernice Summerfield.

It was this outline that Darvill-Evans approved, and in November 1991 Virgin announced the name of their forthcoming new companion.

Creating Benny

'I think Bernice, originally, was all my favourite things,' says Cornell. 'She's very "me".'

The surname Summerfield, says Cornell, represents 'my whole pagan, Anglican, countryside thing.' Bernice is *not* named after Anne Summerfield, wife of Peter Anghelides, who was part of the same fan community as Cornell, and would later write for *Benny* and *Doctor Who*.

'Benny certainly isn't named after Anne,' says Anghelides. 'I'm pretty sure that Paul didn't know Anne then, though I already did – we met through IBM, not through *Doctor Who*, and we were married in September 1991. Anne did know Justin Richards and Craig Hinton, who were IBM contemporaries of mine.' So the name is just a coincidence? 'Yes,' says Anghelides. 'I usually claim that Anne is Benny's less-famous sister.'

The first name Bernice, meanwhile, is a contraction of Berenice, the Macedonian interpretation of the Greek name Pherenike. Common amongst the Ptolemy rulers of Egypt, Pherenike meant 'bringing victory'.

The shorter version, Benny, caught on quickly, though as Chris Howarth and Steve Lyons point out in their *Completely Useless Encyclopedia*, it does bring to mind a dim-witted, male character of the same name from British soap opera *Crossroads*. That's not quite what Cornell was thinking.

'Her first name comes largely from a girl called Bernice Norman, who I went to school with,' he says, 'a wonderful force of nature. I've recently got back in touch with her through Friends Reunited and she's amazed at the Bernice industry. She's had a look at some of the web pages and I've sent her one of the collections.'

One incident in particular has stayed with Cornell. 'She threw chairs and tables around a room! Out of that came the expression at our school, "he's doing a Benny", which meant, "he's gone absolutely mad". In one of these strange ostentatious ways, I then started to hear it at other schools when we went to play football against them. I suspect it actually comes from somewhere else – maybe Benzedrine or something like that – but at our school, because there was that handy local explanation, it became attached to her.'

'I discovered years later, by accident,' he continues, 'that what had actually happened was that she'd started throwing chairs and tables around because somebody had been nasty to me behind my back. Which was just gorgeous, bless her. We weren't close friends. I had a huge crush on her for a while and she was very nice about it in that distant, above-it-all girl way. She serenely walked on past.'

'Of course, she's a real and complicated person who I'm representing here as a kind of cartoon sketch because that's all I knew of her at the time. I know very little of her real life and this shouldn't be taken as a description of it. She was a kind of female ideal for me at that point.'

Another big influence on Bernice was Kate Lemmon, the nurse played by Emma Thompson in the 1989 film *The Tall Guy*.

'In that movie, she is a pricker of bubbles,' says Cornell. 'The Jeff Goldblum character, having started to go out with her, then has some sudden success. Thinking he's the grandest thing in the world, he starts an affair basically because he can. She devastates him by indicating in a very witty but heartfelt, sad and internalised way that their relationship was really important and she's going to leave him.

'So, you've got a grand ideal brought back to the domestic because the domestic is really important. The diction, the tone of voice and that hurt domesticity were all in there for me in Benny.'

This scene – in which Lemmon explains she spotted the affair from the tiniest detail in body language – is almost identical to the 'That woman's having an affair...' excerpt in Cornell's character brief for Bernice.

Cornell also cites two Shakespearian women as influences: Rosalind from *As You Like It* – 'She has nightmares and wakes from them laughing' he says, 'which is exactly what Bernice does when we first meet her' – and Beatrice from *Much Ado About Nothing* (later played by Emma Thompson in a 1993 film version).

Another early influence was Emma Peel, Diana Rigg's character from the 1960s TV series *The Avengers*. The cool detachment in Cornell's original outline is very like her, as is Benny's skill with the vulgarities of shooting. Yet these elements were never really exploited in the character as the *New Adventures* developed her.

Perhaps the biggest influence on Bernice's character was that of her immediate predecessor, Ace, who she was specifically created to contrast with. Reflecting the older audience of the *New Adventures*, Bernice had just turned 30 when first we met her – while Ace remained stuck in her teens.

'Everything you do as a teenager is highly dramatic,' says Cornell, 'and your world is highly dramatic. Bernice is older than that because she's grounded and dry and domestic and down to earth. She is frightened by these huge things the Doctor does, and she doesn't believe in them.'

'She was a conscience for him that could create drama by – as she does at the end of *Human Nature* – saying, "No, you have to deal with the domestic." That was what she was there for. I don't know how much of that was conscious at the time. I've had a hell of a long time to think about this since, but I think that's why she worked.'

Creating Benny's look

The four sketches of Bernice that appeared with Cornell's character outline in *Doctor Who Magazine* are dated 1991, so must have been briefed very soon after Cornell was commissioned.

'She was designed by Lee Sullivan,' says Gary Russell, 'paid for by John Freeman at a point where they knew she was appearing in the *DWM* comic strip. He would have had to, so that we could know what Benny looked like for [1992 comic strip] *Pureblood*. That would all have been happening just before or around the time that I joined *DWM* full-time.'

Sullivan had produced numerous strips for the magazine since 1988. His first story, *Planet of the Dead* (issues 141-142), included likenesses of all seven Doctors, and it was soon clear that Sullivan could add a depth and reality to the characters.

'Lee provided so much of Bernice,' says Cornell. 'There's some of Lee Sullivan's wife in Bernice, certainly in her initial hair-do.'

'My wife was not a model for Benny,' Sullivan says himself, 'though I can see a similarity.' Pushed, he will admit that, 'I was told by writer pals of mine that all the women I drew were actually my wife. But it wasn't intentional!'

'Paul's instructions to me,' he continues, 'were really along the lines of, "she should be like Emma Thompson", an actress Paul was rather stuck on. Which is kind of what I drew without referencing her directly. She was also to be strong, practical and wear cardigans of a hideous style.'

Cornell is not to be swayed. 'Those mad triangular earrings!' he says. 'Which were a huge feature of the early days, they were something Lee's wife wore.'

'I can't remember any instructions about earrings,' says Sullivan, 'but it may have been suggested in the text. I thought that, despite being a great example of a post-liberation female, Bernice would still have a few traditional female foibles. She's probably got cupboards full of shoes at home too!'

'I also specified small breasts,' laughs Cornell, 'because I knew how this would go – with a comic artist, especially!'

'I can't remember the "small breasts" detail!' says Sullivan.

Cornell was also keen that Bernice was a futuristic character – to differentiate her from Ace. 'That's where that mad, space warrior outfit came from,' Cornell continues, 'with the shoulder pads that make her look like something out of *Flash Gordon*. That's where the *DWM* comic strip was then, and that was the kind of shape Lee drew. But at the same time, he also put her in jeans and gave her a trowel. Oh, and a hooded top. Which was very much his wife back then.'

As well as designing Benny for the character outline, Sullivan also painted the cover to her debut, *Love and War*. 'One wonders,' said Peter Linford in his review for fanzine *DWB* #106 (October 1992), 'why Lee Sullivan has depicted the Hoothi as giant testicles.'

'The art brief was extremely tightly delineated,' Sullivan remembers. 'It's exactly what was asked for in every detail: bright colours; man-in-a-rubber-suit bollock monster. I think Paul and Peter Darvill-Evans were after a traditional monster design. I wouldn't have come up with such a specific scene; I prefer a more collage-of-images style.'

'Everyone was happy with it when I delivered it,' Sullivan continues. 'Unfortunately, we were the only ones who liked it! Technically, it was the best I could do, and actually I still like it, but it looks more like a junior title rather than the adult novel it undoubtedly is. I wasn't approached to do any more, unsurprisingly, given the audience reaction.'

But Sullivan would continue to contribute to the look of Bernice for the next 15 years.

Available now…

The Two Jasons

A novel by Dave Stone

ISBN 978–1–84435–279–1

'Oh, bloody hell,' she snapped. 'Listen: me no wantee good time jig-jig all same, okay?'

When Bernice Summerfield first met Jason Kane, she failed to spot his many fine qualities and assets. Over the course of many subsequent adventures, including marriage and divorce, she continued not to see them…

'You're not Jason,' she said. 'Who the hell are you?'

When Bernice Summerfield met Jason Kane 2, he was disguised as a critic of the work of Jason Kane. Benny saw through the false moustache and literary pretentions, and had him and his other clones expelled into space, there to make their own fortunes. One Jason Kane was, she felt, rather more than enough.

Now something is astir in the universe, a plot that threatens Benny and all she holds dear. If she stands any chance at all, she needs all the Jason Kanes she can get…